Three Paths to Coruña

Mark Woodburn

DEDICATION

This book is for my brother, Scott Woodburn

CONTENTS

i

ACKNOWLEDGMENTS

The author would like to thank Stephen Walker for the cover art.

ABOUT THE AUTHOR

Mark Woodburn was born in Edinburgh, 1968, and grew up in Scotland, Canada and South Africa. His colourful employment history includes work in forestry, pet food, ladies' fashion, risk analysis, COVID-19 cleaning and as a part-time soldier in the Royal Corps of Transport. His first novel *'Winston & Me'* ("Woodburn offers an excellent portrayal of Churchill... a novel not to be missed" - Finest Hour magazine "Memorable, eminently readable, and thoroughly enjoyable" - Undiscovered Scotland) was published by Valley Press in 2012. The revised second edition was published in December 2018. Its sequel and his second novel *'The Finest Years and Me'* ("First-rate...If you enjoyed Winston & Me, you will find *The Finest Years and Me* equally satisfying" - Finest Hour Magazine) was published by Valley Press in November 2015.

He lives in Livingston, West Lothian in Scotland with his wife and daughter and is a season ticket holder at Heart of Midlothian Football Club.

'Three Paths to Coruña' is his third novel.

Three Paths to Coruña

Lisbon

'His Majesty having determined to employ a corps of his troops, of not less than thirty thousand infantry and five thousand cavalry, in the north of Spain, to co-operate with the Spanish armies in the expulsion of the army of France from the kingdom, has been graciously pleased to entrust to you, Sir John Moore, K.B., the command of chief of this force.'

Lord Castlereagh to Lieutenant-general Sir John Moore, K.B., September 25th 1808

Chapter One

Sir John Moore laid the letter from the King of Sweden down before him on the bed. It was delivered earlier personally by the adjutant – general of Gustavus IV.

'Mr Thornton, They say he is mad. I now have proof to that effect.'

The British general yawned wearily. It was past midnight and he usually retired to bed at precisely 10 pm. It was a ritual inculcated rigidly throughout years of bachelorhood.

Thornton, the British minister in Stockholm, urgently summoned to his countryman's side, picked up the letter. He could not but glance over again the last words:

'...that he should not leave Stockholm without the Kings permission.'

They were in Moore's lodging house in the Swedish capital. The Scottish Lieutenant-general was recently appointed the commander in chief of a British army of over twelve thousand men, sent to assist his country's sole remaining European ally. The force at present lay idling in convoy ships berthed off Gothenburg harbour, two hundred and fifty miles to the west, having been refused permission by the Swedish monarch to disembark.

'He is placing you under arrest, Sir John, right enough,' agreed the diplomat succinctly. Thornton was a Yorkshireman of good stock. Educated at Cambridge, he'd risen steadily through the diplomatic service to his present position but retained the cadence of his native shire. Consequently, he was able to slip from court manners to plain speaking with alacrity. Like the general he was unmarried, in his middle forties and greatly sympathised with the military man's plight.

'I shall require to send a note to Hope. He must be forewarned regardless of any action I decide to undertake.' John Moore announced.

He climbed out of the bed in order to use the chamber pot. General John Hope, an old and trusted friend was Moore's second in command.

The June night had cooled somewhat as the general returned to his bed after urinating. Thornton prepared to take his leave. He understood Moore's inference and wholeheartedly agreed with his sentiments, which undoubtedly pointed to the general taking immediate and irrevocable action. He'd grown to admire the man during the short period of their acquaintance.

'I shall endeavour to learn more, Sir John. Whether the king decides to confine you in some manner is, of course, his prerogative. He is quite disturbed as you rightly say, having some history in these matters. The Russian minister Count Alopaeus was allowed no contact with anyone, not even his valet and was confined under a guard numbering upwards of two dozen.'

Moore pulled the covers round him and doused the candle. He was relieved that the diplomat delivered such a forthright summing up of the situation. It was refreshing to meet a member of the Foreign Service so uncomplicated. And so competent.

'Then I shall pray that I should be more fortunate than the noble count. Thank you for your concern, Mr Thornton. Good evening to you, sir.'

John Moore lay awake.

He was unable to fall sleep, his mind alive with the recall of recent events. This latest debacle was yet another result of Castlereagh, Britain's minister for war's vague and contradictory orders. Sweden was nominally Britain's ally. Recent incursions by Russia, now Bonaparte's friend, into Swedish Finland resulted in an offer of assistance from Great Britain. But that assistance did not include any such help in ejecting the evader. The fleet was to guard against any sea-bound invasion. That was clear and defined. But the army was the real issue. The orders from London to Moore advised that he was not to place the army under the command of the king even if requested by the monarch himself. Further, if Gustavus expressed any desire to involve the British force in any action threatening its existence, for example, attempting to expel the Russians in Finland or mount an attack on Norway, Moore was to withdraw it immediately. Those orders had leaked to his Majesty. In his fury, he announced that his country required no such foreign aid. Therefore as his land was but a poor one and unable to supply subsistence for so large a horde, the British soldiers must remain aboard their ships, consuming their own victuals until the Swedish king decided otherwise.

In response, a flustered Lord Castlereagh forwarded fresh orders which appeared to give in to all Gustavus' demands. But as before, they contained a worrisome element of confusion, leaving them open to interpretation. Castlereagh stated that the king's desire to have full control over British land forces *'presented some difficulty,'* but Sir John was to consider himself under the command of the Swedish monarch while *'serving in his dominions.'* Under no circumstances was he to involve the army in operations in Zealand or Norway. If he received any orders that differed principally from his *'original instructions,'* he was to inform his Majesty that he must advise London before submitting to them. On reading this communication, Moore was left astounded though hardly surprised at such obtuseness.

He turned his tired mind back to his earlier meetings with Gustavus.

The fourth of that name, the pale Swedish monarch was thirty years of age, moustachioed, styled his hair short (powder was no longer in general fashion) and swept back in an attempt his critics claimed, to gain the illusion of greater stature. It was no secret that he based himself on his illustrious ancestor, Charles XII, dressing in imitation of his predecessor while retaining a semblance of consistency with contemporary fashions. It was believed his failure to marry the granddaughter of Catherine the Great led to her demise as she suffered a stroke on hearing the news of the snub to her family.

Their initial meeting was held at the palace at Royal Haga, less than two miles from the capital. Originally bought from the church by his father with grandiose ambitions to enlarge it, Gustavus had less ostentatious ideas for it than those of his sire who planned a pavilion to equal that of the Prince of Wales in Brighton. But he never succeeded in his dream due to the fact that he was assassinated. To John Moore, the white country house style resembled any respectable hunting lodge visited in his homeland. The modesty of the surroundings seemed to belie the rumours of mental imbalance surrounding the king.

On making first acquaintance, it quickly became apparent any modesty previously assumed of the sovereign was a false one. After receiving his credentials, Gustavus took the British general aside, declaring that he'd never requested outside help. At present he was not inclined to permit any army onto Swedish soil as the forces of his nation were sufficient to carry out his plans. Plans that involved attacking his enemies on all fronts.

Moore listened. He could do little else as it was the role of kings to expound their wishes and the place of subordinates to execute them. The immediate assault on the Danish island of Zealand was imminent, Gustavus declared. Plans were already in effect to that end.

John Moore, in all his history, could never be other than plain speaking when folly was presented before him. Finally able to respond after the king's interminable discourse, he announced any attack on Zealand was contrary to his understanding of the situation.

'What do you mean?' Gustavus snapped back. They spoke in French.

Moore replied with as much mildness as he could summon. 'That your Majesty should ready himself for invasion of your own lands and prepare your armies accordingly.'

'General, I believe your Foreign Office acts under a false assumption,' the king retorted. 'My country has no fears of invasion. On the contrary, as I have mentioned to you already, we have plans to attack the Russians in Swedish Finland. We have plans to invade Norway. Zealand you appear to be aware of. Had you forgotten already the former? Were you listening to me?'

Now on dangerous ground, Moore quickly switched tack.

'Might I ask his Majesty whether the peasants I saw drilling this morning outside the capital on my journey here will form part of the invading force?'

Back on happier ground the king responded breathlessly. 'Undoubtedly. Fine specimens I believe and there are plenty more. They adhere to perfect discipline and are highly motivated.' Gustavus added the last in an exultant tone.

Moore nodded, grateful for the opportunity now entered into the conversation that allowed him time to think. But the king himself then continued. 'I am aware of your reforms and ideas for your own army, General Moore. I have studied them with great interest. But I believe such enlightened thinking dangerous in the extreme. There is no place for such beliefs in my country. My generals and soldiers are after all, the heirs and descendants of Adolphus. Perhaps you are a student of his?'

Gustavus then went on to repeat that the British army sent to aid him was not needed at present and for reasons of economy was required to stay on board their ships. His temper flaring, Moore was able to contain himself. But just as he believed the intolerable interview near over, Gustavus announced a new plan to invade the Russian capital.

At that, the British general came as close to exploding and committing *lèse majestie* as he ever had. Barely containing his passion, he spoke as clearly as possible, assisted by the fact he was speaking in another language.

'Your Majesty, are you aware of the military resources available to Russia in comparison with your own? Do you believe the coast of that land to be left so unguarded, as to be unable to resist any such attack? The numbers at their disposal make it unlikely they would have to draw from their forces in Finland. Surely that is the object of the king's strategy?'

The monarch dismissed any such fears and announced that General Tibell the quartermaster general, awaited an interview with Sir John in order to discuss the logistics of his plans.

'I will send over the general to you on the morrow. We shall discuss your conclusions at the Royal Palace in the city in the afternoon. That will be all, General Moore.'

With that the Scot left the royal presence, relieved the meeting was over but with his mind in turmoil.

It was happening all over again.

General Tibell, a smiling gallant, very knowing of his sovereign's peccadilloes, had served six years in the French army and there were whispers he served them still. On arriving at the New Town lodgings of John Moore in the capital, he appeared sympathetic to Moore's dismissal of the king's strategy as being somewhat fantastic. In particular, the plan to invade Russia in the hope by doing so that country would be forced to draw on forces already committed elsewhere, received deserved opprobrium. Tibell recognised it was not part of the British general's remit to aid any such attack. But the inference was obvious. Gustavus would request that General Moore offer every military assistance within his power.

'I must inform you, Sir John, I have no intention of advising the king in matters in which his mind is already made up.' The quartermaster general ended his discourse unhelpfully.

'Then I must inform my superiors accordingly.' Moore replied bluntly. After dismissing Tibell, he dictated a letter. He advised the British government that unless a direct order came through to him from London, he would under no circumstances place any part of his army under the control of the king or government of Sweden.

That afternoon, Moore attended to the monarch, as Gustavus explained in further detail the various strands of his strategy. Sir John endured the meeting, offering guidance where he thought appropriate while committing himself to nothing. It appeared to Moore what was left unspoken between them was his concurrence to the wishes of the king. He did nothing to disavow the monarch, holding his fire until receiving a response to the urgent dispatch sent off that morning.

Moore got out of bed. Daylight was showing through as he opened the curtains. He admitted to being impressed with the Swedish capital. There was as a fine harbour deep enough to receive ships to the quayside. His lodgings were more than adequate. He was recommended to the Burgher's Club for dining where he was introduced by a member, partaking of the food and finding it excellent. The centre of the town, where he was based, was all brick buildings with not a wooden dwelling in sight. His military assistant, Major Colbourne, remarked more than once on the carriages passing along the streets containing the most exquisitely beautiful blonde females he'd ever seen. He was rising exceedingly early each morning in order to attend classes in Swedish, as invitations arrived daily for the good looking major. Moore was greatly amused at his young aide's speedy progress with Stockholm's ladies.

In the days following his first meeting with Gustavus, he wandered the capital and attended the houses of distinguished citizens. He was propositioned on no less than three separate occasions, each more difficult than the last to decline. But he'd greatly enjoyed the flirting involved which helped to take his mind off more pressing concerns.

He was in receipt of twice weekly reports from Hope on the condition of the army. The second in command ordered regular excursions to the shore for the confined men with sports and concerts on board ship to alleviate the tedium. At least Moore could reflect on that account, his good friend relieved one burden from his mind. Hope added they were well supplied despite the king's entreaties to the contrary.

As the days wore, on he reflected on the vagaries of his original instructions from London. As he'd discussed with his lover, Lady Hester Stanhope at her home in Montague Square shortly before he left the country, it was apparent the government had no real plan for the army other than to send it to Gothenburg and await events. Hester worried he would be blamed by Castlereagh should matters develop less than favourably. It was well known Moore had no interest in the government. But he had sufficient at Court. At a meeting at the Duke of York's office where Castlereagh was present, it was made clear by both the commander in chief of the army and the secretary of state for war that Moore was not intended to be placed under the command of the King of Sweden. Nor was he to engage without further orders from London in any enterprise that would lead the army into the Swedish interior or beyond direct communication with the naval squadron.

Colonel George Murray, Britain's military envoy in Stockholm brought dispatches to the attention of the British commander. They were from King Gustavus to Count Adlerberg, the Swedish ambassador in London, outlining his desire that British forces arriving in his country were to be used for offensive operations against his Danish enemy in Zealand. They were not required for 'defence' or any other similarly useless endeavour. The dispatches were sent without consultation with London, who on learning of them would refute their contents entirely. Adlerberg, obviously distressed, said nothing, fearing if he did his country would be left unassisted by its ally.

Making matters worse, was a letter from the monarch himself disavowing three of the original conditions of the British promises of aid. First, that there should be a longer term of notice of any possible recall of the army. Secondly, that the army could not be allowed to act only in conjunction with the attached fleet. Finally and most tendentiously, that the force be immediately placed under the command of the King of Sweden to do as he saw fit.

Now Castlereagh had caved in to the mad monarch and left his commander on the ground in an impossible situation.

Adding to Moore's anxiety was Murray's confidential report on the state of Swedish defences. It made lamentable reading. Zealand itself was defended by a force of thirty thousand Danes with anything up to forty thousand French and other allied armies prepared to reinforce them at short notice. According to Colonel Murray's report, the Swedish army totalled twenty-eight thousand men and an untrained militia of recruits numbering less than ten thousand.

After washing and shaving, Moore dressed and readied himself for breakfast. He did not know how long he had before the knock came to the door. But as his journey to the fleet was imminent, he made himself best prepared. He then set out for the Burgher's Club.

Colonel Murray was apprised of the situation and already on his way to the palace to seek further news along with Mr Thornton. Moore wished both good fortune. As he strolled in the pleasant June morning sun, he recalled the events of his final meeting with the king.

He'd answered the summons to the Royal Palace, but unlike previous meetings, on this occasion they were not alone. A number of Swedish military men and officials were present including General Tibell. The demeanour of all spoke volubly as Moore steeled himself, though he was stiffened by the presence of the reliable Mr Thornton at his side.

'Sir John, it has come to my attention that you have disobeyed ours and the orders of your own superiors. Will you explain yourself?' The king began without preamble.

Before Moore could speak, Gustavus who stood behind a small deal table flanked by his officials, lifted a letter and read from it. It was a copy of Moore's last letter to Mr Thornton for presentation to the monarch. In increasing tones of excitement, the king read out each point, the tension in the room and within Moore becoming ever more palpable.

After he had finished, Gustavus dropped the letter to the floor. One of his people stooped to pick it up.

'Leave it! It is trash, full of lies and where it belongs. In the gutter! The king exclaimed furiously.

'You Majesty, I cannot be permitted to accept such slander on my honour!' Moore declared hotly.

'Honour? You have none! Did you not stand along with me merely a few days ago and personally approve of my plan to attack Vasa?'

During their second meeting, the king waxed lyrical about attacking the Russians at Vyborg. The British general was forced to show some interest in the absurd plan. After examining the map laid before him, he stated that Vasa offered a more viable starting point for the offensive. Moore was unwilling to believe for a moment the king would ever undertake such a hazardous venture.

'I do not deny that I stated I believed such an attack on Vasa more advisable than on Vyborg. Any small British force landing at Vyborg should be overwhelmed due to its size and proximity to the enemy capital.' Moore explained reasonably.

'Then you do not deny it!' Gustavus roared triumphantly.

'I deny that at any time I offered the forces of the crown of Great Britain to undertake any such rash action, and reiterate any such action is contrary to my original orders.'

There was a pause. The officials stood frozen. None had ever heard there monarch spoken to in such a fashion. It was new to the king also. Evidently routed on his first point, he now changed his line of attack.

'Sir John, I shall be informing his Majesty King George of your conduct. You have failed to observe the spirit of your instructions. The king will not require me to advise him that the defence of the nation is best decided by myself. Nor will he be pleased that you, his servant saw fit to offer me advice on such matters which was not formerly requested. You *presume,* Sir John! You presume too much in your arrogance!'

Moore's temper was long beyond him. But there was an inherent sarcasm within that poured out when under attack. It was a weapon used before to great effect and no lasting damage had yet arisen from it.

'Your Majesty, I admit I have erred. I believed myself summoned here today to listen to your latest commands. Obviously, I presumed incorrectly. You have nothing new to say to me. Therefore, I offer my leave.'

The king's face paled further, his colourless eyes appearing to bulge markedly.

'No! You were brought to me that you should be made aware before witnesses of your calumnies so that King George may be fully apprised of your disobedience! You state one position while alone, yet in company and in letters, you declare the opposite!'

Moore then affirmed that he'd been in King George's service since the age of sixteen. He was sufficiently known to his Highness to leave behind any apprehension that he should ever be considered only as someone who spoke the truth. Any statement made by him should be treated as such. On no occasion had he ever made any such falsehoods on behalf of the king, including any private meetings held with his Majesty.

Somewhat mollified, Gustavus turned to discussing the conduct of his Norwegian campaign. He then attempted to blame Thornton as an accomplice in concocting the letter to the detriment of the king. He asked one of the officials to repeat back to him the words used in the letter, where it stated unless Gustavus allowed the army to disembark from their ships, General Moore intended to recall the army and return it to England. To the official, but not to the king's great embarrassment the poor man was forced to admit that no such passage existed.

There was a deeply uncomfortable silence. Thornton then interjected on Moore's behalf.

'Your Majesty, it may be best if Sir John issues a fresh dispatch to London listing your concerns. I am quite certain the authorities there shall alleviate them to your satisfaction.'

The king accepted the suggestion then waved away the Britons dismissively, glad to be rid of both.

'No good shall come of this.' Thornton warned gloomily as they boarded their coach back to his residence and Moore's lodgings.

And indeed none had. Events took a dramatic turn when Mr Thornton, after leaving Moore's lodgings late that night, drew up a letter to the Swedish Foreign Minister, Baron Ehrenheim. He warned him that the outrage inflicted on the person of King George's senior representative was such that the insult to his Majesty's government was deemed too great. There was no other recourse but to declare a state of war between the two countries, should Sir John's arrest order not be rescinded with immediate effect.

The letter remained unanswered. On returning after breakfast, Moore found Colonel Murray, waiting frantically at his lodgings where he had returned from the palace to advise the Scot he must indeed consider himself under arrest. Moore replied to Murray the only logical response lay with his escape back to the fleet. He still remained free and unconfined but such was the feverish unpredictability of the king, his physical arrest may only be a matter of time away. Murray begged him to reconsider as Gustavus and the government may not take kindly to the back-street flight of a Lieutenant-general. Moore gave his reply.

'The fact of the matter, my dear Murray, is that my arrest is now public knowledge. It may be agreeable to ministers of England to hush up the affair. But they remain the fellows who landed me in this predicament.

The behaviour of this mad king would not have been out of place during the reign of Robespierre. It has no place in a civilised country. It therefore behoves me to accept that civilised standards do not apply to this situation. Our sovereign king of course will not apologise. I shall no longer "await events" as our masters in London are much in thrall to. I've already prepared my escape plan.'

The same day, after further vain remonstrance on the behalf of Sir John Moore by Colonel Murray at the Palace, a tall gentleman in civilian clothing boarded a curricle outside his lodgings at the invitation of a British resident of the city, Mr Oakley, in order to take some country air. Two days later, where just the evening before, the naval commander, James Saumarez hosted a ball for the good people of Gothenburg, officers on board HMS *Victory* were astonished to see a small fishing boat lie up alongside Nelson's flagship.

Captain George Napier of the 52nd, on seeing a gentleman climb out of the boat onto the deck of the ship, could only exclaim in amazement and some pleasure at the safe return of the army's much admired commander in chief, Sir John Moore.

Chapter Two

The light but intermittent rainfall and cooler country air made a pleasant change from the unusual summer heat of London that year.

John Moore was walking with Jane, his sister through the gardens of Brook Farm in Cobham, their absent brother Graham's home. Graham was three years younger than John, who was the head of the family. The younger Moore was now a distinguished naval commodore with a small fortune in prize money safely banked away.

Jane, a spinster, and the eldest of the Moore brood, split her time between watching over bachelor Graham's home and tending to their elderly mother, who divided her time between all her sons. There were three other male Moore's. John was referred to as *Jack* by the family.

Graham originally wanted to buy a farm of his own with his winnings but settled for stables for his horses and the pursuit of a wife now his future was settled. He and John were very close and both dreamed of serving together one day in some great joint military or naval endeavour. John was also close to Jane and while their mother detected strain in him, her son laughed her concerns away by opining that mad kings are best dealt with from a safe distance.

Jane understood there was more to the remark than jest. She was a woman who long accepted she was never going to marry. Now in her early forties and with no fortune, her only true regret was the want of children. Happily, her hands were full with a growing brood of young Moore's among her sibling brothers. She retained high hopes for Graham to expand on the score while her ambitions for Jack still remained limitless.

'Now will you tell me?' They had walked well away from the house and settled together on a garden bench flanked by blooming July roses.

John sighed. 'Is my disposition so obvious?'

'We may be locked away in darkest Surry but our senses are not addled, Jack. You have a face that is plain to read at the best of times. Was Sweden so very awful?'

'Not for Johnny Colbourne.' Her brother smiled ironically.

She was beginning to find his reticence irritating. 'You always used to tell me everything. Is that right now reserved solely for Lady Hester?'

'Lady Hester was not at home when I last visited.' He spoke regretfully. In the absence of Graham, Jane was now his sole confidant.

'The military are no longer in fashion?' Jane asked coyly.

'Evidently not.' John replied, off-handed.

Hester had set out for Wales. She was chronically in debt and required an inexpensive bolt hole while gathering herself for her next assault upon her creditors. John Moore offered her assistance in the past but she always refused him. Generous, adorable, profligate Hester. Wales! And on horseback, he learned. What a woman!

Jane spoke her mind. 'Lady Hester is too *fast* for you, Jack. She always was. She plays on your kind nature in order to use you for her selfish, egotistical whims and ludicrous grudges.' Meaning Hester's financial imprudence and her well known vendetta against Canning over the early death of her beloved uncle, the late prime minister, William Pitt.

'And her *scandal* is not to be born!' She added the last a little too censoriously.

Amused rather than offended, John replied mildly, 'Janie-lassie, no man or woman alive ever need make use of me to advance their causes unless I believed it deserving. There are aspects of Lady Hester's views on this government which match my own, that is all. Anyway, there is enough in this old brother of yours to go about for a dozen Hesters.'

'Oh, Jack, but why do you quarrel with them so? It will lead you nowhere. You have no friends among them. Can you not emit a little tact from time to time? It can only do you good.'

He now became irritable. 'Let us not speak of this any longer.'

'Not until you tell me what Castlereagh told you!' Jane replied stubbornly.

Her brother drew another sigh and relented. 'Do not tell Mother until I am in Portugal. Promise me.'

She leant over and kissed his cheek. 'I promise.' She had got her way with him.

He stretched out on the bench and folded his arms. 'The commander of the army of Portugal is to be Sir Hew Dalrymple. Harry Burrard is second in command.' Moore could barely speak the last name. Burrard was a nonentity but a guardsman and friend of Court. Dalrymple was experienced, but not in battle. He was an administrator. They were a safe and highly uninspiring pairing.

A new man of note, Wellesley was to serve under them. That man seethed as John Moore did as they were alike in many ways. They'd never met but he knew enough to be impressed. The feeling was reciprocated, it was said.

'When I returned to London and reported to Castlereagh, he only enquired about Sweden. He refused to apologise for the errors made and only spoke of the "unfortunate behaviour of the king." He chastised me cleverly but with great sensitivity over my escape. I was greatly angered at this point but restrained myself. As for the future, all he said was that the army was due to leave very soon.'

'Is that all?' Jane asked incredulous.

'My dear, that was but our first meeting. Afterward, I took off for St James to present myself to their Majesties. The king was gravely concerned and spoke of his great sadness at my travail. The duke was more guarded. It was he who told me about Dalrymple and Burrard.'

Moore was bitter now. 'I fear the duke no longer has much influence. The scandal of his mistress can no longer be ignored. As a result, the paper warriors of Whitehall are currently in the ascendancy.' The Duke of York's mistress, Mary Ann Clarke was using her influence in the purchase of commissions for army officers. It was believed the duke was aware and pressure was mounting for him to face a parliamentary committee in order to explain himself.

'Any fool could see that I should lead the army with Wellesley at my flank.' Moore continued, his tone becoming increasingly excitable. 'But we are two of a kind, Sir Arthur and I. Our tongues run away with us and the little gnomes burrowed away in their quills have ways of making us pay for our honesty.'

'I had no idea of your unhappiness. But is that the only reason? Surely there must be more?' Jane pondered.

'Gordon advised me I was the choice of the duke.' Colonel Willoughby

Gordon was a friend of Moore and also military secretary to the Duke of York. 'The king sympathised but H.R.H. now has little say in such matters. Portland is a poor, weak vessel and Canning has always despised me. The fools!' Moore spat. 'That poor men must suffer and die for the sake of interest and stupidity!

'I was summoned to Downing Street. Castlereagh advised me that Sir Arthur had sailed from Ireland and was expected within a week at Lisbon. He was ordered only to attack the French should he construe the risk acceptable. If not, he was to await my arrival.' He stopped abruptly.

He found it difficult to speak, the shame and anger within him resurfacing. He gathered himself and continued explaining to his sister that the secretary of state for war then advised him for the first time what he only learned the day before from the king.

'Oh, Jack! Please tell me you did not argue and row!' Jane pleaded.

'Well, of course I did, damn it!'

There was a pained silence. Moore was annoyed at his temper flaring before his beloved sister. Jane was upset and chastised herself for goading him.

'I am so sorry.' She apologised.

He patted her knee. 'No, girl. There is nothing to apologise for. My rage will out. It is I who should be ashamed. But those men... are vile! Fops and boudoir bravoes who've never heard a musket shot in anger and would run faster than coursing hares should they ever!'

There was now little to say between them. 'Let us now return to the house.' Jane announced resignedly. 'The rain does come on heavier. Do not add a cold to your list of miseries.'

John Moore dined with his mother and sister before awaiting the coach to carry him to Portsmouth. He'd no real home of his own and when in England usually lived at his mother's house in Kent.

She fretted for his safety as if he were still a child. Now in her sixth year of widowhood, her husband, Dr John Moore, was an eminent surgeon and author of novels who left his wife well provided for. His estate was worth the enormous sum of £30,000 which was divided among her and their children. John and Graham received less than the others, though this was already agreed prior to their father's demise and never a concern to the Moore elders. Graham was now rich, though their younger brother Frank, employed in the Foreign Office, earned more than John did as a lieutenant-general. He'd also made a scandalous marriage to the notorious Lady Eglinton. James was a doctor, but the youngest child Charles, was a concern as he suffered from mental incapacity.

When John Moore was twelve years of age, his father left their family home in Dunlop Street in Glasgow and took his older son on a tour of Europe. Dr Moore recently become known to the mother of the teenaged Duke of Hamilton, one of Scotland's richest noblemen. The young man's older brother had taken ill and Dr Moore was recommended to the boy, who sadly succumbed. Dr Moore's kindliness and professionalism throughout the traumatic period was noted, and when the new sixteen year old duke professed a desire to broaden his horizons, Dr Moore was confirmed as a suitable travelling companion. A payment of £500 was awarded plus a yearly annuity of £100. Dr Moore, deeming such an opportunity would be in the best interests of his eldest son's development, allowed John to accompany him and the duke on their adventure together.

The young Moore was a stocky, hazel eyed and rosy cheeked youngster with brown hair. He greatly looked forward to the tour but knew that as it may last the best part of five years, he would miss his mother deeply. At the time he was too young to consider the loss of her husband to his mother, but as he grew older it weighed heavily on his thinking on the subject of marriage.

That his father and older son could be taken from her so readily (and so willingly on their behalf) as an adult, made him look at his father in a different light. He idolised him as a child and saw only his virtues. But only now could he view his father for what he was. An extremely ambitious man with a streak of ruthlessness that allowed nothing to get in the way of advancing himself in society.

While they were abroad, his mother ran into financial difficulties. The family's bank went broke, all their savings were lost while Dr Moore had issued a letter of guarantee for £2000 to his brother in-law. Mrs Moore was pregnant and the strain was becoming too much. Matters were made worse when letters to Scotland failed to arrive. It was suspected the money for the postage was kept, the letters thrown away by the servants who were supposed to take them to be mailed.

Dr Moore was just able to resolve the financial issues with assistance from the duke's mother. But the stress it had caused his wife was too great.

Her child was born a boy but died only days after.

While this was happening, the little party were residing in Geneva. Young John was greatly concerned for his mother's plight. The duke, a kind and generous young man, gifted the boy money and presents in sympathy. The noble was enjoying life greatly as he pursued a number of dalliances, becoming the talk of the city, invited everywhere among society.

It was during this difficult period that John asked his father whether it was necessary for them to return to Scotland in order to assist his mother. His father became testy and advised they had a duty and commitment to his Grace, which must remain paramount before all other considerations. John never forgot his father's words. Throughout his life, he never forgave his father either.

The tour encompassed Paris where he dined with a number of senior French army officers. Then on to Italy. In Florence, John met the young pretender, Charles Stuart, now a debauched wreck, on a walkabout, though the duke only had eyes for Bonnie Prince Charlie's remarkably beautiful new nineteen year old wife at his side. On a trip to Mount Vesuvius, the young Moore burnt himself when venturing a little too close to the volcano's fiery entrance. Onwards into Germany, he saw the King of Prussia, met many dukes and barons, then on to Vienna and returning to Italy to Venice. In Rome, John received word the Duke of Hamilton succeeded in obtaining an ensigncy in the 51st regiment for him though he was only fifteen years of age. The matter could be surmounted by his taking a leave of absence from the regiment which was stationed in Menorca, until he had reached his sixteenth birthday.

John kept in correspondence with his brother Graham, who'd joined the navy at the age of twelve as a midshipman. His meeting with the dashing French officers left a marked impression on him, though he learned tales while in Prussia of that country's savage system of military discipline that alarmed him somewhat. But on professing an interest in the military, his father discussed the matter with his oldest son in forensic detail, leaving him convinced the boy's desire was genuine.

Though money available for the commission was tight, the duke's influence and always generous assistance on that account was crucial. With great excitement and no little trepidation, John Moore joined the British army.

*

On board HMS *Audacious,* headed for Cape Finisterre, John Moore dwelled on his mortality.

He was not normally introspective on the subject. In a lifetime of service in America, Holland, St Lucia, Corsica, Egypt and Sicily, he'd received a total of seven wounds. None of them were particularly incapacitating. The one that bothered him above any other was a finger hit by a spent musket ball in Holland. He'd suffered wounds in the leg, shoulder and to the head, including being shot through the ear and cheek. But the finger pained him most.

Moore knew he'd killed at least one man. He was a French infantryman at a redoubt at the capture of San Fiorenzo in Corsica. He ran the man through with his sword while leading the attack on the position. He was barely conscious of it until at the end of the action, while breathing great gulps of air and shaking mightily, he focussed on the sword dripping with blood and realised what he'd done. He felt little more than relief at the time, but over the years the effusion of red figured heavily in his dreams. He'd no recollection whatsoever of the face of the unfortunate man whose life he took.

He thought often of Ralph Abercromby. Probably the finest soldier Britain produced at the time, the kindly old gentleman was always remembered with great affection. Never fail to treat the men with decency and honour, he advised his young protégé. The old boy was blind as a bat but when he put on his spectacles he could read a map, view a piece of ground or decipher a captured enemy communication and see in it something no one else could. At Alexandria, scene of his greatest triumph, early on in the battle, Abercromby was hit by a bullet but kept it hidden from everyone. He later died after the battle was won of blood loss, apologising to everyone and begging assurances that his poor wounded men be taken care of.

John Moore did not require Sir Ralph Abercromby or anyone else to teach him about kindness and decency. His name was a byword for those qualities. Flogging men and treating them like animals was an insult to God and to all humanity. More could be gained by tolerance and good treatment. This was inculcated at Shorncliffe barracks when he commanded the light infantry, where the ideas of the inspirational training commander Colonel Mackenzie, were heartily endorsed by his fellow

Scot. The years spent there were the happiest of Moore's life.

Moore believed such a death as Abercromby's was one he would not mind for himself. He was unmarried, there were no children. But he had a mother and siblings who may not be too sympathetic with his views on such a matter. They all loved him dearly, but lately, with this new command and his age, his thought processes turned somewhat morbid. Not so long before, he'd rebuffed a highly attractive young woman who earnestly desired marriage to him. Lady Caroline Fox, niece of the late Whig politician Charles Fox, was now nineteen. But two years earlier while on duty on station in Sicily, the lady, daughter of Moore's commanding officer featured heavily in his life. The subject of marriage, though never openly spoken of by himself, became a common theme among everyone else as the young girl fell madly in love with the tall and very handsome, albeit middle-aged general.

She and her equally alluring elder sister Louisa, called him their 'Candide.' He was always referred to as such at their meetings. Moore could not fail to note the undertone the name inspired. As a young man, Caroline would have been the type of woman he could only dream of. Beautiful, rich and sophisticated, she would have been far out of reach of the then Lieutenant Moore as the moon and stars. He remembered the balls he attended, observing the rich dandy's and roue's of the time attract to the honey pot the beauties of the period. He was Dr Moore's son. Of no consequence. A nobody. The fact that he cut a highly attractive figure, was lost to him completely in his natural and unassuming modesty.

But for him, Caroline was impossible. As he explained to Graham, his brother, much later, he could not marry a girl of seventeen who in the years ahead may grow to contemplate the errors and silliness of youth as she, still young in years, but old enough to have been passed by of any new opportunity, encumbered herself with a man in his sixties and possibly infirm at that. Graham thought him foolish to reason so. She was perfect for him. Older men married young girls. It was a natural state of affairs. John remained obdurate. He would not be responsible for ruining a beautiful girl's future happiness.

Hester Stanhope wished to marry him. They'd not discussed the subject openly but he knew she longed for him to propose. He could not bring himself to commit to her until he returned from Spain. He would remain the bachelor general for the present. It was simpler to put such a decision aside for the time being. But they would write to each other often, sometimes daily.

He prepared his affairs carefully with Messrs Drummond and Messrs Greenwood Cox, his lawyers, before sailing. His estate was valued at £22,000 and particular care was taken to the conditions of his will.

Moore looked out over the Atlantic Ocean. He was alone, on the main deck leaning over a taffrail. He was a good sailor and rarely sea-sick. He'd mended matters somewhat with Castlereagh in a series of letters. One thing remained clear to him. The secretary of state counted on him refusing the commission offered. It was only in respect to the king that Sir John Moore was given the position, a signal of how little the Tory administration cared for their sovereign's will these days. Moore, a member of parliament for a short period during the 1780's, representing the interests of the Duke of Hamilton for the Lanark Burghs of Peebles, Lanark, Linlithgow and Selkirk, was judged to be partial to the Whigs, regardless of his former support for many of the policies of the late, lamented, younger Pitt.

Wellesley was outraged, fully expecting himself to lead the expedition. But ambition overcame Sir Arthur's fury who buckled down. Moore looked forward to meeting the man.

'Excuse me, sir.' He turned and saw his valet, Francois David standing before him with his overcoat held out.

'Oh, Francois, you are such a fuss!' He responded kindly.

'The air is cooling somewhat and I believe it best that you put on your coat.' Francois replied firmly.

Francois first came into his master's service while Moore served in St Lucia in the West Indies. He was the then teenaged son of French emigres and without him, John Moore was lost.

'How are you enjoying the voyage?' Moore asked.

'The food is awful beyond comprehension, the sailors are uncouth brutes. But if you don't put on your coat, I'll really have something to complain about.'

Moore laughed heartily as always at his young valet's superb quips, taking the coat as Francois helped him on with it.

'Not long now and we'll be in Lisbon.' Moore sympathised. 'I believe the food will be much more to your taste in Iberia, my dear *Capitaine* David.'

*

The historical circumstances that would lead John Moore to the Peninsula came about partly due to the fact that Napoleon Bonaparte loved nothing more than offering his brothers and sisters the empty thrones of Europe he won in conquest.

As Britain's oldest ally, Portugal willingly kept its ports open for trade with its ancient friend. After an ultimatum from the Emperor of France to discontinue this practice which went unheeded, the French marched into Lisbon determined to overthrow the Braganza dynasty. Unhappily for Bonaparte, the entire royal family of Portugal along with a large part of its gold deposits escaped only days before, carried by Royal Navy ships in safety to the colony of Brazil.

The Bourbon dynasty of Spain, next for Napoleonic scourging, were corrupt and venal with a decrepit king at the head and a son and heir who's only real ability lay in convincing the Spanish people into wrongly believing his future reign would provide prosperity and happiness. Unfortunately for all concerned, including the heir, Spain was ruled not by the old king but by Manuel Godoy, an ambitious and avaricious libertine from a little-known branch of provincial nobility. Godoy had somehow insinuated himself with the royal family (he was believed to count the queen herself among his many lovers) and was the man who truly ruled the kingdom, though in reality he was nothing more than Napoleon Bonaparte's cat's-paw. In October 1807 the Treaty of Fontainebleau was signed by representatives of Godoy allowing French troops to pass through Spain to join with the Spanish to invade Portugal. The French, supported by a tiny elite of *afrancsados* (pro-French liberals) slipped into Spain bloodlessly. But soon it would be *guerra al cuchillo* (war to the knife) as the proud Spanish people reacted violently to what they saw as a foreign occupation. Ferdinand's principal worry was his fear that Godoy might exclude him from succession and take the Spanish throne himself. Ferdinand wrote to Napoleon requesting his support against Godoy and his father the king. Godoy learned of this letter and the heir was put under arrest for treason.

France and Spain were both enemy and ally during the wars since the French revolution. But where France prospered, Spain suffered ruinously whether friend or foe of its northern neighbour. The destruction of the Spanish fleet at Cape Trafalgar in 1805 effectively bankrupted the nation, which now had difficulty in extracting wealth from its colonies in the West Indies and South America as there were fewer ships to protect itself from British plundering. Spain's empire teetered on economic and military collapse while Spaniards grew increasingly perturbed over Godoy's dealings with Napoleon's atheist, revolutionary France.

On the spurious grounds that due to the fact the British sent a force of seven thousand men to Gibraltar, the Emperor of the French stepped up his campaign to subjugate his ally. A strong force already in Spain in order to 'assist' his friend was supplemented by twenty-five thousand extra troops under General Junot. By now, Napoleon Bonaparte's army in Spain numbered fifty thousand men.

The King of Spain's son and heir, Fernando viewed developments for what they were and decided that action was required. He was known romantically by many nationalist Spaniards as the *El Deseado* (The Desired) and to his liberal Spanish opponents as the *El Rey Felón* (The Felon King). On 17th March 1808 there was a mutiny of Spanish troops joined by Spanish peasants. After a palace coup, the old king and queen were deposed and Godoy was arrested. Fernando was declared king and throughout Spain there was rejoicing while an outbreak of savage attacks began on French interests and anyone connected even in a minor way with the now despised ally. Hundreds of horrific murders were committed while mercy was rarely shown regardless of sex or age.

Ever the manipulator and schemer, Napoleon kindly offered refuge to the former sovereign, his wife and their ministerial favourite across the border in Bayonne. The gesture was gratefully received along with a request that their son, the newly crowned King Ferdinand, join them in order that the French Emperor act as mediatory in resolving the family quarrel that erupted over the deposition of the former king. Foolishly, the new Spanish monarch accepted the invitation. On reuniting with his parents in the French town and been roundly cursed by them in colourful language, Napoleon offered, or rather, imposed on Ferdinand a huge pension in return for his signing a declaration of abdication. Ferdinand would spend the next seven years as prisoner at Talleyrand's estate of Valençay.

As the news of Napoleon's political machinations filtered into Spain, a rumour spread in Madrid that the French commander, Joachim Murat had kidnapped the Princess Maria Luisa and her children. On the second of May 1808 a mob of angry Spaniards assembled in front of the Royal

Palace in Madrid demanding the release of the Spanish prince, Francisco de Paul, Maria Luisa's son. Murat replied with a heavy hand sending French troops to drive away the mob which responded by throwing stones and brandishing knives and swords. Then the fatal order was given to open fire on the people. This led to a frenzied reaction by the Spanish populace in Madrid. Savage street fighting and brutal atrocities against the French erupted all over the city. The French replied by clearing the Puerto del Sol with artillery, killing hundreds of civilians and eventually establishing order by the evening. Madrid was put under martial law, Murat ordering all rebels captured to be executed by firing squads.

With that along with news of other outrages committed against his countrymen throughout the land, Napoleon ordered more troops to be sent into Spain. The Bourbon dynasty was declared at an end. His surprisingly unambitious and kindly older half-brother Joseph, the King of Naples, was to be installed as the latest new King of Spain.

Bonaparte made two basic errors in Spain. First, by deposing the monarchy he inadvertently severed ties with the Americas which ultimately moved towards independence. This resulted in no more treasure ships arriving from the New World to finance his armies. Secondly, he delegated Spain to battle-hardened officers unsuited for the diplomacy necessary to win the people over. In June 1808 after the Spanish rebellion spread, Napoleon organized his army into flying columns to stamp out popular resistance by force. One of these, a strong force of over twenty thousand men under General Dupont, was sent south to the port city of Cádiz where the French navy was isolated. But after sacking the city of Córdoba, Dupont encountered stiff Spanish resistance. French supply columns were attacked and wiped out to the last man. This culminated in the stirring victory at Bailen where admittedly a far larger force of Spaniards under General Castaños defeated the incompetent Dupont who was taken prisoner. This was the first defeat of a major French army in the reign of the Emperor.

The victory was hailed throughout Spain and Europe but was an illusory one. It was achieved through incompetence by the French rather than tactical brilliance on behalf of the Spanish commander. But its effects on the people were as if it had been another Cannae. Unfortunately, a dangerous but heady atmosphere of over-confidence and complacency befell the nation. Instead of announcing a new central government and re-organising the army in order to face the inevitable French response, the nobles and politicians of Spain returned to doing what they did best. Argue among themselves while carrying out petty feuds, empire building and helping themselves to whatever they could in the way of spoils.

Alarmed by the first setback of his martial career, Bonaparte immediately determined to solve the Spanish question personally. Heading up a huge army with his best marshals at his side including Ney and Soult, Napoleon began preparations to march over the Pyrenees and deal with his erstwhile friend and ally.

His ultimate destination was Madrid and total subjugation of the entire Iberian Peninsula. The Spanish were incapable of preventing his entry. Wracked with internal dissension and military incompetence, they could only await events.

John Moore arrived in the Peninsula just as Sir Arthur Wellesley won a spectacular victory over the French at Vimeiro. The news came at the same time as that of the significant victory by Spanish forces at Bailen.

The day after Sir Arthur's victory, a party of French officers lead by the famous General Kellermann offered a parley and terms of a conditional evacuation of the forces of the Emperor of France from Portugal. Dalrymple and Burrard immediately seized on the opportunity presented to them. Less willing was Sir Arthur Wellesley, who was refused permission by Burrard to follow up his victory which may have resulted in the complete expulsion of the French army from Portugal.

The result of the truce was the infamous *Convention of Cintra* which ruled that the army of France should leave Portugal but take with it all its stores, ammunition and the treasures of that land plundered by officers of the Emperor's legions. Sir Hew Dalrymple and Sir Harry Burrard succeeded in kicking the French out of Portugal, but back home they were pilloried and ordered to report to England to explain their actions. Wellesley, an extremely reluctant signatory to the accord, was similarly obliged to return to London.

Shortly before the future Duke of Wellington sailed for England, Sir Arthur Wellesley requested an urgent meeting with Sir John Moore. It would be the only occasion in which two of the greatest soldiers in history would meet.

*

It was said that it was difficult to *like* Arthur Wellesley.

John Moore was willing to look at things differently. The man standing before him seemed a mirror image of himself. Shorter in physical stature, but plainly dressed as Moore was and only a few years younger. Wellesley exuded professionalism. He'd performed miracles in India. The victory at Assaye was an extraordinary achievement. It was said that Wellesley placed logistics above all else. He hanged and flogged as much as the next man but it was noted that his casualty lists were low. The men under his command were well supplied and fed. He never exposed them to unnecessary risk. They didn't like him, unlike Moore, who was adored. But most of them stayed alive. He was a winner. The men forgave his aristocratic disdain for them accordingly. He was after all, a proper gentleman.

Moore was quartered at the palace at Queluz. He was pleased to be joined on his staff by his old friend, Colonel Paul Anderson and his secretary, Colbourne. It was the latter who presented Wellesley before him. The man was all business at first. He shook hands and began immediately.

'The army has nothing to do presently. What is required is change of leadership. I will propose that you lead the charge when I return to London.'

Moore ignored the sporting metaphor. He was not normally uncouth but he believed veracity was required. 'Sir Arthur, you act under a false assumption. Both Robert Stewart and George Canning regard me with contempt. To use ordinary soldier's parlance, they would rather consume their own shite before proposing me as commander.'

He strongly suspected the reason for Canning's enmity was due to Hester ending a brief affair with him on Moore's return from Sweden. John was surprisingly forgiving of her. She was not after all, like most other women. He was also aware that certain members of the Tory cabinet opposed to Moore's Whig sympathies suggested the Swedish mission be undertaken by him to get him out the country in order to give the command in Portugal to the politically more acceptable Wellesley. A man, though a friend of Castlereagh, junior to Moore in the army lists.

Wellesley nodded in sympathy. 'Canning, I grant you. As for my Lord Castlereagh, I believe I have some influence in that direction. Subtleties of distinction are required when dealing with politicians as with most else.' He coughed slightly. 'The matter of offering command to Dalrymple before you is testimony to incompetence somewhere in government.' He conceded somewhat grudgingly.

Wellesley then accepted the offer of port from the Douro valley provided by Moore's valet. 'Ah! The famous Francois! With *Quinta da Pacheca!* Would that I had so devoted a servant bringing me such fine port.' Sir Arthur raised his glass. 'To the very best. Francois! I salute you!' Francois smiled awkwardly and left the room.

The underlying humour Wellesley emitted was further evidence to Moore of the man's peculiar character. Though he viewed it more likely as a clumsy attempt to lighten the atmosphere.

'He's impossible at the best of times, Wellesley. I'm grateful for that!' Moore retorted in mild jest. He felt it necessary to join in the false jocularity. The man had after all, condescended to defer to him regarding political ineptitude.

'A good valet is priceless, Sir John. Now my plan. I will have to mediate with Castlereagh as I am led to believe your last meeting with him was somewhat painful?'

Of the former statement Moore believed the man before him had described Francois as he would a thoroughbred horse. As a Scot, he intensely disliked such lordly arrogance. As to the latter, he had absolutely no idea where the man's intelligence originated but decided best not to probe.

Sir Arthur continued. 'You wrote him a letter where you offered any suggestion that Castlereagh's decision to employ Sir Hew Dalrymple was not viewed as a slight by yourself?'

'Whoever is providing you with such information deserves acclaim.' Moore acknowledged with a trace of annoyance.

Ignoring the tone, Wellesley continued unabashed. 'And that in every instant you would never accept the decision to appoint Sir Hew was an insult to yourself?'

'Never crossed my mind for a moment.'

'Sir John, this is excellent port, by God!' Wellesley declared staring at his glass. 'I am satisfied on two counts. First, I will slither effortlessly out of the Cintra nonsense. And secondly, I can assure you I will convince our masters in government that Sir John Moore is exactly the man to redeem England's honour and lead the army into Spain.'

Moore smiled. 'Allow me to refill you, Sir Arthur.'

The man raised his glass in salute. The bottle and many more emptied that afternoon. But try as he might at the end of their meeting, John Moore could not bring himself to feel any warmth towards the future Duke of Wellington.

In early October of the year 1808, a special despatch was sent by frigate for the attention of Lieutenant-general Sir John Moore. It was dated September 25th only little over a week since his meeting with Wellesley. The letter, signed by Robert Stewart, Lord Castlereagh, secretary of state for war in his Majesty's government, announced the following appointment:

'Sir,

His Majesty having determined to employ a corps of his troops, of not less than thirty thousand infantry and five thousand cavalry, in the north of Spain, to co-operate with the Spanish armies in the expulsion of the army of France from the kingdom, has been graciously pleased to entrust to you, Sir John Moore, K.B., the command of chief of this force.'

Evidently the weight of public opinion regarding the people's favourite, Sir John Moore, along with the nation's scorn over Cintra had swayed the government's decision. Wellesley would have still been at sea, travelling to England on the date of the communication. Any entreaty on Moore's behalf by that gentleman would now be redundant. John hoped Sir Arthur would learn of the appointment as soon as possible in order to spare himself embarrassment.

The new commander of the only British army now in existence marvelled at the artfulness and mendacity of politicians. He only knew one thing of them that was unequivocal.

It was highly likely they would one day be the death of him.

Chapter Three

Robert Craufurd was now a greatly relieved man. But it could all have been so different.

Before sailing from England, Robert received a letter from his old friend, Johnny Moore, containing disappointing news. Moore wrote that he understood what it must feel like to be demoted through no fault of one's own. He'd spoken to the duke and the gentleman recommended Craufurd return home if dissatisfied with his appointment. It was H.R.H who handed out the promotions after all, Johnny reminded him meaningfully. But Moore wanted him on his staff and pleaded with Craufurd to accept the offer. To return home would be a grave error.

Craufurd knew Moore well enough and accepted his friend would have pleaded his case vociferously. But as everyone knew, Moore had problems of his own these days. Robert believed that the man could have done no more on his behalf without threatening his own delicate position.

Robert Craufurd sailed from Falmouth a mere colonel, though formerly holding the higher rank of brigadier which was removed after returning home from the debacle of Buenos Aires. He was now attached to Sir David Baird's division of the army of Spain and fretted constantly over the inequities of *interest*. Baird, the hero of Seringapatam, who led the successful storming of the Tippoo Sultan's fortress, sympathised greatly with Robert's plight. But he was powerless to assist in this instance. David Baird was a friend whom he first met at the Cape prior to the South American fiasco.

The packet only just arrived from England with the letter from his old mentor, former secretary of state for war, William Windham by way of his Majesty, the Duke of York confirming Craufurd's now official rank of brigadier.

His remaining hope was Windham. And the old boy saw him through. He served in the coalition government of Grenville, the so called *Ministry of all the Talents* but was ousted by Castlereagh when that administration fell in 1807. Evidently, he still retained some interest.

Robert Craufurd was a member of parliament for four years like John Moore, though unashamedly Whig. He'd been known in the House as '*the Colonel*' and shared Windham's passion for army reform. That was how he met Moore while he commanded at Shorncliffe, where they regularly exchanged ideas and letters on the subject closest to both their hearts. Admittedly, they disagreed on many points. Moore's paramount concern was the welfare of the men, primarily in pay, pensions and abolishing cruel punishments. Craufurd's was over enlistment duration and organisation of the militias. But they saw eye to eye on most other things. They'd recently been called together at the trial of General Whitelocke over the South American fiasco. Moore serving on the court martial board, Craufurd as a witness.

Robert was walking alone around the centre of the town of Coruña. The British force, after being penned up in their transports off the Spanish city's harbour for two weeks while awaiting permission from the authorities to disembark, had finally received clearance to leave their ships. Robert Crauford was an impatient man with a temper. But his commanding officer, Sir David Baird, was more than his match.

The second in command of the army, Sir David Baird, never a good sailor, suffered as most others including Robert Craufurd on the voyage over through sea-sickness. The relief of arriving at the port was tempered quickly when it became apparent that they were not expected by the Spanish authorities.

'*Our Davy*' as he was known, grew up among a family of fourteen children in the Gordon House on Edinburgh's Castle Hill. The building was divided into apartments containing various different strands of the capital's society. Lower middle class businessmen mixed with genteel spinster ladies, shopkeepers and tradesmen in a uniquely democratic fashion, leaving a lasting impression on the young David. He would carry it with him in dealings with all classes of people whether high born or low throughout his life.

His father, a successful merchant from Haddington in East Lothian, died when David was eight. His formidable mother, who achieved the remarkable distinction of not losing any of her offspring through stillborn birth or early infant mortality, ensured all her children grew up into adulthood to make their way in life.

As a child, David was the one member of Alice Baird's brood who would cause the most concern. A women who believed that any show of affection was a sign of weakness, her children were used to receiving beatings and bread and water diets for any misdemeanor, no matter how trivial. Davy, even as a youngster, stronger and with a greater physique than most other children of his age, despised injustice, spoke freely in defence of the underdog and believed he should follow his own accepted truths rather than submit to those of others. This inevitably brought him into conflict with his mother. Though he accepted his punishments as a fact of life, he received his regular hidings with a cheerful *sang-froid*.

He never lost his affection for her despite his harsh upbringing. She'd kept them all fed, clothed, educated and alive. When he received his first command, Baird set to music the songs she sang to her children when they were young. The band of the 71st Highlanders were ordered to play them exactly as they were sung by his mother.

As for his choice of career, there was never any doubt that soldiering was his preferred option. As a child he would watch the soldiers on the parade ground at the Castle, dreaming of carrying his own sword and travelling far from the confines of the house his family shared with others. The matter of the receipt of his commission was fortuitous, though tragic. Money was scarce but enough was raised for his elder brother, who also sought a military career. Sadly, the young man took ill and passed away though the commission was retained. This left David the next in line and only a few days before he turned fifteen years of age, he was gazetted an ensign in the 2nd Regiment of Foot.

General David Baird would undergo tremendous personal hardship in his chosen career. Far more than most officers who achieved similar rank. He also suffered through lack of patronage and this was to cause him grief beyond measure. While an experienced and successful major general sent by personal order of the Duke of York to India, he was scandalously superseded in command by a mere Lieutenant-colonel whose brother just happened to be the governor-general himself. The Wellesley brothers would leave an indelible imprint on the career of David Baird.

He was venerated by his men, something the great Wellesley never achieved. Baird was loved for his concern for his soldier's well-being, his enlightened views regarding mental and physical health improvements, forbearance with the lash and ability to always see them through to victory.

He also proved an excellent administrator. His highly esteemed, forwarded thinking reforms instigated during his period as both conqueror and then governor of the Cape Colony, left a record of accord and stability behind on his departure. His achievements in leading an earlier logistically trying military expedition to Egypt in 1801 were also noteworthy.

He could be intemperate, quick to take offence and bore grudges though these never lasted long. He could also be mightily forgiving and it was noted that he never fought a duel or ever risked one from any quarrel or disagreement. The fact he was six foot three inches tall, strongly built and broad as he was long, was usually the deciding factor for anyone who wished to try his luck in that regard.

But in this latest campaign, he was initially passed over once gain. Fortunately, John Moore personally requested him as his second in command. If he hadn't, he may well have been left behind completely despite his heroic status in the country after the defeat of the Tippoo Sultan. Baird was grateful to Johnny, whom he first met years before in Egypt. The fact Arthur Wellesley had left India for Europe was an irritant. But there was no brother here now to push his case, no matter how deserved after his victory at Vimeiro. Not that Baird bore a grudge against Sir Arthur. The man had no empathy for others and was quite unaware of how his haughty and disdainful manner affected those he came into contact with. It was like faulting him merely for the size of his over-large nose. He was no more capable of changing his appendage than his personality.

The hero of Assaye was on his way back to England to answer charges. He was now an irrelevance in regards to Baird's new mission.

The voyage out hardly began auspiciously. Originally ordered to sail from Cork, when Baird arrived to embark he discovered there was transport arranged for the men only, not the horses or artillery.

On receiving his latest orders, Davy Baird refused to leave the Irish port, devising a series of excuses not to sail until such transport vessels arrived. In doing so he incurred the wrath of Castlereagh who ordered him to get a move on. Technically, it was insubordination by the general. But he wasn't wrong. No soldier worth his salt wants to be separated from his guns.

Moore, with thirty thousand men was in Lisbon and had arranged to transport the army by sea to meet up with Baird's force at Coruña. While on the voyage over on board HMS *Loire,* Baird suffered the indignity of passing by a division of Marshal Junot's French army transported on British ships to be returned to France as part of the agreement signed at Cintra. Davy's choice of curse and Edinburgh invective that day created naval history.

In early October, the fleet arrived at Coruña where to their astonishment, they received no welcome nor even a reception party. Furious but also extremely concerned, Baird left his ship with an interpreter in tow. Making a request to the gentlemen who represented the Junta of Galicia to be permitted to disembark his army, he was refused as those worthies advised him that for such a major undertaking, the central Junta in Madrid must first be consulted. Davy Baird was so angry he dared not speak lest he offered violence to the men who stood before him.

Returning to his ship, he consulted his senior officers. Castlereagh in his original orders had painted a flattering portrait of the efficiency of Spanish government. Davy decided that clear thinking was required to stave off a possible diplomatic disaster. First of all, the interpreter needed to be replaced as his grasp of Spanish was deemed insufficient. This unforeseen problem took days to resolve before someone suitable was finally appointed. Baird then requested the town officials that until Madrid responded, may he at least disembark his poor horses as an act of humanity? The request was acceded to and an unusually large number of cavalrymen well in excess of the rolls and their grooms left their ships with their four-legged charges.

As no supplies awaited him, Davy was forced to acknowledge he required money in which to make purchases. He had no paymaster and immediately assigned one, ordering him to solicit cash sufficient to buy provisions as the local Spanish merchants were unwilling to accept treasury bills. £5000 was raised but Baird was forced to write to Castlereagh to beg for funds.

He also wrote to John Moore requesting financial assistance and urged him to sail for Coruña immediately. This was a private letter in which he admitted that he found himself in an extremely difficult situation.

A few days later, a ship arrived from England carrying two distinguished passengers. The first was the leader of the Spanish army recently escaped from Denmark while serving as an ally of France. General Romaña, hailed as the saviour of Spain, was exhibited publicly through the city in a flower strewn carriage surrounded by ecstatic local crowds. Privately, Davy thought he resembled a barber. This was uncharitable. Militarily he would later prove highly effective. The other visitor was the new British Minister in Madrid, Mr John Hookham Frere.

There was a warm welcome for the English visitor from the Spanish dignitaries. Baird fumed it was more due to the fact the British diplomat brought with him £500,000 for the Junta in Madrid. Ignoring the niceties, Davy immediately demanded £50,000 from the sum which was grudgingly handed over. The problems with Mr Hookham Frere had only just begun. Though in the new spirit of co-operation the arrival of the Spanish general engendered, the Junta generously made available the sum of 90,000 dollars to the British commander. It was only a loan, of course.

The following day, Davy received important news. In a letter from Moore dated the day the fleet originally arrived at Coruña, the commander of the army informed Baird he was no longer sailing for the port as formerly planned. In order to save time, he was marching with the army out of Lisbon in the direction of Burgos, where a suitable meeting place would be arranged for him to link up with Baird.

Davy Baird understood his friend's reasoning but was a little perturbed. Obviously, Johnny would have received word of the problems encountered at Coruña. Militarily he accepted that Moore's decision was based on encouraging reports on the strength and abilities of the Spanish army. Nevertheless, Moore's decision to enter the Spanish interior before linking up with the remainder of his army went against the spirit of his original orders.

Now aware time was critical and that a courier had only just arrived from Madrid, Baird demanded an answer to his earlier request. Eventually Frere was able to receive permission and the army began to disembark from their ships two full weeks after arrival. Earlier, a horse-buyer was sent out into the Asturias as mules were required for transportation. He had yet to return leaving Baird with the problem of only five animals to transport an army. It would mean that the men would have to set out with only their basic equipment while the baggage remained behind.

Davy required the men be supplied with food and other essentials for the march but became increasingly frustrated with the bureaucracy of the local Junta. Each request presented had to be ratified by anything up to a dozen individuals, any one of which could throw up an excuse for inaction, causing further delay. But he was willing to accept that as these people were so recently mortal enemies of his country, it took time for attitudes to change and strived to keep an open mind.

He was deluding himself.

Continuing his walk around the town, Robert Craufurd concluded that Coruña was not an easy place to defend a fleet. He noted a number of defects. Though the crescent shaped harbour was imposing, the contrary winds and Atlantic breakers could tie ships down inside the harbour while leaving them at risk of foundering if kept outside. The surrounding country was overlooked and dominated by hills that could provide effective artillery emplacements, targeting the port and town. The French could bottle up an army here for years. He quietly applauded his friend Baird's command over his temper in dealing with the Spanish authorities.

Not that Robert Craufurd could claim moral ascendancy in that regard. Early on in his military career he'd established a reputation for himself as something of a martinet. He was a lusty flogger and disciplinarian, feared and loathed by the private soldiers. Though he was proud of the fact that he had never once hanged a miscreant. A dead soldier was no good to him. Keep them upright and fearing the Christ out of you. Lay their backs bare. But leave them alive to carry their muskets.

Or rather, a Baker rifle. Robert was given the light brigade to command. A crack division of three highly specialised regiments. The 95th, the green-jacketed skirmishers modelled on the frontiersmen of the American wars who carried the new and highly accurate weapon, and the 43rd and 52nd regiments of the line, experts in use of the musket and drilled to support the 95th as they made an especial nuisance of themselves before the Corsican's vaunted columns. All three trained by Moore and Mackenzie in new light infantry tactics at Shorncliffe. The brigade was a special gift and Robert Craufurd was acutely aware he had received a specific honour. But until the confirmation of his rank, he was unable to enjoy it fully.

He was somewhat of a depressive. Born in Chigwell, Essex, the third son of a minor Scottish baronet, he was educated at Harrow. He believed learning and hard work would advance him in his chosen profession. Studying at Potsdam as a young man, he received three signed notes from Frederick the Great himself while early exposure to brutal Prussian discipline heavily influenced his thinking. His older brother Charles, a rising star in the military, gained him a place on the Austrian staff where he toured and studied many of Frederick's battlefields. He then became a captain in the 75th Regiment in his own country's army, seeing action in India against the Tippoo Sultan, and fighting a duel, wounding his opponent in the leg. He returned to Austrian service and reached the rank of lieutenant-colonel. He then became deputy quartermaster in general of the British army in Ireland during the rebellion of 1798. After that he was given a difficult assignment in Switzerland, acting as an intermediary in the British government's financial arrangements with Swiss officials in an effort to divert that country away from French influence. He was praised for the manner in which he protected his country's interests during negotiations, but made enemies as his manner was never suited to diplomatic niceties.

He was removed from Switzerland before causing further damage, and given a promotion to the Duke of York's staff in Holland towards the end of his disastrous expedition to the Helder. Though the duke regarded the colonel favourably, Craufurd became disenchanted and considered resigning from the army. He saw no other way open as he believed himself unable to make a difference in a system that was at its core, entirely rotten. The duke was determined to destroy the scandal of influence in the appointments of officers in the army. But his idea of its replacement, namely approving senior officers primarily due to their age, was little improvement.

Doubts assailed him. He began to lose himself, his dark mood broiling to the surface. He was also beset with financial worries, his late father having badly mishandled family affairs. Robert lost most of his own capital investing in a failed enterprise in India. Money was a never ending source of concern for Craufurd.

His life was turned round when Robert met and married Mary Frances Holland, a granddaughter of Capability Brown, whose care and devotion softened him and brought him back into the light. After the Treaty of Amiens of 1802 temporarily placed a halt to the war, he became a much admired member of parliament, working feverishly to make a name for himself. A few of the military reforms he championed became law. He befriended John Moore. But his mood darkened again. His wife realised that a return to the military was required. He re-joined the army and his patron in the government gave him a position on the expedition to South

America with the temporary rank of brigadier.

'Here's tae ye, Boab!' David Baird raised his glass.

The others around the table joined in the toast. They included Baird's senior officers, Major Generals Manningham and MacKenzie and his military secretary, Captain Sorell. Three ensigns honoured to be present gave the company an air of cheerful homeliness. None of them were older than fifteen years of age. Robert Craufurd acknowledged the salutes and downed his glass of rough Spanish red.

'Aboot bluidy time tae, ah ken! But that's the airmy for ye!' Davy was slightly drunk and his Edinburgh accent inaccessible to some of his younger, southern born officers. The older ones knew him well enough and how to handle him. With Craufurd present, they could afford the burden to fall on that man's shoulders this evening. He was content to take anything thrown at him.

'Thanks, Davy, I ken it's about time!' Robert replied, as cheerily as the man was capable. 'It's also about the hour we give these young fellows leave for their beds! Long days march in the morn!'

Born and raised in England, Robert had only ever been to Scotland once, on joining his first regiment, the 75th, at Stirling, when he was twenty four years of age, staying there only a few weeks. Nevertheless, Craufurd could effortlessly slip into his father's vernacular, particularly when in the company of native Scots. It was indicative of his unusual, some considered disturbing dual nature; either displaying his curious, ironic, sense of humour or when agitated and highly emotional, using extremely vulgar Caledonian invective. It baffled those who didn't know him well enough. Unfortunately, there were few who did. There was talk of madness in his family, which offered mitigation.

Not half as inebriated as he appeared, Baird took Craufurd's hint. 'Aw'richt laddies! Aff tae yer beds. Nae mair drink but a guid forty winks for a' o' ye's!'

The three young ensigns, each extremely grateful to be dismissed as they were all about nodding off, gladly made for their billets. The senior officers took the opportunity to depart also. The last thing any of them desired was to see their commander under the table. Again, they had Craufurd to thank and more importantly, to see him off to his own repose.

When the last departed, Baird snapped at Craufurd.

'Now, will you tell me what happened in Buenos Aires?' He'd not felt it proper to discuss the matter before his officers. A court martial was involved.

Robert reached over the table for the carafe of wine. 'Not as sick-drunk as you look, eh, Davy?'

'No, I'm not. But I know how to play these Englishmen well enough. The laddies are only bairns. I've a duty to their mothers not to get them drunk and stay up late. The others pretend to chat to each other. But all they're really doing is listening to and watching me.'

'The exigencies of command, David. That's why we're paid so much.' Robert sympathised.

'Fash!' Baird snorted. 'And pish, too. Stop trying to wriggle out of it, Bobby.'

They sat in the house of a Coruña wine merchant. The man had graciously opened his home to Baird and his staff on the proviso that while the army remained encamped there, they would be good for his trade. At least he was honest. Which was more to be said for the custodians of the country at the present moment.

Robert Craufurd knocked back his glass in one gulp. 'It was as bad as they say. Whitelocke and Gower between them, were every bit as bad as they say.'

There was a silence. Davy looked over bemused. 'Is that all?'

Robert spoke quietly, almost to himself. 'There was a moment. When it was all so clear. When what was required lay before me.'

Baird was unsure whether Craufurd was drunk. He was a man of strange moods. The army knew he did well in South America. The only one to come out of the whole sorry mess with his head held high. He'd few friends though Moore liked and admired him. But Johnny was Johnny and always befriended *collie-dugs*. Soft hearted Johnny Moore. Not like me, Baird thought. Or Bob either.

Or that arrogant snob, Wellesley. 'You mean when you asked Gower for permission to storm the city?' Baird asked.

Robert's head was down. He twirled the stem of the empty glass in his hands while tapping it gently with his fingers.

'Don't go off into one of your morbid tempers, Bobby.' Baird warned meaningfully.

Craufurd seemed to awaken as if startled from a dream. 'Eh? Oh, sorry,

Davy. I was away there.'

'Aye. With the fairies. Pour yourself another drink, man.' Baird ordered sharply. Robert reached over. The carafe was near empty and his glass only half filled. 'I knew Whitelocke.' Davy reminisced. 'Couldn't stand the bugger. Treated the men like muck one minute, the next he was calling them by their first names. Do you know he actually looked up the rolls in order to learn their *Christian* names?'

'Aye. He did that over there too.' Robert replied with a yawn.

'And never anywhere near the front.' Davy continued. 'Yellow. That's a fact. But he was born on the right side of a lord's blanket and so the auld king's bonny son looked after him.'

'All wrong.' Robert slurred. He'd drained the half glass as the drink began taking full affect.

'Still, was he really that bad?' Davy asked, somewhat sceptically.

'What makes a man see something differently from another?' Robert began, looking down at the table. 'I saw what was required. Gower knew it but was too inexperienced to act. It didn't matter about Whitelocke. I could have taken my six hundred into the city. Created havoc. Gower would have been compelled to follow. I would have sent Pack to Whitelocke to inform him. Whitelocke would have *had* to act. Why did I not disobey Gower and just do it?'

The origins of the expedition to the Rio de la Plata would have brought a knowing smile to the face of Sir Francis Drake.

It was a classic example of freebooting. Or piracy, if you were Spanish, made without authorisation or even the knowledge of the British Government. It was the brain child of Commodore Sir Home Popham, who had contacts among South American revolutionaries eager to throw off the Spanish crown. Without permission, Popham set off for Monte Video from southern Africa with his small fleet and sixteen hundred men to conquer a continent. Among them was a regiment he'd sweet-talked David Baird out of while that man was governor of the Cape of Good Hope. The proviso being the Scottish general would receive a generous share of any prize monies won in South America.

In June 1806 the tiny force landed eight miles from Buenos Aires. The original plan was to take Monte Video. But Popham was aware that ships carrying gold to Spain left from the larger city across the Plata and persuaded the army commander, General Beresford, to amend his plan accordingly. The prospect of up to £2,000,000 in bullion docked in the harbour of Buenos Aires focussed the minds of both men and the target of attack was switched accordingly.

Spanish forces in the area were disorganised and poorly equipped. Consequently, the 1600 regulars of the British army were able to march into the city of seventy thousand inhabitants virtually unopposed. The British flag was soon raised above the city. Sir David Baird's cut of the spoils amounted to the then substantial sum of £23,000. He was now a comfortably wealthy man.

The news caused a sensation among the investors of the City of London, who saw great opportunities developing in a new market. The government, shaken by the news but hardly able to ignore the clamour, could not also ignore the large wagons drawing up at the gates of the Bank of England containing gold from the Plata.

It was now necessary to accept the *fait accompli* and the government put together a force of three thousand men under the American born Sir Samuel Auchmuty, to be dispatched immediately in order to augment the success in South America. The newly promoted Brigadier Robert Craufurd was then, thanks to his benefactor William Windham, given command of a force of four thousand men and ordered to sail around Cape Horn in order to subjugate Spanish Chile. The plan was nothing short of madness.

Craufurd was at sea less than three weeks when the shocking news came through that the people of Buenos Aires had risen up and expelled the pitifully small British band left there as an occupying force. Beresford was forced to surrender to the Spanish commander, a Frenchman, General Liniers. Craufurd was redirected to join up with Sir Samuel, the Chilean plan temporarily in abeyance.

The combined force arrived in the Plata and soon captured Monte Video. But events in London then took a fatal turn. The government believed Craufurd, who was senior to Sir Samuel, not experienced enough to command a force of nearly ten thousand men even though he had achieved success so far. In their wisdom, they turned to Lieutenant-general John Whitelocke to command, with the aristocratic but entirely inexperienced Major-general John Leveson Gower, aged only 32, as second in command.

On arrival at Monte Video with an additional force of 1800 men, it soon became apparent that although Whitelocke was unwilling to take advice from anyone, the real power lay with Gower. Whitelocke was inexplicably in thrall to the flattering young noble and deferred to him in all matters. He also took to winning the non-commissioned officers and men over by making jokes and ridiculing the officers before them while calling rankers by their Christian names. This left the majority of the men uneasy and most grew to despise him.

After a survey of the city, Whitelocke made it clear that he had no desire to invest Buenos Aires. Craufurd was left to assume the commander wished to meet the Spanish force in an open fight which would only have one outcome, a victory for the British. Less than a month later, Whitelocke changed his mind, or had it changed for him, and a plan was drawn up to assault the city.

The force, now numbering over ten thousand men, set off in the fleet across the Plata with Craufurd's light brigade first to reach the shore. Whitelocke then chose to divide his force into four columns and with no effective measures put in place to communicate between the separate parts of the army, set out for the city.

In the vanguard, Craufurd's brigade captured the small village of Reduction without difficulty. From there they could see the spires of Buenos Aires before them. Night had fallen and Craufurd chose to stop less than two miles from the city, where he could see the camp-fires of the enemy army. This indicated they were outside the city awaiting the approach of the British.

In the morning, Craufurd received orders from Gower to find a way over or around the *Rio Cheulo* which was now all that stood before the two armies. The Spanish formed a strong defensive position around the main bridge over the river.

Following up a unit of enemy cavalry, a group of British horsemen found their way over a small waterway known as the Passo Chico, previously considered unfordable. It was in fact only three feet deep with a firm gravel floor and only a slight current. Word was passed to Craufurd and Gower who brought their columns over including guns, and found themselves behind the Spanish force with the city in front of them, guarded only by a battalion of Spanish soldiers. Meanwhile, Whitelocke was out of sight, his whereabouts unknown.

Gower now returned to the other column under command of Brigadier Lumley and brought it to the ford. Craufurd noted some heights before the city that were undefended and requested permission before Gower left to take them, which was granted. It was then that Craufurd deduced the forces before him were in such disarray, that a push now on ahead would see them onto the city streets, virtually unopposed.

'Bring those damned guns up now, by God!' Craufurd signalled Major Trotter to his left. Here was his opportunity and he was cursed if he would allow anyone to stop him.

'Pass word to the men to halt and give them water until the guns arrive.' Robert then ordered Major Macleod.

The brigade came to a halt. They hadn't stopped since morning and were glad of the chance to rest. The guns were only just brought up when the Spanish, finally spotting the enemy, opened with grapeshot and musket fire.

At first the barrage from the Spanish side was heavy and the men ran about looking to take cover. Craufurd rode up, hollering to them to form line, which they did with the 95th forming skirmishing order. Soon the green jackets were scoring a large number of hits.

'Fix swords!' Major Trotter roared, after ordered to do so by Craufurd. He had by far the loudest voice in the brigade.

'Prepare to charge, boys!' Craufurd ordered. He got down from his horse and unsheathed his sword. The fire from the Spanish lines was now sporadic as the British sharpshooters aimed at the artillerymen.

'Forward, the light brigade!' With a swing of his sword, Robert dashed ahead as the men of the 95th and the other regiments cheered their excitement and rushed forward towards the centre of the Spanish line while another company of riflemen moved towards their flank. Craufurd's men tore through the hedges and scrub which gave cover, quickly overrunning the first artillery position and killing all before them. As they emerged in to the open facing the square, the second Spanish line fired on them with bullet and shot which blasted into a number of Britons. They stopped and began firing in return. Shots continued from ahead, but it was noticeable now that many in the Spanish lines were turning to flee the fire from the enemy.

In support, the flanking company under Captain Elder began firing ferocious volleys into the Spanish and one of the senior commanders, Juan Pio De Gana was killed. This was the signal for the defenders to turn and run. The light brigade troops followed in deadly pursuit.

On reaching the former Spanish second line, Robert stopped as his men poured after the fleeing enemy, mercilessly bayonetting and mauling all they caught up with. He looked back at the fallen men of his brigade, some being helped by comrades as the screams and shrieks rent the air of the killers and the killed. Robert walked back through the bodies and the guns as Major Macleod who was mounted, pulled up beside him.

'Sir, I request most earnestly that you retire! We can ill afford your loss.'

'Dinnae be daft, Willie! Look over there! That's Liniers scuttling off like a minister from a tart's mattress!' MacLeod could make out a group of spectacularly dressed officers grouped together, making away from the city back towards the Spanish position.

'All we need to do now is form back up and march in.' Robert Craufurd exclaimed joyfully. 'The city's ours, lad! We've won a great victory! We have *won!*'

Robert sent a messenger to General Gower requesting permission to move into the city. But the officer returned with an order from the second in command to fall back immediately to Corrale instead. In disbelief, Robert sent the man back to plead his case. This time Gower followed the officer down from his position to personally confer with Craufurd.

Having had time to calm himself, Robert stood before Gower. 'I must inform you, sir, that it is my opinion, that should we advance now, we will invest the city as the forces there are clearly not in strength or organisation to oppose us.'

Gower looked over at the heights where he saw redcoats forming up and buildings of the city in clear vision. 'I think not, General Craufurd. We shall first await orders from Sir John.'

Still in control of himself, Robert continued. 'It's imperative that we advance now. Sir John, would he be here, I'm certain would be in full agreement.' Craufurd looked over at the small figures running back towards the city. What an opportunity!

Gower looked ahead. They were both on their feet having dismounted. 'I'm convinced that if we enter the city with so small a force, we should be overwhelmed. We still await word of Lumley's division's whereabouts. Auchmuty remains with the rearguard at Reduction. No. We shall await junction with Sir John's forces before plotting further strategy.' With Whitelocke's location still unknown, Gower's caution was understandable with night now falling.

Losing all restraint, Robert exploded. 'But that is madness! They are not formed up! We have ample force to enter the city and build up strongpoints! Can you not see, damn your eyes, man!'

'That is enough, sir!' Gower replied furiously. 'I will not risk the army for your impulsive folly, Craufurd!'

'Damn ye to hell, you rich *hoor's* abortion!' Craufurd swore savagely, his accent heavy. He turned and mounted his horse, riding over to where the light brigade was now formed up again following their rout of the enemy. A group of officers having witnessed the scene, stood together in shock.

'You heard that, MacLeod! Trotter! The fool will bring us nothing but shame!' Craufurd roared breathlessly.

'Robert, I ask you to appeal to General Whitelocke!' Lieutenant-colonel Lancelot Holland, his aide and also his brother-in-law, pleaded.

'Ach, shite, Lance! He'll no listen tae the likes o' me!' Robert spat. He turned his horse and looked back. He could see clearly the way open to the city. Gower, by now, had returned to his position and begun marching his column towards a flat plain in the city's suburbs known as the Corrale. Almost beside himself over the lost opportunity, Craufurd reluctantly ordered the brigade to advance towards Gower's position.

Craufurd threw his glass to the floor. He raised a hand to his face.

'Few know the shame, Davy. That's the worry. To hand over your sword to a rabble. Whitelocke preferred shame. Why are there such men?'

Baird knew that Craufurd was aware that in India years before, David Baird was captured by the forces of Hyder Ali. He'd been chained in a cell for four years.

'Change is needed in this army, Boab.' Davy sympathised. 'That's for sure. We're all sick fed up with rakes, drunkards and the *gets* o' high-born trollops buying their way in. Oh, aye, now and again you get someone competent. But there's not enough of them and damned too many of the other.'

'I shouldn't have broken the glass.' Robert brooded. 'It wasn't my property.'

'It's only a glass, man.'

Craufurd rose unsteadily. 'I'll away to my bed. Not as young as I used to be.' A servant brought a fresh decanter through and placed it on the table. Baird reached over for it.

'Aye, none o' us are. Good night, Bobby.' Baird filled his glass and was left alone. He lit a cigar and thought of the morning ahead.

Robert Craufurd knew the following day would be a long one, but couldn't sleep. Some poor ranker would pay for his bad head in the morning.

He was grateful Baird got him alone before mentioning Buenos Aires. On the voyage over, he heard whispers of '*that's him*!' and '*well, ask him, damn it!*' but so far none dared approach him. He was a natural scowler, of medium height and somewhat stooped. He could do nothing with his beard, no matter how often he shaved. He always carried a dark shadow which gave him a piratical look, though he in fact appeared younger than his actual age of forty-four. His countenance declared to the world: keep your distance.

But he did not want to be alone. He had a desire to be heard and ideas he wanted to share. He did well in parliament and was widely respected. But when things did not pan out as he wished he lost heart, questioned himself and walked away. His deep moods of depression left him in despair and he needed someone to bring him out of them. His wife did that now and absences from her were deeply painful to him. If Buenos Aires had been a success, he'd determined to leave the army forever. He was no lover of war or battle and understood his chances of surviving each engagement reduced every time he exposed himself. He now had a young family and must temper his desires accordingly.

His remaining passion was to gain glory while purging the shame of the surrender in South America. Once his goal was achieved and his pain expunged completely, he would return home contented. His rank was confirmed and the light brigade was his to command. This time, he was under exceptional commanders of proven ability. There was the opportunity of encountering Bonaparte himself. A gift only God could have provided him.

He would soon set out on a long and dangerous road. But the path to Robert Craufurd's redemption began on the day he set sail from home, bound for an old Galician port of northern Spain.

Coruña.

Chapter Four

Andrew Berry desperately wanted to become a soldier.

He was not a criminal. Neither was he an orphan, a slum dwelling street waif or an itinerant country yokel. He hadn't left a girl pregnant or abandoned a wife and family he could no longer support. Nor was he a runaway from a brutal father and neglectful, unloving mother.

Andrew lived and worked at his father's coach inn on the new 'great road' recently built to connect Glasgow and Edinburgh in Scotland. The settlement, known as Barbauchlaw, set around the Bathgate hills of Linlithgowshire in Lothian, was rich in farmland, mineral deposits and located twenty miles west of the Scottish capital. The land was recently bought by Sir William Honeyman, an estate holder from Sutherland in northern Scotland, who sought property near Edinburgh for business purposes. Sir William later took a title and the settlement based around Andrew Berry's father's coach house, which slowly began to expand into a town, would become known simply as Armadale, after the new lord of that name.

Business was brisk for William Berry who also undertook the duties of running the toll section, forming part of the new road. He employed all his children, four sons and three daughters. Grateful for his good fortune, William thanked God every day for the providence that allowed him to provide for his family while depositing good Scotch *siller* each month into his account at the British Linen Bank in Edinburgh.

His only concern was his second and best loved son, Andrew.

Each of his male children could read and write English to an acceptable standard. William ensured that until reaching the age of twelve years, his sons regularly attended the house of a teacher in nearby Bathgate for their schooling, for which they travelled the short journey of three miles there and back by horse-cart. Like many Scots fathers, he took advantage of his country's enlightened views on education, at the time the most advanced in the world. But he only desired the laddies to learn so much. Any more and they might harbour ideas about running off and becoming apprentices to firms in Edinburgh interested in cheap, though semi-educated country labour.

He was not a selfish man. He was God-fearing and kindly but was fully aware of the evils that dwelt in the city across the Lothian plain. The brothels, ale houses, the illegal sports. The whores and pick-pockets. The tricksters and confidence men. All such perils and more awaited good, honest lads entering into that haven of iniquity, Scotland's capital.

Those he feared most were army crimps and naval press-gangs. The strong, healthy, well fed young Berry lads were a recruiting sergeant's dream. Even more, that of the crimp, those vile parasites who kidnapped fine young men and sold them on to the army or the militias as substitutes for more affluent young gentlemen called up for compulsory military service. They were the fortunate ones who had enough money to purchase away their duty to their king if suitable and compliant replacements could be found.

Consequently, William was reluctant to allow any talk of his boys leaving his employ. None of the four sons had ventured more than ten miles in any direction from their home in their lives. Happily, three showed absolutely no inclination to travel further, each content with their lot. He was confident his reliable, though entirely unimaginative eldest son Robert would take over the reins of running the business when the good Lord finally summoned him or left him too infirm to continue. The youngest two would do the bidding of their elder brother. Of that, William Berry was also quite content.

But as for Andrew, Mr Berry, though he admitted in his heart was always his favourite, the boy's intelligence, imagination and the desire to visit faraway lands was ingrained too deep. Thus he resigned himself to losing him. His schooling was *too* successful, as it opened his overly intellectual mind a little too much for his father's liking. Though William was honest enough to admit it gave him a certain feeling of pride that his adored second son desired to go out into the world and experience God's creation for himself.

The only problem was that Andrew, in seeking adventure in new lands, saw the army as the path to fulfilling his dream. William Berry did not like to think of a son of his running off to the military. It was the refuge of failures, ne'er do-wells, felons and crossed lovers. His mind recoiled at the very mention of the word *soldier*. It was a subject that still had the power to make him flinch, despite the hard earned measure of contentment he finally enjoyed, after years of toil and painful memories time dulled but could not completely erase. There were those three dead children he and his wife laid in the ground. And there were older matters. Eternally unresolved though forever seeking closure, biting at him, eating away at his soul, remaining unburied within, no matter how much he tried to shroud them.

Travelling recruiting bands were a common sight in those times of conflict. They passed regularly through the Inn on their way to towns in Lothian like Borrowstouness, Linlithgow, Bathgate, the little villages of Livingston, Mid-Calder and others. This latest group, hailing from the county's own regiment, the famed 1st of Foot, spoke of a great open recruiting day to be held in Edinburgh that weekend. Regiments from all over the country, along with naval teams, were gathering together in order to tempt the youth of the Capital with large bounties and splendid uniforms into taking the king's shilling. Andrew listened avidly.

He knew he would not go off there and then with this particular band. He couldn't do that to his parents. But the idea of the army finally coalesced in his mind after he learned of a new Act recently passed. A recruit, instead of signing on for life as was the former and only available stipulation on offer, could instead join for a limited period of seven years only. The sum of eleven guineas was offered as bounty, an enormous amount of money to a working man of the day.

Andrew had no desire to spend all his life in uniform. He was thrilled by this new piece of legislation as he believed the limited service offer was a trade-off he could present before his parents. He could sign up knowing that if fortune favoured him, he would return only seven years later, hopefully by then a sergeant, with captured booty and a wealth of stories he could tell his younger siblings of the glories of Europe. He may even achieve the rank of officer after performing a remarkable feat of daring and courage. He knew that though his father was developing a healthy bank balance, he could never afford the £500 required for an ensigncy. He dismissed this with little regret. He would not have dreamed of asking for such a sum in any event.

The resignation in his father's face was plain to see when he informed him that he was setting out for Edinburgh the following day. His mother was less restrained as were his sisters. Their tears were heartfelt and bitter. He was everyone's favourite, not only his father's.

But he was eighteen years old. His parents were married with two children at an age not much greater. Nevertheless, the dread tangible in his mother and sister's eyes among their tears remained a poignant and deeply painful memory to Andrew in the days ahead.

Andrew was a healthy, broad-shouldered young man, five foot eight inches in height. His hair was brown and dropped just below his ears. He had blue eyes, large and expressive, and a slightly turned up nose. He was pleasant faced and somewhat ruddy in complexion. He smiled often with a ready wit, was expansive and caring in nature. He'd always carried out his duties at home diligently. And as he set out that morning for his nation's capital, his mind was firmly set on avoiding two things: the navy and a cavalry regiment. He desired to view foreign lands, not their ports and he'd had enough of the horseflesh of others. Andrew wanted to march with his own two legs, carry a musket and wear the beautiful red coat. He didn't want to wear a sword or sabre and worry about the upkeep of some spavined, four-legged old nag.

His father paid for the coach journey. Andrew wanted to walk. It would have been an adventure, but his parents insisted.

He arrived in Edinburgh at the Kings Stables Road, in the west end of the city, in late afternoon. He marvelled at the sight of the Castle, towering on its rock above him. Andrew could usually view it in the distance from the hills around his home, including that of Cairnpapple, an ancient burial ground and the highest point in that part of Lothian. From it on a clear day the Bass Rock, far to the east on the Firth of Forth, could clearly be made out also.

He wandered the few yards through the wynd into the Grassmarket where the fair was being held. He'd never seen so many people together before in one place in all his life. This was the city's main gathering point and also where public executions were carried out. Murderers, witches, covenanters and many other criminals met their end there with most of the city's populace in attendance. Eighty years before it had witnessed the notorious Porteous Riots.

Tenements of the poor and townhouses of the wealthy sat side by side. They soared high and somewhat precariously to Andrew's mind above him and he had to crane his neck on looking upwards. The noise and smell were overwhelming for someone who never strayed far from home in his life. There were stalls selling produce to locals and refreshments to the recruiting teams. He watched bands of soldiers in their red-coats, cavalrymen in blue and hussars with pelisses, standing outside an inn called the *White Hart,* playfully swinging and brandishing their sabres before groups of urchins, cheekily asking to be signed up.

Andrew wanted to join a foot regiment and his heart was set on the 1st. He wandered along the cobbled road, avoiding horse droppings and other detritus searching for the regiment of his choice. He stopped to look around and then across the street, he caught sight of a lone individual wearing a black feathered headdress, a red coat with white cross belts and a kilt of darkest green with long red and white cheque stockings.

Andrew approached the soldier. 'Sir, can you direct me to the 1st of Foot?'

'And why would I wish to do that?' The man asked with a slightly ironic smile.

'It is the regiment my desire is set upon.' Andrew replied simply.

'Then you are living under a misconception, my good lad. The 1st are here recruiting and it is within my knowledge to direct you to them. But if I do, I will be responsible to you of a grave disservice.'

Andrew by now had caught sight of a long wood and metal object leaning against the tenement wall the soldier stood before.

'You notice my musket?' The soldier offered, alert to the young man's interest.

'I observe it, yes.' Andrew replied, guardedly.

'Do you wish to investigate it further?'

Andrew could not resist. 'It would be my pleasure, sir.'

The man turned and grabbed the weapon. 'It's not "sir", *buckie.* I'm a sergeant.' He pointed to his arm. 'Three stripes. And in just so many years of honest and fortunate service, you may attain such a rank.'

Andrew only had eyes for the musket held out before him. The sergeant offered it and Andrew took the butt in his left hand and held the barrel in his right. He looked closely at the brass plate that attached the working parts to the wood. He noted the word *Tower* inscribed above the trigger guard which meant it was manufactured by the Ordinance board for soldiers in Britain and not destined for the East India Company's army. Eyeing the crown with *GR* stamped below the firing pan, Andrew ran his hand along the thirty nine inches of polished wood and dull metal, longing for one of his to own.

'It's heavy, but of great beauty and craft.' He concluded happily, handing back the weapon.

The soldier replaced the musket against the building, in plain sight of Andrew. 'Its accuracy is well known to the French. Six men I have dispatched to God with one.' He responded drily. He might have been discussing the weather.

'What regiment are you?' Andrew asked, his curiosity aroused.

'The 42nd of Foot. We are a fine regiment and our honours are many and hard won. But we only accept superior recruits. If you were to approach us, we would have to be convinced of your potential before deciding on your application. We cannot accept inferior material as this would dilute the effectiveness of our regiment.'

Andrew glanced at the soldier. He admitted to himself that though lowland born and bred, the red-coat combined with the dark green of the kilt was a combination that intrigued him. He was also encouraged by the fact the man was clearly only interested in him if he was deemed of good upbringing and respectability.

'I'm here of my own free-will, with my parents blessing. They are good folk of godly disposition. My father is the owner of the Inn on the Barbauchlaw Toll.'

The soldier's demeanour, up till that moment that of a wholly professional recruiting sergeant, aloof but cunningly ingratiating, well versed in the nefarious tactics used to successfully complete the second oldest transaction of all, changed momentarily to something less than certain.

'I know of that house and the... I mean as to say, I have heard of it.' Stumbling to his conclusion, he was momentarily bereft of his former trickiness. Andrew looked at him meaningfully but the sergeant soon collected himself, returning to his former air of self-assured authority.

'Your parents are indeed folk of an honest and industrious reputation. If you are of a similar nature, then I believe we may have a place for you in the 42nd. But even that is not enough. Once joined with us, you will be subject to constant and rigorous examination of your character. The regiments of the highlands do not desire to punish with the lash. They rely on a man's honour and respect for his chief. Thus, flogging is negligible and rare. But there are those who seek advantage from such a lenient regime. I trust you will not be one of them.'

'I will not, sir.' Andrew responded resolutely. 'It is my desire to serve my king and fight his enemies.'

'What is your name and age, boy?' The sergeant asked thoughtfully, looking directly into Andrew eyes, which caused the young man to wonder if his last words were deemed somewhat foolish. Andrew informed him as requested, but now felt a little less confidant.

The sergeant nodded slightly. 'It is beholden of me to advise you, Andrew Berry, that our battalion is due for Portugal presently. What it shall meet there almost certainly will be those enemies you speak off. Do not cozen yourself of tales of Frenchmen's courage not being comparable to that of a Briton. They are a staunch and resolute adversary. I have fought many an engagement and suffered to witness brave lads like you dying most bitterly at their hands. Do not propose to take this step lightly. I will think no less of you if you were to leave now uncommitted and return to your parents in Barbauchlaw. For many a widow and poor mother has shed tears these past years due to the Tyrant's columns, which are as fearsome a vision as any man beheld.'

Andrew was grateful for his honesty while being thrilled at the mention of Portugal. He already decided that he would take up the offer, but the mention of his mother was unexpectedly cutting. He felt a creeping doubt, but stood firm.

'I don't intend to be a victim of Bonaparte, sir. My wish is to inflict that very suffering on those who threaten my country. I would be proud to serve with the 42nd if you'll have me.'

An oddly familiar expression, similar to the melancholy acceptance on Andrew's father's face only the day before, came over the sergeant.

'I will escort you to the magistrate where you will attest and take the oath. I believe the sum of fifteen guineas is offered as bounty. A lesser amount of eleven guineas is paid for short service. Whichever you decide, my advice is to keep three guineas for necessaries, a few shillings for yourself and forward the remainder to your parent's immediately on receipt.'

The soldier placed a hand on Andrew's shoulder. 'My name is Alexander McGillivray. A sergeant of eleven years, corporal of five and private soldier of three. No finer life did ever a man lead than that of a soldier. You have made a wondrous and a terrible decision. Your life will never be the same again. But the army will offer you opportunities should you be prepared to work hard and conduct yourself with steadiness and sobriety, as becoming an upright young man of good character and virtue.'

Listening carefully, Andrew replied, 'I have those qualities, sir. It's my fervent wish that I do not dishonour my parents by bringing them shame as a drunkard and dishonest individual. I've promised my mother to avoid strong drink and disreputable company.'

The sergeant smiled but without trace of mockery. 'Come now, I have fulfilled my quota. I will address you as Mr Berry for the last time. For soon you will bear the title of a king's man, and there is none finer.' The sergeant pointed towards the direction of the West Bow. 'Mr Berry, will you accompany me to the magistrate?'

'I will indeed.' Andrew replied proudly, unable to keep the happy grin from his face.

'One last thing,' Sergeant McGillivray declared, 'you must ensure to avoid drink-sodden, licentious slatterns and other notorious individuals who will endeavour to relieve you of your bounty before we set off for barracks. I've known many fine lads have their pockets picked and their brains bashed in for their money. Beware of such villains, soon to be *Private* Berry.'

Andrew was grateful for the fatherly advice, considering himself in the hands of a decent regiment. He didn't need to be told about sending money home as he planned to do that anyway.

The highland soldier offered his hand. 'Welcome to the 42nd.'

And with that, Andrew Berry became a private soldier of the Royal Highland Regiment, the *Black Watch*.

Chapter Five

John Moore inwardly cursed the British Government, the commissariat, the weather, his lack of money, Sir Hew Dalrymple and everyone else he could think of.

He sat in the throne room in the recently refurbished palace at Queluz, late pride of Marshal Junot. Sparing no expense, the Frenchman had lavished its many chambers with ceilings painted with eagles trampling upon crowns and broken sceptres while spreading their wings over a huge representation of the globe. Each eagle was painted with an 'N' attached to a crown.

The throne was replaced by a dais and a canopied regal chair. Moore sat in the chair while to his side sat his closest aides and friends, Colonel Paul Anderson, Colonel Thomas Graham, Major Colbourne and George Murray, his quartermaster general.

'Gentlemen, I mean to march for Spain but I confess the scarcity of information on Portuguese roads causes me grave concern.' He concluded after their discussion ended.

'Johnny, the blame lies not with you.' Anderson soothed his friend.

'Sir, each day we remain in Lisbon the character of the army disintegrates further.' Colbourne pointed out.

'Yes, I intend to issue an order regarding discipline.' Moore replied a little vaguely to the last.

There was a growing problem with the abuse of alcohol, amongst many others issues with the British army of Portugal. A large, tented camp was built up around the grounds of the palace. With the French now evacuated according to the articles of the Cintra agreement, the British army was left with no thought as to how to maintain its base in Portugal. Before signing the accord, which was of course unknown to London at the time, Dalrymple was ordered by the government to enter Spain immediately after the victory at Vimeiro.

The late summer weather in Portugal brought with it great heat by day followed by freezing cold nights. The men were drinking poor quality water and cheap wine while consuming copious amounts of local fruit for want of little else on offer. Inevitably, sanitation problems developed and an outbreak of dysentery ensued. A few cases of typhus were also reported.

A hospital was hastily built, unfortunately too close to the stores depot which was separated by a ditch used as a latrine by patients suffering from dysentery. Inevitably this resulted in a greater outbreak of the disease. But the consumption of alcohol alone was becoming a major cause of the army's ills. Disciplinary infractions increased as a result for which it was noted by senior figures, the mainly inexperienced company officer corps were usually inadequate to the task of dealing with offenders satisfactorily. It was a portent of things to come.

Moore concluded early that sailing the army to Coruña was no longer feasible due to information received on the inadequacy of the port's ability to supply large numbers of troops. It would have enough problems dealing with Baird's force alone. He received Davy's communication on the problems he was experiencing, dispatching £8000 to assist him. He could barely spare the sum himself.

The British commander suffered from a serious lack of funds. He was left with only £25,000 by Dalrymple, barely enough to cover the soldiers pay, never mind feed and supply an army. But by far the most urgent problem was transport.

The army sent to Portugal was criminally lacking in its military train. Scouring the country, the wagons bought from the populace were too unwieldy and those provided were too few in number. Local carts were found to be unsophisticated and inadequate to the task. With the onset of autumn just weeks away, such poor quality transports would be useless in mountain tracks reduced to mud by the rains that were a feature of the climate.

With one or two exceptions, the commissariat branch was woefully unprepared and subject to the army's scorn. This was unfair on many individuals concerned, though the commissariat suffered from a reputation of corruption and venality at the best of times.

Erskine, appointed Chief Commissary General, who only agreed to take the role on a temporary basis, was in fact merely a comptroller of army accounts. No one else was available to take on the task. He suffered from ill health and was soon laid up with gout.

Fortunately, matters were being organised in a more efficient manner back in Britain. Three months amount of provisions were already at sea in victualling ships along with enough biscuit packed to eliminate the necessity of baking on arrival. Cattle would be procured on the march while further provisions for an army of twenty thousand men to last another three months were being prepared in England, to be sent at a moment's notice.

At present, Moore was without proper transport to carry heavy equipment and baggage. He had no proper store for his artillery, little in the way of medical supplies and worryingly, was unable to leave stores of ammunition at Almeida as he started out along his intended route into Spain. The commissariat was a civilian organisation, answerable to civil servants in London so they could be excused somewhat for their naiveté. But Moore was heard to remark that many of them had spoken of journeying into Spain as if they were heading for a leisurely stroll around Hyde Park.

Another head-ache was the paucity of information on roads into Spain. The commissariat was responsible for mapping the army but the task of scouting suitable pathways for such a large force was disgracefully inadequate. Many reasons were cited such as the lack of Portuguese and Spanish translators and the poor quality of local maps. Indeed, the local Portuguese appeared remarkably ignorant on the subject. It left Moore bewildered at such a lack of preparation by his predecessors.

The news from Madrid was not encouraging. Lord William Bentinck, temporarily British resident in the Spanish capital, wrote privately to Moore expressing his concerns over their Spanish allies. The veracity of Bentinck's fears were accepted as genuine because William was the son of the man who had sent Moore to Spain, the prime minister, the Duke of Portland.

Bentinck warned there was a dangerous unwillingness to act uniformly among the Spanish as each regional Junta looked to itself first. The victory at Bailen was regarded as a solely Andalusian victory, the recent defence of the city of Zaragossa was seen as a fight for Aragon and not Spain itself. No Junta would permit a general from another region to command its army. Most serious was the charge that no local Junta engendered any respect for the central one in Madrid. Stores sent out from Britain to assist were lying in ports unloaded due to disputes over where they should best be directed. There were even reports of Junta's keeping the money intended to pay their troops for themselves.

The principal concern, according to Bentinck, was the inability of the Spanish people to see the struggle as a national one that should unite the country in a common cause. Too many of the problems of old Spain still remained. Factionalism, regionalism, corruption and incompetence.

Moore received daily reports leaving him with foreboding. Talk of Spanish armies being raised to propel the invader from Madrid did not sit with what he knew privately and not so privately. For it was the talk of the army how unprepared and uninterested a large part of the populace appeared to be.

Regardless of his concerns, he was tasked with command of the only British army in existence and though his orders were fairly cogent, he could not help feel that they were now up for reappraisal based on his more immediate knowledge of the situation. Originally, the government's plan was for him to transfer his army by sea to Coruña where it would meet up with Baird and form a secure base. From there he would advance into Galicia, through Castile, and onto Burgos where he would join up with the Spanish armies of the north and west. The fact that once again, London was unable to supply him a true picture of the state of the country's government and condition of the armies he was to meet up with, must be put aside for the present. Though the original plans were drawn up no doubt in good faith on information available to the government at the time, presenting Moore with a cautious approach to operations, events now superseded them. Moore had absolutely no way of knowing if any such army existed except in the deluded minds of Junta officials in Madrid.

He was aware that there were rumblings of discontent over his decision not to move the army by sea. Moore need not explain his thinking to anyone, least of all belly-aching junior officers. The simple fact was that he dared not make it public knowledge for reasons of morale. The deciding factor in his decision to move across land was his receiving a letter from Castlereagh at the end of September informing him that due to a larger number of enemy troops than anticipated, there would be no transports available as all shipping was required to fulfil the articles of Cintra in removing the last French soldiers from Portugal.

Let the men know that and there would be a mutiny. And he, John Moore, might just bloody well lead it!

He desperately wanted to come to grips with the French. But at present it appeared he was on his own if he chose to trust his own instincts in regards to Spanish preparations. And the longer he remained in Portugal, the greater the likelihood he could lose control of an increasingly drunken, ill fed, poorly supplied, diseased rabble of an army.

'Johnny, you're decision on Hope and the cavalry?' Thomas Graham woke Moore from his reverie.

It was already decided that Moore would have to split the army into three columns. It went against all the rules of an invading force in time of war. But the fact was that with so large a force, it would be difficult to feed and supply it if passing through the same villages and lands. And the lack of definitive knowledge on the state of the roads meant that the artillery and cavalry could not travel the same route as men on the march.

Moore decided on the city of Salamanca as a concentration point for the army. It was close to Madrid and an acceptable distance for Baird to march his division from Coruña.

'South.' He replied firmly. 'Marching east from Elvas where he will cross the river *Tagus* at Almarez. Then turning north at Talavera, past Madrid and roads north west from there to Salamanca.'

'A distance of over 370 miles.' Colbourne calculated.

It was a fearsome journey when it was considered that the route to the same city through Coimbra was estimated at only 250 miles, albeit through roads believed unsuitable for artillery and horses.

No one spoke. All accepted the necessity of the decision. But it meant to all intents the British army was left naked and exposed in a country where intelligence of the enemy's whereabouts was scanty at best. It was expected to take two to three weeks before the army met up together again. A message had already been sent to Baird to strike out for Salamanca.

'The brigades of Beresford and Fane will march via Coimbra.' Colbourne continued. 'General Fraser shall command the brigades of Hill and Bentinck on the route through Guarda by Abrantes, carrying with him the battery of six pounders.' These were thought to be the only artillery pieces capable of being transported over such a route and were in effect, the army's only protection during the march.

Lord Edward Paget would tail away from Hope's brigade at Elvas for

Alcantara, leading Anstruther and Alten's light divisions. Edward's brother Henry, who was with Baird, led the cavalry and Moore was grateful both brothers were available to him as they were extremely effective professional soldiers.

The room was filled with cigar smoke as the officers drank from decanters placed before them by Moore's valet. Thomas Graham spoke first.

'It's an almighty gamble you're takin', Johnny. But I believe I speak for every man here, that you've been left wi' little choice in the matter.'

'There is always choice, Tam.' Moore replied purposely, now fully attuned to the moment. 'Our one certainty is that the French are still in the north and they cannot be expected to know of our intentions. We are after all, only here to assist. We have not the numbers to expel the invader on our own. Nor were we ever expected to. But we must endeavour to remember that while we are our country's only standing army, we are duty bound to use that army in the best interests of our country and that of the ally we presently stand shoulder alongside.'

'Stay here in this cess-pit any longer and you'll no' have an army to worry about.' Graham concluded gruffly. 'Sail to Coruña in storm tossed autumn seas and chance our army on the outcome o' that? Not a choice as far as I can see. And it could be worse when we arrive there from what we've learned of our hosts and their inefficiencies.'

'Come now, Tam,' John Moore smiled indulgently at his friend's crusty honesty, 'we don't know how we shall be welcomed. What I do know is that should we sail there, we will waste valuable time while the weather turns worse. I do not wish to be locked up uselessly in a Galician port in winter any more than you gentlemen while awaiting word of Spanish armies that may or may not materialise. But I do believe that a British army can act as a rallying point for all of Spain. The effect that may have could prove incalculable in spurring the people of this land. Therefore it is beholden of us to take the initiative. We can only all of us do our duty. May God watch over us in the days ahead.'

Funny fellow, old Tam Graham.

John Moore sat alone in his room. A candle burned low, Francois having left him a small carafe of port wine as a night cap. Trust Tam to say what everyone was thinking. Then again, Thomas Graham of Balgowan was a man used to speaking his mind. He was a wealthy land owner up till the Great War began. No intentions or desire to become a soldier whatsoever. His wife was the great beauty, Mary Cathcart.

It was a double wedding long ago, as her sister Jane married the Duke of Atholl on the same day. It was his bride's father, Lord Cathcart, who composed the immortal words, *'Jane has married to please herself, John Duke of Atholl, a peer of the realm. Mary has married Thomas Graham of Balgowan, the man of her heart and a peer among princes.'*

The wedding portrait of Thomas' young bride by Mr Gainsborough proved the sensation of its day. There were some critics who considered her beauty enhanced by the dress she wore, enriched as it was with satins, pearls and rich plumes. The painter famously retorted by calling his next portrait, "The Honourable Mrs Graham as a Housemaid" by painting her again in a common cap and gown. It made her look twice as lovely. Legend held that it was Robert Burns himself, after staying as a guest of the couple who penned the term, 'the beautiful Mrs Graham' for which she became widely known.

After twenty years of happiness, Mary become seriously ill. Graham was advised to take her to warmer climes in order to alleviate her symptoms of consumption. It was on board the yacht Tam chartered that she died, just off Toulouse in 1793.

The incident that changed Thomas Graham's life was not the death of his beloved wife. In a scene hardly creditable for one involving so-called civilised nations, a mob of clearly paralytic custom guards and republican volunteers ordered the crate containing her body be opened as they suspected it may contain contraband. Despite fierce protests from the distressed widower, after what seemed an age of wrenching and hacking, the crate was smashed open, where they proceeded to view the exposed corpse of the dead women. The body was so damaged by the battering that a new coffin along with a surgeon were required to make repairs.

Thomas Graham made first acquaintance of John Moore not long after. He became an ordinary volunteer, leaving his wealth behind to carry a musket like any common soldier. He was in his mid-forties and soon distinguished himself. He only ever had one thought in his mind. To personally kill as many Frenchmen as the Lord provided for him.

But he had excellent diplomatic skills, honed in his earlier years as a successful man of business. Moore used him when he needed to mediate disputes, whether between his officers or with Spanish officialdom. If you were wrong, he told you to your face in such a manner that left no one feeling insulted. He was the army's chief scouting officer of supreme ability. A highly dangerous role, Tam undertook it with relish even though he was now recently turned sixty years of age. A tremendously tough, indispensable old warhorse, prone from time to time to violent outbursts of ferocious, highly undiplomatic language in private. He and Davy Baird didn't get on too well. Too similar. Though their verbal sparring could be vastly amusing to others, it was considered best to keep them apart.

Which was why his words tonight provided John Moore with much needed comfort. He knew they didn't like him in London. They'd hoped he'd refused the commission offered but found they'd painted themselves into a corner by appointing the two imbeciles who'd created the situation he now faced. Worse of all, he'd been deprived of Wellesley just when he was needed most to cover his flanks. He knew that every military decision he'd made was the correct one covering the exigency of the moment. None of his commanders questioned anything and he didn't expect them to. There were murmurs from some, like that ass, Charles Stewart, Castlereagh's half-brother, here to spy on him no doubt and report back everything. A conceited, insolent young scoundrel. Nothing more. But one to be watched, nevertheless.

Davy Baird wouldn't be happy about it. But Davy wasn't answerable to a pro-Spanish fanatic like John Hookham Frere, blind to military reality and a government at home desperate for a result now they had placed so much faith in their new ally. They'd a lot to lose, possibly power itself should their latest strategy come to naught.

It could all go wrong. Rain and snows may arrive early and he was marching thousands of men over mud tracks and mountains. There were no guns and cavalry to protect his flanks while his infantry effectively marched blind, deep into the Spanish interior.

But the weather was the same for everyone. The French were too far way to offer any obstacle for the present. It was what he would do once he arrived at Salamanca. He admitted to himself he had no idea as yet, based on the intelligence so far gathered.

This was his chance and he had to take it. Finally, command had arrived. He would never have wanted an officer like himself as a subordinate. He smiled when he thought of those he had quarrelled with over the years.

Admiral Hood was one of his earliest protagonists. Moore collided with the naval hero in Corsica during the siege of Bastia in 1794. The old man planned an attack on the port that Moore initially supported. But John's commanding officer was General David Dundas, *"Old Pivot"* as he was known, for being the author of the innovative new drill manoeuvres for the army, later adapted and improved on by Moore and McKenzie at Shorncliffe. But the plan of attack on the Corsican town was vetoed by Dundas as being too dangerous. Outraged, but with majestic arrogance, Hood summoned the then Colonel Moore to his cabin and asked him what he personally thought of the plan.

'Sir, surely you cannot expect me to answer that!' Moore was almost beside himself.

Hood sat back in the great cabin of H.M.S. *Victory*. He smiled sourly. 'Come now, Colonel Moore. It is common knowledge that you approve of my plan. Surely you can use your influence to present the facts to General Dundas in a more, shall we say, favourable light?'

All John Moore wanted to do was reach across the table before him and smash his fist into the awful old monster's face.

'I cannot and will not do any such thing! Were one of your officers to present himself so to General Dundas, how would you take that?' Moore pleaded, trying unsuccessfully to keep the snarl from of his voice.

Hood laughed but there was no humour to be found in it. 'Why, I would have him keel-hauled.'

'Admiral, your arrogance overwhelms me.' Moore spoke, barely able to contain his feelings. 'I believe you have sufficient numbers in your complement of marines to replace my regiment, should you go ahead with the attack. Despite General Dundas' clear misgivings.'

'You actually believe in co-operation between the army and navy?' The smile was gone from the admiral's face, replaced by the well-known graceless scowl, hated and feared by his unfortunate subordinates. 'Colonel Moore, your naïveté overwhelms me. The army is nothing without the navy. It goes nowhere without the navy. You should remember that.'

'I will not quarrel with you. General Dundas and I would not presume to debate with you the merits of naval matters. You should show us *lobsters* the same courtesy. It is of course, what any gentleman would do at the very least. And now I believe I will take my leave. The atmosphere in this cabin is become somewhat rancid.'

With that, Moore left. Of course, he received no back up from Dundas. The old boy had already planned his exit back to England and his replacement was more malleable to the admiral's will. The plan was eventually carried out to great success by Hood's young protégé, a certain Captain Nelson.

Hood had in effect asked the Scottish colonel to commit mutiny. In his arrogance he assumed that he could bend anyone to his will. Many an officer may have folded under such pressure. But not John Moore.

He was later requested to leave the island after becoming involved in a political battle with its governor. Sir Gilbert Elliot surrounded himself with the more ambitious and Moore believed, disreputable element of Corsican society. Moore sided with the faction led by the great patriot, Paoli. But the old warrior lost in the battle of wills and exiled himself to London. Moore perhaps could have played matters with a little more subtlety, but he had a propensity for telling the truth as he saw it. He also had an extremely naïve tendency to believe that the listener would ultimately accept his point of view, forget about it and move on.

Elliott didn't and it was the king himself who wrote to Moore ordering his recall.

First Corsica, then a posting to Sicily where he fell out with Drummond, the British minister over his relations with the troublesome king and queen of that island and lately his dealings with the deranged sovereign of Sweden. He certainly had his fill of politics and politicians. He was determined not to be hung out to dry in Spain. He would document everything and leave absolutely nothing to chance. Most of all, his plans were his and his alone to make. He would listen to advice but his private council was ultimately to be his only. He would trust his own judgement.

But as he so often reminded himself, for all his rows and arguments, his promotions were never affected and he retained the affections of the Duke of York and the king throughout his career. It was just that very moral rectitude he was known for along with his lack of ambition that attracted him to royalty. You always got the truth from Johnny Moore. It might happen at inopportune moments, best kept for another time. But you knew you were dealing with an honest man who only had the best interests of those he served and more importantly, those he served over at heart. Precious lives were too important to be lost over favouritism and the pursuit of personal glory.

He thought about Shorncliffe often. The happiness he experienced there remained with him always. Men drilled humanely, fed properly, becoming fit and capable of staggering feats of stamina and endurance. Their clear, honest pride as they were awarded their little prizes and precious badges to sew onto their uniforms. Being taught that pipe clay and stocks were not what the army was about. That a dirty uniform was acceptable as long as your rifle was pristine. Abolishing the lash completely at the camp while recording a huge decrease in incidents of desertion, drunkenness and theft.

Talking to the men in small groups about innovative infantry tactics. Listening to their own ideas and discussing them freely as professionals should. Giving poor, uneducated men self-respect and pride because they knew you trusted them. It was so simple, really. Those three regiments were his greatest achievement.

And the old duke. Never was born a more compassionate soul. The stories of his personal generosity and kindness to ordinary soldiers and their families were legion. Poor widows walking miles to ask him for help and his personally arranging their pensions while slipping them a few coins to aid them on the journey home. Old soldiers writing to him for assistance and the duke always responding. Simple but effective reforms like abolishing the awful queue's in their hair that the soldiers loathed and hated above all else. He was a catastrophe as a general, as his failed Dutch enterprise proved. But his true greatness was to realise his limitations and to turn to what he was best at. Reform and how to drive it through.

But his influence was waning through personal scandal and Moore knew he was now on his own unless he achieved a remarkable victory. But that would only happen if fate pushed him towards one. He was never going to risk lives for his own personal ambition. He would think and plan every step carefully and consult only when necessary. He had a precious instrument entrusted to him. On no account would his final monument be to the folly of an overly vain and ambitious general who needed to prove himself, in pursuit of personal aggrandisement at the expense of priceless British blood.

Sir John Moore left Lisbon on October 27th 1808. His division was last to leave the Portuguese capital. He would be travelling with Generals Hill and Bentinck in the direction of Abrantes, along the valley of the river

Tagus. The British soldiers were ordered to wear red cockades in their hats. They were inscribed with *Viva Ferdinand* in gold stamp as a compliment to their soon to be new hosts across the border.

Fully attuned to the possible difficulties ahead, Moore was forced to sign a highly unpopular order before leaving Lisbon. The large number of women and children who followed the army could not be assured of safety due to the lack of transports. Therefore, he ordered those deemed not to be physically robust enough and those with particularly young children not to travel. They would be recompensed and placed aboard ships returning to England. Admittedly, he could not control the carrying out of this order personally, relying on company officers to enforce it.

They failed utterly, due to many reasons including inexperience and plain-soft heartedness. This was an unwelcome indication of the poor quality of junior officers Moore and his immediate subordinates were saddled with. Inevitably, very few women heeded the order. Ordinarily only six wives per company of soldiers were allowed to travel with an army. But this rule was flouted to such an extent, that it was in fact a meaningless regulation unless rigidly enforced, which invariably, it was not.

Hundreds of women, many of them pregnant, and children, some mere babies, joined the army on its march into Spain. The resulting calamity would end in a human catastrophe unparalleled in British military history.

The first twenty miles of the march was pleasant, mainly on paved roads and in fields alongside the great river, with aloe trees a familiar sight for the soldiers though they were rapidly shedding their leaves through the advancing autumnal change. The valley was a vision of colours and aromas, myrtle, sage, rosemary. The soldiers picked flowers to pass to the girls of the villages they passed through while the violet and grey hills of central Portugal shadowed the army's movements.

As they left the valley behind, the country around them became barren and thinly inhabited. The pretty little villages were replaced by sparse and miserable mountain hamlets, where glum-looking peasants in dull greyish brown cloaks and clogs eyed the passing foreigners with suspicion and barely concealed enmity.

They spent their nights under whatever shelter available, castle ruins, churches or stables while the officers were billeted by priests or local officials in private homes. The food offered was usually of poor quality and reminded them of the muck dished out in Lisbon. It was handed over grudgingly and without warmth. The men grew to despise the Portuguese for their incivility, particularly when it was considered that unlike the French who took whatever they wanted from the locals, the British paid for everything.

As the month turned to November, the weather began to deteriorate and rains arrived as the army fell upon the valleys of the Beira. They then began the ascent into the mountains as they left Castello Branco where the tracks there were already turning treacherous. This caused some difficulties for their transport. Bullocks and mules lost their footing as they pulled on the precious ammunition and stores carts, causing numerous delays. Many unfortunate beasts, once starting to slide, could not be stopped and plunged over the edge of the mountains into the abyss below. The men remained soaked for two days, unable to dry out until they reached Guarda where the rains blessedly ceased. Moore stood with his men, talking and laughing with them around large fires as the army took the opportunity to dry itself out.

Light faded early and the nights became long and bitterly chill. The men began to complain of the severe cold, as they were overcome with excruciating circulatory pains when they awoke partly frozen in the morning.

But the ills of the army on this march were as nothing compared to what was to follow.

Andrew Berry marched with his regiment comprising a total of just over 900 men under Colonel James Stirling, who arrived with the 42nd from Gibraltar to serve in General Bentinck's brigade. He was not sorry to leave Lisbon behind. It failed to live up to his expectations as an exotic and exciting city. After disembarking at the *Praca do Commercio,* which the soldiers soon nicknamed 'Black Horse Square' due to the equestrian statue of King Joseph I at its centre, Andrew and the other recruits were marched to Queluz, just outside the capital. Aside from a small garrison complement in Lisbon, this was the main base of the British army in Portugal. Andrew and his regiment were billeted in a requisitioned convent since arrival in mid-September.

On visits to Lisbon, Andrew and his fellow soldiers quickly began to sicken of the constant stench of garlic, fish and oil permeating the air of the Portuguese capital. The city was also filthy and there appeared to be no understanding of basic cleanliness anywhere. Even the square they arrived in was piled up with rubbish and dung-heaps which stank to high heaven. It was not an auspicious beginning and Andrew's illusions were dented somewhat. The smallest Lothian village was a healthier and more welcoming place than this open, foreign sewer.

While off duty, he wandered around the streets in the first few days but soon grew disgusted with the countless beggars and level of squalor. He quickly tired of the inhabitants, the only point of interest in them the peculiarly large cocked hats all the men wore regardless of age, trade or class. The women did offer more. Invariably dressed in red cloth and black velvet, the wrapping of the material adorned round the body left little to the imagination in regards to the figure which were in the main, highly attractive to Andrew. His admittedly inexpert eye inevitably travelled down to the only area of invitingly bare flesh on view, namely pretty ankles and feet.

On a nocturnal wander around the city, he and his companions narrowly missed being drenched by ordure thrown from windows during the evenings. This practice, once the curse of Edinburgh which usually followed the infamous cry of '*Gardyloo!*' resulted in the inhabitants of Lisbon being ordered by a French proclamation to shout out '*water comes!*' three times in order to warn unwary passers-by before emptying pots below. Invariably, the call never happened. Officers took to carrying umbrellas with them on nightly strolls in order to circumvent such deluges.

One day early on in a visit to the city, Andrew was accompanied by his closest friends, Archie, a labourer's son from a farm near Dunfermline and Joshua, a former lawyer's clerk from Newcastle upon Tyne. The Fifer stopped to ask a local where the headquarters of the Inquisition was to be found. Archie, who had a ghoulish streak, had learned the necessary words in Portuguese. The local who was stopped, crossed himself vehemently and pointed in the direction of the *Rocio*, the square where the sinister institution was based. He then scurried off in great haste. Taking the lead, Archie led his two friends to the building.

'Do you think they'd let us in to have a look about?' He asked hopefully.

Andrew on realising where he now was, visibly paled, mouthed the name of his Presbyterian God and told Archie in no uncertain fashion that no power on earth would make him enter such a house of evil. He demanded they leave this place of Satan immediately. Joshua, shuddering inwardly, agreed vehemently and both boys took off, leaving their friend to stare at the building. Archie then caught up again a few minutes later with his companions, somewhat thwarted.

Bored and disenchanted, Andrew asked Corporal McQuater of his company if there were any extra duties he could perform. McQuater spoke to Sergeant McGillivray and he was immediately loaned to the commissariat department where his reading and writing skills were utilised in requisitioning and stores. Andrew enjoyed the work greatly, which took his mind of the disappointments of Lisbon.

Now he was marching with full kit across Iberia, passing through and staying over in towns such as Santarem, Castello Branco, Almeida and Ciudad Rodrigo. By the time they arrived at Salamanca in the middle of November, they'd marched 280 miles.

Everything had happened so quickly since the last day in Edinburgh. The recruits stood before the magistrate who first read the extract from the articles of war relating to desertion, mutiny and the penalties thereof. Then each recruit declared his full name, age and place of birth and that he was not serving already with the army or navy.

Each of the boys could not fail to hide a smirk when next they were made to swear that they *did not suffer from rupture, were untroubled by fits and no way disabled by lameness, deafness or otherwise but had the perfect use of limbs and hearing and was not an apprentice.*

Each then had to sign, or if unlettered, made to make his mark upon the attestation document before swearing the oath:

'I swear to be true to our sovereign lord King George, and serve him honestly and faithfully in defence of his person, crown, and dignity, against all his enemies or opposers whatsoever; and to observe and obey His Majesty's orders and the orders of the generals and officers set over me by His Majesty.'

After the oath was sworn, the ceremony was interrupted with an urgent message for the recruiting sergeant, who momentarily left the magistrates office. He returned to declare that Andrew and the other recruits were ordered to report immediately to the port of Leith, where they were to embark for Portugal. Andrew along with the other young men reacted with great alarm at this unexpected news.

'But what about our muskets and uniforms?' Andrew asked innocently.

'Aye.' Another lad spoke up. 'How are we to learn our drill if we are to board ship?'

Sergeant McGillivray explained that as they were joining up as part of the new fifth company of their regiment already on its way to Portugal, there were sufficient stores of uniform and weapons available awaiting them at the dockside. As for drill, there was enough room on a troopship deck to accommodate basic manoeuvres.

At a loss at the rapidity of events, Andrew pleaded time to write a letter to his mother, enclosing the bulk of his eleven guineas bounty. The other lad who spoke up requested the same. The magistrate kindly leant writing paper and pens and promised to ensure delivery of their letters.

'A receipt will also be required to be filed for each, sir.' Sergeant McGillivray pointed out loudly to the magistrate. 'The lads must be confidant their parents receive their monies.'

'Yes, yes, of course, Sergeant.' The magistrate assured, a little breathlessly. 'I would treat such requests as if they were those of my own sons.'

Andrew was grateful for the sergeant's consideration. But the news meant for certain there was now a very real chance that he may never see his family again. He initially believed that in being billeted in a nearby barracks, he would have the opportunity to say farewell before embarking overseas. Now that was gone. He quaked inwardly and became a little frightened. Now reality had dawned, Andrew wanted to go home to his parents and forget the army forever.

'Now lads, listen very carefully.' The magistrate addressed the recruits, cutting in on Andrew's fears. 'You are starting out on a great adventure. It would be understandable to me and to Sergeant McGillivray, to believe each of you experience some measure of trepidation at the turn of events. But let me assure you of something. You are in the hands of a very fine regiment with good officers, all esteemed gentlemen and a group of excellent non-commissioned officers such as the sergeant here. You will be clothed, fed and paid far better than many a labouring man you may name. Your mothers should have no fears that you have fallen in with a drunken rabble. You most assuredly have not. Now, bear up and remember you are from this moment on, soldiers of his Majesty. I wish you God-speed and a safe return home one day to each of you.'

Their fears assuaged somewhat, the boys were then led through the West Bow up into the High Street, through to the Walk, then down into the port of Leith where they arrived that afternoon at the awaiting troop ship.

The kind words of the magistrate that day were no platitudes. In his military career so far, Andrew had suffered no blows, injuries, bullying or ill treatment. The crossing over on the transport ship, however, was an ordeal he wished to forget. Caught in an inferno of strong gales, deep troughs and huge waves towering alarmingly over the ship during the hellish journey around the Bay of Biscay, the terrified soldiers feared being sent to the bottom as the strength of the waves battered the vessel daily and threatened to capsize the ship. Two men died and were buried at sea, though Andrew was too sick and fearful down in the holds to care.

He wanted to die at one point himself as the misery of the voyage consumed the nerves and health of every one of the redcoats on-board. Whether officer, non-commissioned officer or private soldier, none were spared the horrors of acute seasickness even in calmer seas. This included Sergeant McGillivray, who despite his valiant efforts to ensure the younger recruits were visited regularly by the ship's surgeon, suffered as much as anyone.

The only other physical discomforts Andrew experienced so far came from breaking in new shoes on route marches, and the pounding his shoulder and upper arm received from firing his musket at the range set up outside the camp in Queluz. Though he discovered that he was left handed in its use, Corporal McQuater, himself a left-hander, had shown great patience in drilling the young recruit in the use of the weapon with his right. It did not feel natural, but as the musket was only to be pointed in the direction of the enemy and fired, due to its notorious inaccuracy (despite Sergeant McGillivray's earlier selling points) in reality, it mattered little which arm he used. Andrew quickly proved he was able to fire the requisite three shots per minute with ease and was pleased to note even the gnarled old veterans of his company complained of the kick of the musket. Many a lively discussion was held on how to alleviate the blows with cloths placed under the coat and other measures.

Initially happy as he began the long march through Portugal, enjoying the scenery of the country and the banter between his friends alongside him, Andrew soon began to feel the strain of the sixty pound load he carried.

He was in full marching order and carried everything on his back. Over each shoulder was a leather strap that crossed over his chest and was hooked in place by a breast plate inscribed with the regimental crest. From these straps hung his bayonet and a box containing ammunition. Inside was a wooden block drilled with holes where each sat a single cartridge. Andrew's box contained sixty.

Individually, every man carried his musket, canteen of water and knapsack. All Andrew's personal items were carried in the latter, a canvas and wooden framed holdall connected by a belt across the waist. Andrew found this so restricting that it often left him breathless and in some cases, overcome by an awful sensation of near suffocation. It was poorly designed, highly impractical and universally loathed throughout the army.

Andrew's knapsack contained two shirts, three pairs of stockings, a pair of home–made breeches sewn together from his allowance of plaid in the tartan of his regiment, two shoe brushes, spare shoes, shaving kit, pipe clay and personal items such as a small bible and his diary with pen and ink. Andrew slung over his shoulder a small haversack which contained three days rations which included bread and beef. He carried his own blanket and took turns to carry the section's one and only greatcoat, shared among the men and usually worn on sentry duty at night, strapped above his knapsack.

His section was split into six men which included two of the recruits he joined up with, Archie and Joshua. Each section had its own *kettle* or large pot for boiling water and cooking and a halberd, each man took in turns to carry.

He did not despise the stock worn around the neck as much as many others did. This was a thick, leather collar worn inside the soldier's coat. Its origins were lost in antiquity, but it was believed to be intended to keep the soldiers head upright. A few of the regiment's old salts were experts at shaving the leather down with a knife in order to soften the leather. This was a risky business to undertake for being caught with a shaved stock resulted in a flogging.

Though it often felt like a wire brush rubbing against the chin, some swore by it for its protective qualities against sword and bayonet thrusts. Sergeant McGillivray advised Andrew and his two friends to keep it on as protection against cold. It also aided against sunburn of the back of the neck and sunstroke which was a killer in hot climates. Andrew tugged at it from time to time but did not really mind it too much, though it was constricting.

Despite the annoying and compulsory wearing off the stock, Andrew and his new friends were blessed in one respect: the recent abolition of the *queue*.

This was the revolting and time consuming practice of tying the hair and pulling it up into a pig-tail, the *queue*, then folding it back to form a type of club or in some cases with the aid of a small bag of sand, held in place by a leather board or strap. Substances such as candle grease, flour or cheap pomade were used to keep the hair in place. This could take a soldier anything up to an hour every morning to prepare and it was not unknown for sleeping men to be attacked by rats, attracted to the vile mixture. It's abolition that very year of 1808 was cause for jubilation, though some of the men kept the practice going as many a soldiers wife, skilled in the art of applying the queue, would lose out financially now that it was no longer required. Some regiments were slower than others to eradicate the practice completely but the impracticality of its continued use on long campaign, the exigencies of modern war and the Duke of York's reforming zeal, meant its long overdue death knell.

Andrew loved his red coat and bonnet. The highland headdress was a far more practical and protective item of kit than that worn by southern regiments. It was made of knitted material with a red and white checked border known as a Kilmarnock bonnet, fixed to a sturdy wire cage topped with ostrich feathers. It also had the advantage of providing coolness and shade in warm weather. In the centre of the bonnet was a *tourie*, a small woollen ball. A red tourie denoted a line company, white for grenadier and green for the light company. Andrew wore the red.

As for the vaunted *redcoat*, which was in fact more of a brick red in colour and would soon fade with wearing, the army recently abolished the high collar around the neck and his pride in wearing the smarter, new single breasted, eight buttoned, short tailed tunic was immense. Underneath, a white waist coat with long sleeves was worn. Andrew would often look down at the regimental crest embossed in gold on his belt, the sight filling him with pride.

But he absolutely loathed wearing the kilt.

The new kilts or *philabeg* as they were now known, which replaced the belted plaid of old, was a much shorter and less voluminous version of the former, more practical garment. Adorned with a light brown goatskin sporran, it was ideal to wear in warm climates as it was cooler and aided circulation. But now with the weather changing, the disadvantages of the kilt were mounting up for all to experience. Andrew found himself prone to chills and was constantly needing to urinate as were his two friends. Crossing fields and fences presented difficulties unforeseen previously. But the biggest problem was crossing rivers. Those in trousers or pantaloons could roll them up, but the kilted soldier could either remove the kilt completely and risk pneumonia, or plough through and hope to dry it as soon as convenient. As it was only held in place with three pins at either side, it could fall off altogether if it snagged or caught at anything. This was a matter that played heavily on Andrew's young mind. He thought of discussing it with some of the older soldiers but blanched as they would think him an ignorant *Sassenach*.

Sergeant McGillivray paid a visit at the camp shortly before they left and demonstrated to Andrew, Joshua and Archie how to make a pair of breeches out of their ration of plaid. Each soldier in a highland regiment was issued six yards of the hardy material on joining. McGillivray advised them to each make their own pair and to carry them with them on the march and in the field without fail.

Andrew's feet were a problem as they were for all the other new recruits. McGillivray advised the boys to each make a pair of *moggans*. These were socks with the feet cut from them and were first worn on initial training marches in order to harden the skin on rough roads. They could then decide to switch to their spare socks later. Andrew would discover that many preferred to wear all their stockings in such fashion, but decided only to cut up the one pair to begin with.

He quickly changed back to a whole pair after his first march but found little difference initially. Whether he should wear one type or another became a point of debate with himself and a subject of discussion with others as he marched along, helping take his mind of the ache of his feet.

The men in the main were of the north of Scotland. Many spoke Gaelic though most had rudimentary English. Surprisingly, there were a fair number of southerners including Englishmen, Welshmen and some Irish.

Of his two friends, Archie took naturally to the life. The son of an illiterate farm labourer, he had no letters, though in his spare time Andrew read to him from his bible and tried to teach him a few words. Archie remained a happy soul of eighteen years (so he believed, but was unsure) and uncomplicated in his desires. His food, lodgings and the precious few pennies left after allowances to spend were the summit of his ambitions.

Joshua was educated, having left home in Newcastle to become a clerk in a solicitors firm in Edinburgh. One night when they were alone he confided to Andrew his reasons for joining the army. He had come to the attention of the wife of one of the partners in the firm. The women seduced the young Joshua, but at a later rendezvous, the couple were caught *in flagrante* and Joshua was badly beaten by the scandalised husband. He was dismissed from the firm and his name put out about as a shameless adulterer and gigolo of wealthy women. This was plainly absurd as he was only eighteen years of age, while the 38 year old seductress was a well-known strumpet who rode her way through half the advocates of Edinburgh. Andrew, a virgin, listened to the tale with sympathy and some fascination.

Joshua's widowed mother would not survive his disgrace as she had spent many a precious penny she could ill afford educating him. There were four younger children to support and he could not return to her. As Andrew did, he'd forwarded on the majority of his bounty home and signed on for seven years.

All three boys swore that they would look after each other and form a little brotherhood to assist each if any of the other fell on hard times. It was childlike and innocent, but just such a pact, formed under the barely believable hardship and human misery to follow, would help keep them alive in the bitter days ahead.

Sir John Moore and his division, which included Andrew and his new friends, arrived in the city of Salamanca on the 13th November 1808. Despite earlier fears, Moore noted bitterly that it was entirely possible to have brought his artillery with him as the roads were not as troublesome as originally believed. The six pounders carried on the route all arrived intact. At Almeida, he wrote to Hope advising him of the case rather forlornly, informing him not to turn back but to continue on his present route with all God's speed.

The men's spirits rose greatly once they left the mountains and entered the open Salamanca plain. The soldiers sang lustily as they marched and Andrew Berry realised a dream to finally step on Spanish soil.

But the morale of the army and its chief's exultation at its safe arrival at the great city of learning, was tempered immediately by the dreadful news awaiting the British commander.

Moore received ominous communications earlier while on the march of Spanish defeats in the field. He advised Baird and Hope accordingly and sent out his instructions to them in light of new developments. But on entering Salamanca, he was presented by officials of the Junta with the gravest of all possible tidings.

Napoleon Bonaparte, with an enormous army, had arrived in the country to personally supervise the destruction of the armies of his new enemy while overseeing the total subjugation of the nation of Spain. It was believed that at this stage Napoleon was unaware of the tiny British force in his midst. A force that was now deep in Spanish territory, divided and far from any friendly port where it could escape the web the Emperor was weaving remorselessly over the north of Spain.

And even now he had the capital of Madrid in his sights, only one hundred and fifty miles from Salamanca.

Salamanca

'I mean to proceed bridle in hand; for if the bubble bursts, and Madrid falls, we shall have to run for it... Although we may look big, and determine to get everything forward, yet we may never lose sight of this, that at any moment affairs may take that turn, that will render it necessary to retreat.'

Letter from Sir John Moore to Sir David Baird, Salamanca, 6th December 1808.

Chapter Six

Salamanca is a city that existed long before the Romans arrived in Iberia. It reached its apogee in the fifteenth century when her university was regarded as one of the greatest seats of learning in Europe. Sir John Moore's army entered a city with two marvellous cathedrals, numerous convents, churches and a panoply of exquisite architecture.

Her glories were now clearly of the past, as the city evinced an air of waning magnificence and faded refinement. But Salamanca still glowed in sunlight in the colours of the oranges, lemons and pears growing among many of its tree-lined boulevards. Though the majority of its arteries were narrow and cobbled, many led into the magnificent Plaza Mayor, the new town's beating heart, planned and built only a century before as Europe's finest square. Surrounded by colonnades of arches supporting up to three stories of buildings, the square was decorated with gardens, arcades and avenues where the city's finest would promenade.

Among those worthies now were multitudes of red coats and the detritus of the defeated armies of Spain, seeking refuge after her countries recent military calamities.

John Moore's reception in the city began with some embarrassment. There was a contest of manners between the Marquis de Cerralbo, the city's wealthiest resident and president of the local Junta, and the commander in chief of the British Army. The marquis generously allowed use of his magnificent *Palacio de San Boal* for the general and his staff as headquarters. Situated in the old northern quarter of the city, it bore an imposing exterior of black and white tiles with wrought iron balconies under each window. The interior was more pleasant to view in that it contained a courtyard built in sandstone baked by over two centuries of hot Spanish sun. All rooms were situated on the first floor, artworks and busts decorating each. After voluminous introductions in French, the young nobleman made a startling offer.

'My dear Sir John, the house is entirely yours to do with as you will. My staff will provide every comfort. You need only to ask. You do me such honour by your presence.'

Taken off–guard by such generosity, Moore could only splutter. 'But my lord marquis, are you not aware that I will require my staff with me constantly and there will be other visitors that I shall require to attend to? I cannot possibly put you to such huge expense and inconvenience!'

Entirely nonplussed, the marquis merely smiled. 'In that case, Sir John, if you will refuse me to attend to all your needs, I cannot allow you to dwell in my house!'

John Moore could only smile through gritted teeth and accept the marquis' offer. In reality it was a trifle, but it was indicative of the type of extravagant behaviour he would have to tolerate in dealing with his new hosts in the weeks ahead.

Napoleon Bonaparte had no such qualms in his dealings with Spanish nobility. Lately these were of the most violent and terminal in nature. He himself arrived in Spain, at Vitoria on 6th November. Immediately before that, General Lefebvre began preliminary operations at the end of October, culminating in defeat of Spanish forces under General Blake at Espinosa at the hands of Marshal Junot in mid-November.

Napoleon's original plan involved Lefebvre's corps holding down Blake while Moncey's divisions contained the army of Castaños, victor of Bailen and Palafox, on the Spanish right flank. The army, reinforced by Ney, would then outflank Blake, turn east and assist Moncey in forcing Castaños and Palafox north or east. The way would then be open for Napoleon to drive through the centre and on to Madrid. It was a bold plan bolstered by the overwhelming force the Emperor brought to Spain.

After Espinosa, Soult, newly arrived from Germany, took over from the inept Bessiers and routed the Conde of Belvdedere's army at Gamonal. Burgos was then taken which left the way open for Madrid. With the remainder of his army, Blake began a retreat westwards followed by Soult but the Spanish general was exhausted, his shattered force now merely an army in name only. He was replaced by the gallant Marquis de Romaña.

Ney was instructed to pursue the army of Castaños while Victor and Lefbvre joined their Emperor in his march to the capital. There now appeared little in the way to prevent Bonaparte adding another laurel to his conquests.

David Baird, beside himself with anger, swore and spat disgustedly over on to side of the road.

'I've never in all my life witnessed a shambles to compare! Will ye move that fuckin' cart oot o' the way, damn ye tae hell!'

The unfortunate driver and his aide, bearing the brunt of their general's ire, pulled again at the pair of bullocks. They'd no intention of shifting, planting themselves firmly where they decided to stop, bringing the column yet again to a shuddering halt.

'Shoot the buggers! Do *somethin*'! Christ, if ye have to do a job...!' Davy, who planned to ride in a carriage most of the way, was forced to take to his horse in order to keep an eye on matters. He leapt off the animal furiously and the army was then gifted the unique sight of its commanding general putting his huge shoulder against the enormous, sweating, fly-ridden backside of a Spanish bullock and heaving for all he was worth.

'Move, ye horrible auld besom, or it'll be steaks the night for supper!'

More men appeared from the column to push and pull the animals. The general continued to heave his vast strength as slowly the brutes began to edge forward.

'Thank Christ!' Baird exclaimed with some relief, puffing wildly through his exertions. 'Whoever paid good siller for these muckle buggers deserves to be hanged!'

The men around laughed easily as the column began to move off again. The army was spread out in single file along the narrow Astorga road, running over one hundred and twenty miles alongside mountainous terrain girdled with sheer cliffs, ravines, gorges and valleys. There was little in the way of forage and virtually nothing to accommodate the army on its march.

It was painfully slow. The cavalry under Lord Henry Paget, set out days after Baird. There were grave concerns over the condition of many of the horses and it was decided that the cavalry would move in easy stages, with rest days in between. Even this was too much and many an unfortunate beast was put out of its agony along the way.

Robert Craufurd, who set out well in advance of Baird, had his division ready to march only six days after fully disembarking from their ships at Coruña. Only he could have realized such a feat of organisation. Only the Shorncliffe trained regiments he commanded, could have achieved such a distinction.

Robert took it in turns to both ride and march. He did not mind taking to his feet as it helped set an example. As he walked, he worked out problems in his mind. One of them being march discipline and the avoidance of straggling. This was a particular bug-bear of his. Nothing enraged him more than observing men stop for no apparent reason, fall out and others invariably following suit. His light division consisted of five companies of the 43rd, the first battalion of the 95th, four companies of the 2nd battalion and mixed companies from the 14th and the 23rd Regiments.

Today he was with the 43rd. It was a Monmouthshire regiment, though most of the men were English. There were Welshmen of course, along with an inevitable sprinkling of Irish.

'And how do the 43rd view matters today?' Craufurd asked as he swung alongside the sweating red-coats.

'That the mountains of Portugal are the very devil!' One voice spoke aloud.

'I'd rather have the girls of Portugal!' A wag shouted.

'Oh, give me some fine Spanish wine and rum!' another joked.

'I'll lay bare the back of any man caught with drink on the march!' Craufurd snarled ominously.

There were a few boo's, which pleased Robert greatly as it indicated morale was strong. He deigned to crack a joke. 'What's more, any man caught with drink on the march will exchange his fine Spanish rum for my sour Portuguese grog!'

There were loud laughs and jeers. The men disdained the rough Portuguese port which spoke volumes for how bad it was.

'A song, 43rd!' Robert ordered. 'Will it be said you are not musical? Or has the dago dust clogged up your pipes and the port wine drowned all your whistles? Who will sing?'

'John Porter!' Someone yelled.

'He knows a fair tune!' Another acclaimed.

'John Porter.' Robert addressed the column. 'I have heard there is a merry cove in the 95th who has a voice which soars as a lark on the wing.

When he sings, the sound is so fair, the lassies swoon in ecstasy and give of him their passions freely. For it is said he is not a man but an angel. Can you do better?'

'John Porter has a wife and two children!' an Irish wit declared. 'That's all his voice won for him!' There followed a tremendous burst of laughter from the men.

The object of their humour began to sing a song of his shire as the men joined in happily. His task complete, Robert climbed onto his horse and rode forward to survey the condition of the next regiment.

David Baird was not as content as his subordinate.

It was believed that it would take six days for his column to reach Astorga. He was grateful to return to his carriage after his exertions with the stuck cart. It was the correct action to take for purposes of morale and example, but physically, it near exhausted him. Approaching his fifty-first birthday, the robustness of his youth was long behind him. The period in India, including years chained in a dungeon as prisoner of Hyder Ali, would have destroyed lesser men. Only Baird's inexorable desire for revenge on those who captured and mistreated him gave him the strength to endure the torturous experience.

He added subsequent laurels to his name. But none gave him more satisfaction than viewing Hyder's eldest son, the famous Tippoo Sultan, lying dead beneath the walls of his fortress of Seringapatam. It was almost worth the agony he endured.

But his body was now failing him. He was often short of breath, over-tired and suffered bouts of dizziness. His joints ached and he was prone to headaches. His temper needed to be kept under control as wild rages invariably left him spent. Formerly, his anger was his avenue to releasing stress. Now it was a danger.

He found himself taking to his bed early while in Coruña. He confided in Craufurd that he often felt unwell. Bobby was sympathetic and offered support. A casual word here and there to his staff was usually enough to excuse Davy's absences from dinners and social occasions in Coruña town, while the army awaited permission to disembark.

The carriage, however, was an unmistakable sign not only to his senior officers but to the army in general that their *Davy* was not a well man. The soldiers discussed the matter among themselves. He was a great favourite after all. Nevertheless they all believed whether fit or not, the big man from Edinburgh would see them through as he always had.

The main part of the army, its test of endurance through the peaks and mountains successful, reached the Leon plain and finally arrived at the town of Astorga on 22nd November. There, Baird received the catastrophic news of the defeats of the army of General Blake at Espinosa and at Gamonel from an official of the local Junta. There was now nothing between Baird's force and the French army, barely a hundred miles away. Davy ordered the army to encamp and immediately called for a council of senior officers.

They assembled together that evening. Lord Henry Paget, who had rode a hard gallop to reach the meeting, Craufurd, Generals Warde of the Guards and Leith, met in the office of the town Junta.

'Gentlemen, I have called you all together as I require to impart grave tidings to you and to seek council.' Baird announced, then advised of the military setbacks of the Spanish forces.

Henry Paget spoke up first after his commanding officer finished communicating his report. 'That leaves us bare-arsed to the wind, Sir David.'

'It certainly does, Lord Henry. Let me state that I am most remiss that I have not yet had the opportunity of acknowledging my gratitude for your exertions in arriving at such short notice.' Paget, nodding graciously, was miles back with a squad of cavalry when summoned by a dispatch officer.

Baird then made a request. 'I believe it advisable to first ask each of you on the condition of your divisions.'

Davy Baird arrived with four infantry brigades and three artillery batteries. Paget reported that the cavalry may take upwards of a week to arrive. The others advised the six pounders and remaining infantry would hopefully arrive before then.

'Thirteen thousand men isn't much of a force to take on the entire French army, gentlemen.' Davy concluded forlornly after the reports were completed.

'Have there been any further dispatches from General Moore?' Leith asked.

'Yes, and they confirm the news imparted to me today of the destruction of the Spanish forces.' Earlier that day, an officer of the Junta handed

Baird letters received from Ciudad Rodrigo, where Moore stopped on the march to Salamanca. Davy proceeded to describe the contents of Moore's latest communications.

Johnny recommended caution and advised Baird to lay down a depot of stores at Astorga. The letters, written over consecutive days, spoke to Baird of a man growing ever more concerned. There was a taint of vacillation about them which disturbed Davy somewhat. But he put it down to the fact that Moore may well be receiving conflicting information himself. The time lapse from writing and the receipt of the letters was no help to anyone, especially when there was always the chance a despatch, for any of a number of possible reasons, may fail to be delivered.

After the discussion there was a silence. Everyone in the room knew what was required.

'Your decision, Davy?' Craufurd spoke up on the others behalf. There was no time for subtlety.

'A simple one. I propose we halt here at Astorga and await our forces joining us. We will then gauge conditions and seek clarification of the positions of our allies and our enemies.' Baird looked around each face. He only saw agreement.

'Undoubtedly the correct choice, Sir David,' Paget concurred. 'You have my support.'

The others murmured their assent. The meeting then relaxed somewhat as wine was brought in and cigars lit.

'Do you mean to write to Johnny?' Robert Craufurd asked over a glass.

'Aye, he'll have to know.' Baird replied despondently, though relieved that the tension had subsided somewhat. He was proud of the men that sat with him. All competent, sensible and reliable. But he badly wanted to lie down as his head was spinning, his body ached and his spirit longed for peace.

'I'm not stepping one foot further forward until *all* the army is in one place.' He stated baldly. 'It'll be easier to turn around if we have to. And gentlemen, I think we must accept the distinct possibility that we may be forced into a reverse manoeuvre at any given moment.'

David Baird had good reason for his caution and it was rooted in bitter experience.

He was alone with Robert Craufurd. Bobby was a good listener. But that was only because he rarely listened to what anyone else was saying. He was usually too deep in his own intense brooding over whatever was on his mind at any particular moment. But he had the happy ability to make the talker assume he had their rapt attention. It made him strangely endearing, usually against the better judgment of those who did not really know or had a pre-conceived idea of him.

Davy knew this anyway. He was long reconciled to his friend's peculiarities. Because Craufurd was so different, it was easier to offer up his deepest concerns as Bobby would never reveal them anyway as his sense of honour wouldn't allow it. Though he was known as a 'schemer,' John Moore's own and somewhat valid description, he was not a gossip. He was no threat to Baird as they both desired the same ends.

Rooms were made up in one of Astorga's few hotels for the senior officers of the army. Davy would have liked to have Henry Paget present as he greatly respected the man and hoped it was mutual.

Baird was born far lower on the stratosphere of class than Paget. But the noble lord was a soldier first and foremost. Long before, when Davy began his career, he actively desired to compete against such types in order to prove himself. Ironically, it usually worked out that the highest born officers became his closest companions. The opposites seemed to attract in the less rarefied world of the army, unlike society in general. But that did not necessarily apply when it came to the distribution of commands. In India, he was superseded by the far younger Wellesley due to that man's connections to his brother, the governor-general. Baird was a man who tried not to bear grudges but that one rankled greatly.

Though he classed John Moore as a friend, even with his fellow countryman, there was reason to feel some measure of grievance. Years before, after a period of leave at home in Scotland, he received a letter from a senior captain in Baird's then regiment, the 71st Highlanders, based in India, advising him that their commanding officer had taken seriously ill and was being returned home. The captain advised Baird that if he wanted the command himself, he should contact Horse Guards quickly and plead his case.

Baird arrived in London too late. Another officer had already bought the colonelcy but solely for the honour of commanding a regiment, preferably based in England as he had no desire to serve overseas. Baird met the man who explained he would be happy to exchange commissions for another regiment and sell his on to him.

Davy was tipped off by a friend at Horse Guards about an officer who wanted to buy out and immediately made contact. The man was happy to sell his commission to Baird, who would then swap with the home-loving colonel and the 71st would then be his.

Baird was about to conclude the deal when he received word from Edinburgh his agent had delayed the financial transaction for reasons yet to be fully disclosed. After discussing the problem with his Horse Guards crony, Davy was approached by an officer who apologised for overhearing the conversation, commiserated with Baird's plight and offered to advance the money to him.

Startled by such unthinking generosity, Baird was able to graciously decline the offer. Fortunately the money eventually did arrive. But the delay resulted in David Baird being gazetted on the army's lists behind a certain John Moore. It would bear repercussions for the future as the older and more experienced Baird, due to the iniquities of military bureaucracy, would always be deemed junior to his fellow Scot. Ironically, had he taken up the stranger's offer, with the time that would have saved him, he may have been in Salamanca today in Johnny's place.

Davy certainly bore no resentment towards Moore. For one thing, it was almost impossible to feel any such negative emotion towards the man. He was just not that kind of being. But in the present situation they now found themselves in, he was developing a nagging doubt and mounting anxiety over the predicament the British army faced in Spain. And those doubts extended to John Moore himself.

'I told you about Buenos Aires. Are you going to tell me about Munro and Pollilore?'

Robert Craufurd rarely made such requests of his friend. It was known throughout the army Davy Baird barely ever revealed anything about this defining moment in his life. The discussion that night in Coruña weeks past tweaked Robert's interest but only because Baird asked him inadvertently about his own *ghost*. Robert revealed so much mainly because the generally known facts fitted what he'd disclosed on that occasion. Baird did not need to be told about the characters of the main protagonists. He, like everyone else, merely found it inexplicable how it all could have happened and seeking some kind of comfort, vainly hoped for some hidden piece of information lying at the heart of the disaster.

There was none of course. The whole rotten affair simply boiled down to inept leadership.

'It doesn't work that way, Bobby.' Davy replied, softly.

Baird was tucked up in bed while Robert sat in an easy chair in the upstairs bedroom of the commanding officer. The chamber's only other adornment along with a cabinet of drawers, was a small table that bore a candle and a scattering of the excuses for maps the army was hampered with. Robert had his coat and boots off. His unshaven countenance bore a darkly saturnine quality that never failed to amuse Baird.

'Christ, but ye're a black, miserable looking devil, Boab!' Davy stated pointedly but in a teasing, brotherly tone.

'"*Black Bob*," they'll all be calling me, sure enough.' Craufurd responded wistfully. 'But they have to be alive to call me that and I'm damned sure I'll keep them that way, by God. If I have to flog every man of them along the way.'

'That's a grand name to be known as and one that'll be remembered.' Davy replied cheerily. His friend's gloomy countenance never failed to charm him either. He often wondered what it would be like to share that odd mind for a day.

Davy shivered, not altogether due to the chill of the room. He leaned over the bed and reached out his glass. 'Here. Refill this for me, will you?'

'Only if you tell me about it.' Robert continued in what he would regard as a light-hearted tone.

'Och, ye're an awfy man, Robert Craufurd! I never took ye for a sweetie wife. Do you really want to ken?'

Robert poured from the brandy bottle into Baird's glass. 'They say a man who does not learn from the past, will one day repeat the errors he has made previously.'

'Wise saying indeed.' Davy agreed sagely, taking the proffered glass and drinking deep. 'Jesus, that's rare! About all these dagos are good for, eh no?'

'*India*, Davy. We've got all night.' Robert prodded gently.

'And me wantin' my bed an' a'.' Baird yawned. But he didn't mind any longer. He felt the need all of a sudden. After twenty five years, enough time had passed. Maybe it was his tired and sick mind and body. But all of a sudden he seemed to have less strength in him now to not to want to talk about it than to remain silent.

'Pass the bottle over, *Black Bob* Craufurd. This will cost me. It'll cost me dear. You of all people should know what you're demandin' o' me. Damn ye to hell for askin.' But ye're a friend and you have the right tae ken.'

Chapter Seven

Only a few days after arriving in Salamanca, John Moore ordered the execution of a soldier convicted of stealing. Having read the findings of the court martial and in particular, the details of the character of the private soldier of the 6th Regiment found guilty, he reluctantly accepted there was little in the way of extenuating circumstances permitting him to invoke clemency. The man was a thief, a rogue and a hopeless recidivist, given any number of chances in the past and clearly beyond redemption.

Moore loathed the very idea of hanging a man in order to provide mere example but he was willing to overlook his scruples on this occasion. He believed it necessary to send a signal to company officers that if they failed to keep their men in line, this is what awaited them. He could not believe that any young officer would enjoy organising and carrying out a hanging and this particular example would be a timely reminder to them of their responsibilities to their regiments. He was growing increasingly concerned over the quality of officer he commanded, as daily reports came in of misbehaviour by the men being left unchecked.

Moore fretted. He'd sent out patrolling officers a few days after arriving in the city and awaited their return. These men were the eyes of his army. He was blind without their reports. He also nervously awaited the arrival of the three divisions under Paget, Beresford and Hope. The latter most of all. As well as being a close friend, John Hope had his guns. Without them, he was naked.

Naked and blind, struck in the middle of Spain. Napoleon on the way and hardly a credible word to be heard on the state of the Spanish armies. What a fine pickle!

He was at his desk writing in his journal. He'd finished another letter to London. Castlereagh was proving to be far more sympathetic and competent than initially believed possible. Though the fact of the matter was that Moore was unable to formulate a plan about what to do next. His latest letter to his lordship was a delaying tactic, involving commentary on the administration of the army and advising that he was happy to trust civilians like Frere and Sir William Bentinck to deal with matters in the country. He also opined on his growing concern over the lack of news and the general feeling of unpreparedness of the Spanish people for war.

His journal was his solace. But he had an eye on posterity. His true feelings were poured out onto the paper as consolation but also as exoneration. He'd achieved his life's ambition. He did not want it to go the way of Corsica or Sweden. There he had little control as the politicians and senior officers conspired to thwart and humiliate him. He received little backing from home. Now it was his turn to write the script. He was set a task. It was to lead Britain's only field army on a perilous mission. It was all down to him. He was answerable to orders as always. But there was leeway. Room to manoeuvre. He was to assist the Spanish in any way possible but importantly, Castlereagh told him he was not to suborn himself to them should he believe they endangered his army. He was to contact London first and await a response. Both Moore and Castlereagh learned the lesson of Sweden.

Moore wrote to Lady Hester Stanhope regularly, sometimes daily. He poured out his concerns to her and as with all his letter writing in general, it provided him with an outlet to relieve stress.

Hester's letters to him were filled with a mixture of support, perceptive insight into prevailing political weather, and sound advice. Most welcome of all, were her underlying declarations of love, concern and longing for his return.

He first met her while commanding the infantry school at Shorncliffe. Moore was renting a house on the beach near Sandgate Castle. William Pitt, Prime Minister and Warden of the Cinque Ports often visited nearby Walmer Castle as part of his ceremonial duties. Hester was the niece of the prime minister and moved into Downing Street, becoming his *de facto* housekeeper come private secretary.

She was the object of suspicion, derision and scorn. Her polymath father, the brilliant but tyrannical Charles Stanhope, who famously declared himself the minority of one in the House of Commons for his tireless campaigning on behalf of radical causes, labelled his daughter *the*

Logistician in tribute to her remarkable mind.

She was well educated but the times were not suited to independent female brains. A stunning beauty, at twenty she described herself as having a complexion of alabaster where a pearl necklace at a short distance away could only be separated from her skin by the keenest eye. Blue veins heightened the brilliance of her features, her eyes and lips few women could compete with.

But she believed the position of women should not be about only finding a husband or becoming a well-kept mistress. She was happy in the company of men. She famously enjoyed discussing male pursuits of horses, gambling, politics and ribald jokes.

Her love-life was even by the standards of the period, torrid. She developed an inexplicable attachment for her cousin, the notoriously violent and maniacal Thomas Pitt, Lord Camelford. The young man achieved infamy by driving the famous naval officer George Vancouver to an early grave after sailing on board his ship as an ordinary seaman. He was flogged repeatedly for his consistently appalling conduct. He was known to provoke brawls and duels and had killed a man already before his most famous exploit, where he was arrested in France, accused of plotting to personally assassinate Bonaparte. He'd only been released after calling on all his undoubted persuasive charm to convince Fouchè, Napoleon's police chief, that he was merely a Francophile on holiday.

Hester's personally most damaging liaison was with Granville Leveson Gower, whom even her uncle declared bore the extraordinary good looks of the Emperor Hadrian's lover Antinous while just as venal. She fell obsessively in love with him. Granville was ambitious and saw Hester as a route to political power through the prime minister. He led her on, though he was a known rake and counted among his many lovers the much older Lady Bessborough, mother of Lady Caroline Lamb, who desired him for herself. Alert to a possible scandal and with no doubt a certain element of self-interest attached, Pitt offered the young man an ambassadorship to Russia, in order to remove him from the country and out of his beloved niece's reach.

Granville accepted gratefully and left Hester with a goodbye note. She immediately swallowed a huge dose of poison after sending him a farewell letter. Her uncle called a discreet physician who ministered to her. She barely survived and damaged internal organs left her in great pain.

There was malicious gossip that Hester had fallen pregnant, not once but twice. On the first occasion during her relationship with Camelford, inexplicably, she travelled to Italy where she had a violent row with her brother, Lord Mahon, in Florence. The subject of the disagreement remained a secret and they were estranged for the rest of their lives. The second occasion was when it was strongly suspected that her suicide attempt over Granville was in fact a botched abortion, the laudanum she had swallowed, a known inducement.

John Moore was introduced to her on a visit by Pitt, who personally raised a battalion of militia in Kent that formed part of Moore's area command. She had spoken easily to him of military affairs and he was captivated by her looks and intellect. Her knowledge of politics and her inquisitive mind also left a lasting impression, stimulating him greatly. He longed for a reason to see her again and they began a correspondence. But soon after, he was appointed to serve under General Fox in Sicily where he met his captivating daughter, Caroline.

While in Sicily, young Charles Stanhope, serving as an aide to Moore, informed the general that his sister had taken a house of her own in Montague Square. Charles was at pains to mention that Hester remained unattached but was as impossible as ever.

On returning to England after his service was over, Moore decided to pay a visit. She welcomed him effusively and it was clear that the officer commanding Shorncliffe left a lasting impression also.

Now Pitt was dead, tragically young at the age of forty six. The Government saw fit to award Hester a yearly pension of £1200 in thanks for her service. It was a sum that ordinarily should have kept her in reasonable comfort had she been prudent. But of course she could never be that. She asserted that such a trifling figure meant she could not afford a carriage and she would not be seen in a lowly Hackney cab. She kept an overly large household mainly through kind-heartedness as she could not bring herself to dismiss her loyal servants. But now the enemies she made while serving the late prime minister mobilised. She was viewed as the dethroned queen and rarely received visitors of any note, becoming a social recluse.

Amused, Moore listened to her declare her travails to him and found it difficult to accept that the woman who sat before him could possibly be short of admirers. Dazzlingly beautiful, John Moore's feelings for her increased accordingly.

'Hester, my dear.' He declared, getting down comically on bended knee before her. 'I cannot accept this self-pity! Why, as I turned into the street I was waylaid by a gang of young blades making for your very door!'

She laughed uproariously. 'Moore, you are a liar, but a very dear one. Was Lady Caroline so very lovely that you would prefer her to say, an old dowager like myself?'

He was caught off-guard by the response which admittedly, delighted and excited him in equal measure. As he attempted to rise to his feet, he fell slightly and grabbed his ankle.

'Oh, what is the matter? Is it a wound?' she asked concernedly.

'Mere arthritis. A common complaint of the ancient and impotent.' He rubbed his ankle piteously, while looking at her, the humour in his eyes warming her heart to him even further.

Hester reached over to place her hand on his handsome face. 'Ancient? Why you jest, Moore! Impotence, however, is another matter entirely and there is only one conclusive method of investigating the veracity of such a condition.'

John Moore stayed the night at Montague Street, dispelling the matter of impotence decisively.

He was now forty-seven and Hester thirty-two. Despite her unconventional beliefs, Moore sensed she desperately longed for marriage. She certainly had no desire to be any man's mistress. There was a workhouse not far from the square where she lived. It wasn't only the poor and hopeless who dwelled within its grim walls. There were many discarded women of men cast aside and left nothing to support them forced to enter through its doors.

Her father had blown the family fortune on his scientific obsessions and causes. She'd cut all ties with him and Lord Mahon, but remained close to her two younger half-brothers, Charles and James who were in the army thanks to her influence in gaining their commissions. She was left solely with her pension and debts were rising. But she would be no man's pampered whore to abandon whenever the whim suited.

She did want to marry. But only for love. She was both remarkably modern and surprisingly conservative. She believed that not marrying for love was the route to a private and often a very public hell.

She saw in John Moore the man she now desired to marry. At twenty, she would not have wanted him. At that age she wanted adventure and danger. She wanted Camelford. He was an evil man, irresistible to her. What a silly fool she was. But in that respect she was no different from generations of young girls who suffered from the tiresome preconception that danger presented an attraction that was intertwined irretrievably with the pursuit of true love. When she thought now of them both, she could only see John Moore's sweet, honest face. Thomas' visage presented only darkness. Now long dead after being killed in a duel, Camelford, she desperately wanted to forget. Granville was a greater lover than both and raised her to unimaginable levels of sensuality. But his mind was always on himself and his next conquest.

She still saw her uncle in her dreams. He was her chaperone when she was young. Her father would have nothing to do with his children, treating them dismissively while he attempted to change the world for the better on his one man crusade. It was faintly ridiculous to see the prime minister at some ball, half asleep at three in the morning, waiting for his niece to finish her dancing, gossiping and flirting. Then being taken home by her bachelor relative, the nation's most powerful man.

Now she saw Moore in that place of deep and lasting comfort. That was why she knew she loved him and would marry him. His was a steadying influence and at times his fiery nature though similar in respects to her own, had a not wholly undesirable effect in moderating her more passionate tendencies. She knew he was quick-tempered, could bear grudges and sulked. But he was not like that towards her.

In return, Moore understood that marrying Hester was an assured path to contentment. He found her beauty endlessly provocative and her mind marvellously stimulating. She was an ever available sounding board for his travails at the iniquities of the government and those who stood to prevent him from achieving his goals. He found her agreeing heartily with his opinion of Castlereagh and Canning's political and military strategies. His ideas on army reform and improvement in general throughout society found accord with the daughter of the *minority of one*. He also felt she required protection. Despite her bravado, she was vulnerable. On their last night together before he sailed for Sweden, they talked for hours.

He spoke of his mission, she contributing sensible advice. They lay together after making love for the last time.

'How long do you think you'll be there?' she'd asked before and he'd replied it was impossible to say. That she had asked again, he surmised correctly, was not due to their post love-making warmth.

'No matter how long I'm there, the outcome on my return shall remain the same.' He replied.

'Can anything so wonderful be described as a mere "outcome?" she chided, mischievously.

'It is something you have a very strong desire for?'

'Greatly.'

'Are you certain that the attractions of an old soldier will not diminish through lengthy absence?'

'I am not acquainted with any *old* soldiers. Does the attraction of an old maid diminish through lengthy absence?'

He turned and moved on top of her. 'Lady Hester, I am unacquainted with any such creatures.'

'You are to come back. You are to come back safe to me. To me and no one else.'

He kissed her. 'There is no one else. There never was anyone else. Only you.'

The anxieties of his predicament now consumed him daily. Moore rose each day extremely early, lit his own candles and fire in order not to wake the sleeping Francois and worked alone into late morning. The room he sat in in the *Palacio San Boal* was long, narrow, draft ridden with a window overlooking the main square below. Papers and the awful maps that were all he could rely on lay strewn around tables and desks.

He confided his thoughts and fears to his private journal and to two of his subordinates, Paul Anderson and Thomas Graham. He considered the former his closest friend and confidante, rather than military inferior. They first met in Ireland in the early 1790's while Moore was in Cork with his regiment. Anderson, from Waterford, was of third generation Scottish gentry now intermarried with Irish nobility. He was good humoured, patient, highly efficient at any task undertaken, and enjoyed tremendous personal loyalty from his junior officers while remaining remarkably unpretentious and self-deprecating. He was highly disparaging of social and intellectual snobbery and shared John Moore's ideas on military reform. The two became inseparable and would serve together through most of the following fifteen years, including Corsica, Sicily, Holland and Egypt where Anderson received a bad wound in the right arm at Alexandria. Worse, one of his younger brothers, Robert, serving with the 42nd was killed in the same battle. Though wounded in the same action, Moore wrote a letter on his friend's behalf to his mother informing her of the tragedy.

When Moore finished work after a snatched breakfast, he did his rounds of the city. He enjoyed talking to the officers and men of his army. Most were left thrilled at his interest in their affairs, though few did remark on the general's sometimes snappy responses when he heard anything disagreeable to him. This, to those who knew him better, was out of character.

On returning to the palace and with no news to greet him, he grew ever more morose. He needed word of Hope and to hear from his scouts. After nearly two weeks in the city, the overriding thought now beginning to form in his mind was he had no other option but to order withdrawal.

He looked forward to Hester's letters but by God, would rather she was with him! The prize of his life, this command, came with a heavy price. He had himself been a subordinate, cursing and fretting over his superiors assumed dilatoriness and perceived incompetence in the past. Muttering openly his discontent with others while suffering the agonies of powerlessness to interpose his own will. Now the roles were reversed. He was aware of cur's like that damned fool Stewart, Castlereagh's informant, openly voicing criticism of his indecisiveness and publicly stating that the wrong man was in command. It should have been Wellesley but for the senile favouritism of the king and his corrupt son.

Hester would have damned them all to their faces for disloyal scoundrels, fishwives and whoremasters. Moore grinned at the thought. But only now did he truly appreciate the loneliness involved in the command he craved. Hester was hundreds of miles away. John Moore was on his own.

He rose from his desk. There was a knock and an orderly officer announced the arrival of a gentleman from the Supreme Junta with a report for him. Thinking it may be just another stuffed Spaniard with unreliable information, the general sighed and bid him enter.

The figure who entered John Moore's quarters was no native of that country. An Englishmen in civilian clothing, evidently battered by hard riding presented himself as Mr Charles Vaughan, secretary to Stuart,

Britain's attaché to the Supreme Junta at Aranjuez.

'Thank you for seeing me at this late hour, Sir John.' Mr Vaughan presented a packet of documents.

His eyes on the dispatches, Moore quickly remembered his manners. 'A chair and a drink, Mr Vaughan?'

'A chair, yes. I'll have a drink after if you don't mind.' Vaughan responded, the exhaustion in his voice evident as Moore carried over a simple armchair for the secretary to use.

He walked back to his desk and looked for his letter opener. 'I can very much tell you what they contain myself, General, as it was I who drafted them personally on Mr Stuart's behalf.' Vaughan stated helpfully.

'Hard news, I most earnestly pray.' Moore replied hopefully.

'Hard, yes. But unfortunately, unhappy tidings, Sir John. I've ridden these six days in order to inform you that on November 23rd, the armies of their Excellency's, Palafox and Castaños were defeated at Tudela most decisively. Theirs were to the best of my knowledge, the only forces that stood between yourself and the French. It was a sorry affair and did nothing to add lustre to Spain's glory.'

Moore slapped the dispatches down on his desk. He leant over it, his arms stretched out over either end.

'As long as the army of Castaños remained, there was hope, Mr Vaughan. Do you yourself have any estimate of the numbers involved in the French force?'

'They're all in there, Sir John. Our best estimate is up to one hundred and ten thousand men in total based on the latest information received. Another thirty thousand are due to arrive in Spain imminently.'

'Seventeen thousand Britons are paltry number in comparison.' Moore replied almost absently. 'And now the door to Madrid is wide open.' Tudela was barely 200 miles north east of the Spanish capital.

Vaughan nodded again, but now in a chair and with the blessed warmth from the fire, he was struggling to stay awake from his exertions and barely heard the last.

Noting the man's exhaustion, Moore thanked the secretary, saw to it that was he was provided with suitable quarters and dismissed. He returned to his room and sat in the chair vacated by the emissary and stared into the burning fireplace.

He felt an enormous weight of burden removed from him. His earlier concerns over withdrawal were now justified. There was simply no other option. There was nothing between Bonaparte and Madrid and he Moore, was in no way strong enough even when linked up with Hope and Baird, to take on such a huge force without Spanish assistance. Assistance, like the hope he had spoken earlier of which the news of Tudela now extinguished. He could have stopped to curse the ineptitude of a people incapable of defending their own land but he didn't have the time any longer. The decision was made. He now needed to announce it.

This very evening.

They weren't happy to hear the news.

Colbourne, Anderson, Napier, Murray and Clinton he could rely on. The croakers, centred round Charles Stewart were clearly annoyed and vocally so. Moore showed them the dispatches from Vaughan and outlined his reasons but they weren't placated. Colbourne, though a major of only twenty-one, seething inwardly at the show of emotion, took it upon himself to end the griping.

'Gentlemen. No more!' he roared, then with a glance at Moore, 'Sir John?'

The talk gradually died away. Stewart petulantly sitting to one side in order to avoid Moore's eye.

When he was satisfied that they had settled down, Moore finally spoke. 'Gentlemen, as I have informed you all, I have taken the decision to withdraw the army. I did not call you together this evening in order to request your counsel, or to induce any of you to commit yourselves by offering an opinion on the matter. The responsibility for this decision is entirely my own. All I require from each of you is that you prepare immediately to carry out my order. Thank you all and good night to you.'

That evening, John Moore lay in bed, restlessly thinking over the dispatch from Stuart, the decision it had resulted in and its inevitable effect on the morale of the army. He contemplated the opprobrium of some of his officers and government ministers at home and the effect on the Spanish people. He recalled the personal note attached from the British diplomat and took some comfort in the official's final words,

'I therefore lose not a moment in dispatching this to you, that you may

be enabled to take such measures as, in this state of affairs, become
absolutely necessary for the security of our army.'

Andrew Berry and his two friends were oblivious to the machinations of
their army's commanders or their Spanish allies. They were too busy
enjoying the city of Salamanca.

It was what Andrew dreamed of when he thought of Spain as a child.
The difference between this welcoming, beautiful city and the smelly,
dishevelled and disappointing hovel that was Lisbon, was overwhelming.

The three boys spent time in the Plaza Mayor, buying fruit and
sweetcakes from vendors. They walked the streets, viewing buildings and
entering churches. A staunch Presbyterian, Andrew marvelled at the
somewhat frightening imagery within of lifelike Christs bleeding from
crosses, doll-like saints with black faces encased in gold and gaudily
painted Madonna's dressed in ridiculous costumes. All drenched in the
stench of incense. Most fascinating and horrifying of all, were the perfect
wax casts of parts of the human body, sufferers with afflictions hung up
next to images of favoured saints in the expectation of a miracle cure.
Archie was drawn to such displays and spent a long time gazing at them.
Joshua surmised he was only interested in looking out for certain female
parts in particular. Andrew was left feeling nauseous and vowed to avoid
churches known to display such superstitious vulgarity.

They entered a small art gallery, gazing wonderingly at religious art and
nudes on view side by side. This was Andrew's first sight of a naked
female. Fat, creamy-coloured and not very attractive, though admittedly
he was drawn to the breasts. Alongside this canvas, sat a horrific image of
the arrow-ridden Saint Sebastian. That evening Joshua awoke with a
nightmare after viewing the same painting. Archie meanwhile, dreamed
happily of the nude.

On the fateful night while their commanding general was receiving the
dispatches from Mr Vaughan, Andrew, Joshua and Archie set out to visit
one of the town's brothels.

Andrew was less willing than Archie and Joshua even more reluctant.
Archie, a short and heavy, though powerfully muscled young man left
most of the thinking and planning to Andrew in day to day affairs. Of his
two friends he was closest to his fellow Scot, though not out of prejudice
or dislike for Joshua. It was just that Archie had difficulty understanding

Joshua's thick north east of England accent at times.

On arriving in Salamanca, the knowing winks and smirks about women reached a crescendo with the old sweats in Andrew's company. He was interested of course, but only in the desire to meet a respectable girl. He'd no interest in paying for a whore, the very idea of which appalled him. Listening avidly, Archie was then seen speaking to a scarred veteran of Alexandria named Grant.

He then returned to his comrades. 'Grant says we should await a week or two before we try one. By then all the English will have had their fill, and the prices will drop. He said that Scots get prefer...preferall...' he stumbled over the last.

'Preferential treatment?' Joshua assisted his friend.

'Aye, that's it! That means they like us kilties the best, plus it'll cost less.'

'I still don't want to do it.' Andrew interjected. 'What if we pick up the Spanish pox? All our parts will rot away and we'll die in agony!'

Archie was aware of Andrew's reluctance and looked to Joshua hopefully. He didn't want to go alone, desperate as he was to sample the wares.

The young Englishman's reply was much to Andrew's relief. 'The cheaper the whore, the more likely she'll be diseased, Archie. I don't fancy it either. I'm with Drew.'

Archie rubbed his chin, looking uncertain. 'I'll not go without you. But look, once we get there, I'll find a whore and you can stay and have a drink while I'm away with her, how about that?'

'Away where?' Andrew asked mystified.

'Upstairs with the tart.' Joshua answered shortly.

Andrew thought carefully. That sounded reasonable. And probably sensible because he could see for himself what such a place was like, in order to add it to the list of experiences he wished to gather. He would also satisfy his curiosity in finding out what whores looked like, plus he'd be helping a friend.

'Alright, I'm happy to chum you.' he agreed, finally. 'But only when the prices go down. I don't want you fleeced as well as poxed, Archie.'

Sergeant McGillivray heard about it and was not best pleased.

He'd taken a special interest in his last three recruits. Two of them were respectable, well-spoken lads, both with the makings of fine non-commissioned officers. The other, though he could barely write his own name, was strong as an ox, thick as good Scots mince, and would likely become a reliable soldier.

'Has your friend been speaking with Grant, young Mister Berry?'

McGillivray had cornered Andrew in his dormitory in the convent where the 42nd were billeted. The sergeant watched and waited till the young man was on his own before pouncing.

Every spare moment he found while in Salamanca, Andrew spent with his musket. He adored it. The sleekness, the weight, the mechanism. He was forever cleaning and polishing the firing pan and unblocking the touch hole with his wire brush and picker, pulling through the barrel and polishing the wood. He never tired of working on it. Before he had time to reply, McGillivray spoke again.

'Aye. That's good to see. A young lad taking care of his weapon. Love it dearly and you'll never have cause to curse it.'

'Thank you, Sergeant.' Andrew beamed, pleased at the compliment.

'Though I'm thinking there's another weapon a young buckie has to keep clean or it will cause him to suffer dearly.'

Looking up from his bunk, Andrew asked, 'What weapon, Sergeant?'

McGillivray pointed his right fore-finger towards his own groin. 'This one, Andrew. Respectable lads from good homes do not frequent *hoorhooses*.' Unable to speak at the shock of his denouèment, Andrew merely gaped, his mouth open.

'Am I to have to write to your parents? Just because yon skinny Englishman got caught with his trousers down and that Fife lout misses the sheep on his master's farm, does not mean you have to follow them to an early grave. Lousy with disease, and dying a thousand deaths before the actual one.'

'Oh, Sergeant! I'm only going to have a drink while…while…'

'And drink, too?' McGillivray exclaimed with mock levity. 'My! The young gentleman is quite beyond redemption! And since when have you been drinking? Trollops and Spanish wine! Quite the young rip!'

Red-faced and ashamed, the mention of his parents was an unwelcome one to Andrew, bearing in mind his original statement to the recruiting sergeant about his desire not to drink and associate with bad company.

'It's only to accompany Archie,' he began to explain, now his wits were returning. 'Joshua also has no desire to…to…partake.'

Sergeant McGillivray waved a hand. 'I cannot prevent Archie from dipping his wick but if you and Joshua have the good sense I suspect in you both, then maybe I will relent a little in my reproach. I advise you only as one who has experience in such matters and have seen many a lad wretched with Cupid's pox. There are methods of protection. Sheaths. Though moderately expensive in cost, the use of such can save an even heavier price later. I strongly advise Archie to make use of them. And you, too. Even if you do say you choose not to *partake*.'

With that, McGillivray left Andrew who thought mightily on the sergeant's words.

Grant directed the three boys to the dark side street in the less than touristy neighbourhood of Salamanca where the unnamed brothel was housed.

For once, Archie took the lead. He'd been with a number of farm girls at home and indeed, his reasons for joining the army not only included escaping from the eight children and a drunken sot of a father, but seventeen year old Agnes Ross, whom he'd impregnated. Archie was wiser to the world than his more literate friends imagined. He just didn't talk much.

They passed other soldiers in the streets. Infantrymen from regiment such as the Foot Guards, the 50th, artillerymen and hussars. Whether they had come from the brothel, they knew not. Andrew was content to hang back. In his nervous state he spoke incessantly to Joshua, who though listening tolerantly to begin with, was becoming worn down by the drivel he was forced to endure.

At last they arrived. The doorway was unprepossessing. But on entering they were surprised to find themselves in a tavern as like any other frequented in Salamanca. The exception being there were a lot more women than usual. Archie visibly licked his lips in erotic anticipation.

With the exception of the staff, all customer/clients were soldiers. They sat around tables covered with ale jugs, wine carafes, cups and glasses. Red coats and blue cavalrymen jackets were removed and lying either on the dusty floor or hanging wherever a suitable spot was available. The noise of chatter, a tin whistle played '*The downfall of Paris.*' Female laughter and good cheer. Andrew felt a little more comfortable. Find a place for himself and Joshua, order a drink and let Archie have what he wants.

'Do you see that one?' Archie pointed out a young woman in her twenties sitting on the knee of a private soldier of the 32nd regiment. 'That's what I've come for. That's what I want!' he chuckled happily.

'Pretty but taken, Archie,' Joshua observed sagely.

'Aye. But not for long hopefully! I'll get the drinks in.' Archie offered.

'No,' said Andrew. 'I'll get them. You'll need the money for your girl.'

Joshua and Archie went to look for somewhere to sit. Andrew ordered a jug of watered-down wine. He'd discovered the pain of raw, red Spanish wine early on in the march into that land and wanted no repeat. Joshua was only a moderate drinker.

They settled at a table below a staircase. A couple were coming down. A soldier of the 4th regiment putting on his coat and a fat, hard faced woman of indeterminate age.

'That's the best you'll get, Archie. Grab her now while she's free.' Joshua suggested.

Archie took a deep drink of his wine and rose to his feet. The soldier stopped as he noted Archie waiting at the foot of the stairway.

'She ain't no beauty. But boy, can she gallop, Jock!'

The Lancashire soldier buttoned his shirt as the woman stopped to look Archie over. She gave a half smile and turned back up the steps.

'That's me in!' Archie cried exultantly. 'You two stay sober, I want to make this last as long as possible!' His friends watched as the two walked up to the landing and disappear.

'Always the quiet ones.' Joshua observed mournfully and took a drink.

Andrew wondered how any man could possibly want to do it with such an unattractive specimen. Archie should have waited while a better one became available.

There was a loud noise and scream from across the other end of the tavern. The girl on the lap of the 32nd soldier lay sprawled on the floor. Andrew could only see the top half of her body but he did hear the sound of the kick that followed.

'Bitch! Fuckin' dago bitch! She be tryin' to snatch my purse!'

Andrew heard another voice with a similar accent. 'You rotten bastard, Tom Ford! You've gone and ruined her for me!'

The first soldier then leant down and took a hold of something out of Andrew's vision. There then followed an almost inhuman screech of pain.

'Rip it out the whore!' A third soldier yelled.

Another prostitute from the tavern launched herself at the first soldier. There was struggle as as they slapped and tore at each other. One of the soldier's comrades then grabbed one of her flailing arms and together they hurled her across the table. She crashed to the floor, her skull connecting with a sickening thud.

Andrew was up in an instant, took a few steps and flew at the first soldier who was still clutching a handful of blood soaked hair. His momentum carried him smashing into the man who was knocked off his feet. Andrew felt someone grab his arm but pulled away and lashed out with his right and caught a second soldier a glancing blow to the head. Space seemed to appear in the formerly crowded tavern as Andrew felt himself being pulled and hauled by any number of arms. He caught a brief glimpse of Joshua's shocked face.

'Get Archie, for God's sake. Get Archie!' He knew he had only to hold them off before his friend arrived who would put paid to his assailants.

It wasn't easy. He caught a glimpse of the white facing on the sleeve of a 32nd redcoat and then suffered a thump to the side of the face that left him numbed and feeling sick. He felt his strength weaken and he wondered whether it would be best to try and seek an exit.

Slightly stunned, he lost track of time. He only knew that he had to continue to hang on to dear life to the collar and squeeze as hard as he could to the 32nd soldier he'd knocked over, now sprawled beneath him. The man's eyes were bulging out of his head, his face was turning blue as Andrew heard weird gurgling sounds while others rained blows down on his head and arms. But he refused to let go. He only began to twist the collar harder.

'Stop it, Jock! You're killin' 'im. Let him loose and you can go!' A voice of reason from God knows where made everyone stop for a moment.

'I'll be damned if I will! The bastard's a no good piece of scum!' Andrew screamed defiantly.

He then felt one of those closest to him being pulled away. There followed a fearsome slap then a scream as he turned his head and caught a glimpse of Archie's enraged features.

'Drew! Just leave it out, mate! That's enough!' Joshua voice pleaded.

'Fuck off, you Cornish queers! The fights over!' Archie snarled hotly.

Andrew finally released the soldier who fell to the side with a helpful shove from the Scot. He felt himself being bundled backwards without resisting and then the blessed relief of fresh, clean air hit him as they left the brothel. His face soon began to throb as he stopped to lean against a wall. He felt exhausted and sore all over.

'What a waste of money!' Archie moaned aloud. 'I hardly had my kilt up before all that happened!'

Joshua leant over Andrew, concern on his young face. 'Are you alright, Drew?'

'Aye, just need to catch my breath.' Andrew turned and wiped his lip. 'Do I look bad?'

'I've never seen anything like that.' Joshua replied in genuine wonder. 'You wouldn't let go! They couldn't get you down and you wouldn't let go!

Andrew spat out blood and laughed. 'That was nothing, Josh. You've never seen me on a night out in Bathgate!'

Chapter Eight

'My dear Sir John,

The more I consider our situation, the more I am convinced of the danger that would attend my making, at the present moment, any movement in advance, or attempt to join you, until my force is more collected.

As it could never be intended by the British Government that our army should engage in the defence of this country unaided and unsupported by any Spanish force, I confess I begin to be at a loss to discover an object at this moment in Spain.'

You and me both, Davy, John Moore thought bitterly. You and me *both*.

He was looking back over Baird's last letter, advising him of his divisions halt at Astorga after learning of Blake's defeat. Moore had just finished writing to his friend to advise him of his decision to retreat, based on the latest intelligence received from Mr Vaughan.

Following receipt of Baird's letter, Moore communicated his own concerns to Frere who responded firmly that any suggestion of withdrawal was out of the question. The British army must remain in Spain to fight. After deep sole-searching, Moore reluctantly replied to Baird's letter, overruling Davy's legitimate concerns and instructing him to begin moving his army towards juncture in Salamanca.

Now Moore was countermanding that order. He could just about hear the language from Davy, pitying his poor staff who would bear the brunt of his friend's justifiable wrath.

John Hookham Frere. It all came back to that one man. Another meddler who'd spent too long in the country and was now more Spanish than English. Worse, he was clearly ignorant of military affairs. A firm believer in the ridiculously jingoistic notion that a Briton was automatically superior to a Frenchman at any time. The legitimate concern over troop numbers arrogantly dismissed as either exaggeration or an excuse not to fight. Generals would do anything other than fight? By God, how he loathed politicians!

He took comfort in that the language he'd used in his letter to Baird would find full agreement with Davy along with Paget and Craufurd:

'It certainly was much my wish to have run great risks in aid of the people of Spain; but, after this second proof of how little they are able to do for themselves, the only two they had having made so little stand, I see no right to expect from them much greater exertions; at any rate we should be overwhelmed before they could be prepared.'

He sealed the letter and called for a courier.

Davy Baird took the latest order better than expected.

He'd made only desultory plans to move his division on to meet up with Moore. He knew his friend and anticipated another letter ordering retreat to arrive imminently. Alone in his hotel bedroom, Davy sighed in relief.

After this was over, he decided that he was going to retire from the army. His body was giving out. His temper, usually loud, voluble, always containing humour in order to soften the blow on the unfortunate recipient, was deteriorating badly. The humour was gone and in its place, unvaryingly, uncouth vitriol. He was now in constant pain. Pains in the stomach, probably a result of those years in captivity catching up with him. Pains where he'd been wounded, including a pistol ball in the leg. The onset of rheumatism, caused by sleeping on hard ground on campaigns over the years. And age. Christ almighty. I'm only fifty-one but I feel twice that.

He was aware that he was only ever frightening people now. He remained fatherly to the men when dealing with them, that he could not change. But in regards to his staff and other officers he encountered, he found less tolerance than ever for belly-aching and excuses for not doing anything. He was snapping back over the simplest of instructions or commands. He was wise enough to know that in a commander, that invariably led to trouble. Bobby Craufurd could bite back at him, which was a consolation. He was on good terms with Paget and Leith, thankfully. But he knew that loss of control at the wrong moment could result in disaster and death. Disgrace, too.

He remembered the conversation with Craufurd over Pollilore. It was simpler to recount than he'd first thought. He was relieved of something after. He felt as if being enclosed in a tight space with little air, then a door unexpectedly blew open, allowing him to fill his lungs again. He never need repeat the tale to anyone and he could rely on Bobby's discretion. It was a useful exercise after all. He wondered what his mother would have thought of his candour.

Four years prisoner in that place after the massacre at Pollilore. Eight inches of chain between the shackles on his ankles. Four years of shuffling around a dungeon. When they let him out for exercise, he worked in a small garden. Four years of shuffling around vegetables and weeds. The ball in his leg was only removed after he was released. Four years later.

Hyder Ali. Your son, Tippoo Sultan. I saw your dead body, Tippoo, at Seringapatam. You were brave but you were a bastard. You took four years from me, Hyder Ali. But I took your all.

On hearing that her son was captured and chained in a cell with another prisoner, Baird's mother's famous response was that she *'pitied the poor cheil chained to our Davy.'*

Old bitch. He honoured her, but she was not an easy person to love. Hard as Edinburgh's castle rock and tough as old shoe leather. Unforgiving. Unrelenting. Scottish.

Now he himself was becoming equally unlovable. He must get the army back to Coruña as per Johnny's letter, then home. He remained unmarried but there was time enough to find a wife, if maybe too late for children. Do a little gardening. Find some softness in my life, some peace.

The quiet life. Even generals longed for that.

The young Captain Baird, twenty two years of age, first arrived in India in January 1780. He recently transferred from the 2nd regiment to a newly formed unit from the highlands of Scotland. Their chief was Lord McLeod, previously a Jacobite supporter of the Stuart cause, now returned from exile in Europe after accepting the new reality of Hanoverian Britain.

The regiment, originally designated the 73rd but later changing to the 71st was overwhelmingly comprised off highlanders. Among them the largest minority were from the lowlands with a sprinkling of English and Irishmen. As a newly raised regiment, Davy, in transferring, enjoyed a purchase free promotion to a captaincy. The £2000 required for such an advance would have been well out of his reach.

But he was equally as pleased with the culture and ethos of his new regiment as much as with his advancement. The 2nd was a traditional regiment, filled with savage discipline, flogging and the men suffering the whims of brutal NCO's and officers. His own advancement would have necessitated either raising sums of money he could not afford or filling dead men's shoes.

Highland soldiers were not ruled by fear of the lash. Their motivations went deeper, through both personal and clan honour along with unquestioning devotion to the chief. Far worse than the scourge of a flogging, was the shame that would be brought on a man's name and his family should he disgrace his oath. As a soldier served with those he invariably grew up with in the same villages and hills, it would be simple enough for word to reach home announcing a miscreant's dishonour. In such circumstances, it would be difficult for him to return and consequently he would become an outcast.

The highland code was rigidly honour bound and taught that caution was required when dealing with fellow men. Anything regarded as an insult, however slight, could result in a demand for redress, thus men chose their words and actions with care. A young officer intending to lead such men must understand this necessity and act accordingly. Highlanders were led, not driven.

The excitement of the regiment on arriving in India soon dampened, when, on shown their new quarters in Madras, they found not the pristine barracks they were promised, but a rat infested former granary whose walls were blackened with soot and decades of grime.

The promises of higher pay and allowances were also misleading. Davy Baird and many other young officers were reduced to a state of near penury through being forced to adopt the Indian custom of employing any number of servants.

But by far the worst test faced by either officer or enlisted man was the dreadful heat. Added to that was the constant plague of mosquitoes. The latter resulted in the abandonment of the kilt for the wearing of plain trousers, as the men suffered terribly from dreadful ulcers caused by the tiny varmint's merciless scourging.

In the country itself, events were taking place that would soon drive all such concerns from the minds of the 73rd. Hyder Ali of Mysore, who had recently extended his borders while greatly improving the fighting abilities of his army by employing European officers using the British army as his model, declared war on Great Britain.

Resentful that the British failed to honour a treaty years before and didn't come to his aid in his war against the Mahrattas, he secretly built up an alliance with his former enemy in order to drive the hated British, with French assistance, out of India. A huge army led by Hyder, its divisions split among himself, his sons Kureem and Tippoo, prepared to converge on Madras itself.

The government in that city turned to Sir Hector Munro, who'd led a small army to an extraordinary victory over an immensely superior force at Buxur in 1764, and was seen by many as the man to deal with the new threat.

Unfortunately, British forces, though large in number, were widely dispersed. Sir Hector sent out orders to all commanders to converge at St Thomas Mount, a few miles south of Madras with immediate haste.

Even while these orders were being prepared, the government in Madras was shocked to learn of an urgent appeal for assistance from the Nabob of Arcot, a potentate known to be friendly to the British, who was being laid siege by Hyder Ali. He begged the British to relieve his poor people as soon as possible. The city was well supplied and provisioned, the nabob advised and these could be passed onto the British should they relieve the siege quickly. It was an offer Munro could not afford to refuse. Madras was poorly stocked to equip an army.

The nabob, though friendly, was known in the past to spread his loyalties around. Sir Hector was aware of this but ordered Lord McLeod to march on Conjeeveram. He sent orders to Colonel Baillie, marching with a force of just under three thousand men from Guntur Circar, heading as previously ordered for Madras, to change direction and join up with McLeod. The highland chief was dismayed as this would mean a forty mile march into an unprotected town and for Baillie it would mean adding many more additional miles to his march. Surely it was better to wait the two days until it was expected all the forces would meet as originally planned? His concerns went unheeded.

After gerrymandering the vote of the Madras council, Munro's amendments to his original orders were accepted and he was appointed commander of the Madras army. Hyder Ali, who would have been astounded if he learned of this news, while still believing the British would do nothing until all their forces reached Madras, continued to concentrate his forces, including recalling Tippoo's divisions around Arcot.

Munro, who some voices in the army suspected was not the man he was sixteen years earlier, with a force of nearly seven thousand, began his march to Conjeeveram. They were short on provisions as the city was unable to provide them with more than seven days supplies. Four days later they sighted their destination. The town was set aflame. There was no sign of Baillie's force.

The Nabob of Arcot sent a representative with Munro's army who promised that he would arrange a large supply of provisions for the British force. This turned out to be a lie. Now fully aware of the trap he had allowed himself to be led into, Sir Hector sent off to the governor in Madras a desperate order for supplies in order to maintain his force in the field.

Meanwhile, the force of Colonel Baillie found themselves trapped at the wrong end of the raging waters of the river *Cortelier*, now flooding through mountain rains. He sent a message to Madras asking for boats to be sent to the mouth of the river in order to transport his men over. After a delay of nine days and with no reply from the city, Baillie was able to extricate his force over the water to a small village, only fourteen miles from Conjeeveram.

Here he ran into a large force of Tippoo's cavalry. There was a short engagement in which Baillie had cause to be grateful to his artillery, which saw off the horsemen, but left the British with a hundred dead and expenditure of a large amount of ammunition. Both he could ill afford to lose.

Munro's force heard the cannon fire in the distance. He immediately set off from his encampment and after a few miles, ran into the mass of Hyder's army where he halted. Both forces eyed each other for three days.

Sir Hector then received a desperate plea for help from Colonel Baillie. He was suffering from a large number of wounded and dwindling supplies. *'I am in want of everything, I expect you with anxiety.'*

Sir Hector acted quickly. Summoning his officers, he ordered a relief force of one thousand men led by Colonel Fletcher, including the light and grenadier companies of the 73rd to make for Baillie's position immediately. Baillie would be ordered to rest up a few hours, then with the additional men, make for Conjeeveram. Sir Hector's force would meet him halfway.

David Baird, along with his best friend, Lieutenant John Lindsay, would join the relief force. Davy was both excited and relieved, as three days sitting up in the blazing sun eyeballing the enemy was taking its toll on his health as well as his temper.

The force set out that same evening and after covering twenty miles, they came to a large lake which was in fact a tank, or reservoir, which Bailie wisely cut in order to strengthen his position. Davy and his men waded through the water in order to reach their comrades on the other side.

Grateful to meet his rescuers, Baillie was happy to wait till morning in order that his men be rested as much as possible. The small but now reinforced band set out at 8.00a.m. in the attempt to make juncture with Sir Hector.

They were harassed all the way, making only five miles before Baillie forced a halt. Unfortunately, the force was plagued by camp followers who outnumbered the fighting men considerably, an idiosyncrasy of Indian armies as most of the soldiers were native sepoys. They included numerous women and children and were a hindrance at the best of times, but now as the force was continually being attacked on the march by Tippoo's cavalry, they became a serious liability. Davy Baird swore loudly and often as he lost count of the occasions where his men fought off horsemen desperately trying to capture women and stick children with their swords and pikes. Davy himself had to fight off one determined enemy while carrying a screaming child under one arm, and wielding his sword with the other.

Colonel Baillie had up till that moment acted wisely, making sound decisions. But in ordering a halt, he made a serious error of judgement. Colonel Fletcher argued that they should continue. Attempting to make such a rabble move off again may prove difficult. Pray continue on! There is no time to tarry and delay!

Tired and exhausted, Baillie overruled Fletcher's sensible counsel. The battered force stopped for the night. Observing closely, Tippoo informed his father and prepared for the morning.

After learning his son's intelligence, Hyder Ali continued to monitor Munro's force. He decided against the advice of his French allies who wanted to trap both British forces, and moved his army quietly at 4.00 a.m. the next morning to cut off Baillie's advance and juncture with Munro.

Meanwhile, Baillie marched his force that morning two miles along a road running between two ridges towards the village of Perambakam or Pollilore as the British called it. With none of the enemy to be seen, Baillie decided not to send any scouts and advanced until the column was hit by gunfire and grapeshot volleys from cannon behind the left ridge. Baillie attempted an about turn towards the shelter of some trees, but immediately, fire came from that direction also. Now coming on fire from all directions, Baillie halted and ordered his guns to be turned on the enemy. Soon they succeeded in knocking out two batteries of the Hyder's army.

While this was going on, Captain Baird was preparing his men as enemy cavalry had appeared. Davy gave the order and at forty yards, a crashing volley rang out from the 73rd which stopped the attack in its tracks. Those fallen from their horses were immediately dispatched by highland bayonets.

There then began an artillery duel as Baillie moved the force, dangerously exposed in the open, towards a dried up water-course. Apart from the sounds of cannons, there were no further attacks for over an hour. Then in the distance, the strains of a British marching tune could be heard. The men cheered as redcoats came into view. Munro's army had arrived.

But it was a false vision. Hyder Ali, in using British tactics in his army, also used British tunes for his bands. He units also wore red coats. The dreadful truth now revealed itself to Baillie's men. They faced what was the entire enemy army and only God and Sir Hector Munro knew where the second British force was.

The order was given to form square. At first it seemed the tried and tested tactic was succeeding as the enemy in their confusion, inexplicably began to fire on one another. Numerous cavalry charges were made but were repulsed with savage losses.

Davy Baird kept a cool head, ordering volleys and encouraging the men while remaining unhurt. He began to hope that as long as the ammunition lasted, they could make it through the battle. The enemy couldn't endure such losses much longer. The dead were piled in front of the British square offering a barrier and a defence to the men behind corpses that included those of horses and riders. Munro must hear the sounds of battle and would be hurrying to the front. The stink of gunpowder and the sounds of screaming horses and men, the roaring of elephants that formed part of the Hyder's army, the clashing of metal, the smell of piss and shit mingled horrifyingly in the noon-day sun. Davy Baird prayed in between shouting orders to his men, he would see the day out.

Then an explosion from within the square shattered Davy's hearing as ultimately it would destroy the hopes of the British force. Two tumbrils, or carts containing ammunition blew up, possibly being struck by an enemy missile or through negligence, killing the gunners and a number of nearby unfortunates. The camp followers panicked and ran among the soldiers, screaming, terrified of further explosions. Many sepoys dropped their muskets, shed their uniform coats and ran for their lives, believing the enemy had some terrifying weapon which was honing in on them.

The British attempted to fill the gaps and regroup, but their perimeter was now too small and their ammunition near exhausted as a result of the cataclysmic explosion. With Colonel Fletcher already dead, Baillie, realising that the game was now up, tied a white handkerchief to his sword in order to wave surrender.

An officer from Hyder's army came forward and ordered the British to drop their weapons. But whether this was unnoticed in the confusion or a mere ploy, no one could tell, as a cavalry charge led by Tippoo himself charged the British square. Davy Baird was one of the few left fighting on.

He had by now received sword cuts to the head. At this final charge, a horseman swung a pike at him which caught his right arm, causing him to drop his sword from the shock. Now defenceless, his life was only saved just as the cavalryman pulled back his arm in order to land a killing blow, when Davy was knocked over on his side as he was hit by a bullet in the thigh. The man, overreaching him, was pulled off his horse by Lieutenant Lindsay and bayoneted by one of the few remaining highlanders. David Baird by now, through loss of blood and shock, lay semi-conscious.

Soon after that, it was all over. Colonel Baillie's force was effectively wiped from the face of the earth.

Only a few miles away, Lord McLeod and Sir Hector Munro were involved in a heated argument. McLeod demanded that he be allowed to march the remainder of the 73rd immediately towards the firing. He was refused. For once, Munro was correct not to split his forces. Instead they marched another two miles at normal pace. But then stragglers appeared from Baillie's column. Horrific tales were recounted about the fate of Fletcher and Baillie. The word soon spread down the column. There had been a massacre.

Munro knew the only option now was to turn his force around and retreat. Dumping his heavy guns in the reservoir, he hoped to reach the village of Chingleput where it was believed provisions were stored.

Leading units of Heyder's army now caught up with them and they were harassed all along the march. Arriving at the village, Munro found to his dismay that the hoped for stores were not there. Indiscipline now threatened the army.

The men became demoralised through thirst and hunger. Firing on attacking cavalry became ineffective as panic set in among many of the sepoys. In the three-day march to Chingleput alone, upwards of five hundred men were lost.

After meeting up with another column from Trichinopoly, Sir Hector struggled on and finally arrived back at Madras. His force was saved only by Heyder's inexplicable decision not to turn on Munro, only to harass and not offer battle to his rapidly depleted force while it retreated.

'Thank God for Heyder Ali and his bungling. Nearly, but not quite as bad as ours!' Robert Craufurd exclaimed after Baird concluded the tale.

Davy looked meaningfully at his friend. 'Don't expect Bonaparte to be quite so accommodating here in Spain, Bobby.'

Chapter Nine

News of the retreat order spread rapidly throughout the city. The overwhelming majority of the army reacted with shock and incredulity. The local Spanish were aghast. The British had marched a perfectly fine army into the country. Now Bonaparte himself had arrived and they were turning tail and scuttling back to Portugal.

Andrew Berry and his friend Joshua weren't too concerned. In truth, only Archie out of the trio was keen on the idea of battle. He'd heard old-timers boast about gold and silver available on the battlefield in the form of French officer's watches and purses. English ones too, for that matter, if they happened to fall their way. Archie reckoned if he was fortunate to fight in a battle and survive, he might just pocket easy pickings. He wasn't stupid. He didn't look for a fight. But he accepted that risking your life was the price paid to enrich yourself. You could buy a much better class of whore with French gold in your sporran.

Joshua decided long before arriving in Spain that joining the army was the biggest mistake he'd made since allowing himself to be seduced by his former employers wife. Of course, the pleasure of it had been hugely enjoyable at the time. She treated him as her poppet, lavishing him with gifts, many of which he discreetly sold in order to send money home to his mother. He'd enjoyed staying with her in her Canongate townhouse, whose luxury went way beyond anything he enjoyed in the High Street hovel he shared with three other clerks. Why she had chosen him remained a mystery. He was short, very slight to the point of emaciation and despite his best efforts, could only grow the wispiest of short beards which even she teased him over.

And yet he liked her and evidently, she liked him. He was an extremely bashful virgin and she had introduced him to the arts of love.

But it hadn't been worth this! If only he'd thought things out clearer. He'd put money aside from a present of a moleskin coat she'd bought him. He could have used the cash for the journey home to Newcastle. Or he could have walked and saved most of it. But he believed her husband, Mr Johnstone, when after he had beaten him up, swore he would send word to all the faculties of advocates throughout the land, declaring Joshua Whitfield a dishonest individual and seducer of rich women who should never be employed by anyone in the profession again.

Only now, after giving it careful thought, did he dissect that last statement and accept it for the nonsense it truly was.

Rosamund Johnstone was a notorious nymphomaniac, who preyed on very young men while her husband rutted his way through the Old Town brothels of Edinburgh. He'd heard his fellow clerks, a few of whom were not averse to sampling such delicacies themselves, mention they had often seen Johnstone in the same establishments. What's more, Rosamund's husband was a church elder. It was a well-known fact that Edinburgh's brothels did their steadiest trade during the Kirks' annual General Assembly.

Fool! Damned fool! Joshua had cursed and slapped himself on the head countless times since in his frustration. Why, by God, I could have threatened him! Blackmailed the swine! Instead he ran from his problems by hiding away in the army. His only consolation was that he did not change his name because he could not bear the thought of his family not knowing what became of him. So he wrote to them, telling a lie. He had become bored with the life of a lawyer's clerk and wanted adventure.

His mother's response drove him to tears. He turned to Andrew for consolation, which his new friend gave him. Andrew listened to Joshua pour his heart out one night in Lisbon which sealed their friendship. He then told Archie. That young man merely shrugged and told him not to worry, for though he had no friends now in Edinburgh, he had new ones in the army. They then both went off together. Later, Andrew asked what they had spoken about. Joshua turned red and replied that Archie wanted to know every detail of his liaison with his employer's wife.

'And did you tell him?' asked Andrew. He was keen to know himself what was said but thought it wrong to enquire without invitation.

'Yes, I told him. He's women-crazed is Archie. It's all he thinks about.' Joshua said no more.

It was all Andrew thought about much of the time, too. Especially after observing the girls on view in Salamanca. They were all heavily chaperoned of course, those being the gentlefolk of the city. But he'd caught more than one eye when doing the rounds with his friends. It was true. The Scots *were* popular. But he didn't push it any further. Flirting with barmaids and serving girls were his best avenue. One night he became involved in an extremely long and enjoyable kissing session with a sweet-faced señorita. It whetted his appetite for more but more was not forthcoming. He went back the following night but she indicated kisses were her limit. For the moment. It was enough for him at the time and he was happy to have her pretty face in his mind to dream about. Her name was Gabriela and she worked in her father's tavern.

She was one of the reasons why he disavowed visiting brothels. He'd found a girl and was content. She was incomparable to the harlots in the place he visited where he was involved in the fight with the soldiers from the 32nd. Later, Joshua asked him why he so readily involved himself in another man's dispute. Andrew was slightly put out. Because he struck a lassie, was his curt response. It was that simple.

As for the army, Andrew was beginning to share his English friend's concerns over the wisdom of his earlier decision to enlist. Now that he'd worn the uniform, learned how to use a musket, been on board a ship, visited two new countries and met a beautiful foreign girl (and visited a brothel), there really wasn't much more he wanted out of the life. Along with the stories of plunder, many from the regiment had served in Egypt with Abercromby and their latest commander, Sir John Moore. The men held both in the highest esteem. But when they reminisced about the battle of Alexandria, Andrew listened with unease.

They spoke of receiving cannonades. Men standing in line while round and grapeshot blew them over like skittles. And there was no way to escape. You had to stand there and take it. If you ran, you were flogged or hanged.

Wounds. Having arms and legs amputated. Remember Ruaridh? Aye, he died badly. A bullet hole in the chest and a bayonet in the guts. Squealed like a pig, he did. God rest his soul. Buried him with his brother in the sands of Egypt.

Andrew didn't want his body to lie anywhere but at home in Scotland. He wanted his mother to have a gravestone to visit. Not a dust filled hole in Africa or Spain she'd never know.

The truth was, Andrew didn't know if he could take standing under a cannonade. He didn't know if he could ram a bayonet into another man's belly. He truly hadn't thought of such things back home in Barbauchlaw. Didn't really want to.

With the retreat order, he now felt an overwhelming relief. The news that Bonaparte himself was in Spain was exciting on first hearing. But the initial thrill of facing the great Tyrant of Europe dispelled somewhat when he stopped to consider the implications.

He would put his trust in God. And in his fellow Scot, Sir John Moore.

The army commander was in turmoil.

The retreat decision Moore made was now bearing the bitter fruit of censure, even the early shoots of potential disgrace, if some were to be believed. He was being dragooned, damnit! Dragooned and browbeaten into making a potentially catastrophic decision!

His ire was raised in particular by a letter received from Charles Stuart in Madrid. At least the man had remained at his post. That vile fanatic Frere had shit his breeks, fled the city and was presently spreading his poison from Talavera.

The letter from Stuart, received in knowledge of Moore's decision, begged him to reconsider in light of new facts concerning an upturn in Spanish fortunes. At that time, Tam Graham and two other officers from Moore's army were in Madrid sounding out the situation. Moore placed more faith in a report from them than from Stuart, whom he believed was being pressured by Frere. The letter went on to list various numbers regarding Spanish troops available. But by now, Moore regarded such information at best wishful thinking, at worst, downright unbelievable.

What left him most disturbed was the section of the letter where Stuart made an outright threat:

'You must, however certainly know best the chances of effecting a junction between your different divisions; and it does not become me to hazard an opinion on the subject. With respect, however, to the consequences of their distinct retrograde movements, I can tell you, that they are likely to produce an effect here, not less serious than the most decisive victory on the part of the enemy; and I shall, I own, be surprised

if a change of government is not the immediate consequence, when the reasons for you retreat are known.'

Moore swore again on reading the inflammatory passage. One hundred and ten thousand men to face and *I'm* responsible for changing their rotten government? Why, a blue arsed monkey could run a country better, damn them all to hell!

To add to his concerns, he recently received word from his good friend, John Hope. French cavalry had come within twenty miles of him on his march to meet up with the army. He was on his way as earlier ordered, to make juncture with Moore at Ciudad Rodrigo. An urgent dispatch was sent to Hope redirecting him on to Salamanca. Hope hadn't spared his men or horses who became so exhausted that he was forced to abandon six precious guns.

The calibre of a man like John Hope and I'm here, dealing with trash like Stuart and Frere!

There was a discreet tap on the door. Paul Anderson entered. 'Sorry to disturb you, Johnny. There are two rather interesting visitors arrived from Aranjuez. They've brought a letter from the Supreme Junta.'

Moore sighed. 'I'll see them in the dining room. Have refreshments prepared. I'm sure they'll be thirsty.'

The two gentlemen in question were Brigadier-general Don Augustin Bueno and Don Ventura Escalante, Captain-general of the armies of Granada. They were aged, impassioned, and several levels out of their depths.

Moore observed them wryly. Splendidly attired in Spanish general's uniforms, both immaculately turned out. Evidently, they'd brought their best dress with them to change into before greeting the general who wants to run out on them. This *is* official. Or an act of desperation. The conversation was in French.

'Sir John, thank you for seeing us at this hour,' Brigadier-general Bueno began the formalities after his credentials were read out in the long and laborious Spanish fashion. There were far too many for Moore to remember later.

The other nodded in the direction of the British general. 'I am always honoured to be in the presence of patriots such as yourselves.' Moore replied gracefully.

Bueno returned the compliment by raising his glass. 'And you, sir.'

Impatient to get things over with, Moore spoke plainly. 'What news do you bring from the Supreme Junta, gentlemen?'

General Bueno as if to authenticate his importance, slowly lowered his glass to the table before answering. 'Sir, I bring only good news.'

He snapped a finger. Every British officer reacted in amazement as a Spanish orderly in riding clothes entered with a letter which he handed to Don Bueno. The man bowed deeply, then left the room.

With elaborate charm, the Spanish general rose from the table, walked over to Moore and with the letter in both hands, solemnly placed it before the British commander.

'Sir John, I present to you the communication from his Excellency, Don Martin de Garay, secretary of the Supreme Junta, with my compliments.' With a slight bow, he returned to his chair.

At something of a loss, Moore looked around the table. 'Stanhope, kindly have this translated for me as soon as possible will you?'

'Yes, Sir John.' This was Charles Stanhope, Hester's half-brother whom Moore accepted as an aide. He'd recently allowed James, another brother, to join his staff at Hester's specific request though he didn't officially require any more young officers. James was at sea on his way to Spain. Moore couldn't say no to her.

'Er, we can save you the time, Sir John.' Don Bueno interjected helpfully. 'The letter authorises myself and Don Escalante to discuss the matter of your plan of campaign in order to relieve the city of Madrid. The monster, Bonaparte is now determined on enslaving our country and as he approaches our glorious capital city, a new spirit of resistance burns in the hearts of all Spanish people.'

There was a silence around the table. Moore felt gratified to speak. 'I congratulate you on this new spirit, General. But spirit alone cannot defeat an invader.' There was an uncomfortable pause. All eyes were on the Spaniard.

He gave a short laugh. 'Sir John, I am pleased to inform you that both in spirit and in body, the Spanish people are ready to repel the Corsican barbarian. His Excellency, General Castaños has escaped from his misfortune at Tudela with twenty-five thousand men from his army and marches on northern Madrid. The Estramaduran army of Segovia under his Excellency, General Heredia, numbering ten thousand men, is ready to march for Spain. In Guadarramas, his Excellency, General San Juan has raised twelve thousand men and is defending the Somosierra Pass which has been fortified so strongly that it renders the approach to Madrid impracticable. Ten thousand levies from Castile and Andalusia have already arrived in Madrid and many more are expected imminently.

'General Moore, that numbers nearly sixty thousand patriots. Combined with your gallant twenty-seven thousand, a total of almost ninety thousand men are now available to destroy the twenty thousand French pigs heading as we speak for the city!'

Both Spanish generals had tears in their eyes. It was a little embarrassing to the British. The officers seated next to each of the old men, Paul Anderson and Edward Paget, stood up from their chairs and grabbing the nearest decanters, began to refill the men's glasses.

Just as the general stopped speaking, an orderly appeared to the side of Moore, whispering to him intently. Moore replied and the orderly left the room hurriedly.

'Gentlemen, I am sure we all congratulate you on your news. I am now advised that one of my senior officers, Colonel Graham, has just now returned from Madrid and is eager to report his observations to me. He is invited to join us.'

On cue, Thomas Graham of Balgowan entered the dining room, spurs clinking off the wooden floor, leather riding boots squeaking audibly. His riding cloak was discarded but the smell of horse and sweat was tangible. He looked every inch his sixty years, worn and exhausted, thought Moore. But what can I do? The man's irreplaceable.

'A cigar and a brandy first, young Colbourne!' Graham ordered business-like. The officers at the table attempted to hide their grins, some couldn't.

'And a hello and good evening to you, too, Tam!' Moore welcomed ironically, but not without humour.

'Oh, aye, Johnny. A guid evenin' tae ye! But ye ken I'm no use after a hard ride till I get a drink down me!'

There was now an uncontrollable giggle of laughter. Graham was used to poor behaviour from Moore's young tykes and usually rose to their bait. On this occasion he chose to ignore them. He was too tired and all he wanted was a drink and then his bed. The two Spanish gentleman sat opened mouth in astonishment at the coarse intruder. A mess orderly arranged a chair for Graham between Moore and Don Escalante.

'Christ, that's braw!' Graham now seated, exclaimed after downing a full glass of brandy. There were a few quiet sniggers from the younger officers. Graham then let out a terrific belch. The sniggers grew worse.

'Sorry to interrupt your supper, Johnny.' Graham glanced at Moore. 'I dinnae believe I ken these two gentlemen?' He then lit a cigar.

Moore introduced both to Graham and then asked General Bueno to repeat the news delivered. Graham leant with one elbow on the table, smoking a large cigar, listening in silence as Stanhope translated.

Graham heard them out. There was a pause, then he let rip a tremendously loud fart that cannonaded across the room like a mighty drumroll. Stanhope and the young officers were now in a state of near hysterical collapse in their efforts not to laugh out loud.

'There's as much wind comin' frae that auld pantaloon as fae ma arse.' Tam Graham observed philosophically, the smoke from his cigar so thick it clouded him in a haze.

Equally beside himself with mirth, John Moore struggled to respond. 'What can you mean, Colonel Graham?'

'What I mean is that just last night about this time, I was dinin' with the famous General San Juan himself. Oh, no' as luxuriously as this. It was out in the field right after a squad of French cavalry just chased the entire… what did you say the numbers were, General?' Graham looked over pressingly at General Bueno, who not having any English, looked on with some mystification.

'Twelve thousand I believe.' Stanhope answered helpfully in between a guffaw.

'Oh, aye. Twelve thousand men. Yes. Well, the good lord created the loaves and the fishes for all those folk long ago, but even he couldnae turn a rabble o' a few hundred into twelve thousand men.'

Moore lost all humour. 'What are you telling me, Tam?'

'I'm tellin' you he's lyin'. They're both lyin'. There's no sixty thousand men. They're talkin' a load o' shite.' There was a stunned silence. Graham then began to explain himself.

'Bonaparte has already crossed the Guadarramas.' By this time a staff officer sitting next to Don Escalante was translating quietly Graham's words, though somewhat censored in content.

Don Escalante gasped at this last statement. He spoke over in his native tongue to Bueno who visibly paled.

'So much for General Heredia.' Graham continued sarcastically. 'As for the magnificent "army" o' Segovia, it's presently on the run and retreatin' as fast as possible.'

The two old Spaniards now began to weep, their heads in their hands. Moore could only sympathise with their humiliation. The news of Guadarramas alone was stunning enough.

Tam Graham stopped and took a long draw on his cigar. He did not attempt to look over at the Spaniard across from him or the one at his side, though all eyes were now on them.

'Alright. Apart from that, what good news I have is that there has been an uprisin' in the south. The city of Saragossa in Aragon has seen a defeat of a besiegin' force of Frenchmen. How many were lost, I cannae say because the details are patchy like everythin' else in this bloody country. As for Madrid, I cannae see it holdin' out long. But there is work being done to defend it. Thousands o' people are building a trench around the city. It's a marvel to see. Women of all ages and indeed, children too. Auld men, all gettin' stuck in. They're also preparin' works beyond the trench line. But Bonaparte's wants it and what he wants he usually gets. He's sendin' twenty thousand to take it. There's not much I could see in the way of stoppin' him. But the spirit o' resistance does shine in Madrid. I only wish it existed elsewhere.'

There was another thoughtful silence as Graham's words were digested.

'Well, that's the news. It's no' great but there it is. Now, if you don't mind, I'll say goodnight to ye, Johnny, and to you insolent young toerags. I'm off to my bed.' He rose from his chair stiffly but before he left the room, he turned to Moore.

'Oh, and some advice tae ye, Johnny. Send these two auld rogues back to where they came from. *Pronto.* Good night, gentlemen.

The Spanish grandees left Salamanca the following morning to return to the Junta at Aranjuez, their mission an abject failure.

But John Moore now had at least something positive to consider. The report from Tam Graham on the situation in Madrid matched an earlier one of his staff officer's, Charles Stewart. He commanded the cavalry in Hope's division and left the force to make a detour on his way to

Salamanca in order to report his position by way of Madrid. In the city he noted as Graham had the efforts made by the citizens to defend their capital. Stewart was greatly encouraged by the high state of morale of the Junta and the resolution of the people.

Charles Stewart was one of Moore's loudest critics and at first he was somewhat sceptical of the young man's report. But now that Graham had confirmed it, he was left with food for thought.

That morning after breakfast, Moore received a letter from the Supreme Junta in Madrid, signed by the Prince of Castelfranco and Thomas de Morla. Moore judged it a little more realistic in tone.

'The army which General Castaños commanded, and which amounts to about 25,000 men, is falling back on Madrid in the greatest haste, to unite with its garrison and the force that was at Somosierra of 10,000 men also is coming for the same purpose to this city, where nearly 40,000 men will join them…

'But the Junta hope that your Excellency, if no force is immediately opposed to you, will be able to fall back to unite with our army, or take the direction to fall on the rear of the enemy. The rapidity of your Excellency's movements will be such that the interests of both countries require.'

Moore now felt inexorably drawn to commit himself and the army to attempt some measure of assistance to the Spanish. His earlier argument for complete withdrawal was sound. But he strove to find a solid reason for a swift about turn to prepare for his masters in London. The truth was he just couldn't settle on one solid answer that would not be thrown back at him. Stuart and Frere were too powerful and influential with the cabinet back home. Moore could well imagine the tone of their reports concerning him. The Scot did not require reminding that he was not popular with the government. And yet his latest communication from Castlereagh was heartening:

'You will keep in mind that the British army is sent by His Majesty as an auxiliary force, to support the Spanish nation against the attempts of Bonaparte to effect their subjugation.'

While as ever playing both ends, Castlereagh still allowed him enough leeway to protect both himself and the army.

To be given such a weapon as he had and not use it in any way seemed wasteful. If the people of Madrid believed a British army was on its way to assist them, surely that could only bolster their determination to resist? And if he did make some token show, would that not at least remove some of the criticism attaching to him, while offering Castlereagh something he could fight the cabinet with?

He was aware of his limitations. He knew he could be almost insanely stubborn when he believed himself in the right. In Corsica, Sicily and Sweden. Damn it all! He *had* been right as events proved. But the damage it caused! In thinking back, he accepted that he should have shown a little more subtlety. God knows, there were enough people around him advising him so. By Christ, he must have come across as an utter prig! He hated to think he was considered so by anyone. One of his great qualities was that he bore no grudges. None that lasted, anyway. He had met people he plainly disdained, even disliked. Hood, William Drummond, Gilbert Elliott. But those three weren't liked by anyone, damnit!

John Moore laughed to himself. I know I'm a bit of a prig. Can't help it. All that honour and respect taught by his father. He came from a humble background but when died, he could have bought and sold any number of lords and ladies he'd served throughout his life.

I'm too touchy and I'm moving in circles that only see me as a surgeon's son from Glasgow. A tradesman.

Hester doesn't see me like that.

He thought about her. From her letters she was still championing him to everyone. But what did she really think? She just wants me home safe. So do the families of all my soldiers. They want their sons and husbands home *safe.*

They don't think I'm as good as Wellesley. They wanted him for that reason and because he's a penniless Irish lord's son and I'm not. He's a gentleman and I'm one step up from the gutter. Wellesley knows that too. I saw it in his eyes. His father didn't have a pot to piss in and never did a hard day's work in his life. His son believes the revolution in France changed nothing. He's wrong. I know it changed everything and the day will come when the duke's and lords of this country will go the way of the French aristocracy. Maybe in not quite so dramatic a fashion. But already they're being replaced by men of science, of medicine, philosophy and engineering. And these men, these *new men*, will one day be the rulers, replacing the old down at heal feudal anachronisms. They will decay and disappear in the modern age.

He, John Moore, was one of the new men. He'd exhibited it at Shorncliffe. He wasn't an engineer like Watt or a philosopher like Hume. But he was an engineer of *men* and a philosopher on the science of war. He created something modern and revolutionary. Soldiers did not have to march in line and column as unthinking automatons and be blasted to death by wrote any longer. New weapons, grooved rifles and rockets were changing the face of war and he was in the vanguard of those reacting to that change. *Embracing* the change. Even David Baird, that bad-tempered, irascible but lovable old devil, had remarkably forward thinking ideas on fitness and hygiene. These meant far more to him than pipe clay and pigtails. Nelson. Yes, his old protagonist from Corsica, was another. A parson's son. Yet his genius, his modernity, was unquestionable.

The Wellesley's wanted the world to remain as it is. Moore knew it was changing. He was part of that change. His system at Shorncliffe was not universally popular. It was barely understood in some military circles.

Moore did not want his legacy to be solely that of an innovative trainer of soldiers. He wanted to leave behind an honourable and distinguished record as a leader of men. He had no doubt that after the Cintra enquiry, Wellesley would be back. Possibly in a stronger position. Moore would not allow himself to be superseded the way Baird had by that man and his family connections in India.

He made his decision. He was going rescind the order to withdraw and instead, march the British army to the aid of the people of Madrid and Spain.

The following morning he called his senior officers together and advised them of his decision. They were to prepare to leave the city as soon as General Hope arrived with the cavalry. Each and every man rose to his feet, applauding and congratulating their general in the heartiest and happiest manner possible.

He no longer looked for God's assistance. Logic, science and Hester's love were now his guides.

Chapter Ten

John Moore's decision was put to severe test late that same evening under circumstances he could never have foreseen. John Hookham Frere was the root cause.

An intermediary in the form of a messenger between the two men arrived in Salamanca. This was an individual whom Moore considered so base and calculating, that he came as close as he ever had to physically assaulting another human being and beating them to death with his bare hands.

Monsieur le Colonel Venault de Charmilly, Knight of the Royal Military Order of St Louis, suffered a most exhausting day. Presenting himself at the *Palacio San Boal* in the evening, he arrived hot from Talavera with important intelligence on the situation in Madrid, corroborated by a written communication from the British representative, Mr Frere.

He was refused admittance at first.

John Moore had dealings in the past with the '*Colonel.*' He first encountered the name years earlier in the West Indies. Moore was serving as temporary military governor of St Lucia shortly after the British take-over of the French colony. An *émigré*, Monsieur Charmilly, approached him offering his services. After some discreet enquiries, Moore learned Charmilly's name was connected with horrific massacres in Saint Domingo in the early 1790's. There was also rumours of unpaid gambling debts.

John Moore promptly 'chased' Mnr. Charmilly.

He later emerged in London. He had been a merchant of coal, a distiller, a serial gambler, money lender and ultimately, a bankrupt. Along the way he made a scandalously good marriage to Lady Dufferin's daughter. A file was opened on him in Whitehall. He'd even tracked Sir John Moore down and had the effrontery to ask him advice on raising his own regiment. Now he was here in Spain.

'A most insistent fellow.' Paul Anderson complained of him.

'Ask him to give you his letter from Frere and I'll read it up here alone.' Moore's irritation was clear from his voice. He was busy composing a letter to Davy Baird, explaining fully his decision but would now only have time for a quick note.

'Afraid I already did and he refused.' Anderson replied regrettably. 'He said the letter was there to confirm the message he and only he is able to deliver. Damned peacock!'

'Suffering Christ!' Moore swore, accepting the *fait accompli* with ill grace. 'Send the bastard up then!' Anderson left with a wary look and a few moments later, the man John Moore remembered from St Lucia entered the room with a flourish of bows.

He was of a similar age to Moore. Tall, clean shaven, deep set grey eyes, cavernous features, balding. He was dressed in expensive riding clothes. Whatever his new business was here in Spain, he appeared to be prospering.

'Sir John, I present Colonel Charmilly.' Paul Anderson introduced the visitor. He remained at the Frenchman's side. He trusted him about as far as he could spit.

'Ah, we have met before, Sir John! Twice we have made acquaintance and had a most interesting discussion.'

'Yes, er, Colonel, I believe we have.' Moore wanted this over as quickly as possible. 'You have some communication for me?'

Trying to appear not too put out by the lack of formality, no offer of a chair, or refreshment. Charmilly's continued in the same ingratiating manner.

'My dear General Moore, may I request we be alone? I have ridden far and under difficult circumstances. I am in need of nourishment. Forgive me, but I must be perfectly clear in what I must tell you.'

He stopped speaking and there was an awkward moment. Moore loathed the very sight of the creature. To have him here now under such circumstances, was deeply wounding to him. It was indeed better to be left alone.

'Colonel Anderson, please allow us this room. And can you send up some wine and something to eat for our guest.' Sensing that it had taken a lot out of his friend to make such a request, Paul acted as instructed.

Once his aide left the room, Moore showed the visitor a chair. There was a silence as the British commander sat behind his desk. Oblivious to the effect his presence was having, Charmilly looked around, showily.

'It is not the room of a general. It is the room of the *man* himself. Am I not correct?'

If there was one aspect of the French character that Moore detested most, it was the false intellectualism they were prone to indulge in. Moore gave a shrug. 'It serves a purpose, no more.'

'Ah, yes! A soldier's response. Simple, but devastating in its effect. I congratulate you, sir. They say Bonaparte is a genius. But for me there is genius and there is vulgarity. To flaunt one's genius is disgusting. A man should have simple tastes. Then he has more time to contemplate the important things in life. No?'

Wondering where the hell the orderly was, Moore remarked that it is was an interesting concept.

Charmilly beamed happily. '*Enchantè*, Sir John!'

There was a knock and at last Francois himself appeared with a tray of cold chicken and a decanter of wine with glasses. He made space, removing papers and other objects and laid the tray on Moore's desk.

'Thank you, Francois.'

The valet gave Charmilly a chilly look and left the room. Moore tried not to smile. He was certain his young servant was now standing outside, listening for the first sound of any trouble, preparing to burst into the room in order to save his master's life. Francois remembered Charmilly all too well from St Lucia.

The colonel stood and without permission, poured from the decanter into both glasses, one of which he handed to the Scot. He then grabbed a chicken leg and returned to his chair.

'I am aware that you have ordered a complete withdrawal of your army.'

Ignoring the remark, Moore replied. 'What is the message you wish to give me?'

Charmilly took a bite from the chicken leg and chewed. It was evident he was famished and Moore had to marvel at his earlier self-control. This *must* be important.

'I apologise, Sir John. Once I am finished eating, I will reveal all.' He then took a large gulp of wine. When he had finished the chicken, he reached over and laid the bone back onto the tray.

Moore observed in fascination, slightly annoyed at himself. Charmilly then took out a pink handkerchief from inside his shirt and wiped his mouth and fingers.

Noticing, Charmilly smiled. 'A present from my wife before I left. Ah, just like a woman! So delicate and yet so strong!'

'Yes, indeed.' Moore agreed. 'Now if you'll forgive me, Colonel, I am extremely busy.'

'*Eh voila!* Yes! Now I am suitably refreshed. I am most grateful for your kindness, Sir John.'

He then reached inside his shirt again and removed a parchment which Moore recognised as the style of letter he usually received from Charles Stuart and John Hookham Frere. Reaching over the desk, Charmilly handed it to the Scottish general.

'The letter is sealed. It is undisturbed.'

Moore looked over the letter. 'Yes, I can see that.'

'Good. Please open and it and review its contents.'

Moore opened the letter. It was from Frere. It confirmed Charmilly's credentials and went on to say that based on a report received by himself from the colonel on the new found resolution of the people of Madrid, it left him entirely confident that its citizens were fully prepared to defend it to the hilt. In conclusion it read:

I cannot forbear representing to you in the strongest manner the propriety, not to say the necessity, of supporting the determination of the Spanish people, by all means which have been entrusted to you for this purpose.

I consider the fate of Spain as depending absolutely for the present upon the decision in which you adopt. I say for the present; for such is the spirit and character of the country, that, even if abandoned by the British, I should by no means despair of their ultimate success.

Rage and anger broiled within Moore. He was barely able to read through to the end of the letter, which mentioned changes within the Supreme Junta. Finally and with magisterial self-control, he placed the letter carefully on the desk before him.

Moore's countenance revealed little to Charmilly.

'Sir John, such *sang froid* is admirable! I can only confirm that the pride and patriotism I recently witnessed in Madrid was truly overwhelming. The people have taken to arms. The women, even the children, carry pikes, staves, rolling pins! From all around the environs of the city, peasants flock to offer their labour in digging and building defences. The pavements of the streets have been broken up and large stones and rocks taken up to the roofs of houses in order to be used as missiles!

'In regard to the Supreme Junta, I have secret information which as you have noted, Mr Frere only hints at. The Junta has left the city for Badajos. The Duke of Infantado has now assumed the presidency and thus, responsibility for the defence of the capital. This can only strengthen the resolve of the defenders that such a man has taken control at this critical hour.'

Charmilly then stood. 'Sir John, I have spoken with his Highness, the Duke himself. He has a message for you. It is his pleasure to announce that you have been appointed commanding general of the forces of Spain. Please allow me to be the first to congratulate you on this signal honour!'

Charmilly leaned over with his right hand out. John Moore did not utter a word throughout the entirety of Charmilly's speech. He could not trust himself to.

He took the hand and shook it gracefully. He then stood himself.

'Colonel Charmilly, I have been most remiss. You must be extremely tired after such a journey and desire to rest and refresh yourself. I commend your zeal in foregoing such before seeing me.'

Moore then walked around the desk. He took Charmilly's arm and led him to the door.

'Have you suitable quarters?' Moore asked solicitously.

'I have found rooms in the merchant quarter of the city.' Charmilly replied, evidently charmed by the general's solicitude. 'Is this the end of our interview?'

'I have much to do this evening, Colonel. I'm sure you understand. Shall we meet again, tomorrow morning, say eleven o'clock?'

The colonel was pleased to confirm the time was suitable and with that, John Moore showed his visitor out.

Back at his desk, Moore cleared his mind of Charmilly and Frere and completed his note to Baird. In it he gave a brief outline of the situation in Madrid. With regard to Frere, he merely mentioned "representations" from the gentleman compelling him to act in reverse of his earlier decision. He now requested Baird cease his retreat to Corûna and return immediately to Astorga to await fresh instructions.

He then composed a letter to the Marquis of Romaña, the sole remaining Spanish leader left with a strong enough force available to put into the field. Moore was aware that his new strategy, though sure to be welcomed throughout the army, would soon be questioned once the initial exuberance wore off. Mindful of Castlereagh's advice regarding Britain's army to be used as an auxiliary force only, he knew that twenty seven thousand men could do little on their own other than form a rallying point. If he could achieve juncture with Romaña at Madrid, or thereabouts, it would serve as a beacon to all of Spain that here was a united force prepared to confront head on the hated invader.

The hour now very late, he ordered couriers be made ready to leave that night with dispatches for Baird and Romaña. He then took to his bed.

He lay for a while, reflecting over the day's events. He felt a sense of relief, but also the kernel of an idea beginning to form in his mind. It was one to be pondered very carefully as it involved a gamble. John Moore was not a gambling man. Far from it. It would be dangerous. In fact, extremely hazardous. But he was confident it was a stratagem that if successful, could potentially seal the fate of the French in Spain.

Along with securing Sir John Moore's place in history.

Colonel Charmilly seethed with indignation.

He stood in the hallway at the *Palacio San Boal* at precisely 11a.m. the following morning. He was disturbed to discover that according to Captain Percy, aide-de-camp to the general, his Excellency was presently indisposed and would the colonel care to try again this afternoon?

Stressing the urgency of the mission, Charmilly stated that time was of the essence and if Sir John were unavailable, he would try two other gentlemen of his acquaintance, namely Generals Fraser and Beresford.

Harry Percy had neither the time nor the inclination to advise this increasingly insufferable foreigner that the forenamed gentlemen were not to be found in the city at present. He merely replied that he would make Sir John aware of his presence and wished him a good day.

Colonel Charmilly left the building in torment. His mood had grown more perturbed as he observed the bustle and activity within the army headquarters, which he naturally assumed was due to the retreat order given by General Moore.

On calling on General Fraser, he was advised he was unavailable. He asked the same aide if General Beresford could be found. With apologies, the young man advised the general was not at that time present in the city.

After visiting a coffee house, (always an invaluable source of intelligence) he noted to his satisfaction, the obvious disquiet among locals regarding the British general's order to retreat with the army to Portugal.

On finishing his coffee, he decided to give it one more turn back at Moore's headquarters. It was now after 1p.m. and even generals must stop work for lunch.

Colonel Charmilly presented himself again to the same insolent young pup, who unfortunately had to report there was nothing further he could add to that given earlier that morning. The general was preparing important letters for dispatch that evening to London and could not be disturbed. The look of horror on Charmilly's face at the last could not fail to register with Captain Percy.

'Are you, well, my dear Colonel?' the young man asked, feigning concern.

Composing himself with all the strength of character he could muster, Charmilly summoned every ounce of his knowledge of the infernal English language, along with every reserve of remaining patience, in order to respond to this impudent rascal.

'It is absolutely essential that I speak with the general immediately. I have another dispatch of very great consequence from Mr Frere on my person that Sir John must be presented with urgently. I beg you to allow me to gain audience with him this instant!'

In order to rid himself of the damnable Gallic reptile for once and for all, Harry was willing to be accommodating. 'I'll see what I can do.'

With a smirk, he turned away, leaving the Frenchman in the hallway. After climbing the stairs, he saw Major Colbourne leaving Moore's room.

'I say, Johnno. That ghastly Frenchie, Charmilly's back. Says he's got another letter for the old man from Frere.'

Colbourne reacted with dismay. 'Christ! Moore will tear him apart! He presented a letter from the bugger last night and I've never seen the chief so pissed off! You mean to tell me the sod's holding back another?'

Percy shrugged. 'Devious swine, these Crapauds. Never trust 'em. No matter if they've got a grudge against Bony. A Frog's a Frog and always shall be. Like my old dad says.'

Colbourne thought for a moment. 'Hold fast to the bastard, Harry. I'll let Johnny know first. Need time to prepare for the roof to fall in!'

With that, Colbourne left Percy, returning to Moore's room. Curious to listen in, Harry pressed his ear against the closed door.

'What? You mean to tell me he's withheld another *fucking letter? Christ almighty! I'll skin the lying, double-dealing, mendacious bastard alive! Then I'll horsewhip him, by God! No, I'll have him bastinadoed, by Christ! Then fucking crucified upside down!'*

Grinning widely, Percy then heard what he deduced as placatory words from Colbourne. There followed a tremendous crash involving what sounded very much like a glass object hurled with great force against a hard surface.

'There goes mother's crystal.' He muttered quietly to himself, just as the door opened with Colbourne standing in the doorway looking highly flustered. Percy was only just able to move back a step in time.

'I say! Oh, hello, Harry. Do you mind escorting Colonel Charmilly up? The general would like to speak with him.' Percy returned downstairs to the hallway and motioned Charmilly over.

His face impassive, he announced, 'Colonel. Sir John will see you now. Come with me, please.'

The relief etched over the Frenchman's face, Charmilly thanked Captain Percy profusely, and followed him along the hall and up the stairway to the general's room. Leaving the Frenchman standing before his commander, Percy left promptly and after closing the door behind him, thought, *rather you than me, Colonel Frog-legs, old man.*

Moore was in no mood for formalities. He immediately came to the point.

'What does this mean, Colonel Charmilly? Another dispatch from Mr Frere? Can you explain why you did not give it to me last night?'

Holding the letter in his hand, Charmilly squirmed inwardly, but held firm. 'Sir John, my instructions from Mr Frere were that I was to allow some hours to pass before I handed you the second communication.'

Looking hard at the Frenchman, Moore snapped, 'Is that the letter?'

Before Charmilly could reply, Moore ripped it from his hand.

Turning to look at the letter front and back, Moore then ordered the colonel to remain by the room's blazing fire while he read the missive.

Now stood at his desk, he tore the seal open and read. It was only a short note of a few lines. But when he finished it, he had to read it again because he could barely believe that anyone could have the temerity to write such a letter. He fell down into his chair and concentrated solely on one thing and one thing only. Remaining calm.

Sir,

In the event that I did not wish to presuppose, of your continuing the determination already announced to me of retiring with the army under your command, I have to request that Colonel Charmilly, who is the bearer of this, and whose intelligence has been already referred to, may be previously examined before a Council of War.'

I have &etc,

J.H. Frere.

Moore then slowly rose from his chair and walked around the desk to stand before the colonel at the fireplace.

'Did you know the contents of this letter?' He asked in a surprisingly measured voice considering the circumstances.

'Yes, Sir John, I did!' Charmilly answered spiritedly.

Saying nothing, Moore walked over to the door. He opened it and ordered that Captain Percy and two of the sentries standing at the entrance to the building be sent up immediately. The general returned to his desk.

'I am within my rights, General!' Charmilly reminded Moore. 'You must allow me to address your senior officers according to the terms of Mr Frere's dispatch. They must be asked whether the decision to withdraw the army is acceptable to them. If it is not, they are to disobey your order and you are to be removed from your command!'

'Bollocks!' Moore roared back angrily, all passivity now long gone. 'What you want will be viewed as incitement to mutiny and then I shall be "within my rights" to damn well hang you, sir!'

Charmilly, now crimson with passion, screamed back. 'How dare you threaten me? I shall appeal to Mr Frere! To Mr Stuart! To the government, sir!'

Fortunately, Harry Percy now arrived with his military escort.

'Captain Percy.' Moore ordered, once Charmilly had ended his diatribe. 'This man is to be ejected from the city forthwith. If he is found anywhere near its environs, he is to be arrested, locked up and shackled hand and foot! It is your personal responsibility, Captain, to see to it that I never clap eyes on him again!

Shortly after Charmilly was bundled unceremoniously out of the commander-in-chief's presence, John Moore sent for Thomas Graham. Aware of the exertions his friend recently put his ageing body through, Moore apologised profusely and requested Tam make another reconnaissance mission to Madrid and report back on what he found there. Moore admitted that in his heart he did not believe the city could hold out long. He handed his friend a letter to be passed to two senior members of the Junta, the Prince of Castelfranco and Thomas de Morla.

Graham agreed it was a wise decision to send him and pooh-pooed any suggestion of exhaustion. After they shook hands, he left immediately to prepare for his journey. Moore hated sending old Tam off so soon again. But he needed the letter delivered by someone wholly reliable who would also be able gauge the Junta's appetite for resistance.

The following morning, Moore wrote a more detailed letter to Sir David Baird providing further rationale for his decision. In his letter to the Junta handed to Graham for delivery, he advised of his decision to await Hope's arrival with the cavalry, due any day now and his then leaving of the city in order make juncture with Baird. He confirmed he was in communication with Romaña, presently in Leon and that he endeavoured to unite with the Spaniard's forces in order to *'undertake such operations as are deemed best for the interests of Spain, and for the relief and assistance of Madrid.'*

Lastly, and more than a little grudgingly, he wrote a letter to Frere. He advised the diplomat of his intentions and of his hopes regarding the Marquis of Romaña and Madrid. He left his Majesty's representative in Spain little doubt of his opinion of the creature Charmilly and advised Frere never to use such types again in his dealings with Sir John Moore. He merely referred to the two Spanish generals of indeterminate age sent by the Junta as *'two weak old men, or rather, women.'*

After completing his dispatches, he left on his rounds of the city to view the progress the army was making in preparation for the march to Madrid.

Chapter Eleven

David Baird flipped over the clearly hurried first letter from John Moore and then looked over again at the longer one, written and sent the following morning. If the letters indicated anything, it was that his old friend was suffering from an extreme attack of anxiety and stress.

Davy sat in his room in the old chateau built by the Duke of Alba in Villafranca, fifty miles west from Astorga, on the road to Lugo and Coruña. He stopped there to work on plans to build entrenchments and defences while he waited for the Marquis of Romaña to build up enough forces to join up with him. It was never his considered plan to fall directly back on Coruña. He thought it militarily wasteful. Strategically, he believed it sounder to build up a stronghold in Galicia with Coruña at his back, rather than hightail it all the way to Portugal.

No Spanish general or grandee inspired him with much confidence. Romaña, whom he requested to fall back on Galicia in order to replenish his forces, he only trusted slightly more than the rest. He'd sent engineers out along the road to Coruña for the purpose of ascertaining which bridges could be destroyed, and to note suitable mountain passes that could be blocked in the event of a hasty withdrawal.

Ordering an army to retreat, then ordering a complete reverse, would tax the patience of a saint. The supply line of guns, wagons, horses, provisions, camp followers-on and God knows what other odds and ends picked up along the route, stretched from the harbour at Coruña, all the way to Astorga. Part of Baird's force had almost reached Vigo at St Jago, only a day's march from the port. He would now have to order an about turn that would take them a hundred miles back to his present base.

Baird began to write a letter to Moore, offering ideas from his own personal observations and thoughts on strands of tactics other than that of retreat. He was concerned about the army uniting at Astorga, as the French were sufficiently strong in the north to take the city of Leon. They could then push on into Galicia and effectively cut off the escape route to Corûna. Bonaparte's objective would then be to annihilate the British army in Spain in the open.

Davy suggested the way to avoid this possibility was for himself to remain at Astorga and Moore, by a flanking movement, joining him on his right along a strong position by the river *Esla*, which could potentially be held for some time. Should the enemy build up in sufficient strength to dangerously threaten the army, then with Spanish assistance, they could fall back on Galicia with the option of Corûna still available to them.

Shortly after starting the letter, the catastrophic news of the defeat of Castaños and Palafox reached Baird. Consequently, Moore wrote his original retreat orders to Davy. As for Baird's suggestions, he was forced to tear up the letter as events had clearly overtaken him.

Johnny's latest note still left Davy feeling uneasy as to Moore's strategic thinking. To meet up with Romaña and then what? Madrid may have fallen before then. Try and retake the city? He talked about the people of Madrid being *'enthusiastic and desperate and certainly are resisting the French.'* He admitted he could not foresee the result of their defiance on Spain as a whole but if the *'flame catches elsewhere, and becomes at all general, the best results may be expected.'* But he thought what happened in Madrid one way or the other may be decisive for the fate of Spain. The British army must be on hand to offer aid and take advantage of whatever happens.

This is vague, Johnny, all so *vague*. Then as if to assuage his old friend's concerns, Moore wrote,

'I mean to proceed bridle in hand; for if the bubble bursts, and Madrid falls, we shall have to run for it… Although we may look big, and determine to get everything forward, yet we may never lose sight of this, that at any moment affairs may take that turn, that will render it necessary to retreat.'

He made the suggestion to Baird of continuing to send stores of provisions and ammunition along the road from Villafranca as a reserve. He then went on to request Baird send him two cavalry regiments and advised him to forward his remaining division on to Benavente.

Davy lay down the letter and then picked up the one he had just completed to Moore. He wrote that he was acting as instructed under Sir John's last dispatch regarding his latest orders. He now offered suggestions regarding the situation in Galicia. He reiterated his earlier suggestion in the torn up letter that Moore march to Astorga and with a strong defensive position behind it, the rear could be covered *'until it is seen what efforts the Spanish nation is disposed and determined to make in the defence of national independence.'* He remarked that the road between Astorga and Corūna, though mountainous, was a good one, the country abounded with cattle and that bread and other supplies could be ordered from England by way of transports ships. Galicia would have time to arm itself and would become a rallying point for all of Spain.

He was not trying to cover himself from every angle. He was concerned about his friend's state of mind and reasons for his decisions. The fact he had countermanded his original retreat order did not concern Baird too readily. With the pressure bearing down on him from Frere and the Spanish, it was only to be expected he would be unable to resist them indefinitely. But Davy was certain Moore was not being pressured by London directly. Johnny never hinted at that in any letter he'd written. And Baird had intelligence sources of his own. Rather, he was concerned that Moore may be attempting some quixotic gesture before the people of Spain that had not been properly thought through. Or as more likely, he was just going to march his army towards Madrid and await events. It wasn't the John Moore he knew. But then again, he'd never known Moore as a commander of an army, only as a friend.

But those few words about proceeding with bridle in hand did bring some measure of comfort to Baird. Johnny wasn't making a head long rush into anything. He was already laying down a possible escape route. But David Baird's nagging worry was that it could be an escape route that could turn into a death trap if fortune turned in Bonaparte's favour.

And then there was another factor. The Galician winter.

Tam Graham fell gratefully into the chair offered and then leaning his tired, aching body over, rubbed his stiff and frozen hands before John Moore's fireplace.

'Too auld, Johnny. Too damn slow an' a'. They nearly got me outside

Talavera. I had to make a smart turnabout after givin' one o' the buggers a bloody slash across the face his mother would be ashamed o'.'

Graham came perilously close to capture by a French patrol and was unable to reach Madrid. Stopping at Talavera, he met two deputies of that city who informed him of the shocking news that Madrid had capitulated to the enemy on the 3rd of December. Sir John Moore's letter to Castelfranco and de Morla was ultimately an epistle to traitors. The two men conspired with the French to allow them possession of the Prado and Retiro districts of the capitol while refusing to allow General San Juan to enter the city. Horrifyingly, the citizens in their rage turned on the brave and unfortunate San Juan, murdering him out of spite.

'Suffering Christ!' John Moore swore indignantly. 'Those two bastards only wrote me on the 2nd and then opened the gates to the French the following day! Is there anyone in this accursed country to be trusted?'

'That's put paid to your hope to use Madrid as a focal point.' Paul Anderson, the only other presence in the room, pointed out.

John Moore rubbed his chin. 'It has that.'

Francois entered with a tray of food and drink for Graham. He was extremely fond of the old man, and like Moore, worried about him when he was away on his missions.

'Ye're a fine, upstandin' laddie, Francois. Thanks, son.' Graham accepted the tray gratefully and sat with it on his lap. Soon the only sounds in the room were from the fire and the noise of Graham eating and drinking.

Moore was standing over his desk peering intently at a map of Spain. He must assume that Bonaparte himself would by now be in Madrid but the main part of his army was still making its way there. That meant the supply line from France was stretched and potentially vulnerable to attack.

Graham's last report mentioned encouraging news from the south of Spain where disparate forces were making life difficult for the French. True figures on the enemy strength were scarce. The general belief was that they were relatively fewer than available Spanish numbers.

Whatever the amount of troops involved, their hosts were making a better fist of it there. But now that Bonaparte had taken the capital, only the south remained to be pacified and that surely would be the Emperor's next intention. Oh God, to meet that man in the field! Please give me that one chance!

Moore received a report that the French had recently left the town of Valladolid. This bolstered Moore's own belief that Napoleon was convinced the British army was retreating to Portugal. After all, it was the only logical military solution to his enemy's predicament.

'I'll offer you something to think over, Tam.' Moore thought out loud.

'Aye, more chicken would be nice.' Graham muttered from underneath his glass. 'And the wines no' bad either.'

'A diversion by this army.' Moore explained carefully. 'A march in strength, east to Valladolid and then a push across Castile. That by any definition, would be seen as a threat to Bony's tail. He would have to react. Turn back from Madrid, cross the mountains at the Sierra de Guadarrama and look to catch up with and have his way with us. Only, we're not going to let him catch us. We run like the devil for the sea. Bonaparte's stuck in the north while the southern patriots gather their forces. We send a message to have the transports ready at Vigo or Coruña, and Bony's caught with his army there through the Galician winter.'

'Is that what ye've planned or is it just your belly rumblin'?' Graham, now finished his meal, asked after a round of belching. Anderson smiled knowingly. He too was used to the old man's way of plain speaking.

'It'll work if we have luck and beat the snows in the mountains. My worry is not the French, Tam. It's the weather.' Moore admitted openly.

'Aye, the winters here are gey cauld, that's for sure.' Graham agreed. 'You've a helluva lot o' women and bairns wi' ye, Johnny. Your boys were too damn soft on that score.'

Moore was deeply worried about the army's camp followers and was not grateful for his friend's reminder. He cursed himself for not taking a firmer line with those company commanders incapable of carrying out his original instructions concerning families. But that was in the past. They would have to keep up or be left behind.

While slowing the army down?

If the weather holds, we'll make it in good time.

There aren't enough wagons.

We'll have to travel as light as possible.

With women and children?

'Damn it all!' Moore exploded out loud.

'Nae use greetin' now it's done.' Tam Graham clucked sympathetically. 'They'll have to manage. You just worry about gettin' us there, that's your job.'

Moore now believed he'd unburdened himself enough to his friends. He was relieved somewhat on hearing the news of Madrid as he had never truly expected the city to hold out. His ideas were always fuzzy and poorly formed on that account, relying too much on Spanish "what-ifs" and he thought Davy Baird may have felt the same way on reading of them. Now he had a definite plan. Hope's artillery had arrived in the city at last. It was a march east, timing his moment to perfection. Then such a dash across a country as never seen before. He now had his guns. He had Davy Baird who led a remarkable march across the Egyptian desert and barely lost a man. He had the finest cavalryman in Europe, Henry Paget. He had the greatest light infantry on earth, *his light infantry* led by the firebrand, Robert Craufurd. He couldn't ask for a better set of commanders.

'No more prevaricating, Tam,' Moore concluded and there may well have been just a hint of desperation in the tone.

Thomas Graham nodded. He understood that for his friend, the moment of decision had now arrived.

'No more awaiting events.' Moore continued. 'We're going to create the news. We're going to shake up this land and kick Bonaparte's arse so painfully, he'll never recover from it. We'll lay the groundwork for the army in Portugal to sweep in from the south and chase the French out of this country entirely. It'll be close, damn close! But with the Lord's grace, and good fortune, we'll make it.'

Tam Graham rose from his chair and offered his hand. 'May God go with us, Johnny. Ye're takin' an almighty gamble with a lot o' soldier's lives. Women and wee bairns, too. But wi' His blessin' and good fortune, we'll see it through.'

Moore took the proffered hand and kept it in his grip. 'What Wellesley began at Vimeiro, I'll continue. Or by Christ, I'll die trying.'

Retreat

'Moore is the only General now worthy to contend with me. I shall now move against him in person… If only these 20,000 were 100,000; if only more English mothers could feel the horrors of war!'
Napoleon Bonaparte, Madrid, December 19th, 1808

Chapter Twelve

The December weather was dull and drizzly, but winds were fair and there were no squalls or gales on the horizon to upset the Irish Sea. They would make good time of it, the ships master promised confidently. Just as well. The man lying on the cot in his tiny accommodation cabin was burning with enough rage to broil a hundred oceans.

Not that anyone of the small packet's crew, plying regularly from Holyhead to Dublin and other Irish ports carrying passengers and a few trade goods, would have noticed anything other than an unyielding patrician disdain for the goings on of a mere merchantman. This particular passenger could have accepted a more appropriate vessel. A Royal Navy frigate was offered. But that would have resulted in a lot of damn fuss and nonsense. And worse, delay. Sir Arthur Wellesley had absolutely no interest in ships and those who sailed in them. The vessel was a mere contraption, a machine, whose sole purpose was to transport him from one lousy seaport to another in order that he may travel on to his final destination. He gave it and the human beings aboard her as much consideration as we would the sole of his boot.

And yet the source of his anger may have confused anyone bold enough to examine the reasons for his well concealed ire. After all, Wellesley was recently exonerated in glowing terms by the enquiry into the Convention of Cintra scandal. The Board, only recently concluded at the Hall of the Royal Hospital in Chelsea, deemed Sir Arthur's conduct honourable and his actions while commanding his Majesty's forces a great success. Parliament voted him thanks for the victory at Vimeiro. The Board voted by a small majority in favour of the Convention. Any and all blame for the subsequent disquietude in the country over the scandalously favourable terms towards the enemy reached at the agreement, fell subtly on the shoulders of the main protagonists, Dalrymple and Burrard. Sir Arthur Wellesley was in the clear.

Wellesley's resentment was in the main focussed on the fact he was now returning to a paper shuffling role as Chief Secretary of Ireland. It paid well but he found the work no longer rewarding and now utterly stifling. Dealing with civil servants and their petty, pedantic and parsimonious ways drove him at times to distraction. There was always a reason for *not* doing something. The internecine politics, empire building and lack of ambition to achieve anything in Ireland other than to maintain the status quo at first angered, then depressed and now merely bored him. He'd shown a surprising sympathy for the native Irish and their plight. He genuinely believed in trying to better their lot. But his hopes were shattered by the sheer futility of trying to buck an obstinate and inflexible system.

The army was the place where he'd proven he could bend the will of a system. On *campaign*, at least. He had no influence in London where the real levers of power were held and believed now that he never would. Which was why he was so incensed over the opportunity lost in Portugal. He chased the French army handsomely in his first battle and if not for the untimely intervention of a doddering Scotch meddler, he would have kicked Bonaparte's legions out of that country at the end of a bayonet. Certainly not as guests of King George's navy with their treasure, their strumpets and their hides intact.

Now he would be back at a desk while the real action was happening in Iberia and only God knew when or if the king's ministers would send for him again. He won support from the Tories in Parliament, but he still had enemies who saw him merely as the *sepoy* general, one who owed his attainment to his now discredited brother's influence. A lowly member of the Irish aristocracy. A nonentity.

And he was returning to *her*.

His wife, Kitty. She was his first love. Indeed, the only one and the true inspiration of his life. For when the young Arthur had asked her family for her hand years before, he was rebuffed by the Packenham family in an unforgivable manner as unsuitable due to his lowly position as a penniless junior officer of no influence, albeit a gentleman of some breeding. The ridicule and scorn he suffered and worst of all, the desolation of his beloved Kitty, tore at him. The formerly feckless young man strove to prove himself worthy of her love by ruthlessly stamping out all feelings other than those of relentless ambition, in order to achieve personal glory to win her family over.

Of that, as history would prove, he succeeded. He returned from India, a general, *Sir* Arthur Wellesley, lionised for his victories over the barbaric Tippoo Sultan. In a moment of unthinking exuberance, he wrote to Kitty's family asking again for her to become his wife, the offer this time being accepted.

It was all he desired. He wanted her now more than ever. She was his real prize. Not the honours, the fawning attentions of society trollops or even to wipe away the stain of dishonour thrown at him earlier by the Packenhams. All that genuinely meant little to him now. He only wanted the lovely girl of his youth.

It was an unmitigated disaster. The pretty, vivacious teenager, was now a dumpy, dishevelled and unlovely woman who was dull, unlettered and worst of all, useless in society. Arthur's shock on first seeing her again was tempered by the realisation that there was no going back. He'd pledged his troth and was duty bound to carry it through. How a man of such measure, so meticulous and careful in his behaviour, could strive to make such a serious error of judgment was beyond comprehension.

Worst of all, she adored, venerated and worshipped him. Their wedding night admittedly, proved spectacular. This divine being, this incredibly handsome man of the moment was all *hers*! She retained few of the friends of her youth and spent her years in needlework at home or tending to her little dogs while suffering the cutting remarks of family members. And now this! But her splendid husband palled quickly, embarrassed by her ignorance of important matters, her inability to improve her dress, her weight, the simpleton remarks in company. He did not detest her, he could not feel that for her, ever. He was incapable of that. Rather he loathed himself for his folly, his momentary lapse, his sentimentality. All highly unsoldierly attributes.

Not even being provided with two sons could temper his feelings towards her. After the second boy was born, he stopped sleeping with her completely and sought distraction elsewhere.

He rarely considered his children. The sooner they were off to school the better. He bore them little feeling, viewing them as the product of his stupidity, little versions of *her* in male form. His disdain for innocent children was a constant reminder of the emotional instability he knew he suffered from himself, but put aside as a vile weakness to be expunged from his soul. When he did think of his sons on occasion, he did feel some small measure of warmth and affection for them. But the battle within him was one that he would prefer not to fight. It was simpler to ignore them.

Wellesley turned on his cot. The damnable tub rolled like a Bengali whore. Another few hours and landfall was expected. Though part of him did not want the voyage to end. It was easy just to lie there. To leave everything to someone else.

He then thought of Moore. Wellesley had little respect for few, if any officer in the army. Old Abercromby was a kindly old stick. And damned effective. But he could not imagine with his dying breath, uttering concerns about his soldier's welfare. Damning the drunken swabs to hell, more likely.

But Moore was very much alive and Wellesley had to admit to himself that he was the one man in the army he did respect, even fear. His talents were many, even with the ridiculous sentimentality he shared with his fellow Scot Abercromby over his men. Light skirmishers were all very well. Necessary? Wellesley accepted grudgingly that they had their uses. But training them at Shorncliffe and asking them to learn to think for themselves? Preposterous! Rewarding them with badges and other trash while banning the use of the cat? Almost *Jacobin* in its systematic destruction of everything Wellesley believed in. Dangerous ideas in a dangerous age that should be stamped out. As far as he was concerned, those villains in redcoats existed only to stand as they were ordered to stand and to do as ordered to do unquestionably, whether it meant being rained on by shot and grape at his express orders, or being flogged or hanged at his immediate will. Moore and his mollycoddling! It was positively *unenglish,* by God!

Of course, they must be cared for. But only as dumb animals are. They needed to be fed, clothed and quartered decently in order to get the best out of them. Husband them too. A dead soldier was no use to him. They had to be kept alive so as to continue to fight on to the next battle. But that was the extent of his feelings towards his soldiers. Vicious brutes, the lot of 'em. The officers were worse. The scum of the earth. A bunch of degenerate, scrimshanking scoundrels in the main. But they couldn't be flogged. Instead he spent much of his time sorting out their ridiculous squabbles and jealousies. Very few of them could he tolerate.

Was Moore a gentleman? His father was *surgeon,* by Christ! Did that explain his revolutionary thinking? A lower class fellow with pretentions of modernity. And yet he liked Moore on meeting him. It was rare for Arthur Wellesley to like anyone on first acquaintance. Or on second either.

Damn this ship. And damn Sir John Moore, too. Wellesley dropped off to sleep and suffered a recurring, blood soaked, battle scarred dream. Another man struggling in the middle of a turbulent sea.

Chapter Thirteen

Andrew Berry was sorry to leave Salamanca.

As part of the brigade under the command of Sir William Bentinck, now returned somewhat hastily from Madrid where he carried out diplomatic as well as his ordinary military duties, the 42nd marched in the right hand column that left the city on the 12th December, in the direction of Alaejos and Tordesillas.

The 4th and 50th regiments marched alongside as the column was protected by a cavalry screen under the command of Charles Stewart. The left hand column of the army under General Moore himself marched in the direction of Toro. Sir David Baird's cavalry under the command of Lord Henry Paget, awaited them there.

The affairs of lofty and high born men were beyond the ken of Andrew and his friends. When he asked Sergeant McGillivray why the general changed his mind about retreating, the sergeant merely responded that the changing of one's mind was the prerogative of generals and that private soldiers like Andrew should mind their own business first and foremost. He also warned Andrew that the prospect of a long march with a battle at the end of it was very much a probability. He was to pay particular care to his feet, his footwear and to his musket at all times.

Andrew was not pleased to hear this, nor was Joshua. Archie pumped his fist in elation at the mention of a likely battle. He began to spend in his mind the plunder waiting to be won.

The boys marched through an increasingly bleak, cold and frosty landscape, often never seeing as much as a bird or any other living creature. Even the trees seemed alien, undersized, dried up, lifeless. Broken up gorse and dry, dusty patches of light brown, sunburnt and exhausted earth abounded. It was a foreign landscape to Andrew and Archie, coming from the rich, green and hilly pastures of Lothian and Fife, where fat cattle and even fatter sheep thrived healthily alongside lively villages and towns of brick and stone built dwellings. There were few signs of human habitation anywhere, other than the odd dirt–poor hovel built with mud walls emitting dirty grey smoke. They passed many left abandoned. For the first time, Andrew understood why it was said that Spain was one of the most backward and poorest nations of Europe.

Which made such a marked contrast to the city of Salamanca. Andrew loved his time there, leaving it with deep regret. As they marched out of the city, the streets were aligned with well-wishers cheering them off. A girl leapt from the crowd to hug and kiss him. It was Gabriela. He looked into her pretty, tear filled eyes and longed to stay with her. She handed a small item to him and clasped his hands in hers before parting to return to the crowd, now somewhat distraught. He marched on, a feeling of such loss as he had never known in his young life previously. On opening his hand, he saw her present was a small silver cross on a leather chain. It was an evil, papish, idolatrous symbol, unworthy of a good Scots Protestant to own. But he held on to it and placed it in his sporran. A few men around him grinned but none made comment. The older men reflected wistfully, pitying both youngsters.

Andrew thought of Sergeant McGillivray's warnings about imminent battle. The sergeant was on his mind a lot recently.

After Andrew and his friends returned to the convent after their visit to the brothel, Andrew entered the washroom with a basin of water to clean his wounds. Joshua owned a small mirror, won in a card game. Andrew was discovering as he grew to know his new friends better, that not only Archie had hidden depths. Joshua was a fair hand at the cards. He'd learned the hard way, supplementing his meagre income during his former employment in Edinburgh. He was not in the slightest way boastful of his ability, rather there was an air of regret in his admitting to the skill as if it was something to be ashamed of.

To Andrew, of course, cards *were* shameful, like drink and visiting women of ill-repute. He was slowly accepting that though he had taken the lead in the triumvirate, both Joshua and Archie deferring to him without demur, he was still very much the virgin in so many ways compared to both.

Nevertheless, the mirror, though won in dubious circumstances, was a useful item and each of the boys in turn used it in order to shave. On this night, Andrew was disturbed to note that he had the makings of a blackened left eye, the upper lip had grown in size exponentially, and various cuts and abrasions scarred each side of his face down to his neck.

'You look like a Hottentot!'

Turning around, Andrew was horrified to discover the sergeant peering back at him with a look of utter disdain.

'Oh, Sergeant, I can explain...' He began painfully.

'Explain? Explain? You'll try to explain to your mother and father how in visiting a house of prostitution, you were beaten black and blue? How will you explain that?'

'I was protecting a young lady, Sergeant. I did what any man of decency would have done.' Andrew answer was supplemented by a mild tone of moral righteousness. He was beginning to tire of this. What on earth was it to McGillivray anyway? It was none of his damned concern! He hadn't went there to buy a girl. He was annoyed that the sergeant still didn't believe him.

'Ach, pish! A sassenach belted a wee *hoor* and you felt it necessary to defend her honour. Oh, Mr Berry, you're some boy, so you are!'

'How did you know that?' Andrew asked with some mystification. The sergeant invariably seemed to know everything about him.

'Your wee pal, Joshua Whitfield told me. And if it wasn't for that huddy Miller, you could have ended up receiving a hammering! For what, Andrew? For *what*, lad?' His tone was of bewilderment. McGillivray was clearly perplexed by the young man. Miller was Archie's surname.

Now somewhat mollified and even a little pleased, Andrew dried his face with a small handkerchief Gabriela had given him.

'Oh, that's pretty! Did one of your strumps give you that too?' McGillivray added caustically.

'She's not a strump!' Andrew replied furiously. 'She's a respectable young lady. One that I would be proud to introduce to my parents. I ask you not to impugn her honour again or for shame, you will answer to me!'

The 42nd was a highland regiment and McGillivray had overstepped a delicate line. He recognised it, and offered immediate redress with something of a flourish.

'I wholeheartedly apologise for any suggestion of mine that Donna

Gabriela Vasquez is anything other than a young lady of excellent repute, from a good family.'

'How did you know her name?' Andrews asked, now shocked not only that he had threatened the sergeant, but had so readily escaped unscathed.

'Never mind that.' McGillivray then reached into his sporran and produced a small jar.

'Spread this balm on the cuts on your face and neck. They may well fester and scar, thus reducing your chances of taking Gabriela's hand in matrimony. Should she, of course, ever forgive you for visiting houses of mucky women.' He passed the jar to Andrew.

'Ask Joshua to rub it on. The lad has light fingers with cards and with other things too, I'll warrant. You are more likely to poke your own eye out. Though you're one-eyed enough as it is. You'd put John Knox himself to shame with your sanctimony. Goodnight to you, Mr Berry.'

The division led by Sir John Moore left the city on December 13th in the direction of Alaejos, and arrived in Toro two days later. A large crowd gathered to welcome the British. Burning torches were mounted on balconies all around the town's main square to honour their presence. Though there were available barracks, many private houses opened up to their British guests. The men were well fed on pork, and a few officers took the opportunity to make sketches and paint watercolours of the town's castle and the river *Duero*.

The following morning John Moore received two dispatches that were to result in another alteration to his strategy. Captain Dashwood, one of Charles Stewart's scouts, had rode in disguise into the village of Rueda, halfway between Alaejos and Tordesillas. To his shock, he discovered around eighty Frenchmen comprised of cavalry and infantry. Racing back to Stewart, the general, unable to believe his luck, organised an immediate assault on the village. That evening after surrounding it, he charged in, killing twenty of the enemy and taking over thirty prisoners.

As John Moore read this in the dispatch, he cursed Stewart once again for an arrogant upstart. There was no need to risk lives and worse, to alert the French that a large British force was present. The prize was not worth it.

But as Moore read on, the letter mentioned after the prisoners were interrogated, it was apparent that the French still believed the British were retreating in the other direction to Portugal. They had no inkling of Moore's change of plan.

This was heartening news, Stewart redeeming himself somewhat. Though Moore could just about hear the boasting that young man would be making of his triumph in his next letter to his half-brother.

So far, his plan was working. The French thought he was heading south west to safety when in fact he was heading directly for them. But even better news was to come. A second letter arrived that afternoon from Stewart and its contents were pure gold.

He had just given the order for the army to leave Toro when the courier brought the despatch to him. A note attached explained that a Captain Waters had bought the information from the villagers of Valdestillos near Segovia, just north of Madrid, for the sum of twenty dollars. A French officer rode into the village and was subsequently murdered by the inhabitants due to his *"haughty and arrogant manner."* He was carrying a sabretache which contained a despatch from Marshal Berthier in Madrid for the attention of Marshal Soult, presently based at the town of Saldaña on the river *Carrion*.

The captured despatch contained the latest analysis of French dispositions in Spain. But the most significant feature of the letter from Moore's point of view was mention of Soult's position. The marshal led two infantry divisions and four cavalry regiments, a force of some eighteen thousand men. With this force, the marshal was ordered by the Emperor to advance on Leon, Zamora and Benavante. He would remain unopposed as the British were now reported to have left Salamanca on their retreat to Portugal. The remainder of the French forces were split between Bonaparte in Madrid, Lefebvre's at Badajos, Mortier's in Aragon and Junot's in the direction of Burgos.

At this moment, Soult's force was barely 130 miles north of him, with no support and in total ignorance of the true British position. It was a gift from God! Only Junot could possibly reach him but as he had not yet crossed the *Ebro*, it meant Moore had enough time to intercept Soult and bring him to battle. Once juncture was made with Baird, he would have a superiority in numbers over Soult of nearly ten thousand men.

Then he returned to Stewart's first letter and cursed aloud. News of that attack must reach Madrid imminently. A few of the French had escaped and would soon be telling their Emperor of the British cavalry they had just fought who were not where the French believed them to be. Moore had no doubt that Bonaparte would realise he'd duped and would quickly plan a reckoning.

The captured despatch made it clear that there were now upwards of three hundred thousand French troops in Spain. Moore's force was but a fly-speck in comparison. Even the twenty thousand that Romaña was boasting off, together with the British force combined was still less than fifty thousand men. It was now evident Moore had acted correctly in his earlier judgment that retreat was the safest option available. But the fortune of war had brought a real opportunity to give the French a bloody nose while escaping afterward to fight another day. It would also set down a marker to Bonaparte that in the British, he faced a formidable enemy.

He now had to act. He had an army to unite and an enemy to fight it with.

Lord Henry Paget cursed as foully and as frequently as any of his troopers. He cursed them, too. But the more he swore at them, the louder they cheered him back. They knew he wasn't a flogger like his brother, Edward. The twisted face of fury he affected, was just that, a mere artifice for public show. Many were the times when he'd sworn and damned them for an ungodly shower of vagabonds and then turned away, his hand over his mouth, almost helpless with silent mirth. For Henry Paget loved his hounds dearly and thought it the most amusing thing on earth to cuss, moan and yell at them. Especially if it meant helping to keep them alive.

He was commander of the British cavalry, much admired by his officers and men. But he was unable to command one of his subordinates. Lieutenant-general John Slade was everything Paget despised about the army. A loud, vainglorious, inept, old fool, gifted command of the 10th Hussars, barely able to ride a horse and unable to follow a simple order without bungling it.

And now Paget was forced to trust the man in order that his plan be realised to duff up a large French column of cavalry outside the town of Sahagun.

His problems with Slade came to a head while the brigade was attempting to cross the *Esla* at the bridge at Castrogonzalo. In open country and with concern that the French may be close, Henry Paget cursed as only he could as he waited for Slade to arrive at the pre-arranged meeting point.

Finally, Slade arrived with his contingent, the 7th and 10th very late that evening.

'And where the devil have you been, sir?' Paget, uncaring that his officers heard the anger in his voice, confronted Slade, at last presenting himself.

'We were misdirected, sir! Damn fool of a local lost his way. Can anyone be trusted in this country? Oh, it is too much, Paget, too much!'

'Damn your excuses, sir! You have outriders, you have scouts have you not? You should not rely on any one man. Can I not trust a senior officer with a task any of my troopers could perform?'

Despite his generally recognised incompetence, Jack Slade was beloved of his men for his kindness and good-nature. His only desire now was to redeem himself.

'Please, Lord Henry. Accept my most abject apologies.' He begged gracefully. 'I will never employ the man again. As for now, what are your orders that I may have my men ready?'

Fortunately for Slade, Paget was too professional a soldier to waste any more time with the dolt. 'Though we marched today in open column when the ground permitted and made steady progress, we will now have to ride with our gun's portfires lit.' He announced sombrely. Paget was now deeply concerned about riding head-on into a French patrol. 'I cannot accept anything other than the possibility that we may be called to arms instantly.'

A look of alarm came over Slade. 'I confess I find that a most disagreeable manner of proceeding, Paget! Though I accept the necessity in order to cover any possible enemy movement, should they be close to us.'

Paget bit back a sarcastic retort. 'Then be off with you, General Slade. You have your orders.'

Relieved to be dismissed, Slade turned to leave and rode to rejoin his men. But just then Paget called one of his aide's to him.

'Hodge, for God's sake ride after that damned stupid fellow. Make sure when he announces my orders to his troop commanders, he does it correctly and commits no more blunders.' Slade undoubtedly heard Paget and so did every officer within earshot. But he said and did nothing in response, pressing ahead in the direction of his squadrons.

Thinking back on the incident, Paget accepted he should have held his tongue. But this was war and there was no time to humour buffoons, no matter their rank. Too many lives at stake for niceties. In the days after the incident, they received word at Medina de Rio Seco that a French force numbering six hundred men had only left the village less than an hour before the British arrived. Slade took off in pursuit but unfortunately, according to a staff officer, he chose the longer route, thus the French escaped him. Henry Paget nearly swallowed his cigar in disgust when informed by Captain Gordon.

For Paget it was the last straw. He couldn't sack the idiot but he did take away from him the 7th Hussars and gave command of them to Charles Stewart. Slade was now left with only the 10th and 15th regiments.

Learning that the French brigade, now known to be under the command of General Debelle, was sighted near Mayorga, Paget and Slade took off in pursuit but the weather closed in and a snowstorm halted the chase. They found a convent at Melgar de Arriba where Paget was happy to drop off Slade, who was pleading exhaustion. Paget moved off again and halted a little further on at Melgar de Abajo where he settled in for the night.

But an idea was forming in the cavalry commander's mind. It was now known that the French force had arrived in nearby Sahagun. Paget summoned all officers of the 15th Hussars.

'Gentlemen. I have called you here to propose that tomorrow evening, by force march we come upon the French as they lay asleep after humping each other in Sahagun, and cut them into pieces.'

There was an outburst of cheers and hurrahs. They were wearied of Charles Stewart endlessly recounting his earlier success at Rueda. They wanted a victory of their own.

'My plan is this.' Paget continued after the cheering settled. 'General Slade with the 10th and two guns are to ride west and follow the river *Cea* along its right bank. They will then proceed to attack the French in the town from that direction and drive them onto us as we await at the opposite end. The French fox will be met by the English Hussar and the day shall be ours!' There were loud roars all round once more.

The following day, the regiments rested and prepared their horses and equipment. There was now an air of excitement and anticipation. They'd spent days frozen in the saddle in pursuit and now the opportunity had arrived at last for real action. Scouts confirmed the French were still in Sahagun and making no plans to leave that anyone could observe. They were clearly oblivious to how close the enemy were. A complacent idiot, was how Paget contemptuously regarded Debelle, his immediate opponent.

Troop officers gathered for their orders at ten p.m. that evening. At one a.m. the regiments assembled in order to strike out for Sahagun. The 10th were late.

General Slade was addressing his regiment. He sat before them on his horse and gave them the speech of his life. He promised the enemy only 'blood and slaughter' and then, after about half an hour past the starting time of his original orders, he set off along the *Cea*.

The going was painfully slow. One man fell off his animal and broke his leg. Horses stumbled continuously and streams could only be crossed where the ice was thick enough. Freezing wind blew in their ears. The land was entirely snow covered. There were occasional lightning bursts to illuminate their path in the gloom. The bitter cold pierced through each man so deep, they could barely hold onto their reins. As they were so close now to the enemy, many of the men carried swords which froze to their fingers. Then another snowstorm blew up, blinding the men and horses to all but a few feet before them. But they rode on doggedly, relentlessly, for the enemy were at hand and would be made to pay for their ordeal.

Paget and the 15th suffered equally. Arriving at a forward post before the town, they charged French piquets and killed a pair. First blood. But enough ran off into the night back to Sahagun to give warning.

'My lord, we have killed two and taken six prisoners. A fair start to the night!' Captain Gordon reported triumphantly.

'That damn fool Slade worries me more than the odd French piquet.' Paget replied morosely. 'Do you suppose he will make the start line on time?'

'The best laid plans and all that.' The Scottish officer muttered philosophically.

'Yes, indeed. I suggest we send out skirmishers.' Paget ordered. 'We cannot depend on Jack Slade, but we may depend on news of our little brush here getting back to Debelle in good time. No one runs faster than a Frenchman who's just been *skelped* as you Scotch savages say!' Gordon grinned malevolently.

The order to mount was given and the 15th moved off back into the night.

In the lead column, Paget could now make out before him in the near distance the walls of Sahagun. But he was unaware the alerted Debelle had assembled his entire brigade outside the town's east gate. It was now six a.m. Still dark, but day slowly beginning to break.

If he could see it, Paget would have been pleased to note the French regiments leave their assembly line at the gate and move off east in the direction of the bridge over the *Valderaduey*. General Debelle hoped to catch the enemy in the open, as they then stopped by a dried river facing across land filled by vineyards. Paget could discern in the distance movement to the east, but was it Slade or was it the French?

The enemy thought similarly. From out the dark came skirmishers *'Qui Vive? Qui Vive? Who goes there?'* No one in the British line dared reply.

Debelle had not wanted to stop where he did but his force was being slowed down by the conditions. He was now certain the enemy were before him but believed them to be Spaniards. He prepared his regiments for action. Carbine and musket shots then rang out, following the cries of the skirmishers.

'Damme, it's them alright! The French!' Captain Thornhill, part of Paget's escort, exclaimed excitedly.

'By God, it is!' Paget replied, equally thrilled. 'Screw that old bounder, Slade! I'll not wait a damn second longer.'

'But sir, General Slade must wait until 6.30 as per your order!' a young aide cried out.

'Blast it, boy! That was if the Frogs hadn't known we were coming! No, lad, this is it.'

Then as the light improved, Paget saw before him about eighty yards away, the French begin to move in column.

'15th Hussars, left face! Form open column of divisions!' Paget quickly ordered aloud.

The 15th wheeled to the left to confront the enemy. Sabres were unsheathed and shouldered. The men now began a strange, unnatural humming, turning the hairs on Paget's neck. He saw the cold breath in the icy air from hundreds of men and horses form a single long, white, vaporous cloud that seemed to float around each living being in an unearthly mist before the column. He heard the dread-filled hooves of the entire line of animals scratch impatiently in the snow-covered earth. He felt the elastic in the human catapult being pulled tight beyond all endurance. Elation overcame him as he looked either side, his eyes wide as those of his horse.

Bugles sounded, and then Paget screamed in exultation the name of a triumph of the regiment in an earlier war: *'Emsdorff, 15th! Emsdorff and victory!'*

Paget's excited animal, alongside Thornhill and the seven man escort, soon raced to a gallop as hundreds of horsemen leaped forward as one. Paget heard the hideous high pitched tone of his men screaming their death charges aloud and joined in. This was the moment he was born for. He felt the ecstasy of freezing cold air in his face only for a few seconds before he and his force smashed into the static line of French cavalry, six deep.

There was some desultory carbine fire from the French line, but now the *chasseurs* in the front rank were driven crashing back against the second line of dragoons behind them. Paget could see men flying off horses while animals were knocked over like skittles, the shocked beast's legs kicking in ridiculous and horrific contortions. The noise was hideous.

Men's voices yelling in pain and horses screaming in terror. The jangle of belts and stirrups, of swords striking together. The odd pistol shot. Shouts for friends, screams for mercy. Paget was aware of a trooper being set upon by two French dragoons. The man swung his sabre desperately as each of the horsemen fought to get either side of him.

Paget tugged the reins and nudged his horse forward. The battle between the three men seemed almost personal, as a large space opened up in the crush to accommodate them. A Frenchman scored a hit on the trooper's right leg. The slash caused the man to scream and swing wildly. Paget tried to remember his name to rally to him. Corcoran! Yes! A steady Irishman with a family with the army. A good man with a clean back.

'Hold fast, Corcoran! I'm coming!'

The animal leapt forward as Paget brutally dug his spurs into the horses flanks. He was now on top of the man who cut Corcoran's leg. Paget raised his weapon and with the flat of the blade, dashed it off the steel helmet of the dragoon. The man, shocked, his sword in his right swung blindly but Paget parried. The swords clashed repeatedly, before Paget thought to reach into his belt for his pistol. He released the reins, pulling out the firearm and cocked it hurriedly, aimed, but it misfired. Paget then threw it at the Frenchman who ducked, but the Englishman sabre in hand again, was then able to score a serious wound with a hack to the man's shoulder. The Frenchman frantically reined away to his right and nudged his horse forward in order to escape. Meanwhile, with the assistance of another trooper, Corcoran saw off his other assailant.

'God bless you, your honour!' The Irishman thanked his commander, breathlessly.

'That's tomorrows grog ration you owe me, Corky!' Paget laughed gleefully.

'You're honour knows that I do not drink! Which is not like your worship to forget a tee-totalling man such as myself, there being so few in this regiment!' Corcoran replied, with just enough respect to deflect from his genuine sense of mystification and some little hurt, that his lordship should not properly remember every trooper among five hundred.

'Sorry! Slipped my mind, old man.' Paget apologised. 'Now, shall we return to the fight, my fine fellow?'

Chapter Fourteen

For the first time in weeks, Sir John Moore was in a contented mood.

Chewing over a piece of excellent pork in his quarters in a Benedictine monastery in newly captured Sahagun, he thought back on events of the last few days with great satisfaction as his plan began to coalesce.

There was his meeting at last with Davy Baird on the 18th December at the small village of Villalpando, a few leagues south of Sahagun. It was a particularly happy occasion for Moore to meet up again with his second in command. Davy cursed in humorous terms in a fashion only that man could, about the country, the populace, the weather and his aches and pains. Moore was never so happy to see his friend, but beneath the bonhomie he sensed Baird's unease with the situation and with Moore himself.

The army was set to join up together at Mayorga over the next day or so. At present, Baird's division lay at Benavente while Moore had rode up from Castronuevo with Tam Graham. The encounter was testy as the two veterans eyed each other warily while giving the other a cagey welcome. Moore was unable to stifle a grin.

'Ye get uglier by the day, Tam. Hello to you.' Baird welcomed his adversary sourly.

'If ah had a face like yours, Davy, ah'd cut ma ain throat.' Was the pleasant rejoinder.

'Ah'll lend ye ma razor.' Baird retorted.

'Och, that's enough lads! Ye ken ye both love each other dearly!' Moore now rollicking with laughter, put an arm round both and led them to over to a smiling Francois, waiting patiently with refreshments.

Late that evening, in counsel with both of his friends, Moore explained his strategy in full. Graham remained silent throughout but Baird fidgeted with a wine glass, tapped one foot off the floor sporadically and tugged his collar more than once. Moore finished and there was a silence.

'I'd have expected something like this from Tam the Bam here. Not you, Johnny.' Baird pronounced in judgment.

'Nevertheless, Davy, they are my plans. They are my orders.' Moore countered mildly.

'I'm no' too happy either. But Johnny never had any other choice.' Graham interjected. 'He's been dealt a rotten hand. Each one of his decisions, I've backed to the hilt. They were all correct based on the intelligence provided.'

'He's cutting it too fine though, Tammy!' Baird complained loudly. 'Puttin' the eggs in one basket right here. And those eggs are his Majesty's only army in the field anywhere on earth at present.' He turned to Moore. 'Johnny, let me head back to cover you at Vigo or Coruña before the weather gets worse. Please let me do it!'

'No, Davy!' For the first time in the discussion, Moore displayed exasperation. Christ! Can the old bugger not see the opportunity? It wasn't like him to be so conservative. Maybe the rumours on the army's grapevine bore substance. Baird was getting old, becoming too cautious. Talk about his health. His temper worse than usual.

John Moore had a quick temper himself. But he knew he must rein it in. Risking discord between himself and his most senior subordinate was a recipe for catastrophe.

'Look, Davy. Whatever the governments original instructions were, are null and void now. Events have overtaken them. The moment Bonaparte personally took an interest and crossed the border, the situation changed irrevocably.'

'The Spaniards...' Baird began.

'At present cannot be relied upon, yes. I agree.' Moore cut in. 'I've some measure of faith in Señor Romaña, but he is only one man. I've more confidence in the southern patriots who appear to be making a little headway. If I can draw Bonaparte's teeth to the north, while inflicting a defeat or two on him along the way, embark the army back to Lisbon or at worse back to England, we will have struck a hugely significant strategic blow. I plead with you to see the sense in that.'

There was a silence. Davy Baird emptied his glass and laid it on the table.

'Aye, Johnny. I can see the sense. But supposing it all goes to plan. What kind of army do you think you'll have left to transport? Over this land in midwinter? Run ragged by the French? A bunch of spoiled mummy's boys passing as company officers? Christ! You should see some of them I've been lumbered with. Barely able to wipe their own arses! Never before have I seen such poor material. And the laddies? Too many green recruits. Too many from the prisons, from crimps. A lot of trash among them. Not enough decent non-coms. You'll have a hard time keeping them in line if it all goes to shite! Aye, it's some army!'

'He's right about all that, Johnny.' Graham admitted unhappily.

'And I'm telling him all the risk has been factored in!' Moore finally exploded. 'It'll be as I say and that's enough from the pair o' ye's!'

There was a highly uncomfortable silence to follow. Baird refilled his glass and drank deeply. Graham lit a cigar. No one spoke. Francois entered the room to clear up and place a fresh carafe on the table before them. Moore thanked him. When the French valet left, he reached over for the wine.

'Lads, let's not fall out over this. We can't afford to. We have a battle before us. Possibly in mere days.' He turned to Baird. 'Davy, I'm dividing the army into four divisions plus the cavalry. You are the second in command of this army and it falls on you should anything become of me. But I'd rather you were given command of the first division rather than sit on a horse behind me all day long. Will you accept?'

Baird laid down his glass. 'I will. Thank you, Johnny. That's very kind of you. And forgive me for this now. It's just that…well, I'm just a wee bit more cautious about matters these days. I look at the faces of our boys and I only see their mothers worrying over them. I keep thinking of my own mother, the horrible auld bag! I miss her greatly. It's my duty to fight but it's also my duty to see the laddies home. It's just that I was never more aware of the inconsistency of both those views till now. Must be getting old.'

Tam Graham, after a short pause, replied solemnly. 'It's no' an easy thing to admit to, Davy. But I respect you for it.'

'Why, a miracle!' Moore exclaimed happily. 'The two of you finally agree on something. Indeed, a fine omen!'

He raised his glass to his friends who followed suit, though rather more thoughtfully.

*

John Moore's greatest cause for satisfaction was the sight of his army with the light of imminent battle in its eyes. The grumbling which reached a crescendo on the leaving of Salamanca, had vanished into the Iberian air. Officers with springs in their steps dashed around his headquarters ensuring orders, requisition slips and all other paraphernalia of the bureaucracy of war, were dealt with to the extremes of efficiency and effectiveness. Non-commissioned officers marvelled at formerly listless and disinterested private soldiers furiously pay attention to their kit and their muskets, chatter and joke together happily, and yarn of previous engagements and absent comrades. Surgeons prepared their gruesome instruments for the coming maelstrom of blood and gore. The guns of the artillery were off ahead of the infantry to their positions. Cavalrymen sharpened their already blooded sabres.

It was six Spanish leagues to Saldaña from Sahagun, roughly the equivalent of twenty-five English miles. The army, divided into two corps, would that night march to Carrion de los Condes just south of Saldaña on the river *Carrion*.

Colonel James Bathurst, assistant quarter master general of the army, on a reconnaissance patrol with men of the 15th Hussars, on the morning of the 23rd spotted the position of the French army under Marshal Soult across the *Carrion*. Hurrying back to make his report to the commander, Sir John Moore advised Bathurst his plan to force the bridge at Carrion and present the army to Soult for battle the following morning.

Scribbling a final letter to John Hookham Frere, Moore, advising of the army's march to Saldaña, warned the British diplomat it was a highly dangerous undertaking. He had said little to anyone other than his immediate circle of commanders of his plan. He said nothing to anyone, even Tam Graham, of his fears.

His first taste of high command of an army. Yet he did not think many of his peers or predecessors ever found themselves in quite a fix as this one. A man who was his own worst critic, he replayed time and time again the thought processes leading him to each of the decisions made since arriving in the Peninsula. To those who complained he lingered in Salamanca longer than necessary, he would answer he was forced to delay his departure in order to a) await his army coming together and b) to gain as much information on Bonaparte's movements as possible, in order to formulate his own plans. He got away with the gamble he took in sending Hope's artillery by a torturous and dangerous route. If he had ignored local advice and went with his own gut, he wouldn't have ordered that one. Then he and Hope would have arrived in the city together. His misgivings about his Spanish allies? He allowed too much to diplomacy. But he was only following his orders to the letter in that regard. He hadn't been sent to Spain to take on the French himself alone. He was sure he acted correctly though his instincts told him the Spanish at present were a forlorn hope. But he had to allow every possibility resistance would fuse together. That it had come in the south, and only in spurts, set his mind to his strategy. There was no deviating from it now.

He knew Hester would approve. There was just the right amount of devilry and cunning in his plan to thrill her. Wellesley? He didn't think the gentleman would have acted any differently from himself. Castlereagh and the government? Provided he succeeded and brought the army home in the best condition possible, he knew he would be safe. The future? He would leave that to the gods of war.

He looked out the window of the sprawling monastery of Sahagun which spread over half of the town. There were no long streets like many Spanish settlements. But there was a lovely fountain in the middle of the large market place where soldiers were carrying out last minute ablutions. Moore smiled at the normality of the scene. His face then turned to a grimace in recall of a sight he witnessed on first entering the town. A dozen bodies of dead Frenchmen were laid stripped naked by locals, almost covered by the winter snow. Whether they were killed in Paget's victory or garrison troops murdered in revenge, no one was saying. To his and to the horror of the officers he rode with, they could clearly see that one of the bodies belonged to a woman, quite possibly young, but difficult to tell, as her face was deliberately smashed beyond recognition.

Harry Percy, riding alongside John Colbourne behind their commander, vomited into the bloody snow.

Robert Craufurd certainly had the light of battle in his eyes. But no one who came into contact with *Black Bob* as the army was now calling him, would ever have accused him of radiating glee.

The cloaked and saturnine figure mounted on his sorrel, wearing a black fore and aft bicorn hat, leading his light division, the vanguard of the army towards Carrion was admittedly, by his own peculiar standards, experiencing an almost ecstatic high of exuberance. Not that any potential straggler behind him would notice should they be found guilty of carrying out the gravest offence in the general's rule book, namely falling out of the column without first seeking permission. Euphoric or otherwise, Black Bob Craufurd would have flogged the hide from his back.

Robert fully concurred with Johnny's plans, himself being among the chosen few allowed into the inner circle. The prospective battle in the morning was a God given opportunity to lay down a marker to the Corsican after Vimeiro that there was more than one Briton capable of besting the Ogre. He was enormously proud of his friend, greatly admiring his flexibility of mind and strategic vision. But he worried about his army.

He was concerned that when, and not if, the bubble burst, the army may not live up to its commanders, and indeed his own, high standards. There were too many warning flags for Robert Craufurd to ignore. On the transport ship over to Coruña, he was greatly disturbed by the number of untrained boys sent on board literally moments after making their attestation marks. Superb instrument that the light division was, it was not exempt from similar concerns over recruiting. There appeared to be a tougher element than usual to the usual former prison complement. Hardened thieves, dangerous recidivist criminals, smugglers, even a few murderers and rapists were released to the bosom of the army. There were not enough of the healthier sprinkling of down at heal petty criminals or the best type of recruit, those unfortunates who found themselves in jail for debt. They were usually better educated, accepted their lot and proved reliable.

The standard of junior officer was also a worry. He discussed such concerns with Davy Baird and it remained a nagging doubt. Non-commissioned officers, the backbone of any army, as always would be relied on to pick up the pieces. But he noted signs of slackness in some, particularly in regards to untrained youths and hesitancy towards the worst of the prison scum. They were not receiving enough training and attention. All that seemed to matter was they knew how to fire a musket. They were then ignored and left to their own devices.

He caught young boys on guard and picket duty with no clue as to what they were doing. Lads who could barely buckle on their own knapsacks. Robert did not punish them, preferring to admonish them in a constructive manner, but went searching angrily for their corporals to demand answers. None he received were satisfactory.

The obsessive nature of the man meant Robert Craufurd was prone to brooding. But tonight he must try to concentrate his mind on the clash ahead. Battles could be great levellers. Men, and indeed boys, could behave unexpectedly. Natural warriors often appear from unlikely source material. Existing leaders may prove themselves incapable. He also had to trust to the god of war. And John Moore.

He glanced behind him. The men looked good. Marching in column perfectly. There was no talking. Never at night. The old lags made it clear to the new men. Shut up. Well, at least that was something.

Don't think about South America. Don't think of Mary Frances. Both extremes reflected his strange, dual nature. Stay in the middle ground. You don't have useless *hoormaisters* commanding you now. You have to get through the next day if you want to see her again. Then you can think about her. To your black heart's content.

Robert allowed himself the merest twitch of his lips in a smile at the last. Why that blessed girl ever entangled herself with the likes of him, he'd never understand. All he knew was that he thanked the good lord every day for her. The depths of the troughs he'd fallen into were only made manageable by her presence in his life. And his children, too.

No. Stop it, man! You'll weaken. You'll go under again. His own personal horror was that he had passed his melancholia onto his beloved young sons, Charles, Robert and Alexander. Mary comforted him in her letters that the only issue with the boys was that they badly missed their father when he wasn't home. As did their first child, Louisa.

Don't think about it. Robert rubbed his eye and turned to look over his shoulder again. *Aye you buggers! Ah'm watchin' ye's! Ye want to win and stay alive? Do what I say.* He ploughed on ahead. They'd travelled only a few miles. The night was freezing. The tracks they marched over would turn to icy slush for those that followed. Thankfully, they couldn't make out the menacing, snow-capped hills around them. They weren't the green hills of home. These hovered ominously in the shadows, ready to rip and tear out your heart and guts. No trees or forestry worth a damn either. Miserable scrub. It might have been a desert, the entire damnable country. He heard the sound of a galloper behind him. By Christ, this better be important.

Robert pulled up to halt. The horseman, a dragoon stopped alongside him. 'General Craufurd, sir? An urgent despatch from Sir John Moore, with his compliments. I am to advise you are to act on its instruction with immediate effect. I must then return the order confirmed by yourself to the general.' The man handed over the despatch.

'And how am I to read it in this light, son?' Robert asked.

'Sir! I...I,' the normally coolly efficient young man was temporarily at a loss. For a dreadful moment he feared the notorious general was going to pull a Nelson at Copenhagen on the army.

'Don't fret. You'll have your piece of paper returned to you.' Robert called for a small lantern to be lit and brought to him. He would just have to take the chance of it being seen in the mirk.

A soldier of the 95th brought forward the light. Robert told him to lay it down and return to the column. He climbed off his horse, picked up the lamp and walked over to the side of the road. He crouched down. Removing his gauntlets, he slipped a thumb under the seal of the letter and opened it.

What he read in the chilly gloom curdled his blood.

Chapter Fifteen

The news sent a wave of shock so profound it shook the entire army to its core. Soldiers were dumbstruck, left in confusion and despondency in their disappointment. A terrible cloud of depression grew exponentially as the former elation of an army poised to fight, turned to shattering despair as it was now ordered to full retreat. It was believed by many to have been one of the main harbingers for the horror that was to follow.

The expected battle with the Duke of Dalmatia, or Marshal Soult as he was also known, was abandoned and the army was to turn back for Vigo or Coruña for swift embarkation. Only hours before, John Moore was poised to leave his headquarters in Sahagun for the *Carrion* as his army began the march to imminent battle. Instead, a messenger sent in great haste from the Marquis of Romaña, the only Spanish general on whom Moore could rely, brought devastating tidings.

According to reliable agents of the marquis, the entire French army in Madrid was now marching in the direction of Sir John Moore's force. Originally, Bonaparte believed Moore was making for Portugal and ordered forty thousand men on standby to head west. But he received enough intelligence reports, including statements from British deserters to confirm in fact the British army was in the north, poised to attack Soult. The Emperor then informed Marshal Ney to abandon all his plans in the south and to head north to support Soult who was to force Moore towards Burgos. The Madrid forty thousand turned north. Napoleon himself with his Imperial Guard would strike at the British flank. Such was the efficiency of planning of the Corsican that by 22nd December, the elite Guards cavalry reached the pass of Guadarrama. Over eighty thousand men were in hot pursuit of a force much less than half its size. If they caught up with them, the only British army in the field would be annihilated.

There was less cause to doubt the veracity of the letter when only a short time later, a scouting officer arrived at Moore's headquarters to confirm Romaña's warning was indeed true. He had come from the south where he personally viewed Marshal Ney's force heading in this direction.

If only Moore had known that Napoleon believed him to be in Valladolid, not Sahagun, some fifty miles south of where he in fact was. The British army was in reality, 120 miles ahead of the French. It was just enough if their luck held to make the difference.

John Moore dismissed the messenger and called for an immediate conference with his senior commanders. Unfortunately, John Hope and Bobby Craufurd were already on the road to Carrion. He began hastily drafting despatches to both, explaining the urgency of the new retreat order.

While he awaited the arrival of Sir David Baird, Lord Paget and the others, Moore composed in his mind his plans for the retreat. He was aware that the route he would be taking through the Galician hills offered opportunities for defensive holding actions. There were routes and passes where a couple of handily placed cannon could hold off an army for some time. Gorges and torturous mountain roads that were a sharp shooters dream, where he envisaged a company of Craufurd's 95th picking off targets at will. But with the onset of deep winter and the deadly pursuit by the enemy now undoubtedly making progress, he believed speed and haste were the best guardians of the army.

The only doubts that stabbed at him were the discipline of the army and the women and children camp followers. He wasn't in any way certain of the former, and the latter was a given that tragedies would occur along the way. The baggage train, due to the poor quality of carts available in the country, was a serious concern. The army was not clothed for a winter that was never foreseen. Even Moore had no idea Spain could prove so cold. No. Unless absolutely necessary, there would be no stopping or slowing down anywhere along the route. It was full ahead to the ports.

The moment of crisis in his plan had arrived. But he was greatly heartened to learn that Napoleon Bonaparte had taken the bait, stripping the south in pursuit of him. In every way his plan was succeeding. He remained confident he would get the army home. How intact that army would be at the end, only God knew.

Andrew Berry was uncertain of his emotions.

He prepared himself, as the others in his company had for the march to Carrion. He listened carefully to veterans talking about Alexandria and previous battles. Sergeant McGillivray and other NCO's blew through the regiment like whirlwinds ensuring supplies of kit, ammunition and rations were all in order. He stopped to offer a pep talk to his three new recruits at 8p.m. that evening of the 23rd of December, just before the men were due to leave the monastery to form outside for marching orders. It had been a good billet. A large store of flour was found hidden and fresh bread and cake was baked which made a pleasant treat from the hard biscuit of their rations.

'Lads, we are off to battle.' McGillivray began. 'You may think it strange that so many look kindly upon it, and indeed, anticipate with great relish such an event before us. It will be terrible to experience and you will all be tested to the limit. But there is a strange exultation in battle that grips a man. It is indefinable, but no less real. There are great opportunities to be had to gain merit and recognition. But undoubtedly, there are great perils to be borne also, pain of wounds, of mutilation and of death. I ask you all to put these things from your mind, particularly of death. If it is your fate that it should come for you, do not dwell on it as it is usually quick and over before you know it. But this I must ask of you. Hold firm at all times. Though you may see your friends fall around you, you must stand up to the challenge.' He looked at each boy. 'Andrew. Joshua. Archie. You have each other. You have myself, Corporal McQuater and others to steady you. Remember above all, your drills. To correctly prime your musket each time you load. The rule of battle is the same of practice. Three rounds a minute. You are each capable of that.'

'How long does a battle last, Sergeant?' Andrew asked, trying to keep the quiver from his voice.

'No one can say, son. Do not burden yourself with such worries. It will be over when it's over.'

'And is it true you can gain great plunder on the battlefield?' Archie enquired eagerly.

McGillivray grimaced comically. 'Trust you, Mr Miller! The greatest treasure to be taken from the battlefield is your own life, Archie. Concentrate on that above all other matters.'

He looked at Joshua. The Newcastle lawyer's clerk was even paler than usual and remained silent throughout the talk. 'Joshua, more cheer from you, my buckie. You will not be alone. You have fine comrades at your side. Make it your purpose to ensure you look after them also.'

'Yes, Sergeant.' Joshua replied but the words caught in his throat.

'Now, gentlemen.' The sergeant turned to leave. 'We will soon be off to pad the hoof to meet old Marshal Salty balls! You boys give him what for. I'm counting on you!'

But when the final order arrived to parade outside before their divisional commander, the address from Sir David Baird stunned everyone present. Keyed up as Andrew was, he could not decide later whether the stronger emotion he felt was one of relief or disappointment. He was an honest and guileless young man and understood that at last the moment had arrived to genuinely earn his king's shilling. Where he would truly face the ultimate test of his manhood. That for all his time in uniform, from that last day in Edinburgh, the journey to Lisbon, the adventures he experienced along the way, his new friends, his exotic love, Gabriela and above all, he Andrew Berry of Barbauchlaw being part of historical events, the time was now upon him where he must make payment for it all. And such payment could result in him losing everything he had.

On returning to their billets, the men of the regiment furiously threw their muskets to the deck in their rage at the change of plans. This normally would have been unthinkable, verging on mutinous conduct, but such were the depths of their anger and feelings of betrayal. Archie admitted to Andrew he was scunnered by the whole thing. What was the use of being a soldier if you were denied the right to face the enemy in a fair fight? He saw his chances of earning a small fortune and finding himself a beautiful señorita with it vanish.

Keeping his own counsel, Joshua said little but the young man was as relieved to hear the news as most were outraged by it.

Sergeant McGillivray ordered every man to carry as much warm clothing as possible in their knapsacks and around their persons. Every spare shirt, pair of stockings, plaid and blanket available was to be utilised for the coming days. He warned everyone they were facing an ordeal far worse than any battle. They must prepare themselves accordingly for insufferable hardships the like of which they would never have experienced before.

Andrew and his friends took great heed to this advice, packing away as much as they could carry. They wore their plaid trews, made originally under the sergeant's supervision, under their kilts. Archie fashioned scarves out of old blankets for himself and his two friends to wrap around there necks and to utilise as face coverings in severe weather. He bitterly regretted none of them had mittens to wear, but cut out long, thin pieces of blanket to use for binding around the hands and as protective coverings for the working parts of their muskets. Joshua was grateful for his friend's prescience as being city bred, he would never have thought of any of it. Andrew busily assisted Archie, for once, taking the lead.

It wasn't till the early hours of Christmas Eve, 1808 that the boys concluded their preparations and bunked down for their last night in Sahagun. In his bed, Andrew could not sleep. He thought of Sergeant McGillivray's words about the ordeal ahead. Would they make it to embarkation? He and his friends were young, well fed and conditioned. But what of the women and children following the army? They would struggle against snow and ice through mountain passes, roads, dirt tracks and gorges. What terrible sights would he witness? Would he be able to bear them? If he saw distressed females and bairns, he would go to their aid. Unquestionably. He simply could not walk by. He knew Joshua was of the same mind. He understood Archie would always defer to him. But in the coming days he would have to rely heavily on the Fifer, as his brute strength and mental toughness, despite his easy going nature, could be the key to all three's survival. He knew Archie had a ruthless streak. He wasn't so sure he would be so accommodating to anyone other than Andrew or Joshua. Archie once told him candidly he would always look out for his two pals, but wouldn't waste much breath on anyone else. That was just the way it had to be, he explained.

Andrew turned over in the bed. He shouldn't worry about such things. Nothing had happened yet. That was just talk from Archie. His thoughts ran to something more personal. He'd written regular letters to his parents and received only one in return. He told them of his adventures (not all) but mentioned Sergeant McGillivray often, along with his two friends. Praising the sergeant's care and diligence towards his recruits, he asked the question in a letter to his parents about who '*Sandy*' was.

It was the name in guarded moments throughout his life, his parents, whenever they argued, brought up. He would listen to their not infrequent squabbles and if ever the name was uttered, there was an immediate hush, followed by lowered voices and whispers. He now knew this was deliberate in order to shut down the conversation from others in the household.

There were no clues at home. Nothing written anywhere that Andrew was aware of. The subject was spoken of among the siblings, but no one dared approach their parents with the question. It wasn't done. Their parents past was an impenetrable wall that was not even to be attempted to be scaled. If they did, the risk of the consequences were dire. Despite his still virginal state, Andrew believed he now had the right to know more about his mother and father. Of his grandparents, only his maternal grandmother survived. She lived with them but the reticence to ask a question extended even to her. One evening a row erupted. The old lady was knitting and Andrew summoned up the courage to finally ask, 'Granma, who is this 'Sandy' they keep mentioning?' the old lady threw her knitting to the floor, and told him in no uncertain fashion to mind his business and never to ask about such matters again.

Andrew still awaited a response to his letter.

Davy Baird felt little satisfaction.

What he feared most of the British army in Spain had come to pass. An ill-planned and potentially catastrophic retreat through fearsome terrain during a harsh winter, was the stuff of nightmares. That evening, Davy spoke hurriedly to the men gathered eagerly to march to battle, informing them that the army was instead to turn to retreat immediately. He was under no obligation to give the reason but later wished he let the men into his confidence. The divisions of Hope and Fraser would start out in the morning, the 24th December. Sir David Baird's division including Andrew and his two friends, would begin their march on Christmas Day.

Word got about, of course. Bonaparte with a huge force was only fifty miles away. It did little to assuage the men. They feared no one. Not even the Corsican monster.

On returning that night to Sahagun, Craufurd was ordered not to stand his division down. Given an hour's breather, they were back on the road, heading for Castrogonzalo to meet up with the other divisions at Astorga. It was on this march that the legend of Black Bob Craufurd was born.

Chapter Sixteen

As he trudged through the awful winter weather, Andrew Berry thought back to previous marches, beginning in Lisbon.

The journey to Salamanca was one of the most pleasurable experiences of his life. He traipsed blissfully through Spain experiencing new sights, sounds, scents. Fresh vistas. New ways of looking at the world. The early autumn conditions afforded reasonably pleasant marching weather. He wore out two pairs of shoes but there were plenty of supplies. Indeed, his only recollection of anything less than delightful, was breaking in new footwear along with the pain of inevitable blisters. But rarely did a day pass when his heart was not filled in exultation. He thought of the stories he would tell one day when he finally arrived home from his travels. Of camping out under Iberian skies. Of cheerful banter at the campfire. Good comradeship, songs, rum (which he didn't drink) and fresh meat.

Then the leaving of Salamanca and on to Sahagun. He happily recalled the tryst with Gabriela and his adventures in the city. He fantasised about returning to marry her and finally realising the ecstasy of two souls joyously making love together. He would take her back home to Scotland, away from the dirt and superstition of Spain. Away from *war*. She was the only girl he ever kissed and held in his arms. He was completely in love with her. In the dreadful days ahead, she would become a distant, almost faceless spectre, the only record of her existence the little silver crucifix the boy now wore around his neck. He wouldn't even be certain what she looked like.

On this latest march, circumstances could not be more different from earlier journeys. Temperatures plummeted to near freezing, the rain incessant, as was the wind. The rain then turned to sleet driving into the faces of the men as they slogged along with their heads down as far into their collars as their stocks would allow. The dirt roads they trampled along became mud and slush filled quagmires.

And then it began to snow.

The route the division was to march was west by way of Valencia de Don Juan, then across the river *Esla* to Benavente, making junction with the army at Astorga. But the first stage, a distance of four Spanish leagues, or less than twenty miles in advance of the starting point, was a portent of what was to come.

The division of eight thousand men carried a large number of women and children camp followers. There was little in the way of transport for them. What carts available were mainly to carry ammunition and by now rapidly dwindling supplies.

The column arrived intact at the ferry point at Valencia. But only just. Andrew's heart sank when he saw the river. The march was hard on him. He'd hated it and wanted it to end. The river looked formidable, and in the poor weather which was starting to cause the water level to rise dangerously, it appeared more malevolent in the early evening light. He was cold, wet, tired and hungry. And also a little frightened.

'We'll never get across that!' Joshua declared morosely. He was nearly in tears from exhaustion. Never the most robust of souls, marching even in the best of conditions taxed him heavily.

'Aye, they'll have to find somewhere crossable along the river. No other way for it.' Archie pondered aloud.

'Surely they'll have a map or a guide?' Andrew voiced anxiously.

'I hope so. Don't fancy swimming.'

There was no more talk as the boys began to consider what would happen next. They were then approached by Sergeant McGillivray.

'Are you well, lads? That was a fair jaunt! How are your feet? Don't hunker down too long now. The general's found a wee ford along the way he thinks will get us across. Just bide you here for the moment.' The sergeant walked off to spread the news to others. Andrew and his friends were once again grateful for McGillivray's ability to keep them abreast of matters.

'How are you feeling, Josh?' Andrew asked.

Joshua had taken off his knapsack and sat down on it. He removed his bonnet and dried his face. 'I hope we don't have to go much further the night. I'm ready to pack it in.'

'Me too.' Archie declared. 'I'm dead beat.'

Andrew didn't believe Archie was ready to stop and was showing solidarity with Joshua. Andrew grew fonder of his friend and his inner strength, thanking God yet again for his presence.

'I think once we cross the river we'll bed down for the night. Stands to reason.' Andrew announced confidently, unstrapping his knapsack. Archie followed suit and they both dropped to the ground beside Joshua. The boys then took the sergeant's advice and inspected their feet and shoes. They each had an old pair amongst their kit. McGillivray insisted they carry a spare set. All three wore full sets of stockings tied with ribbons, along with gaiters. They were soaked through, but would have to do till they crossed the river.

Andrew's left shoe was fine but the right was beginning to split at the instep. It wasn't too serious and he reckoned it would hold for a while yet. Archie's left heel was worn and he didn't expect it to last too much longer, especially if the weather didn't improve. He'd have to think about that.

Joshua's shoes were in the best condition. He was much lighter than the other two and his tread less heavy but his feet were not in good shape with the constant soaking that day. There were blisters on the heel and ball of his right foot. Archie inspected his friend and popped the blisters with his bayonet point. He took a small cloth from his knapsack and dried Joshua's feet before attending to his own.

'Let them air a bit.' He told the grimacing clerk as he massaged his feet. Archie didn't have blisters. They ached, but they were hardened from a life of hard work in all weather and long treks to retrieve lost farm animals through the snow and ice of the Fife winter.

Soon they were up again as the division was led to a ford where the water was low enough to risk crossing. Two barges available to them at the ferry point were utilised but it would have taken too long to get the entire division over using them alone. Large groups each then made the perilous crossing through shallow, though fast moving waters. Soldiers carried women and children on their backs. The rest of the army attached their ammunition to the tops of their knapsacks to avoid getting wet. As they reached the far bank of the river, they became caught up in mud banks up to their waists. Here, Joshua lost one of his shoes. He was unwilling to duck into the mud to retrieve it. Many others suffered the same. Some lost both.

Pack animals, mules, horses and carts then followed. Miraculously, all crossed safely just as the water rose to hazardous levels. On the bank of the river was a tiny village named Villamanan. General Baird ordered a halt. Pickets were set and the army began to bed down for the night. Fortunately, Andrew and his friends were not called to duty.

They now had mud encrusted clothing to contend with. Andrew never felt so miserable and demoralised. He tried to scrape it off with his bayonets edge but it had soaked into the wool. It was like being wrapped in dirty, smelly, wet and uncomfortable rags. Sensibly, he gave up. With his strength waning and with concentration levels sinking fast through exhaustion, he had enough wits remaining to remove his stockings and leave them over his knapsack to dry the best they could. Struggling now to stay awake, he began work on getting his shoes into reasonable shape.

The rain turned to sleet again. There was nowhere near enough accommodation in the village for eight thousand people. Andrew and his two friends were forced to bed down under the awning of a peasant hut along with many others. It offered little protection from the night. The rain and sleet never let up.

After a hurried meal of biscuits and oatmeal, they toasted each other with Yuletide wishes and drank their rum ration. Many quietly shed tears at being parted from their loved ones at such a time. Andrew certainly did. He found it impossible to sleep. He just wanted to go home. To be with his family, to marry Gabriela and never leave Scotland again.

They covered themselves with every piece of clothing they owned, and tried to get through the first night of the retreat. It was the 25th December, 1808.

Setting out alongside Lord Paget's cavalry, Robert Craufurd, commander of the light brigade, was as reasonably content as he could be since arriving in Spain.

John Moore laid his plan out to him. Bobby's division along with Lord Paget was to act as the army's rearguard and travel by way of the bridge at Castrogonzalo. After Benavente and once together again at Astorga, he was to veer off and cover the army's southern flank, in the direction of Vigo.

Johnny sugared it the best he could, but Robert, sympathising with his friend's plight was quietly satisfied he now had a definite goal to achieve and was trusted to get on with it. Moore advised him to expect a lot of straggling and to act as he saw fit, but to try to use restraint and humanity at all times. It was a telling comment to make to Robert Craufurd, indicating Moore's grave concerns about the army's conduct during the coming retreat. He further ordered that Robert keep the French back but not to offer any major confrontations. Skirmish if unavoidable, allow Paget to enjoy himself and do what he considered necessary. But speed was to be the main tactic used in the withdrawal. *Dinnae stop tae dawdle,* Johnny grinned knowingly to his saturnine friend.

Moore would ride with the reserve under Paget's brother, Edward, and meet up with the rear-guard either at Benavente or Astorga. Robert was confident that Johnny would never interfere with his running of the division. But restraint? *Humanity?* He would have to consider those suggestions in as wide a context as possible.

It wasn't long before Robert sensed the change in the men. They marched out to Saldaña in the best of spirits. But they were too infuriated to think of much more than their own disappointment when ordered to return to Sahagun. Now a creeping sullenness and resentment was beginning to set in among them. When he rode or walked along the column to ascertain morale, he could tell immediately something wasn't right. There was a low grumbling instead of the usual cheery sound of the tin whistle and easy chat. They were unwilling to look him in the eye. They stared down or away from him and some would spit. All done in a clever, devious fashion a lesser officer wouldn't notice. Robert Craufurd was not that type of officer. He vowed to take the skin off the back of the first man caught wrongdoing.

His attention wasn't solely aimed at the men. There were officers whom he believed fell well short of his own standards, who required watching. He caught one early on in the march, who pleading illness, allowed his men to break ranks and march around a small brook instead of going through it, thereby wasting valuable time. The officer was made to walk over the brook back and forth again before Robert was satisfied he had learned his lesson.

By the third day of the march, the 28th, the division reached the bridge at Castrogonzalo. Lord Paget, furiously keeping the ever encroaching French cavalry at bay, sent a message to Robert to prepare the charges for demolition of the bridge for that evening. He hoped to lead his cavalry over it followed by the infantry. Destruction of the bridge would be accomplished by midnight.

The rain was falling in torrents. Robert sheltered behind a hastily built defensive barricade constructed from trees trunks, branches and broken off timber from carts. He stood alongside men of all three regiments as rainwater ran through the barrels of their Bakers and muskets. They looked to the east where they could clearly make out the firing and shouts from skirmishing cavalrymen. He ordered two men from the 43rd to scout ahead. When they returned they were in a shocking state, having been attacked by French cavalry, bloodily cut about and fortunate to be alive. Robert sent out more pickets and after a time, he himself went out to gain a personal view.

He took to carrying a wooden canteen containing rum. It was for his own use but also handy for rewarding the men. He offered a drink to the pickets who reported small groups of French cavalry attempting to charge British positions. They were repelled, but Robert cursed Henry Paget to damnation to hurry the hell up.

Eventually to the great relief of everyone, his Lordship arrived with his brigade, Robert stepping out to greet him.

'Cutting it a little fine, Harry?' He reached up to the cavalryman with his canteen.

Panting heavily, Paget took a long drink. 'By Christ, that's good! Better late than never, eh Bob, old chum? Frogs kept you busy?'

'Yes, but not as much as you, I'll wager. Very well, man. Get your smelly old beasts across the bridge and don't forget to take the horses with them! My laddies have stood in the rain long enough waiting for you prince's dolls!

Paget laughed, grabbed his reigns and swung around. 'Harsh, Bobby. Harsh words indeed! See you on the other side.' With a bellow he ordered his horsemen across, as Robert stood and watched the flow of men and animals pass by with a satisfied scowl.

By midnight the explosive charges were in place around the bridge. Robert then ordered his men across before watching the destructive blast blow the two arches of the bridge and a connecting buttress down into the water.

*

Trouble flared the following day.

One of the purposes of the rearguard was to collect stragglers and the injured from the columns ahead. The light brigade had not caught up yet with Baird's division while Hope and Fraser were further ahead by about twenty four hours. Benavente lay just before Craufurd's men. This strategic town was a lynchpin to Moore's strategy as each division made its way through it on the road to Astorga. If Bonaparte got there first, 'the race to Benavente' if won by the French, would have had catastrophic consequences for the British army.

By the early morning of the 29th, the weather conditions and supply situation now began their inexorable effect. Most of the men hadn't eaten anything in 48 hours. The cold and relentless rain the day before, where most had to remain at the stand to awaiting a possible clash with the French at the bridge, had a further desultory effect on the division's health. Men were wracked with colds, coughs and agonising rheumatic pains were beginning to appear. Their feet were starting to cause issues as shoes and stockings began to rot. Horrifyingly, some of the men were now marching barefoot through the snow and ice. Inevitably, some fell by the wayside.

Camp followers were suffering the most. Forbidden to march along with their menfolk, they were forced to remain in the rear. As the already poor roads grew worse under the tread of thousands of boots, and as only a fortunate few found spaces on carts, the majority of the women and children had to walk, enduring the worst of the conditions as they struggled to keep up. They would be the first to begin to fall behind and die.

Whether mounted or on his feet, Robert Craufurd was seen continually moving up and down the column, keeping a careful eye on march discipline. At first if he saw a straggler he confronted the man, ordering him to return to the line or reap the consequences. Trying to bear in mind Johnny Moore's words on restraint, Robert's temper smouldered.

As he was walking back from one sojourn, he found himself alongside men of the 95th. He noted one private, a Yorkshireman named Rook. Normally considered a steady soldier, he was regarded as something of a terror when drunk which a few hundred strokes attested to.

'You, there. Rifleman Rook! Pray, where is your knapsack, man?' The men continued to march as though hearing nothing, Rook among them.

'I said, Rook!' Robert repeated even louder. 'You! Where is your knapsack?'

'Chucked! Like this whole rotten army has by lyin' Scotch bastards!' The unmistakable Yorkshire accent was heavy with anger and resentment.

'Halt! Stop, I say!' The column slowly came to a clanking, nervy standstill.

The mood was unrepentant. Robert could feel the antipathy smouldering like the stench of sweat, leather and unwashed bodies wafting from the men. But it was lesser now, worn down by fatigue. The extreme rage of Sahagun had dissipated somewhat. But it was still palpable.

'Rifleman Rook, step out!' Robert ordered. By now two non-commissioned officers who usually remained close to their commander for protective purposes, hurriedly appeared at the general's side.

Rook slowly eased his way out from the column and stood before the general. Robert looked at him for a moment. He was a man in his mid-thirties, of medium height, with receding, sandy hair. His nose was red and his eyes streamed. Evidently suffering from a severe cold or other form of neurasthenia, he certainly didn't look a healthy specimen.

Robert spoke calmly. 'I asked you twice what has become of an item of your kit. You refused to reply. Will you answer me now?'

Rook looked down. 'Ah told thee. Ah threw it away. Tha's the thing't do wi' rubbish!'

Robert remained impassive. 'You have two choices. Either you go back and collect it from where it was discarded, or I offer you something else to carry on your back. The decision is yours.'

The Yorkshireman spat to the side of the general. 'Thee fookin' decide, *Scotchman!*'

Robert stepped back. 'Column will stand down to witness punishment!'

The two non-coms grabbed Rook at either arm and led him to the side of the road. There was now a very evident change of mood in the column as not a sound could be heard. Robert paced slowly a few steps along the men of the 95th then turned around and walked back to where he began. He rubbed his chin slowly, studying the faces of the men who were now all looking to the front.

'Listen to me, you bastards. You believe because you are riflemen you are above reproach. You believe because you were trained to think and fight differently, you should be treated differently. Well, I am going to demonstrate to you how you should be treated. You are no better than anyone else and by God I am going to ensure you understand me!'

Rook was led away and a square was formed around a small tree to which the rifleman was tied. He was then given one hundred lashes by the 95th regiment's senior sergeant, witnessed by most of the column.

Later that morning, the rearguard of the British army marched into Benavente. The race was won.

Chapter Seventeen

'The commander of the forces has observed with concern the extreme bad conduct of the troops at a moment when they are about to come in contact with the enemy, and when the greatest regularity and the best conduct are the most requisite.'

John Moore stopped writing to peer out from the flap of his tent at the gloomy scene outside. He was camped on the plain of Benavente, just outside the town. The damp and thickening fog enveloping the skies matching his mood perfectly.

He closed the flap. Sighing heavily, he returned to his small fold away desk and lifted his quill. The paper before him was a proclamation to be read out to every man in the army.

'The misbehaviour of the troops in the column which marched by Valderas to this place exceeds what he could have believed of British soldiers.'

The conduct of his troops on entering the town of Benavente was nothing short of scandalous. None of the divisions passing through escaped censure. Even Craufurd's men, some of whom were literally on their knees as they entered the town, weren't entirely without blame. If Bobby couldn't control his men, all may be lost.

It pained Moore most that many of his light infantrymen were amongst the worst offenders. The 1st battalions of the 52nd regiment and his pride, the famous green jackets of the 95th marched alongside him in Edward Paget's reserve. He'd shown consideration and concern for their welfare, only for them to repay him with behaviour that would have rivalled the depravities of Attila.

That the men were more than just half-starved offered mitigation. But their preference even in their deprived state, was as always, for alcohol first. The trouble began when men from the 52nd broke away from the column to ransack a religious house, searching for wine before entering the town. The friar attempted to deny them entry and when they forced the doors he tried to explain that they held nothing of value. Ignoring him, they swarmed through the building and eventually found hidden vats. They then threw the poor man into one and proceeded to get violently drunk.

Many from the rest of the column on entering the town, took this as their cue and began a systematic ransacking of every building in the hunt for drink. A few valiant officers attempted to restore order, but it was noted that most took little action at all and indeed, a few joined in the rampage.

'It is disgraceful to the officers, as it strongly marks their negligence and inattention.'

A storm of looting began and reached its crescendo when a large underground vault was discovered filled with wine barrels. These were taken into the streets and shot through with muskets in order to provide holes to extract the liquid. Sadly for the revellers, it resulted in the barrels bursting, releasing a veritable river of wine through the lanes and streets of Benavente. Undaunted, hundreds of soldiers got down on their knees to drink and attempt to collect what they could from the flumes running over the cobbled stones. Many Spaniards also joined in the fun.

Private houses were broken into and their cowering occupants terrorised. Women were mishandled and there were rumoured to be instances of rape. Men who attempted to protect their women folk were clubbed to the ground. Everything that could be consumed was removed, as if a swarm of red-coated locusts had infested the small town.

Even the local castle, in reality an attractive little palace owned by the Duchess of Ossuna, fortunately absent in Madrid, did not escape wanton destruction. Valuable furniture and artworks were smashed to provide fuel for fires to warm looters. The interior of the fine old building was now little more than wreckage.

Not all soldiers were party to the excesses. Most in fact did not join in and many intervened in order to assist the town's citizens. But John Moore knew he had temporarily lost command and control of his army. And they were barely a quarter of the way to any ships.

They were sleeping it off now. God knows what state they'd be in the morning. He daren't remain much longer as intelligence reports were telling him Bonaparte was picking up the pace. There had already been a fierce cavalry engagement near the town. Once again Paget prevailed, but on this occasion he lost fifty valuable men. Moore simply couldn't afford the eyes and ears of his army to be whittled down any further.

But that encounter resulted in the commander of the British army being visited by a distinguished guest. During the action, Paget's men, after seeing off the enemy cavalry, pursued stragglers to the river's edge. One of the fugitives got into difficulties trying to ford the *Esla* and was forced to turn back to the British side. A German trooper took him captive and was handed over to the 10th Hussars, who were both astonished and delighted to have in their possession none other than the Emperor Napoleon's most favoured aide de camp, and reputed nephew of the Empress Josephine herself, the dashing Comte Charles Lefebvre-Desnouettes, General of the Imperial Hussars.

On being presented in his quarters, Moore noted the magnificent scarlet, gold, white and olive uniform of his regiment. He also could not fail to observe an effusion of red, namely the blood that was streaming down his captive's face from his brow where he suffered a blow during the battle. The British commander called for a cloth and personally cleaned off the Frenchman's face and forehead. Soaked from a ducking in the river, he was then presented with items of Moore's own personal attire to change into, until a truce could be declared and an aide sent into the French camp at Castrgonzalo to retrieve the general's baggage.

A table was set and food and wine offered to the guest, who throughout the occasion emitted an air of dejection. Later in a private moment between the two generals, Lefebvre-Desnouette confided to Moore that there were rumours, though unsubstantiated, that the Emperor himself witnessed the lost cavalry engagement. He was not a man to forgive failure, the Comte opined dolefully and feared his future was now bleak.

Regarding his erstwhile allies, Moore remained in contact with the Marquis of Romaña, pleading with the Spanish leader to maintain his harassing actions against the enemy. It was believed the marquis had upwards of ten thousand men with him. A sizeable force, but how battle worthy was open to speculation. Romaña was requested to avoid leading his army to Astorga in order to avoid congestion on the roads and leave the town to the British.

'It is impossible for the general to explain to his army the motive for the movement he directs. When it is proper to fight a battle, he will do it; and he will choose the time and place he thinks fit.'

Moore poured wine from a jug into a glass left by Francois. He'd taken to the local pork but forbade the lad from entering the town on a foraging expedition. It was too dangerous. He picked over some bread and cheese earlier but his appetite was similar to his mood. Much reduced.

And yet the instance that left a singular impression on his piece of mind was as he watched Davy Baird lead his battered division into the town. They'd camped out in the open two days after crossing the *Esla* in order to cover the other divisions approach. It never stopped raining. They'd eaten little also. A number of camp followers were left behind to catch up later. Many soldiers joined the lists of stragglers. They stopped to rest, some gave up the ghost and at the side of the road, or on a slope or hill vainly trying to find shelter, succumbed and died. Others would be butchered mercilessly by French forward troops and patrols.

But it was when the 42nd trudged into Benavente that Moore personally realised the human cost of the predicament of his army. Very few of the highlanders broke off to join the miscreants bedevilling the town. Instead, they stumbled along, wearied to the limits of their endurance, starved and bedraggled. Their kilts of dark green now almost black with the effluent from the land and the weather's pitilessness.

He observed three boys together, one at each side of the other, using their arms to form a chair to carry an exhausted friend, his bare shod feet dragging listlessly through the mush. His face a ghastly pallor, a sad attempt at a beard, his head hung down. Eyes closed. One of the friends, a short, ox like youth, his face pale though emitting an air of quiet determination, his eyes fixed on the town ahead. The other, a sturdy, reliable boy, his faced half concealed by a scarf to protect him from the hellish sleet, carrying both his own and his sick comrade's musket. Clinging on to his own dear life itself as well as his distressed friend. But never, *never* letting him go.

John Moore wiped his eyes, dipped the quill into the inkwell and continued to write.

'The army may rest assured that there is nothing their general has more at heart than their honour and that of their country.'

For the first time in his young life, Andrew Berry contemplated the reality of imminent extinction.

It wasn't in his mind's eyes view of what a battle involved. For all his worries before Saldaña, he was comforted that he always had a chance to survive a battle as the casualty figures for every engagement proved. There were the dead, the wounded and uninjured and there was a very high probability of avoiding the first should the fortune of war favour him. His conception of death was as an old man, lying in his bed, awaiting the good Lord's call, tearful, loving wife and children with him at the end. Even as a soldier, that remained his expectation.

Now during this dreadful march, he'd discovered how fragile a shell a human body was. Apparently fit and active young men, within a few days, deteriorating into shuffling, gibbering, mindless wrecks. The speed of the disintegration was staggering. The effects, devastating.

He witnessed terrible scenes. Those he dreaded viewing the most, the sufferings of women and children, drained him emotionally as he feared.

A women lying dead along with her equally lifeless new born baby. As he marched he looked over to the awful sight and left the column to run over to them. He would never forget the feel of her cold body as he gripped her shoulder to try and shake her into consciousness. It was like grabbing an alabaster statue. He pulled his hand away in horror.

Iain Colquhoun, an older man Andrew befriended early on with the regiment, brought him back to the column. Taking an arm, he rubbed it with his hand. 'Don't think about it, Drew. You must remove it from your mind. It'll do you no good to dwell on such things.'

But dwell on it, he did. He saw other sights, too. Dead animals left where they dropped from exhaustion. A fortunate few women and children, lucky enough to fetch a ride on wagons were now forced to come off them and walk past the dead beasts that had pulled them along. Many unfortunates soon fell by the way side and were left to catch up with the column. Some never did. Men lying in the road pleading for a good hearted soldier to help them. At this early stage of the retreat, many stragglers were assisted. Later, no one would have the strength to help anyone but themselves. But a number beyond succour were left for the elements to dispose of. Above all else, Andrew was mortally afraid of laying unburied, scavenged and gnawed by wild beasts.

By the time the division laid up after Villamanan, Joshua's condition was causing his friends concern. The spare shoes in his pack proved useless. They were in poor shape anyway and soon discarded. Andrew and Archie tried their own pairs for size. Though short and slight, Joshua had a long foot, and as his two friends were smaller, their own pairs had to be stretched somewhat which could potentially damage them further. Most shoes issued were of one size but by moulding and adjusting they eventually fit of a fashion.

'Remember if we use our own, we'll have none left for ourselves.' Archie warned.

'Surely we'll be resupplied up ahead.' Andrew reasoned.

Archie cut the front of the shoe to let Joshua's toes breath. They fit comfortably for a time, though the water and ice seeping in soon made his condition worse.

As he stood with eight thousand others, awaiting the approaching divisions and any sign of the enemy for the two days at the river, Joshua began to experience agonising pains in his left heel and the instep of his foot. He could not stand and had to go to ground. Corporal McQuater ordered Andrew and Archie to remove him to the rear for medical attention. The surgeon diagnosed a tendonitis and advised him to rest until the division was ordered back on the road. This gave him some relief but there was nowhere under shelter to lie up. Andrew took out his blanket and along with Archie's made a small tent or *basha* for him to rest under out of the wet. Joshua was pathetically grateful for his friend's consideration.

'You just lay back and dream of your bint in Edinburgh rattling you stupid!' Archie's cheerful farewell brought a smile to them all as he and Andrew returned to the company.

As they walked back, Archie voiced his concerns. 'He's not coping well. Have you a plan?'

'We'll carry him if we have to.' Andrew declared resolutely. 'He's not going to be left behind to freeze to death and be devoured by animals.'

'Won't be much left of him to eat.' Archie philosophised. But he was equally steadfast in staying faithful to his pal.

When eventually they arrived in Benavente, it was still recovering from the army's excesses. The town was designated as an advanced stores depot but the distribution of supplies was chaotic as the commissariat lost control of distribution. As a result, wagon loads of goods such as food and items of clothing were dumped outside the city, free for anyone who passed to take whatever they wanted. On learning this, Archie told Andrew to stay and watch over the now sleeping Joshua and emptied all three of the boy's knapsacks. He strapped his own on and carrying the other two by hand, made for the supply area.

He returned with a treasure trove. Salted meat, biscuit, shirts, blankets, shoes and stockings for each along with two bottles of wine. Andrew marvelled at how he was able to haul the load by himself after such a punishing march.

'What riches! Well done, young Archibald!' Andrew hailed his friend.

'Aye, no' bad for now.' Archie wheezed, surveying the stash.

'You're not going back for more are you?' Andrew tried to keep the expectancy from his eyes.

'Of course I am. You just keep a watch over this lot and I'll be back shortly!'

Joshua Whitfield now believed he could not suffer through another ordeal like the one he had experienced since leaving Sahagun.

He lay on a Benavente side street, covered with blankets Archie had taken from the dump. There was not enough enclosed areas left for the men of the 42nd to shelter inside. Many others in a similar state to Joshua lay alongside him, overseen by the regimental surgeon and his assistants. After explaining his symptoms, Joshua was ordered to rest as much as possible while Andrew was told to ensure his friends feet were cared for as best they could. A small bottle of beef extract was left with him. A few drops a day were prescribed to help rebuild his strength.

Joshua didn't think the little bottle sufficient to provide the impetus he required to carry on. His dilemma was he could not bring himself to confess to Andrew or Archie that he believed himself finished. It would hurt them terribly to leave him behind. Andrew, the friend he was closest to and one of life's great worriers, would be particularly distressed.

He was in a state of delirium and remembered little of the final stages before entering Benavente. Both his feet, ankles and shins hurt so much he could no longer stand unaided. He suffered terrible pains in the head which the senior surgeon, a notorious drunk named Ogilvie, described as a rheumatism caused by the severe cold. Joshua was perplexed on being told this as he wore his bonnet and head dress at all times.

Alongside his sick friend, Andrew sat and munched on biscuit and drank from his canteen of water. He still refused to imbibe strong drink. Archie poured wine into his canteen and sipped from the other bottle as he chewed on beef. Joshua accepted some wine but could not bring himself to eat anything.

He felt at rest at last. Lying prone meant his feet and legs didn't hurt as much. He was lightheaded with hunger and exhaustion and this resulted in a mild euphoria, leaving him a false sensation of contentment. He could allow himself to relax a little as he didn't think the army would be going anywhere that day. He was in God's hands now through the will of his two friends and the decisions of his superiors.

Archie brought back more useful items from his scavenging at the dump. He and Andrew discussed how they would divide everything between them to carry, as they now accepted Joshua would have to travel light. Sergeant McGillivray, on his rounds, spoke to them at length about their own state of health and how they intended to deal with Joshua.

'We're not leaving him.' Andrew asserted strongly.

'Aye. Out of the question, Sergeant.' Archie affirmed in agreement.

McGillivray smiled. 'Fair enough, boys. I'm glad to hear that. But I have to warn you. The rumour is that we won't be staying here long. It's likely we'll leave tonight for our next stop.'

'Where's that?' asked Andrew.

'I believe it will be the main supply depot in Astorga. The commander will want us there in two days at the most. The French are gaining but if we reach Astorga in good time, then conditions for a battle may suit us more favourably.'

'A battle!' Archie perked up.

'Yes, Mr Miller. A right auld *stramash* may be had! But what I must do now is find out first if we can spare any room for our sick and injured on the transport wagons. It may be I can find room on a cart for your friend here. If so, I will let you know. If not, then I most heartily endorse your plan of action around Joshua. You have my permission to carry his kit and musket. See he is watered and fed and that his feet remain in good repair. By all means, yes, take turns to give him a *collie buckie*! I am sure you lads will be in fierce competition over who carries him furthest.' Both boys grinned widely.

'No showing off now, Archie. Allow Mr Berry a victory somewhere along the line!' Archie punched Andrew's arm playfully.

'Now, I am off. Oh, and Private Miller. That canteen of yours. I saw what you did with it. I strongly advise you to find another and fill it with water. You're not an old enough soldier yet to march while consuming *unwatered* wine!' McGillivray then left for the commissariat to discuss transport.

'Trust him to spot that.' Archie grumbled ruefully. 'The bugger's got eyes everywhere!'

'Could be good news about Josh if we get him on a cart.' Andrew said with an air of relief.

Archie rubbed his nose. 'Aye, it certainly would. But it's another kind of wagon McGillivray's got in mind for me!'

The sergeant's words proved correct. General Baird announced the division would leave Benavente that day for the next stage to Astorga. John Moore was setting a great pace. They were now trying to outrun the weather as well as the Corsican. Rain, sleet and snow falls had bedevilled them. But so far they'd been spared the extreme blizzards and drifts of mountainous, northern Spain.

The Emperor's troops were now approaching Castrogonzalo, only fifteen mile behind the British, now leaving Benavente. Marshall Soult, robbed of his date with destiny with John Moore, confronted three thousand men of the Marquis of Romaña's army's 2nd division, guarding the bridge at Mansilla, northwest of Sahagun and made short work of them. The rest of the marquis' force along with the sick and injured were sent ahead of the division while the defeated remnant remained to cover their advance. The French now marched unmolested into the large town of Leon to resupply. But as two thousand typhus ridden soldiers of Romaña's army were left there to do nothing more than die, Soult didn't linger.

Davy Baird's last discussion with John Moore in Benavente was most congenial. For all his bluster, Davy could never personally feel anything but fondness for Johnny. At the mention of possible battle at Astorga and his opinion of it, Moore allowed him as always to speak freely.

'Avoid it like the pox, man! If I were you, the only thing in my mind would be which port to make for. Vigo or Coruña.' They were both astride their horses on a gander around the town.

'I haven't decided yet about a fight.' Moore explained himself. 'It will depend on a number of factors. The food supply, condition of our transport system, whether I judge Astorga as being a suitable spot to pitch ourselves, and of course, where the French lie. Also, there's an element of guile here, Davy. The army marches better to battle. If rumours spread about that's where we're headed, it'll put more than just a spring in their step.'

'Devious, Johnny. But clever! Battles are gey risky matters. Those factors you mentioned better come into play, for it's my sure belief you don't want to risk a fight here. And I wouldn't blame you.'

'You're auld blether, Tam Graham, shares your opinion.' Moore chuckled. 'Dinnae ken where I'd be without my favourite auld uncles!'

Baird stared at the nearby hills. He shivered involuntarily. 'So. It's for the off today then?'

'Aye, Davy. With all haste, I beg of you. Don't hang about. There'll be the devil to pay in those Galician hills once the heavy snow begins. And my bones tell me that's not far off now.'

Chapter Eighteen

The town of Astorga was reached in two days on December 30th just as Sergeant McGillivray once again correctly predicted. Perched prominently above a sandy plain, it was renowned far and wide for the quality of its white bread. The town walls, twelve feet thick, dating from the Roman era, were buttressed with solid, elevated towers. Its gothic cathedral was highly regarded for its valuable gold and silver relics though these had now vanished, removed to a place of safety. Shops were plentiful and normally well stocked. Religious houses abounded, as with all large Spanish settlements.

The town itself could not be described as greatly defendable. But the surrounding countryside offered opportunities for ideal defensive positions. Known as the gateway to the Galician mountains, two great passes, the northern defile of Manzanal was the greater, but easier to circumvent while the Foncebadon, in the south, though shorter, was treacherous, rugged and tough to crack.

Joshua rode on an ammunition wagon the entire journey. He had Sergeant McGillivray to thank. His friends also had much to be grateful to him for as it meant being spared lumping Joshua's kit along with their own.

The 42nd suffered another ordeal. The twenty miles marched on the second day were particularly awful as the gradual incline of the road into higher terrain also saw an increase in snowfall. It was Andrew who suffered most this time. He began to feel numbness and tingling in his toes and fingers. He also found it difficult breathing as hard snow blasted into him mercilessly. Archie and Colquhoun steadied him on more than one occasion. Corporal McQuater kept a watchful eye over everyone. But eventually men of the 42nd started to fall out and go missing as in other regiments.

When they arrived at the walled city, footsore, starving and exhausted, they were greeted by a scene similar to a Breughel inspired nightmare.

Unheeding of John Moore's advice to avoid Astorga, the Marquis of Romaña brought the remnants of his shattered force to the town, where they were met by the newly arrived divisions of Generals John Hope and Alexander Mackenzie Fraser. General Baird's division was due to enter next. Unable to do anything about the *fait accompli*, Hope and Fraser were horrified to discover the condition of the Spanish 'army.' Dead soldiers, victims of typhus, lay on every street and corner. All of the buildings were crammed with wounded and dying men. Most of the town's provisions were consumed by the starving Spaniards. Those still on their feet were half naked and without shoes. Many had no weapons and wandered around the town in a dazed state of hopelessness.

The British were appalled at the suffering they witnessed. But they began to feel less sympathy when stories circulated about Spanish soldiers committing crimes against the citizenry in the quest for food and alcohol. The mood changed and unfortunately for the inhabitants of the town, the British began themselves a systematic looting and pillaging on a similar scale to match their outrages in Benavente. Their officers were as useless as before, once again unable to restore order. Though it had to be said, officers were now suffering as much as the men in the conditions.

Disturbances now occurred between the British and Spanish over spoils. Soldiers from one army would arrive at a store being pillaged by those of the other and fights would break out, leading in some instances to fatalities. Spanish soldiers made for the British supply wagons and in one containing their beloved rum, the commissariat, in order to stop it falling into Spanish hands, smashed each cask open. A repeat of the scenes of flowing streets of alcohol in Benavente ensued.

A more significant catastrophe for John Moore ensued when jobsworths in the commissariat, for reasons known only to themselves, in a panic, started destroying priceless supplies of shoes, though most of the army were in desperate need. On word spreading, hundreds, if not thousands of men made for the warehouse where the shoes were set on fire, desperate to get a pair before the entire supply was destroyed. When he learned of the fiasco, the language emanating from Sir David Baird succeeded anything previously recorded by a considerable margin.

Fortunately for Andrew, Archie and Joshua, each had two pairs of shoes thanks to Archie's foresight in Benavente. But they'd taken a battering on the latest march and Andrew was now suffering the consequences.

On arrival in Astorga, the 42nd like most others were unable to find shelter. For many of their men this was the last straw and groups left to find and take what they could. This was a low point for the regiment but Andrew and Archie did not take part. After meeting up again with Joshua, attention now turned to Andrew's welfare. On removing his shoes, they noted the toes on his right foot were very white and cold to the touch.

Joshua asked Archie to empty some of his remaining wine into a cup, then used it to massage Andrew's toes and feet, drying them thoroughly after. Archie looked on, his face etched with concern. They were sitting outside a large building in the town, awaiting the return of Sergeant McGillivray and Colquhoun, desperately seeking to commandeer lodgings for the regiment. Once finished with Andrew's feet, Joshua gestured to Archie to come away with him.

'I hate to have to say this, Archie, but I believe that's the early stages of frost bite in his toes.'

Shocked, Archie stared at Joshua. 'How do you know?'

'When I was being seen in Benavente by the surgeon, I watched him checking another bloke's feet and they were in a similar condition to Drew's.'

'How did he say they should be treated?'

'Rub them with alcohol and keep them warm and dry.'

For the first time since he'd met him, Joshua saw anxiety in Archie's face. 'How do we keep them dry marching on such roads? They're nothing but snow and ice!'

'If not, they'll blacken, become gangrenous and have to be cut off. In the meantime he'll suffer the pains of hell.'

'God almighty! Poor Drew!' Archie wailed. 'How are you feeling?'

'I wasn't bad on the wagon. But as soon as I got off and started walking, my legs hurt again. But I'm going to ask Sergeant McGillivray to give Drew my place on it.'

'But he said we're going to fight a battle here!'

'No chance!' Joshua spat contemptuously. 'This is a bloody plague town! Those dagoes have typhus! That's a killer. We can't stay here long or we'll catch it too.'

'Does *anyone* know what's going on with this army?' Archie howled in frustration.

'You won't get your battle here, mate.'

'Aye. Probably not.' Archie sighed. 'Let's get back to Drew.'

Sir John Moore's first and only meeting with Don Pedro Caro y Sureda, the Marquis of Romaña, initially proved unpleasant. The British commander was in a sweltering rage at the marquis, his own army's conduct, and suffering the symptoms of a very bad cold. The marquis was deeply embarrassed and shame-filled at the condition of his own forces, indeed, at the state of Spain in general. This combined to set the scene for a decidedly edgy confrontation.

Moore and the rearguard were last to enter Astorga. What he witnessed there convinced him, if he had ever any doubt before, he could be sliding ever closer to disaster. Astorga contained two days' supply of food that should have sustained his army before the main depot at Villafranca was reached, fifty miles further distant. But the town was stripped bare by looting and pillaging and denuded by the imbecility of the commissariat department. Of the latter, hanging was too good for the incompetent scoundrels.

The presence of the Spanish army was the thunderbolt that crystallised Moore's ultimate decision. After a distinctly cool shaking of hands with Romaña in the town magistrate's office, Moore kept his face suitably dead pan.

'You're Excellency, a pleasure. Though I must say I did not expect to meet you here.'

Romaña, a man similar in age to Moore, had gravitas and fortunately lacked the usual stuffiness and arrogance for which the Spanish nobility were notorious. While still nominally an ally of France, his fourteen thousand strong army was sent to Denmark as part of an international force defending that country, then in conflict with Britain. Soon after receiving news that the Emperor of France had turned on Spain, employing guile and some èlan, the marquis brought every man back on a fleet of ships under the very noses of the Danes. But that triumph was now very much in the past.

'Thank you, Sir John. I beg your indulgence to forgive the decision circumstances forced upon me to make, for which I fully accept, places neither of us in an advantageous position.'

Somewhat placated at the dignified response, Moore offered his condolences. 'I was sorry to learn of your reverse at Mansilla. It was a gallant affair.'

'It was a gamble, sir. But one the exigencies of war compelled me to take.' He referred to the leaving of the best part of his army to cover the crossing of the bridge at Mansilla. Moore knew in his heart he would have acted exactly the same if facing a similar dilemma.

'If I may be permitted to enquire the intentions of his Excellency now?' Moore requested, moving on.

'As you are aware, the condition of my army at present is a regrettable one.' Romaña began. 'Unfortunately at this time I am not confidant of finding new recruits locally. Nor am I in receipt of any indications from the Junta of supplies or reinforcements marching to my assistance any time soon.' Moore nodded in sympathy. 'Sir John, may I be as bold as to make a suggestion?'

'I am always open to suggestions from friends, your Excellency.'

Romaña smiled gracefully at the compliment. 'There are two mountain passes outside the town. Manzanal and Foncebadon. They represent formidable obstacles to an attacking force. If you were to post your army between both, no general on earth, not even the Tyrant of Paris, would make headway.'

John Moore had already decided to confide in Romaña. The reasoning for his candour was purely political. His almost overwhelming disdain for Spain and its efforts to deal with the invader, their inability to be honest with him at any time over their intentions, and the reality of the situation and loathing he held for Frere and the government in London, were all now clouding his thinking. He understood that even if he got the British army home intact, he would inevitably face a maelstrom of criticism and undoubtedly, a court of enquiry. He would have to explain his interpretation of his original orders. He would have to account for every decision, every piece of lost equipment, lost men, lost monies. He would be held to account for the disgraceful behaviour at Benavente and now here in Astorga. Even his friendship with the duke, as well as favoured status with the king, may not be enough. Such friends might now cut him loose.

Then be damned to them! I was given ambiguous, imprecise orders. Our

Spanish allies have been at best unreliable, at worst an ungrateful parcel of worthless, untrustworthy ingrates. The army I've been given is officered by the most useless articles ever foisted on a commanding general while the men in the main consisted of elements of the worst scum ever to wear the British uniform. And they dare criticise me!

As for Romaña's idea, utterly ridiculous. They would achieve little except allow the enemy time to encircle his army, before putting end to what weather and starvation had begun.

'Your Excellency, I have already decided what I shall do and it does not involve awaiting total destruction of my army. I intend to make for the coast with what is left of my force and there remove it to England.'

Momentarily stunned, Romaña confused his languages. '*Diablo*! Pour Quoi?'

'I believe I just told you why. I will not oversee the destruction of the only British army in existence.'

Gathering himself, the marquis responded. 'Sir John, the Spanish people will never forgive an ally who runs out on them. Your name will forever be enshrined in ignominy.'

'I think not. Perhaps I am in a fortunate position of receiving more encouraging news from the Junta than his Excellency does.'

Moore went on to explain the position of the southern patriots and Bonaparte's denuding of his forces throughout Spain to pursue the British. He outlined his strategy from Salamanca onward and how it was now playing out exactly as planned.

'But Carrion, Sir John! You were prepared for battle. Did your plan encapsulate that eventuality?'

Moore explained the situation with Soult at Saldaña was a blessing the fortunes of war had bestowed upon him, until the news of Napoleon's advances scuppered it.

'It would have been better for the honour of England that you confronted Soult that day.' Romaña replied in a tone of regret mixed with something more personal.

Taken aback, Moore replied, 'What are you inferring by that remark, your Excellency?'

Romaña could not fail to note Moore's testy response. 'That you have not yet crossed swords with the Corsican, yet you plan to scuttle back to your ships like startled curs!'

'I'll be damned to hell if I allow any man to speak to me in that fashion! Yours are the curs, sir. There isn't a single backbone in this entire bloody country!'

'And *your* army Sir John? I have only just learned of the outrage of Benavente. And now here, too. In Astorga The theft of property. The destruction of the homes of decent citizens. The drunken debauchery of the swine that laughingly call themselves disciplined soldiers!'

Rather heroically for a man with such a volatile temper, Moore paused to turn and walked over to the door of the room and opened it.

'Colonel Graham. Will you join us, please?'

Tam Graham along with John Colbourne, Paul Anderson and Harry Percy overheard every word raised. All in shock, Graham's face remained impassive as he entered the room.

Moore closed the door after him. 'You heard all that, Tam.'

'Aye. And it was unseemly from the two o' ye's. You both should be ashamed.'

Remembering his manners, Romaña, spoke for himself and Moore. 'I offer my sincere apologies for this most unfortunate altercation, Colonel Graham. It is war. The base instincts of man are certain to arise on occasion. Sir John, can you please forgive me?'

There was no more relieved man in Spain than the British commander. 'Of course, you're Excellency. As I pray you will accept my apologies.'

Romaña bowed. 'Naturally, sir.'

'Gentlemen. May we all sit down?' Moore, relieved mightily, gestured to a table where food and wine lay prepared for the meeting. As they sat, Tam looked around for another seat. The table was set for two only.

'Colonel Graham, it would be an honour if you will take my chair.' Romaña presented it to Tam who graciously accepted. Moore at something of a loss, scurried over to the door. Just as he was reaching out for the knob, Harry Percy, carrying a chair, pushed forward against the door from the outside, almost bowling the commander of the British army over.

'Christ's sake, Harry! Mind yersel' laddie!' Moore barked at the unfortunate young man.

'Oh, terribly sorry, sir! Thought you might need another one of these!'

'Carry it over to his Excellency, then bugger off, son. Will you?'

After doing as ordered, Percy departed gratefully. Now seated, each man picked out food and Graham poured each of them wine. The temperature in the room now lowered somewhat.

Moore was first to speak. 'You're Excellency. I believe my reasons for every decision I've taken on entering Spain have been the correct courses of action based on the intelligence presented to me. I plead with you to accept my sincerity. If I were to lose the entire army, my government may think twice over allowing another to leave its shores so readily again. My responsibilities are grave and consequently, I cannot countenance such an eventuality.'

Romaña sipped from his glass, then placed it on the table. 'Politics. Invariably it always boils down to the whims of scoundrels.'

'Aye, it is that.' Tam Graham agreed. 'We've all got our lords and masters to obey. If you'll forgive me, you're Excellency, Sir John here has tried to lead this army with one hand tied behind his back. No man ever had a more difficult command. But I for one believe he's made the right decision to evacuate. I'm certain that if you were in his shoes, you'd come to the same conclusion.'

It was Thomas Graham, the diplomat. With just the correct wearied tone and subtle pronouncements he knew were close to every soldier's heart, the wily old man of business played back the ball to the Spaniard perfectly.

'From your point of view, Sir John, I accept Colonel Graham is correct.' Romaña gave a gracious nod to Tam. 'It is a bitter pill to swallow for myself, a Spanish patriot. But I must forego my personal feelings on the matter to the greater good.' He picked up his glass and raised it to the Britons.

'To Scotland!'

Ignoring the carefully hidden barb, Moore and Graham raised their glasses and offered a toast themselves in return to Spain.

'Now, Sir John. Please may we carry on our discussion of your plans?'

'I'm grateful for your understanding, your Excellency.' Moore now in a munificent mood, explained he was sending the light brigade to Vigo to cover any possible advance to Coruña, where he had sent an officer to report on the port's facilities. He advised the marquis to take his army along the way to Orense. He then asked if he could provide the Spanish with anything they required.

The marquis though for a moment. 'Orense, would be a suitable choice. It is a longer route but the terrain is less difficult. I will leave my rearguard at Foncebadon to cover our withdrawal. As for more provisions, sadly you have witnessed personally my army's dishevelment. Clothing, shoes, blankets and a musket for each man would be of great assistance.'

The meeting ended with wine and cigars, Moore and Graham both hugely thankful the prickly affair was at an end. But there was a new and pressing concern on the British commander's mind.

How in the name of God do I provide the supplies to the fellow I promised?

Robert Craufurd never felt so much rage.

He'd brought the rearguard through to Astorga. Bullying, flogging, cajoling, mothering them the entire journey. They repaid him with being part of the japes at Benavente and now here.

He brought them to steep, precipitous ravines where the only way through was for them to sling their Bakers around their necks, sit down and slide through the snow and ice to the bottom. Then back up the other side, the remarkable sight of so many in men in red and green coats scrambling like ants up a steep hillside. They lost many of their horses as they slipped, fell over and spun hundreds of yards below to the starting point. Many wagons and other transport were left abandoned.

Robert personally went up and down the same ravine twice, kicking some of the men and encouraging others with his canteen of rum. He made it his business to be everywhere.

But some of the scenes he witnessed along the way, came perilously close to breaking him. The worst in a catalogue of nightmares were the women and children forced to walk when transport broke down. In his heart he knew he could have allowed them to march with their menfolk. But he understood if he did, it would slow the column down dramatically, causing a knock on effect throughout the division. He was forced to harden an already calloused heart further, despising himself all the more for it.

In Benavente, during the worst of the outrages, he led a small team of ultra-loyal non-coms and private soldiers. These were men he knew and trusted as well as he knew and trusted himself. They prowled the town restoring order in any way they saw fit. Smashing drunken rioters in the face with rifle butts while Robert made good use of a billy club he carried in his baggage. Men of the light brigade caught misbehaving were hauled back to their billets and names recorded for future retribution.

He hoped they'd learned from their folly, but now in Astorga the same villains were performing the same villainy. He sent his squad out again without him this time as he had to attend a hurried commander's conference. On his way now to the magistrate's office, he bitterly regretted the fun he was missing with his chosen men.

'Welcome to you all, gentlemen.' John Moore brought the meeting together after handshakes and the inevitable catch up chat. The room was filled with Henry Paget's cigar smoke. He was suffering from ophthalmia which was affecting him greatly.

'Harry, I'm sorry to learn of your misfortune.' Moore commiserated.

'Damnable luck, Johnny! Means you've got a rotten decision to make.' This was regarding the new temporary commander of the cavalry while Lord Henry recovered his health.

'And you know what that is to be?' Moore replied sorrowfully.

'I do. That bloody fool Slade. Oh hell, he's a pleasant enough chap, but damned stupid! I shall have to rely on Stewart to keep him right till my eyes get better.' This was Charles Stewart, Moore's erstwhile critic and spy for the government.

'I'm sure he will, Harry. I'm sure he will.' Moore agreed. 'Now my lords and gentlemen. I've summoned you all here to impart an update on the situation and provide you with your latest set of orders. I'd like to begin by thanking you all for the fine achievement of bringing your divisions here as scheduled. Unfortunately, the behaviour of this army is deteriorating daily. The scenes in Benavante were abhorrent, only for them to be repeated here. I ask you all to lean heavily on your officers to deal with such issues more effectively. Damn it all, it's part of their duties! We could sully the name of the British army for a hundred years if we don't get to grips with the problem quickly.

'I mention this first because it is highly relevant to what I have to communicate to you now. After great consideration over every issue, I have decided the army will retreat immediately to embarkation at either Coruña or Vigo.' There was a low murmuring among the generals.

Ignoring it, Moore continued. 'I will explain my reasons. First, the situation in regard to supplies is now critical. There were to be two days of food and bread awaiting us here in Astorga. That has now been reduced significantly. You all know why. The issues around transportation and the commissariat are chronic. We have lost many animals and wagons. Too many carters, muleteers and waggoneers are either sick or deserted while the commissariat is no longer worth its name. When we return to England I intend to open up an investigation into that department.' There were approving thumps of the table at the last.

'Secondly, we could not defend Astorga for long for the already mentioned reasons of supply. As for the enemy, there is the great risk Bonaparte may outflank us by taking the road to Pueblo de Sanabria. And gentlemen, I have to state in addition, something obvious to all present. This army needs to recuperate. It cannot rest if it is strung out along two of the most treacherous passes in Europe while awaiting a far superior force in numbers during a harsh winter.

'But my overriding reason for retreat is this. We have achieved our goal. We have brought all of Bonaparte's army in Spain on to us. This will give the Spanish patriots time to reorganise, reform their armies and plot an appropriate strategy. We will embark our army, regenerate a new one from it and return soon to re-join the fight.'

Moore looked around the table. Tam Graham sat next to him and he knew he'd be watching closely various reactions. Moore then gave out his orders for the route of the full retreat. General's Hope and Mackenzie followed by David Baird would leave first light in the morning for Villafranca. The rearguard would now be commanded by Lord Henry's brother, Edward. Robert Craufurd along with Charles Alten would split from the main force and make for Vigo to the west to cover the main body's southern flank against sudden attack. It meant over 3500 of the army's best soldiers struggling on alone.

The Marquis of Romaña had graciously offered his artillery complement of forty-five guns to the British. These would follow with the main body but as each gun took up between 6 -10 animals to pull, meant ammunition wagons would need to be drawn by a collection of horses, mules and oxen. Alongside their own cannon, this meant they would now have to sacrifice most other transport in order to haul their guns. An audible gasp around this last piece of information could be heard among attendees.

'Jesus Christ, Johnny! What do we do with the wounded and the women? It's a death sentence in those hills for the sick!' This from Robert Craufurd.

'Bobby, I've been advised that many of the roads and paths in the mountain are not wide enough for the wagons. Only for smaller carts. We couldn't take them even if we wanted to.' Robert shook his head sorrowfully and reached over for a wine jug to refill his glass.

'I know, gentlemen.' Moore sympathised. 'We will have to leave the most serious cases of our sick and injured here and hope the Emperor provides.'

'Damned if I will!' Davy Baird roared. 'I've seen what those murderin' swine do to our stragglers. I'll carry the boys mysel' if I have to!'

There were grins, *here heres*! and banging of the table all round. Whether this was in jest or in support of the fiery Baird was open to question. Probably both. It certainly relaxed the atmosphere somewhat, which was tense for a time.

'In that case, I leave it to each commander to decide. I wouldn't want to leave any laddie behind either. But we must be pragmatic, gentlemen. I think that's all. Now my friends, to work. And see you all again in Villafranca! General Craufurd, might I have a word with you, please?'

Returning from the conference, Robert was mindful of the last words John Moore said to him after the meeting closed.

'Don't stop, whatever the reason, Bobby. I'm taking a gamble breaking up the army but I believe I have no choice.'

'I see the sense in it, Johnny. Dinnae fash yourself too much.'

Moore drained his glass. 'I'm beginning to think we might just pull this off. It could be tight, but if every part of the army works together, we'll do it.'

'No one could have played such a shitty hand of cards better, man.' Robert commiserated. 'You'll get my backing every step of the way. Especially with those bastards in London.'

Moore grimaced and it wasn't caused by the rather weak wine. 'Christ, Bob, did you have to mention that crew?'

They had one last drink together, shook hands and said their farewells. The two old friends would never meet again

Chapter Nineteen

Napoleon Bonaparte, Emperor of the French, leaned forward on his white horse, staring ahead to the walls of Astorga. *That's it. There's no more to do in Spain. I've learned all I need to know.*

He certainly wasn't about to enter this latest Spanish hovel, infested with typhus along with the usual filth and lice. At halt on the Astorga road less than a kilometre before the entrance to the town, he'd ridden on ahead of his staff officers. They knew their Emperor and when he desired a moment's contemplation on his own, they were well practiced in allowing him the luxury of space and time. Anyway, there was no danger. The English were gone.

If he could, Napoleon would have saluted his latest opponent. Of course, he had quickly grasped what the Englishman's intention were from the very beginning. Incorrect. *Scotsman.* That would have been regarded as an insult to him. Similar to describing himself as French. Not that he ever thought or cared much about his native land. Or his adopted one, for all that either.

It could have been Prussia or Austria. Spain, or Russia. But not England. They've never raised large enough land forces there. An accident of fate made it France. Lucky France. It was the right moment. They were the right people. They understood glory. They understood…

What does it matter? I'm sitting on a horse in Spanish Galicia, freezing my arse off, scratching my piles.

He recalled intelligence reports on the British commander, Sir John Moore. It was one of the very few he'd read that impressed him. An interesting character. He was a '*new man.*' Son of a lowly physician. No real interest. Yet had a fine record of service. Radical ideas. Napoleon regarded himself as the ultimate new man. He knew another when he saw one. This Scot did things differently, thought differently and fought differently. Napoleon knew all about Moore's training of light infantry, the ideas inculcated, the tactics involved. Of course, he had his own, the *Voltiguers*. But Moore was unique, no question. Napoleon shuddered. I don't want to face men like that if I can help it.

Ah, well. He's good. Very good. I'll give him that. Not that Napoleon had any fear or even respect for the English army. The defeat they recently suffered in South America, where they were vanquished by a rabble of half Spanish, half native savages, left him gaping in disbelief on first learning the news. But properly led, any army should be respected. It was his fortune that his enemy's armies were led either by incompetents or dotards. That may not last indefinitely. He was getting older, too. Nearly forty…

Enough of that.

The beautiful white horse was feeling the chill. It won't be long now, my old friend. Don't get anxious. We're going home soon. He looked back towards the army and the staff officers staring at him. They're no longer anxious. They know me so well. He'd learned what he needed to know about his soldiers. On making through the Guadarrama Pass in pursuit of Moore, he and the Imperial Guard endured hellish suffering during terrible blizzards. He'd got off his horse and struggled like everyone else most of the way. He passed down through the column encouraging the men, laughing and jesting throughout the horrendous snow storm. At one point, he put his shoulder against a gun carriage and heaved like any common soldier when it stuck in the road. He hadn't enjoyed himself so much in years.

But there was a purpose to his tom-foolery. He must be certain they could do it. He had to know the limits of glory. With these men, he now knew there were no limits. What was in his mind about the next great challenge ahead was beginning to form splendidly.

He'd secured his empire's western flank in Spain. But what a despicable, degenerate race of superstitious peasants to lord over! Joseph, his beloved brother, wouldn't have too much trouble with them now. Time to start enjoying the perks of kingship again. Not jumping at every shadow. He'd been making headway among the women of his new court to such an extent, one of the many nicknames he'd acquired was *'the cucumber.'*

Napoleon smiled. Filthy sod.

And the English? No need for eighty thousand men to freeze their bollocks off any further. Ah, he's going to get way alright. It looks like it now. Pity though. He'd never fought the British face to face since Toulon. This fellow would have been interesting. Maybe the best yet.

I'll leave it to Soult and the Red-Head. Twenty-five thousand men plus a small reserve should be sufficient. The rest back to Madrid and the south. After all, I left it open, just as you wanted me to, eh, Moore? Clever fellow. I'd like to meet you one day. Share a glass of wine or your vile whisky and discuss infantry tactics. But how are you going to explain it all when you return home? Those petty minded, paper pushing, closed-minded bureaucrats could never understand the brilliance of your strategy. But I did. I took the bait after all. I admit that. Well done. I think I quite admire you, Sir John.

He already had his excuses prepared. Task fulfilled in Spain. The stench of plots in Paris. Austrians getting uppity. Need to return to France urgently to deal with it all. Josephine. A reckoning was required there, too. Napoleon shivered, took a deep breath and sighed. May I never again see this awful country.

But perhaps there shall be a next time, Sir John Moore. That would be quite something.

Chapter Twenty

Unfortunately for Andrew and Joshua, neither of them would be allowed the luxury of riding on transport. There was only enough wagons and carts for supplies and ammunition. Any few spaces remaining were reserved for women and children. Even the sick had to walk now. The days ahead for Andrew Berry and the rest of the army would be regarded by those who survived the ordeal as the true beginning of the retreat.

Since leaving Astorga, they worked their laborious and agonising way up a twelve mile gradient to the summit of Monte Teleno, before entering the Manzanal Pass after which they would gradually descend seven miles into the Vierzo valley. In the mountainous landscape of twisting and treacherous roads already knee high in snow, Andrew, his two friends and the regiment grew to negate everything inconsequential in their lives barring the placing of one foot after the other into the snow and following the men before them. Their ordeal on the roads was complicated further by the amount of abandoned human beings and wreckage from the divisions ahead of Sir David Baird, left strewn in their wake.

Bullocks lying dead beside their carts, the sick and injured occupants unable to leave them unassisted, their hopeful pleas to passing soldiers for help now disregarded. Horses and mules either slipping or shot then pushed over hanging peaks to end up lying in grotesque attitudes below, further hampering the army's progress. Officer's baggage discarded. Equipment thrown aside. Men, woman and children falling away in ever increasing numbers at the roadside. So many to die, victims of the savage elements.

On Andrew marched. He had no thought of anything in his head other than to try and stay alive until the next stop. No one knew when or where it would be but as night fell, on that first day, conditions became more extreme as the temperature plummeted further. Groups of men who stopped to light a fire were ordered to continue on by officers and non-coms. They were encouraged by being told that the next town was up ahead, just a mile or so after the turn in the road. Andrew told himself that he only needed to make the next few hundred yards and he would stop. When the halt failed to materialise, he was at first baffled, then concerned as unwelcome thoughts intruded he could not block out. We're lost. They don't know where they're going. We're going to walk around in circles in the dark till we freeze to death.

The conditions made men thirsty. Those who still carried water or alcohol were the fortunate ones. Others lacking that luxury made the understandable, though potentially fatal error of sucking on snow. Inevitably, men soon began to suffer the early stages of dysentery. Their famished and slowly emaciating bodies, rapidly shedding natural fat, became an ideal breeding ground for the dread illness.

Fortunately, Andrew and his friends, under strong advice from Sergeant McGillivray, stuck to their own canteens supplies and used them sparingly. He warned they couldn't be refilled until they halted at the next settlement.

By late that night they approached a dark, soulless collection of mountain huts and fouled walkways that was the village of Comarros. Already hundreds of men before them had passed through. The remaining stragglers and the sick had already pulled off all the residents doors, stolen furniture, smashed down fences and taken anything else combustible to build fires. The luckless inhabitants stood outside their homes as soldiers entered uninvited, looking for a space to drop down and collapse in exhaustion.

Standing outside one such dwelling place, Archie, with his arm around Joshua, who was slumped against him with his eyes closed, turned to Andrew.

'We've got to get him indoors or near a fire or he won't last the night.'

His mind numb with fatigue, Andrew focussed on one of the smaller children standing next to his or her parents. He couldn't tell if it was a boy or a girl, but its face stared in large eyed puzzlement at him. He looked across to the child's father whose eyes seemed to plead *there is no room here. Please go away and leave. The French will punish us if we help you.*

'None of the three of us will make it.' He answered almost to no one. Then he composed himself. 'We won't get in here. Best to try and find a fire and stay close to it.'

'Here. Hold him will you?' Archie passed Joshua over to Andrew. He then unslung his musket and Joshua's and unfastened his own knapsack. 'Right. Take these. I'll have to carry him.'

Wearily, Andrew grabbed the equipment and Archie took hold of Joshua who was barely conscious, by the lapels of his coat. Andrew took both muskets by the straps in one hand and carried the knapsack with the other.

'Joshua! Joshua! Wake up!' Archie urged. 'Oh, come on, Josh. Wake up, man!' He shook him gently back and forth until finally there was a drowsy response.

'What do you want now? I need to sleep. Just to sleep…'

'You need to get on my back first, then you can sleep. Come on now.'

Somehow between the three of them they managed to get Joshua loaded onto Archie's back, giving him a *collie buckie*. Before they began to leave to search the village for somewhere to shelter, they heard a voice shouting Andrew's name repeatedly. The young man, barely cognisant at first in his exhaustion, turned his tired head side to side to locate the sound.

'Where are you off to, boys? Is it another wee stroll in the darkness, you're wanting?' It was Killane, a burly, steadfast Irishman from County Longford and best friend of Colquhoun. They were both married men with children who wisely insisted their dependants remain in Lisbon after they left for Salamanca.

'Oh, Tomàs! We're trying to find somewhere to rest up.' Andrew replied, much relieved to see him.

'Well, I'm thinking you won't be finding it over there with them from the 50th.' Killane pointed out. 'Come over with us, your own good muckers. Your sergeant sent me to find you.' He then noticed Joshua. 'Ah, the wee fella isn't looking too healthy. Here, hand him over to me, Archibald. You look well out of it yourself.'

Archie was happy to pass Joshua over to the huge Irishman, who took him in his arms as if a child.

'Right. Follow me, *a grà*. Your stately home awaits. There's no maid, mind ye. You can't have everything in this man's army!'

There was no shelter, but the next best thing. Sergeant McGillivray, Corporal McQuater, Colquhoun and two of the company officers stood warming themselves against a fire created from detritus foraged from the village. A kettle heating merrily was being stirred by one of the company men, Willie Angus, with his bayonet.

'Welcome to the mansion house, my children!' The boys were greeted warmly by Sergeant McGillivray. The officers chuckled heartily.

'And where have you three been, Mr Berry? There's nae lassies to be found here!' Captain Crozier of their company, joked. Andrew and his success with Gabriela in Salamanca had evidently reached the officers mess.

'No such luck, eh, Archie, lad?' McGillivray nudged the Fifer in the ribs.

'I ken, Sergeant. Maybe in the next town!'

'Aw, the laddie lives in hope, boys!' McGillivray joshed.

The cheer and fellowship was as an elixir to Andrew's failing spirits. He looked over at the sergeant's smiling face and experienced a strange, *familiar* sensation come over him about the man. It was a feeling of comfort, of security and safety. Almost as if as long as this man was close, he would survive. He'd see him home.

'What'll we do with this bundle of bones, Sergeant?' asked Killane, standing with the sleeping Joshua in his arms.

'Oh, aye. Put him down here. Aye, close to the fire. Andrew, Archie. Make his bed roll up. Quickly now, lads.' The two boys kicked away a pile of snow where the sergeant pointed and made up a bed with the blankets from Joshua's knapsack.

McGillivray complimented their efforts 'That'll do grand. Just lay him down, now. No. Dinnae bother about something to eat. He's out cold, the laddie. Let him sleep.'

Content that Joshua was well wrapped and close to the fire as possible, Andrew stood and put his hands out to warm them, Archie following suit.

'I'm afraid it's just a wee bitty oats, lads. But it'll warm yer bellies.' Angus stood with the boiling kettle. 'Bring ower yer mugs.'

Nothing had tasted better in his life as the smooth oaten porridge slid warmly down Andrew's throat. He licked every morsel and left the mug clean. He remembered he still had some bread in his knapsack. That would have to do for breakfast.

'How far to the next halt, Sergeant?' Archie enquired after finishing his porridge.

'There's a town ahead called Bembibre. We'll stop there, but only for a rest because we have to make Villafranca soon, as that's where the food stocks are. Another day or so maybe, boys. Now, you two get to your beds. No duty for you tonight. Just plenty of shut eye and no snorin', the both o' ye's!'

Grateful to obey the sergeant's order, Andrew, in his exhaustion had just amount of strength left to remove his shoes and stockings, laying them over his knapsack close to the fire to dry off. Archie followed his lead. They then pulled off the tattered foot wear of Joshua who was hard asleep and soon after, they joined him, dead to the world.

Chapter Twenty - One

The following morning, the 31st December 1808, Andrew awoke to the usual sounds of the regiment preparing to move out. His entire body felt chilled on awakening, his blankets crackling with frost. He sat up and rubbed his arms, scratched at what he hoped wasn't the onset of lice, and immediately felt the familiar strange numbness in his toes.

He pulled across the blanket and examined his feet. He noted the tips of his third, fourth and fifth toes of his right foot, cold and lifeless over the last few days, now bore a faintly blue tinge. He rubbed them gently but there remained little sensation. Andrew wondered if this indicated something malignant. The toes on his left foot were red and sore and a couple of nails were hanging loose to the side. He picked these off with a grimace from the sharp stabbing pains incurred.

'I'd watch those if I were you, mate.' Joshua, lying in his blankets across from Andrew, observed.

'I've never seen my feet like that before.' Andrew indicated the right foot. 'What do you think it could be?'

'Wouldn't like to say.'

'Have you any idea? Do you think its frostbite?'

Joshua sat up on his elbow. 'I think it is, Drew. I'm really sorry.'

Andrew bowed his head. 'I suppose it shouldn't be a surprise. What must I do?

'I believe you need to keep them dry and warm. Rubbing them with snow helps. But it's best you see the surgeon.'

'They cut your toes off if they get frostbitten.' Andrew mused dolefully.

'Not necessarily, mate. If you catch it in time, you should be aw'reet.' Joshua assured him. 'Dinna think like that, man.'

Wanting to change the subject, Andrew turned to Archie's empty bedroll. 'He's up early.'

'Aye. He's away to talk to McQuater about something.'

'How are you feeling?'

Joshua head dropped. 'I'll be fine.' Just as his name was brought up, Archie arrived back with news.

'I've just spoken to the corporal. He says Captain Crozier's given permission for us to discard anything from our kit we don't need. We're also allowed to help each other carry our stuff. Muskets included.'

Andrew perked up from his gloom. 'That's good to hear.'

Aye,' Archie agreed. 'I've been thinking. My knapsack's ready to fall apart. What I say is, we rummage through our kit, throw out what we can't use, keep the necessaries and stuff the rest in the other two and dump mine. That way one of us always gets a break from carrying it.'

Joshua nodded in agreement. 'Makes sense.'

'Right. Let's get to it. Oh, and another thing. McQuater said there isn't any food left, so whatever you're carrying has to last till the next stop. This Bembibre place.'

The morning played out as the day before. They continued to snake around mountain roads as the wind dropped and were hit again by the return of sleet. Andrew hated sleet more than rain or snow. It was as if being pelted by tiny musket balls, which, no matter how he turned his face to avoid the merciless sting, always got through, leaving him sore and tender.

The roads had hardened and the ice made them deadlier to navigate. Many slipped including Joshua and Andrew. Joshua was not carrying a knapsack and fell hard on his unprotected back. Archie pulled him up onto his feet, but he had bruised himself and stretched muscles around his spine and under his right arm.

This proved a minor disaster. Joshua wasn't carrying any kit as he was struggling again with pains in his head, shins and ankles. Andrew and Archie walked at either side of him, taking it in turns to swap Joshua's musket between them to carry. They were forced to march at his pace, which in reality was a pain wracked amble, and became tedious as he often had to stop to rest up. It would be a hard march to Bembibre, 20 miles ahead. With the fall, there wasn't an area of Joshua's body that didn't now cause him discomfort. A sharp ache in his side developed. This, along with a sore back and legs, growing hunger and thirst, was wearing him down. He also developed a painful cough.

But he was not alone. Everyone was slowing down. More men fell behind. Officers continually moved up and down the line, offering encouragement. But many stopped and wouldn't get up for all their superiors efforts to assist them.

They halted for rest at midday, just as Joshua's head pains worsened. Archie went off to speak with Andrew.

'I think we need to start carrying Josh now. How's your feet?'

The question was a surprise to Andrew. 'Did he say something to you?'

Archie's face grew stern. 'Look, Drew. You shouldn't be keeping things like that from me. This is serious. I have to know how you are.'

'I'm alright. Don't mind me. How are you doing?' Andrew replied sarcastically.

Archie took a deep breath. 'I only asked you. Don't get cheeky with me, Drew. This is about living and dying and we can't afford to fall out over daft things. Do that and none of us will ever see home again.'

Andrew cursed himself for his stupidity and immediately apologised. He then revealed his fears. 'You asked about my feet. Josh thinks its frostbite.'

'Aye, that's what he told me. Are you going to see the surgeon?'

'I'll give it till we get to the next place.'

Archie peered hard into Andrew's eyes. 'Be sure you do. Are you up for carrying Josh, though? Can you do it?'

Andrew spoke honestly. 'I've sworn to myself that I'll never leave him. I won't leave either of you. Sergeant McGillivray's counting on me. But I promise to tell you everything from now on. You're right. It's too dangerous to keep secrets from each other.' He stuck out his hand and they shook solemnly.

The fading embers of their childhood had now turned to ashes. Out of mortal necessity, they attained wisdom. The boys had become men.

As they approached Bembibre that evening, Joshua's condition worsened. He now couldn't walk on his own and both pairs of shoes had fallen to pieces. It was Andrew who was carrying him as they began to discern feint echoes from ahead that grew louder the closer they advanced towards the town. As they made their exhausted approach to Bembibre, the sound revealed itself to be the drunken revelry of thousands of men and women drinking themselves collectively into a stupor.

The divisions ahead, starving, exhausted, resentful, had discovered the wine vats of Bembibre were kept in underground vaults under its main streets. They were quickly unloaded and there began an orgy of drinking, looting, sexual licence, either willing or decidedly not, violence and mayhem that made the despoliations of Benavente and Astorga pale in comparison.

Soldiers lay about in heaps, so drunk the alcohol was running red from their noses and mouths. Couples lay copulating freely with great abandon. Shrieks and screams, shouts, curses, drunken singing rent, the evening air. There wasn't an officer in sight. They had abandoned all vestige of responsibility in order to seek a billet for the night in yet another crowded little town. They were becoming expert in doing so.

Sir David Baird, at the head of his division, gaped at the scene in astonishment. For a man normally so loquacious, he was quite literally, speechless. He finally broke his silence.

'There'll be hell to pay for this.' He turned to his staff officers riding with him. 'If any man from this division is found among this rabble, I'll have him flogged till there isn't a scrap of skin left. I'll take the fuckin' lot off the bastard!'

He rode on through the human detritus, lashing out furiously at any drunken figure who came too close. His rage was elemental because he believed all of it avoidable.

The 42nd were ordered not to enter. There wasn't anywhere left for them to bed down anyway as they laid camp outside the town limits. Colonel Stirling, a good man, beloved of his regiment, declared Bembibre out of bounds on pain of dire punishment.

Bitterly disappointed at having to spend another night in the open, Andrew vented his frustration at Archie.

'What a bloody shambles. Outside in the night with no shelter again!'

'Mister Berry, 'tis a sin so it is! Do you wish to address your concerns to the colonel? Or does a man like yourself wish to put his complaint in writing?'

As always, Sergeant McGillivray was lurking. But Andrew was beyond caring. He'd had enough of what he considered the general incompetence, inefficiency and downright mismanagement as he saw it of the army.

'Pish to that! We're starving, freezing, and they expect us to camp without cover again! Joshua needs shelter! He can't go on like this! *We* can't go on like this.'

'You'll go on like this until we tell you different, lad. That's what it is to be a king's man.' McGillivray replied evenly.

'I didn't enlist to become a mindless slave!'

'Alright, Andrew. That's enough. I want you to start making camp. Check your muskets are clean and dry, then start looking over your feet. You've still got a way to go yet and they need to be cared for. So stop wasting breath letting your belly ache and start behaving like a soldier. Don't make me ashamed of you, Private Berry!'

Tired to the depths of his soul, Andrew was able to mumble an apology. He knew he could be flogged for his outburst. Fortunately, the 42nd was not that type of regiment.

'That's alright then.' McGillivray acknowledged Andrew's contrition. 'I know you're exhausted. We all are. But think about the scum displaying themselves in the town like wanton savages. No respect for anything. Not themselves, not their mates, their superiors, their country or their king! We are not like that in this regiment. You certainly are not. Keep the head, lad. Save your anger for the French. They are the real enemy you must direct your ire at. Now, remember it's Hogmanay. A happy new year to you, lads. Stay sober!'

McGillivray left to organise the regiment's encampment. Wearily, Andrew and Archie followed their by now well practiced routine of assisting Joshua before they themselves saw to their own requirements. It was just another day to them.

Despite Sergeant McGillivray's belief in the strong moral character of his regiment, that night saw a number of men of the 42nd break ranks and enter the town seeking the pleasures it had to offer.

Colonel Stirling was deeply hurt to learn of the betrayal. He spoke to his senior company officers and demanded a detachment from each be sent in to bring the offenders back to face justice.

Captain Crozier summoned Sergeant McGillivray immediately and translated the colonel's wishes to him. Outraged, McGillivray immediately searched out Corporal McQuater, Colquhoun, Killane and two loyal bruisers, Dod Melvin and Hugh Scott. The group entered into the town armed with clubs and halberds.

Andrew lay awake. It was too cold to sleep despite the fire burning merrily near him. They fed that evening on a quarter of a loaf of bread and a few scraps of pork. In the two days since leaving Astorga, they had eaten barely enough in total to call one average meal. He was deeply disenchanted and desperately wanted to leave the army when he returned home. How he would achieve this was a conundrum that wracked him to his core. Desertion was out of the question as the punishments were dire. He thought about his toes. If they were frostbitten and had to be amputated, was that a price worth paying for a medical discharge? But what would he do then, return home to sweeping out stables? Only now as a cripple. Who would want him? Would Gabriela? She would now be beyond his reach forever.

He thought of how they tried to communicate their feelings towards each other, though neither could speak each other's language. He was in love with her and told her so. He learned the Spanish words for 'I love you.' She had told him the same in English. But had he presumed too much? What could he offer her? He was a poor soldier after all. He wished Joshua was well enough for him to confide in. They spoke often of such matters. He couldn't do the same with Archie. All he wanted was to winch lassies. That's all they meant to him. He then realised that though he now hated being in the army, it had brought Gabriela into his life. Thinking of her made him feel valued. He was important to someone on this earth who was not of his blood. He was foolish to think that he would never see her again. Of course he could! The army would return to Spain and they would undoubtedly pass through Salamanca and he would meet her there. Then he would marry her, and take her with him like so many other soldiers did. She would accompany him back to Scotland as his wife when the war was over and they would live happily together.

He lay smiling at these happier thoughts, and eventually drifted off to sleep. It was after all the dawn of a new year. There was always hope.

Sergeant McGillivray returned from his efforts to bring back the pleasure seekers badly beaten and carried semi-conscious over Killane's shoulder.

They hadn't been long into their search when Scott thought he saw a 42nd bonnet ducking into a side street. The patrol turned into it and hadn't gone twenty yards when they found a group of drunk and semi-inebriated soldiers from various English regiments. A fracas soon broke out after Sergeant McGillivray asked them if they'd seen any men from the 42nd. In response were drunken mutterings of all Scotch bastards should fuck off back to the shit hole they came from, when Melvin received a punch from a man of the 38th regiment and a vicious brawl erupted. The attackers, a group of a dozen or so, laid into the highlanders armed with musket butts, clubs, fists and anything else they could lay their hands on.

The 42nd contingent used their halberds to deadly effect, inflicting real damage on their attackers. But McGillivray early on in the fray received a terrible crack from behind on the skull from a musket butt. He then suffered a brutal stomping as he lay on the ground. Colquhoun leaped to protect the stricken man while McQuater and the other three formed a defensive shield.

Eventually they made their way back to the main street, the alcohol consumed by their assailants and a ferocious fight back, particularly from Killane, Melvin and Scott, having a decisive effect on the encounter.

The battered and bruised party along with their seriously injured man returned to the encampment outside the town, and immediately sought the attention of the surgeon.

The drunken riots aftermath lay for all eyes to see that New Year's day of 1809. Little effort was made to rouse the intoxicated, whose numbers ran as high as a thousand. The sickness of retreat had now affected the officer corps, effectively abdicating all responsibility for disciplining their men. Hope, Fraser and Baird all demanded more from the regimental colonels who passed down orders from the company commanders to the army's weak link, the junior officers, whose role was to enforce order. In the main they failed in this regard entirely. The results of their incompetence were lying about in puddles of alcohol and vomit throughout the town, and along the trail from Sahagun in the form of stragglers, dead women and children and tons of lost equipment, supplies and animals.

There were a small number of regiments who remained disciplined. The Guards, of course. The reliable 20th regiment under the impressive Robert Ross. The artillery. The reserve under Edward Paget. The German legion's conduct was impeccable. Up until Bembibre, the 42nd behaved with great credit. But their reputation was now sullied. Colonel Stirling rounded up twenty-five of the miscreants and would exact suitable punishment that day.

Hope and Fraser's divisions were due to set off for Villafranca that morning. Baird's was to await sight of the rearguard under Moore before starting out on the next stage of the retreat. Andrew and his two friends took advantage of the extended rest they now enjoyed by paying close attention to their deteriorating kit. Archie was granted permission to enter the town and fill canteens with alcohol. There remained a veritable river of wine available and Archie took full advantage. In the absence of supplies, a tot from their canteens was all that would sustain the men for the next hike. The Fifer became a popular figure for a time.

Captain Crozier was pleased with the reports he was receiving from McGillivray and McQuater on Andrew and Archie's military progress. Two fine lads with leadership qualities who would make excellent non-commissioned officers. Assets indeed to the regiment. It was about the only modicum of positivity Colonel Stirling enjoyed at present.

Sergeant McGillivray certainly featured highly in Andrew's thoughts. The news of the evening's events had trickled through. Concern for his welfare plus extracting retribution on the scum who beat him was the talk of the regiment. McGillivray was highly respected and well liked. Andrew learned that Captain Crozier found a space in the town's makeshift hospital for the sergeant. He was treated by the surgeon and though not in any immediate danger, was not to be moved for at least 24 hours.

By midday, Sir David Baird's was the only division left in Bembibre. Moore's reserve were not expected till late afternoon. Joshua was left to rest and sleep under Andrew's supervision. But that young man worried over McGillivray. There was a very real possibility he would be left behind and taken prisoner by the French should he not recover his strength in time. Andrew wanted to request permission to be allowed to stay with the sergeant, to watch over him in the hope he would improve enough, then assist him back to the column.

But that meant leaving Archie with Joshua. He didn't know how to disentangle the problem until it was resolved for him after speaking with Killane. The big man was sorting through his bedraggled kit when Andrew approached him.

'Good day to you, Tomàs.'

'Why, it's the bold Drew Berry. How are you, my bonnie lad?'

'Fine. Is there any news on the sergeant?'

The Irishman was attempting to stitch the soul of a shoe hanging loose. He placed it on the ground beside him and sighed. 'It's the bare feet for me, *a grà.* That'll never stick.'

'Sorry to hear that. I'm reduced to wearing my spares now. But I heard there'll be plenty in Villafranca.'

'And palaces and golden carriages and fine ladies for us all. Never believe what a general tells you, Andrew.'

'Tomàs. The sergeant. Have you heard anything?'

'He won't die but he won't be back on his feet for a few days. Dod and Hugh are going to stay with him as long as they can while rounding up as many of the drunken fools as possible that have shamed the good name of this dear regiment. The bastards can look forward to getting their arses kicked all the way back to us, before the colonel strips the meat from their backs.'

'Is he going ahead with the floggings?' Andrew asked in some trepidation.

Tomàs looked at him directly. 'Oh yes, lad. You can be certain of that.'

Andrew was relieved to learn a plan was in place for the sergeant but less pleased to hear about the mass punishments. He along with the entire regiment would have to witness them. He had never seen a flogging. In fact, the number of floggings in the army in recent years had declined somewhat. The reforms of the duke were bedding in and new, younger generals with different ideas were beginning to have affect. They still occurred however, and there was as yet no indication they would not continue to do so.

After he left Killane, Andrew returned to Joshua. It was early afternoon. All he had eaten so far that day was the other half of the now stale loaf he'd started on the day before. Deciding for reasons of research to try the contents of his canteen Archie had filled, he sipped a few drops of the strong drink he previously abhorred, and found it surprisingly refreshing. He was not fooled. He understood the demon was clever, that continuing to swallow a little more of the apparently pleasant but harmless juice, led to shame and ungodliness. So he wisely quit while he was ahead.

'You're not weakening and looking for comfort in strong drink are you, Private Berry?' Andrew looked up at Corporal McQuater staring down at him.

'Certainly not! I was merely investigating its properties.' Andrew replied, greatly put out at the notion.

'I'm glad to hear of it, for what would Sergeant McGillivray say if he knew you were imbibing?'

'I'm not! There isn't anything to tell him.'

'Then you can assure him yourself in person. He wishes to speak with you.'

'Is he much better?' Andrew asked hopefully.

'You can find that out yourself. He's waiting for you. Take your canteen. It's thirsty work walking the long, lonely steps to the infirmary.'

Andrew jumped to his feet. 'Can Archie come with me?'

McQuater put an arm out. 'No, Drew. It's you alone he wishes to talk with. Private Miller will remain to watch over Mr Whitfield.'

Andrew replaced the lid of his canteen, put on his bonnet and followed the corporal to the hospital.

Chapter Twenty – Two

It was in the offices of the local council, filled to bursting. Fortunately, befitting his rank, Sergeant McGillivray was given a room to himself, albeit a small drying cupboard, where a cot was set up for him. It wasn't much, but it was dry and warm. Best of all, it was at the end of the building, looking out behind the town and not into the bedlam of the main street.

They entered the room where a candle lay burning, providing an eerie light. McQuater knelt down at the side of the cot.

'Xander. Are you well? Andrew's here.'

Unprepared for the sight, Andrew gazed down at a man with a bandaged head in a dirty white shirt, the sleeves rolled up, propped up in bed with his head slumped forward to the right. His face was scratched and bruised, his top lip heavily swollen. There was stitching above his left eye, the knuckles on one hand red and angry.

McGillivray, slowly stirring, moved his head round to the front and opening his eyes wearily, gazed upon on the young man standing before him.

'Andrew. Good day to you. Bless you, Donald McQuater. May I trouble you for some water?'

'I have some wine in my canteen, Sergeant.' Andrew offered quickly.

'Picking up bad habits, Drew?' It was the first time the sergeant referred to him in the shortened, more intimate form of his name.

'I tried a few drops. I'm only going to drink it if truly necessary.' He hurriedly confessed.

'It's necessary now, lad. Pour me a small one, if you will.' Andrew did as he was asked into a small cup by the bed. He handed it over.

'Do you want me to help you?'

'Eh? No. I've been drinking for years.' McGillivray took a sip and painfully replaced the cup on the floor beside him. 'Quite the expert now.'

'I'll leave you to it, then, eh, Xander? Anything you need, just ask mind.' With that McQuater took his leave.

Andrew stood awkwardly at the door of the room as the corporal left the two alone. He looked about him in the candle light and saw only murk and sickness. What an awful place to lay ill, he thought.

McGillivray noticed the boy's disquiet. 'Aye. It's not quite your father's house with the fine view of the hills, is it?'

'No.'

'William was content to stay there. No place else interested him. Your father had no ambition. Nor imagination either.' McGillivray sighed. 'But he was trustworthy and honourable. And the first born.' He smiled slightly. 'I see some of him in you.'

Andrew moved towards the cot. 'Who *are* you?' He whispered.

'You've suspected something about me, surely?'

Andrew thought of the first time he met McGillivray. How discomfited he appeared when he mentioned where he came from.

'Are you from Barbauchlaw, too?

McGillivray smiled. 'Alexander Berry was. I am not.'

'Who was that?'

'Look at me, Andrew. Forget the scars. Have you ever really *looked* at me?' Andrew stood still, unable to move. 'Come over and sit by me here. Don't be a stranger, lad.'

He made himself move the step or two forward and sat over the edge of the cot. The candle was only a few feet from him as the bed-ridden man followed his every movement.

'You have the same eyes as your mother. She's the one you resemble most. Maybe that's why I've felt close to you. More than you being my brother's son.'

Andrew felt a chill run through him as though he were naked and sprayed with the sleet of Galicia. Then, as he thought on what he just heard, he knew many questions were now about to be answered.

'You're *Sandy*.'

McGillivray smiled in recollection. 'I was called Alec by the family. Sandy was Libby's name for me.'

'She calls you that still. You are my *uncle*!' Andrew said in astonishment.

'I am that, Andrew. But she would rather you never knew. And your father certainly wouldn't. I wronged him badly. He didn't deserve it. He was born an inoffensive soul. I was the opposite.'

'What happened' Andrew asked.

'I'll need another drink first before I tell you. Hand me the cup, Drew.'

Andrew was perceptive enough to understand he should not have asked the question. That its answer may reveal something to him he was better not knowing. That he would carry with him forever, like a canker. Like frostbitten flesh.

McGillivray drank from the cup. 'Does it hurt badly?' The young man enquired.

The older man rested back on his pillows. 'The skull is broke and there is a concussion. If I get up to walk, I may swoon like a lassie. In a day or so my strength may return. But I will suffer spells of sleepiness and may fall unconscious for a while. Not ideal with the French army about to arrive anytime.'

'Dod Melvin and Hugh Scott are to remain with you until you regain your strength.'

'Most kind of them.' There was a silence. Andrew was grateful for though he desperately wanted McGillivray's explanation in full, he dreaded it also. He decided to come in at a slant.

'Why did you choose a different name? You are Alexander Berry. Not McGillivray.'

'I took the name from a stone in Bridgecastle Kirk yard. He too was Alexander. It seemed predetermined to me.'

Andrew seized the moment. 'You were going to tell me how the predetermination came about.'

'Oh, yes. The *scandal*. That's what it became known as, I believe.' McGillivray stopped speaking, formulating the explanation in his mind. 'Your father was betrothed to your mother. I am William's younger brother. But I watched her eyes fall to mine more often than they fell on his. The inheritance of the business would be William's of course. It was her prize. Her security. But her heart was for me. Always.'

McGillivray then confessed his life's one secret. 'Your brother, Robert. I am *his* father, not William.'

Andrew stood up from the cot in shock. 'How can that be? You lie! My mother is not wanton. How dare you accuse her so?'

McGillivray observed Andrew's reaction with bemusement. 'That's your father. You're Billy at this moment.'

'Be damned to you! I am my own man. Any loving son of his mother would react as I do. You are mistaken. Your unnatural desire for her blinds you to reason!'

'You wanted to know, Andrew. And I've told you. It's a bitter thing to learn but it should not remove in the slightest the joy of the purest form of love possible you have for her. She was, and remains, the love of my life. I wish dearly it wasn't the case, for I should be a happy man today. She is not to blame. William is not to blame. The fault lies entirely with myself.'

Andrew sat down again, absorbing what he had heard. It did explain much. He knew in his heart his mother bore no real love for his father. All she had borne for him were children. But not the first. There was so much to ask, but he began with the obvious.

'Does my father know he's not Robert's father?'

'Yes. He knew.'

'Who else?'

'Does it matter?'

Andrew thought. 'No. Probably not.'

'What more do you wish to know?'

'Why have you told me all this?'

McGillivray stared at Andrew for a moment, then pointed across the room. 'Bring my knapsack over to me.'

Andrew turned to where he indicated to a French infantry soldier's knapsack lying on the floor at the side of the door. It didn't resemble the British version and was of a more practical design. Regarded as a prized item, veteran soldiers looked to retrieve them first from French corpses before raking through their usually empty pockets.

Andrew lifted it and handed it over. 'Where did you get that?'

'Alexandria. It is yours for the moment. You can give me it back when I re-join the column.'

It was a valuable gift as they were coveted by soldiers who suffered the awful British version. Andrew was pleased to accept it.

'Thank you, Serge…Uncle.'

McGillivray looked up with a grin. 'Never call me that in public, lad.'

Andrew watched as his uncle rummaged in the knapsack. Wondering what on earth he was looking for, his curiosity was then answered when a letter was handed to him addressed to his parents.

'I want you to take that home with you when you return. Give it to your mother first and allow her to decide if she wishes your father to read it. It is my testament. It is the truth of my life. I know I broke her heart. She should know that I carried on. That I bettered myself and found a modicum of peace.'

'They know you went for a soldier. That's why they had such an objection to me joining.'

'Andrew, you bear the finest qualities of your mother and none of the poor ones of your father. You have none of my faults but you do have my inquisitiveness and ambition. The desire to go out into the world and become what you want to be. You are a better man now than either myself or your father were at your age.'

Andrew now understood a little better why his uncle revealed himself. But his puzzlement remained. Did he have a premonition of death? Did he believe he had to present his truth before Andrew learned another version of it? It seemed unlikely that his parents would change and reveal the truth of their lives to him. Why should they? He admitted he was tempted to read the letter himself. But what more could his uncle reveal that was less shocking than he already had?

He was glad he had told him. It did explain the strange feeling of disconnect he always felt for his brother. Though only a little less than two years older, they were worlds apart in outlook, their minds entirely different. It appeared to be a case of history repeating itself. But not quite. Andrew could never envisage himself taking his brother's wife. Or could he truly be certain of that?

'I think it best you return now, Drew.' McGillivray was now tiring, his head sinking down on the pillows. 'It is indeed encouraging that the two lads will be here to look after my welfare. Do not fret over me. Set your mind to the march and get home. Stay close to Archie. A strong and reliable young man. I will pray for Joshua. Pray for you all. With God's grace, all three of you will come through this challenge together.'

Andrew strapped on the knapsack, his mind reeling. 'Goodbye, Uncle. I will pray for you. Night and day. Thank you for all your kindness. I will see you at Villafranca?'

'Aye, lad. Watch for me coming down the road.'

*

The reserve finally arrived at Bembibre with Sir John Moore and Edward Paget at the head of the column, Thomas Graham close behind. It was late afternoon, 1st January 1809.

Containing the best behaved and most disciplined regiments, it experienced very little straggling. Part of its duties was to round up laggards from the divisions ahead and integrate them until the army reformed again. They assisted as many women and children left behind as best they could, but their numbers were dwindling. The men of the reserve encountered many frightful scenes of souls beyond nothing but God's grace that would remain with them until their dying days.

Ordering the halt, Moore, Paget and Graham unhorsed and were greeted formally by Sir David Baird, not far from where the 42nd were encamped. Andrew and Archie were keen to witness their meeting, as they only ever had fleeting glimpses of their commander. From a distance all they would observe was a small group of men shaking hands. One in civilian clothes, stood off them, leaving Andrew wondering who he was. There then appeared to be a heated discussion between Baird and the man Andrew assumed was Moore. The man in the civilian clothing then stepped forward and was seen to harangue the two arguing with each other, like naughty children reprimanded by a parent.

'What's going on?' Archie asked. 'It looked as though they were about to have a fight!'

Andrew found the scene both fascinating and disgusting. 'They're not really much different from us, are they? They squabble and shout at each other like everyone else. And yet we're expected to kiss their boots if they order us.'

'Still fed up with the army, Drew?' Archie chided playfully.

'Behaviour like that doesn't exactly inspire confidence in our noble leaders.'

'No. No, I suppose not.' Archie agreed. The scene troubled him also.

The boys watched as the men remounted. Moore and the civilian then rode of at a brisk trot into the town. Baird following slowly and somewhat forlornly after them.

John Moore surveyed the main street of Bembibre, sprawled with bodies either comatose in drink or emptying out whatever was left of the contents of their stomachs on to the cobbles. The stench was overwhelming as emissions from other bodily functions mingled with vomit to create a ghastly stew.

That an army under his command should be reduced to such a deplorable condition hurt him deeper than any previous episode in his not uneventful career. He was seeing before him the bitter fruits of his policy. He was reaping the consequences of his secrecy in not revealing his mind. Moore remained unable to comprehend that had he opened himself up and informed the army of his thinking, it could have given company commanders a weapon to deal with the indiscipline and insubordination. If the men understood why they were turning tail to the French at every opportunity, they may have behaved in a better fashion.

Thomas Graham knew this. He cursed himself for not saying something after Benavente. It might have saved this latest outrage from happening. He stood with Moore, surveying the disgraceful spectacle, equally shocked but not in any way surprised. He knew Moore now must start going against the grain and begin setting examples. Christ, how he wished Bobby Craufurd was here!

Moore spoke quietly almost to himself. 'When we reach Villafranca, I'm going to demonstrate to them that I'm no longer prepared to tolerate any more of this. The army together shall witness collectively what awaits any man who behaves in this manner. Enough is enough.'

'I just hope it isnae too late.' Graham replied.

'It will be for anyone who thinks he can do what he pleases. I only wish I could flog a few officers alongside them. They're the ones responsible for this. Such incompetence has brought shame on us!'

Graham didn't respond. Moore was only partly right. Tam was disturbed by Moore's delusion and inability to self-analyse. Maybe he did. Quietly, on his own. But Moore usually confided everything to him. He didn't want to accept Johnny truly believed himself faultless.

Moore turned his horse around. 'I don't want to breathe this stink in any longer. We'll camp outside the town tonight.'

They rode out of Bembibre together, neither speaking. Outside the town they came upon the 42nd regiment, witnessing punishment.

Everyone who could stand was ordered to attend. Even Joshua. Archie loaned him his shoes and stood barefoot. Andrew would remember his first view of a flogging for reasons other than merely witnessing an extreme example of military justice.

Twenty-four of the twenty five men arrested waited in line under guard. The twenty-fifth was incapable of standing punishment through the effects of his debauchery. He would experience his taste of the cat at a later date.

It was performed efficiently, almost surgically so. For a regiment with very low instances of awarding flogging as punishment, it was almost as if they wanted the unclean act completed as quickly and professionally as possible. Get it out the way and do not speak of it again. Each man was given four dozen lashes, a fairly lenient sentence by the standard of the day.

Andrew was standing side on, so fortunately, he did not get a clear view of the lacerations inflicted. He did note with interest how some men he expected to howl remained silent and others he expected to be stoic, screamed holy murder. It was an interesting exercise in studying human nature. A man's size, strengths, the outward appearance of his character to his fellows, meant little in the end. He wondered if the same applied in battle.

But the episode that burned deep in his memory would not involve violence. Not actual physical violence, that is. As the floggings were being carried out, his eyes flickered to Colonel Stirling, his adjutant and other officers including Captain Crozier, representing Andrew's company, witnessing the scene. They were directly opposite him, standing on the road just outside the entrance to Bembibre.

From the town, Sir John Moore and the civilian rode out together. Andrew could clearly make out Moore's expression. He appeared enraged, his face flush with red. He stopped his horse next to Colonel Stirling and his officers. Barely twenty yards away, Andrew heard every word that followed.

'Good day to you, Stirling. I see you're dealing with your miscreants. How many are there?'

'Good morning, Sir John. Twenty-four shall this day feel the lick of the regiment's favourite moggy!'

'What? Twenty four? As many as that? Are you unable to maintain line discipline in your regiment, sir? Moore was aware the 42nd hadn't officially entered the town.

'Line discipline?' Stirling responded in bemusement. 'Our discipline is excellent, sir. These men are undergoing punishment for breaking regimental orders.'

Moore leaned back on his horse. 'And what were they?'

'They entered the town against my express command and proceeded to enjoy the effects of alcohol, with the result they became unfit for duty.' Some of the younger officers struggled to stifle their amusement.

'And how many licks are they to receive for behaving like vile beasts?'

'Four dozen per man.' The colonel replied.

'Suffering Jesus! Have you seen the condition of this place, Stirling? Less than fifty lashes for carrying on worse than savages? Is that considered appropriate for such crimes in the 42nd? Or are you so afraid of your highland blackguards, you fear to award a more deserving punishment?'

Andrew heard the man in civilian clothing exclaim blasphemously to the heavens.

The colonel of the 42nd reeled in shock. 'What did you call my boys?' He gripped his sword handle. 'Blackguards, did you say?'

Ignoring Graham's entreaty, Moore carried on the unseemly rant. 'I did, sir! *Hoorsons* fae Angus and Dundonian guttersnipes. That is your regiment, man!'

'By Christ, I'll allow no bastard speak such calumny of my laddies! You shame me, sir! You shame yourself!'

'Begone with you and your scum, Stirling! It is you who have shamed Scotland.'

Colonel Stirling spoke firmly. 'You are the one who must depart, sir. This stretch of earth with its colonel and his officers present, constitutes the headquarters of the 42nd regiment in the field. You are not welcome here. Leave immediately. For your own good and that of this regiment. Go now, I say.'

Moore dismissed the colonel with a petty flick of his hand. He and Graham then rode off to re-join the reserve.

Andrew felt sick. And it wasn't only from the town's stink or the blood and gore from lashed bodies.

Chapter Twenty – Three

A pattern was forming. Each town the British army stopped at it ransacked, looted, burned and despoiled. The next in line was Villafranca.

The commissariat waiting to resupply the divisions arriving were overwhelmed by demand. Riots occurred when men turned up at storehouses demanding food, shoes, blankets and warm clothing. They were unwilling to wait in line with requisitioning orders confirmed by their officers. They wanted them immediately.

Of course, many were already drunk after plundering the town's alcohol supply. There was nowhere safe for its luckless inhabitants as they suffered an orgy of violence, assault, rape and mayhem. Everything breakable was smashed for firewood or for the sheer drink fuelled pleasure of random destruction.

Villafranca was set in beautiful surroundings at the base of a mountain with a nearby stream flowing between pleasant, leafy banks. The close by castle of the Duke of Alva was previously used as a barracks by Baird's division when it originally left Coruña to join up with Moore. Now there was something of the abattoir about the place.

Many of the remaining pack animals had either died or been mercifully destroyed on arrival at the town after suffering terribly on the march. In the narrow streets, bullocks and mules lay dead among groups of drunken soldiers. Carts and wagons were broken up. Stores of ammunition were thrown into the stream. A large number of horses were led to the water's edge and shot.

Andrew Berry believed it like a scene from the Inferno as he and Archie wandered through the town together. They lost out at the commissariat. By the time they arrived the jostling crowds were too deep, too angry, the atmosphere sulphurous. Archie was particularly desperate to find shoes. They'd had nothing to eat since leaving Bembibre that morning, having eaten little the day before.

They did have shelter. Colonel Stirling, it was said at gunpoint, requisitioned a church in the town for the regiment. Space was tight but enough straw was scavenged to lay on the floor to remove some of the chill. He ordered his officers to bed down with the men, refusing them permission to seek quarters of their own.

Andrew and Archie returned to the church, cold, starved and disconsolate. Archie hadn't even bothered to fill his canteen with the wine that was freely available as in Bembibre. They found their spot beside Joshua, now very weak and sat with him.

'Did you get anything?' his voice was now a whisper.

'Nothing. It's madness! A complete breakdown of order.' Andrew complained.

Joshua said nothing. Archie rearranged his blankets around him. 'How are you, pal?'

'Just the same, mate.'

'We have to go out again, Drew.' Archie's exhausted eyes bore into his friend's. 'We can't continue like this. We have to find something.'

'Let's rest up bit, first.' Andrew was so tired, all he wanted to do was to stop and close his eyes for a moment. A wave of fatigue came over as he sat down, threatening to overwhelm him. 'This is the biggest depot outside Coruña. We'll find something.'

Just then two men stood over them. There arms were filled with bread, biscuits and pork. Iain Colquhoun bent down to Joshua and dangled a new pair of shoes above him before dropping them in his lap.

Tomàs Killane looked down at them with a beaming smile. 'Listen, *a grà*. We're missing somethin' for our feast, here. I'd be truly grateful if one of you charmin' young gentlemen might be so kind as to nip out and fill a few canteens with Villafranca's finest. We can't wash this lovely grub down without a drink now, can we boys?'

Archie was not long in returning. He carried three canteens of rum and two filled with well-watered red wine. Andrew deemed the latter acceptable as it sweetened the water without the consequent effects.

Colquhoun advised Andrew and Archie to eat slowly, chewing small portions as their starved bellies would revolt at large quantities in their present condition. Sipping from the canteen, Andrew broke off chunks of bread and meat into balls and lovingly rolled the morsels around his mouth, sucking every titbit of goodness from each piece.

Killane soaked small hunks of bread through with watered wine and passed them into Joshua's mouth. He took an age to chew on two before he painfully gestured with his hand not to pass a third. Tomàs grew concerned. He put his ear down to Joshua's face, then put his hand under the blanket and gently prodded his sides. Joshua jerked and gasped in discomfort.

The Irishman rose to his feet. 'I'm going to talk to McQuater. The lad needs to see the surgeon now.'

Andrew and Archie, their mouths full, looked at Joshua then at each other. 'Can't you eat anything, Josh? Archie asked.

Joshua gave a slight shake of his head. It was then he started coughing violently. Colquhoun bent down and held him round the shoulders. He then vomited the pieces of bread along with blood and green slime. Iain turned the stricken boy's face to the side to avoid messing his blankets.

'Lean back, laddie. Rest up, now. Drew, pass me his canteen.' Colquhoun pulled a cloth from his sleeve and soaked it. He wiped Joshua's mouth and face, then held his head and passed a trickle of liquid into his mouth.

'Aye, just wee sips now. That's a good lad.'

Killane returned with McQuater. The corporal bent down. 'How are you Joshua, son? Not too good, eh?' Noting the blood and green mess, he turned to the Irishman.

'I see what you mean, Tomàs. I'll grab the assistant surgeon, Mr Innes. He's good wi' the laddies. Ken's his stuff, tae. No' like that auld windbag Ogilvie. Drunken auld sot. Bide here, boys. I'll bring him the now.'

It was nearly an hour later before the assistant surgeon arrived. He was a dark haired, good looking man in his late twenties. According to regimental gossip, he was the son of wealthy Edinburgh merchants with a beautiful, aristocratic wife waiting for him at home. He'd temporarily put behind his life of privilege to pursue his main passion, anatomy and the study of disease.

'Gentlemen, if you'll allow me some space to examine the soldier?' Andrew and Archie, along with Killane and Colquhoun, made way for the surgeon. He bent down, removed the blanket covering the boy and opened up Joshua's shirt front where he proceeded to place a listening instrument on his chest. He held his head there some time before asking the boy to take a number of breaths, as deeply as he was able. After a couple of efforts, he began to cough again and more blood and mucus was expelled. He lay back exhausted, his face colourless. Mr Innes then removed the instrument and fingered the secretions, rubbing and sniffing. He wiped his hands on his apron, then lifted each of Joshua's eyelids. He then prodded the boy's side and received the same reaction previously as Killane had.

'How long have you had that pain?'

'Three...three days, sir.'

'Have you suffered extreme head pains during that period?'

'Yes, sir. They've been really bad, sir.' It clearly exhausted him to speak

Andrew and Archie were aghast. Joshua hadn't told them, though they'd carried him on their backs the previous two days.

Mr Innes placed his hand on Joshua's forehead for a few seconds, then put his nose to his mouth and sniffed. He then raised himself up, putting both hands on his hips. He appeared to be attempting to come to a decision.

'You men are to remain here and keep this lad comfortable and warm. I will consider my evaluation and then refer to Captain Crozier in the first instance. I'll try not to be long.'

The mention of Crozier sent warning signals through Tomàs Killane and Iain Colquhoun. Andrew and Archie were oblivious to anything other than their shock at Joshua's confession. If only they had known sooner. They believed his legs were the problem.

'Alright lads, let's finish our supper.' Colquhoun broke the heavy silence. 'Joshua's had enough excitement for the day. Let's give him some peace and make ready to hunker down for the night ourselves. Another hard day tomorrow.'

Killane left to find a container of water to clean up Joshua's bed. Colquhoun asked him if he needed to urinate. He replied that he did and Iain lifted him from the bed to take him outside the church to the temporary latrine area. Iain spoke with Andrew before he left.

'Smarten up his bed and take that spare blanket from my knapsack. He'll need it tonight.'

'Do you think it's serious, Drew?' Archie asked as they tidied Joshua's bed after Colquhoun left, careful to avoid the vomit.

'We'll have to wait for the surgeon. If only he had told us sooner.'

'Why? Do you think it's a sign of something serious?'

Andrew shook his head. His eyes were wide and his face pale. 'I pray to

God it isn't.' He then stopped what he was doing, surveyed the scene inside the church and shivered.

'I feel a coldness growing within my soul. As if something evil that's been chasing us is about to catch and destroy us. And we can't fight back. It's unrelenting and won't be stopped.'

He stood up. 'I don't like being in this popish chapel. It's bad luck. I tell you. It's bad luck.'

Archie, whey-faced, shivered in the chill.

Andrew lay on the church floor, cold, despite the straw, staring at the ceiling above. He imagined Satan and his angels circling his sleeping body, carrying him in their talons to the fires below. He knew he wouldn't sleep that night. It meant he would be sick in the morning. That always transpired when he suffered a bout of insomnia. He was a little confused as he must have dozed off at some point as he noted Colquhoun and Killane's bedrolls were empty. He remembered they were together when they bedded down after cleaning up Joshua.

Archie was out sound. The noise from inside the church of hundreds of men snoring, talking, moaning in distress or pain would never have let him sleep anyway. But Archie could sleep through anything. He heard sounds approach and turned to look up at Tomàs Killane. His face was ashen.

'Andrew, awaken Archie. You are both to go to speak with the assistant surgeon.'

Andrew pulled himself up, stiff and aching from his blanket. He nudged Archie and after yawning and rubbing his eyes to wake himself, they both wandered barefoot to the small vestibule inside the entrance to the building where the surgeons had set up their makeshift infirmary.

Soldiers lay asleep everywhere. The boys had to step over many a body before they came to Mr Innes, who was sat on a stool writing out a report or journal entry. There was a wineglass filled with rum resting on the small foldaway campaign table he was using.

They stood behind him. 'Mr Innes, sir?' Andrew asked quietly.

The surgeon put down his pen and turned round. 'Good evening, lads. It would be a fine thing to offer you a seat for what I'm about to tell you, but alas, there is literally no room at the inn.'

He was not facetious. He was tired and somewhat disillusioned. He was a single human being attempting to clear up the results of a torrent of incompetence, ignorance, violence and death. Tomorrow and the day after, he would have to do the same.

'Which of you is Andrew?' That boy indicated himself. 'And you are Archibald.' Normally his full name emitted smiles and sniggers, but not tonight.

'I have concluded my diagnosis of your friend, Joshua. The reason I took a little longer than I'd hoped was that I needed to eliminate a suspicion forming in my mind. Thus I had to consult a volume and some notes I made previously. I believe now I have successfully done so.' Mr Innes was initially concerned over the possibility of typhus.

Archie and Andrew said nothing, though both were now beginning to tremble involuntarily as their feet chilled through the straw on the church stone.

'Boys, it is with deep regret that I must pronounce it is my firm belief that Joshua has pneumonia which has now settled on his lungs. It has advanced to such an extent that it is too late for any remedy to alleviate the symptoms. Unfortunately, I must state with a degree of certainty, based on previous experience of this affliction, that Joshua will probably not live through this night. As is common in such circumstances, he is likely to pass unto God's mercy in the early hours of the new morning. He will not be leaving this place.'

Andrew could only gape in shock, his mind closed to any form of response. He was paralysed, unable to formulate words in his mind. Next to him, Archie began sobbing uncontrollably.

'The three of you are the pride of this regiment' Mr Innes declared solemnly, in an effort to comfort them in their distress. 'Your sense of duty, your devotion to each other and to your comrades, has inspired everyone. Sergeant McGillivray praises you highly and your conduct has reached the ears of the colonel himself. He knows your names and follows your progress with great interest.'

Andrew hardly took in a word that was said. He wanted to cry, to weep like Archie but he was too numbed. He was unaware of himself shaking, of his bare flesh growing colder. The goose pimples breaking out all over his body. Joshua, dying this very night? How? *How?*

An object was being held before him. It was the glass of rum. For the sake of doing something, anything, he took it and drank. He swallowed but the bite of the alcohol made him screw up his face as he felt molten heat pour down into his stomach.

'Just as they say. You're not a drinker, Andrew Berry.' Mr Innes confirmed with a tired grin.

More conscious of matters now, Andrew put his arm around his weeping friend to console him. 'What do we do now, sir?'

'Now? Well, as you are here and it is fairly peaceful, I may as well take the opportunity to examine you both for my reports. I especially wish to study the condition of your feet.'

Mr Innes carried out his examination. He listened to their chests, asked a number of questions regarding the state of their health and finally looked over their feet. Archie's were blistered and sore but in reasonable shape despite the punishment endured. Andrew had one question to ask about himself.

'Yes. I'm afraid it is frost bite.' Mr Innes confirmed. 'Still at early stages, but the blueish colouring and the lack of sensation are unmistakeable.'

Andrew asked what he should do.

'Colonel Stirling believes there may be another ten days march ahead. I believe in another few days, if the weather conditions continue, your feet may begin to blister. Which is not good. The traditional way of treating the ailment is to rub the affected areas with snow. I discount this entirely. Snow can be rough and cause the skin to break. It is my theory that heat is the main factor in alleviating frost bite. Therefore what I am about to say to you will sound strange, but this is what I recommend. When at rest, clean and dry your feet thoroughly. If you cannot find heat from a fire, you are to lie across from Archibald and lay your foot on his bare stomach or chest. He must then gently rub your toes. Remain like this as long as possible. Such transference of heat from another body to the afflicted area over time, may assist in the healing process.'

Andrew made an attempt of levity to try to comfort his devastated friend. 'You hear that, Archie? I'm to rest my foot on your belly every night!'

Archie made a brave attempt to snigger. He dried his eyes, composed himself and faced the surgeon. 'Sir, what do we do tonight for Joshua?'

'I will come to that in a moment, Archibald.' Mr Innes leaned down to a set of saddle bags under the campaign table. 'This is among the last of my supply. It is rubbing alcohol. You will use this, Andrew, on your feet every night after you have cleaned them as I have described. You have proven to me you are tee-total, therefore I trust you not to consume it. But I must strongly advise you not to give it away to anyone. If you do, you may be at risk of losing your toes and feet.'

Andrew took the bottle of clear liquid and thanked the surgeon.

'Sir?' Archie had as ever, waited patiently.

'Yes, lads. Tonight. The best you can do for your friend is to see to his comforts. Keep him warm, wet his lips as he may become dry. Tend to his needs. Talk to him of happy times together. When the end comes, if God is merciful, he will slip peacefully from us. This night will be a long one for you. I will come and check how things are during my late rounds.'

The night was indeed long. Colquhoun and Killane stayed with them throughout. Joshua's breathing became heavier and his coughing fits longer and more painful. These exhausted him greatly. He was now barely lucid. Then at three thirty in the morning he asked for Drew.

Andrew reached over and took his hand. Archie took the other.

'Drew.'

'I'm here, Josh. I'm here.'

'My mother. Tell my mother. My pay. Give my money to her.'

Tears streamed down Andrew's face. 'I will, Josh. You know I will.'

'Tell her I'm sorry. That I love her.'

'I know you do, pal. I know you do.'

And at the time the assistant surgeon predicted, Joshua Whitfield was delivered unto God's grace, enveloped in grief, cushioned in tenderness and cherished with devotion by his beloved friends.

Shortly after, Colquhoun and Killane left the church together. Outside the town a patch of earth was marked out for burying the army's non-catholic dead. Heretics were forbidden to lie in consecrated ground. But Iain and Tomàs had no intentions of leaving Spanish peasants to dump their young friend in a pit to lay with strangers.

The task was brutal as the ground was solid from the cold but they were able to hack away their grief, preparing a respectable burial site before returning to the church. Andrew and Archie remained awake beside their dead friend, still tearful. Killane bent down and put a hand on each of their shoulders.

'We'll put him in the ground now, *a grà*. No one but us has that right. It's better we do it while it's quiet. It'll allow his soul a free run to heaven, so it will. Better you boys stay here. Remember him as he was.'

Killane lifted Joshua's body with its blanket and left with Colquhoun to lay him in his last resting place on earth.

As the morning proper arrived, the entire army was ordered to view the spectacle of an execution.

On arriving with the reserve late the previous night, General Moore ordered that a miscreant was to be found and handed over to the provost martial. Later, lurid speculation would circulate over the method used to choose the unfortunate individual. Many believed three random drunken figures were hauled out of the gutters of Villafranca and made to draw lots.

The truth was that the man chosen, a light dragoon, had stolen food and property from a local house and when challenged, struck an officer. That act alone was a death sentence in any army. Consequently, every man under Moore's command was lined up in the towns Plaza Mayor as the prisoner was marched towards a small tree with one branch. He was made to kneel facing it, the order was given, and he was shot dead from carbines by members of his regiment.

Andrew was oblivious to the event. He stood in the rear column with Archie with their eyes downcast and minds elsewhere. Neither did they take in much, if anything, of the subsequent speech made before the army where Sir John Moore castigated them for a drunken, cowardly, disgrace and prayed his head would be blown off in battle before he ever lead such a rabble again.

When it was over, they returned to the church. As their division was due to march out at midday, they concentrated instead on arranging their kit for the next stage of the retreat.

Archie took the shoes Colquhoun had brought for Joshua. His own were finished. These would have to last till their final destination was reached. Andrew had the melancholy task of looking over the dead boy's belongings. Earlier, Killane handed Andrew two items. One was a small gold band and the other, something of an enigma.

Hanging on a gold chain was a miniature portrait of a beautiful woman in her thirties with deep black curls, wearing a satin blue and white dress. A string of pearls hung round her very white throat. Ordinarily it would have been deemed an extremely expensive item, way beyond the means of a lawyer's clerk. Could it be of his mother? It was more likely to be the woman who was the cause of Joshua's disgrace in Edinburgh, the advocate's wife. If it was, how strange that he should carry it with him still. Neither Andrew nor Archie had any idea it was in his possession, for all their supposed closeness.

Andrew handed it to Archie to keep. He couldn't risk sending it home to Joshua's mother. He did think it ironic that the first item of value Archie gained, for all his dreams of winning a haul of gold and jewels from a battlefield, should be something from his friend's dead body.

Along with his purse containing a few little coins and a small bundle of letters, these were the only possessions of value remaining. Andrew kept the mirror for himself and Archie to use. His back pay would be sent home. So little to show for a promising young life.

They handed in his musket to Corporal McQuater, then the two boys left the church. They did not speak but both knew instinctively where they were headed. They wandered over to the Bembibre side of the town, to wait hopefully for a glimpse of any stragglers returning to the column. Three in particular.

Andrew decided not to tell anyone the truth about his uncle after last speaking with him. It was too personal for discussion. Neither Joshua nor Archie mentioned his going off alone to talk with the sergeant. Andrew was unsure how they would react to his revelation. Close as he was to them, this was something he could not bring himself to share. It was his family's business and no one else's.

But it was important now for Andrew to talk to his uncle. To explain his sorrow and pain. He needed the comfort of a blood relative, particularly one who would understand such a loss and how to come to terms with it.

Archie stood, sipping from his canteen. His initial devastation was wearing off. His life, after all, has been an unforgiving one. Brought up on a farm, his father was a drunk who spent most of his life beating his children and lying on top of his wife in their tiny bothy, given them to live in by the land owner. Children came and went. Many died in childbirth or as babies. Archie felt little affection for any of them. His way of escaping was wandering the hills around Dunfermline and the coastal paths towards Kinghorn and Aberdour. He was at his happiest when he was tracking stray sheep, lambs and calves. Many a time he carried an exhausted animal home wrapped around his neck. Carrying Joshua was little effort to him. It was nothing.

He would look down on the river Forth at the ships sailing in and out. He dreamed of getting on board one and travelling far away to the Indies or Tahiti where the women were beautiful and free with their charms. Then he would return to the joyless hovel he lived in, to his father either humping or thrashing his mother, unfed children crying and indescribable filth.

He had no real friends. He was unlettered as the landowner refused to allow him to be schooled as he was needed for his labour from an early age. He would usually end up fighting with locals whenever he went into a village. They looked down on him. Invariably they ended looking up at him with bloodied heads. He could take care of himself.

But when he joined the army and met the two boys who became his first real friends, he cherished that friendship more than anything, even more than money in his sporran. They worked together. They helped each other. They shared everything. Archie was happy to defer to Andrew as the natural leader, but Drew was always willing to seek the advice of the farm labourer. To talk through a problem. To discuss the issues of the day. For the first time in his young life, Archie was respected and regarded as someone of worth.

Joshua was a wealth of fascinating information on Archie's favourite subject, women. Things he would never tell Drew, he confided in the lad from Newcastle. Joshua cut an exotic figure. He'd never met an Englishman before. Joshua had lived in a big city and tasted its forbidden delights. He was an object of awe to Archie. Now he was dead.

He swore as he sat with Drew with Joshua's body that night, they would both live through the ordeal of the march. Their friend would have died for nothing if they didn't get home. For then, who would be left to remember him? He would carry Drew all the way if he had to. He had to stay alive so he could honour Joshua's memory.

The morning passed but no figures yet emerged on the road. The weather turned bad again as snow began to fall. The rum in his canteen warmed Archie but Andrew was beginning to feel the chill. And they still had a march ahead.

Andrew was about to ask Archie if he wanted to return, when in the distance his eyes caught a speck of movement. He started walking in its direction to try and get a clearer view. Then more specks appeared. Hobbling creatures, waving their arms. He began to hear sounds of cries and shouting. He ran on ahead, Archie following behind. They came to the first apparition.

Andrew came close to vomiting. It was a soldier in a redcoat. Except the red was mainly blood. The man's head was blackened and looked like he'd stood too close to a flash of gunpowder. His hands were cut and fingers were missing. His lower lip was torn and hanging off. There lay a trail of red in the snow behind him from his bloodied, bare feet.

He was gibbering in shock, a form of pleading, as he fell down at Andrew's feet. But soon more figures in a similar horrific state advanced towards them. Andrew turned round to see men running from the town in their direction.

Andrew broke away from the man. 'Sergeant McGillivray of the 42nd! Does anyone know him? Has anyone seen him?'

The men, all in *extremis*, fell down into the snow. Soldiers from the town arrived to assist and remove them to safety.

'Melvin! Scott of the 42nd!' Archie shouted, but there was no reaction. 'Hugh! Dod!' They walked on ahead, passing other figures but they could see no one in a kilt. Just as they were about to turn back, Andrew saw them.

Two figures arm in arm, struggled to help each other forward. Even though they were bent in their exhaustion, Andrew could tell by the bulk of Scott and Melvin's red hair that it was their friends from the company. There was no sign of a third man. The two boys ran to them.

'Drew, is it you? Drew!' Scott slumped to his knees. Archie caught Melvin as he was about to fall. He pulled out his canteen and fed rum into his mouth. Melvin coughed and then dropped on all fours, panting heavily. Archie passed the canteen to Scott, who drank deeply.

'Christ! What happened, Hugh?' Andrew asked anxiously. It was now that the boys could see that the two men suffered similar injuries to the first man they'd met.

'Dragoons. French dragoons rode in to the town. Thrashin' away like devils! There was no escapin' the bastards.'

Archie tried to get Melvin to speak. 'Dod, Dod! Where's Sergeant McGillivray? Where is he?'

Scott rose painfully to his feet. The rum had now effected a return to some modicum of sense. 'He wanted to leave the hospital to get some air. To see if he could walk again. We accompanied him. We were only a few yards down the street when the horsemen arrived. I got slashed across the arm before I even saw them. Doddie leaped for cover. They must have thought Xander was just another drunk in the street with that bandage on his head.'

Dreading what was to come, Andrew could only listen.

'I was on the ground tryin' to avoid the hooves.' Melvin recounted. 'I looked up and the sergeant was wanderin' across the street, in a daze. I screamed at him to get down. A dragoon hacked at him and cleaved his head through. The man was dead before he hit the dirt.

'That's it, Drew. That's what happened. He died there and then in that stinkin' Spanish hovel like a dog. Like some poor, bloody dog.'

Coruña

'I hope my country will do me justice.'

Sir John Moore, Coruña 16th January 1809

Chapter Twenty – Four

Robert Craufurd was cold, hungry, miserable and exhausted as anyone else in the army. He had given up his horse to a fourteen year old ensign of the 43rd and a ten year old drummer boy he'd found close to death, freezing and huddled together for warmth. After mounting them on his reeking sorrel and wrapping them in a blanket, he was now struggling through the snow, ice and sleet like any other ranker.

What drove that strange man? It was a question in the minds of many who knew him. How he could mercilessly flog a soldier one moment and the next, give away his horse to children, was emblematic of his strange psyche. He had difficulty reconciling his own duality himself. It was as if he had to balance every action he took with the opposite extreme in order to maintain some measure of equilibrium. He knew he was hated, feared, admired and regarded fondly in equal measures. He was mercurial, savage, compassionate and deep. In another word, unfathomable.

No man brooded more on his perceived personal failures, the lost opportunities, ideas that never gained acceptance. Why can't they see it's all about winning while keeping as many men alive as possible? Johnny Moore was as close as he had come to finding a true kindred spirit. The only subject they disagreed on was flogging. Moore loathed it, but it was not that Robert possessed a fetish for watching a man being stripped of the flesh from his back. He was no psychotic who enjoyed inflicting pain. But it was only that he believed he understood men a little better than Johnny did. The soldiers themselves were philosophical as much as any basically illiterate, uneducated beings could be over the lash. They would rather be flogged than receive most other punishments, particularly stoppage of drink and fined their pay.

You had to keep brute beasts in line. He knew what they were capable of when discipline lapsed. They were addicted to alcohol. The slightest whiff of it and they became unmanageable. Johnny would argue, so what does flogging achieve when they care for nothing but getting themselves as drunk as possible and damn the consequences? Drunkenness was the army's biggest problem, not flogging. It hadn't yet found the answer. But Robert knew that once a man felt the lash, it focused the minds of the better type among them to avoid it at all costs. The scum among them, always present, were beyond redemption.

The problem for Robert and indeed for John Moore, was this particular army had a higher quota of scum than normal. Though circumstances of this army were extreme, a long retreat would test the mettle of any force. As far as Robert Craufurd was concerned, John Moore's army failed him in Spain in this regard. He attached no blame to Moore. When he thought of the fine army he was part of in South America, he could have and indeed did, quietly shed tears of frustration at the difference. If John Moore had led the Rio del Plata expedition, Britain would now own a brave new colony at very little cost.

Sir John Moore and Sir John Whitelocke. Never were two commanders so different in character. Robert reviewed over and over again in his mind the moments he would wish to have acted differently in the Plata. His greatest personal regret was not speaking up when Whitelocke, who had virtually conceded authority of the army over to his second in command, approved Leveson Gower's plan for the attack on Buenos Aires.

The devilishly complicated plan Gower conceived involved the army being split into thirteen columns, comprising between two hundred and six hundred men. One of the columns would head for a key position, the Plaza de Toros in the north east of the city while the other columns would aim for specifically selected target areas. They would smash their way into buildings and set up defensive positions, command the rooftops and await further orders. No one bothered to speculate what these orders would be. Gower laid emphasis that he did not want any column to make for the Plaza Mayor, the city's main square, believed to be the heaviest defended part of the city. Nor was anyone to deviate in any way from their chosen route. Most controversially, he insisted the men enter the city with unloaded muskets as he didn't want any stopping to pick off defenders and risk being bogged down in street fighting. Whitelocke approved the plan unreservedly and set the time of attack for midday.

The American, Auchmuty was astonished and argued that setting off at such a time when the city was fully alive was highly dangerous. Gower agreed and the attack time was put back to dawn the following day.

Plodding through the slush and ice, Robert cursed himself again. I said nothing to this. I never spoke up. I know why I didn't but that doesn't mean it was right. Denis Pack, one of the more experienced brigade commanders, never spoke up either, though he knew the city well and understood how it could be turned into a defensive bastion. The plan had major flaws. Division of the force in enemy territory and reducing the British army to the lottery of street fighting instead of using it to its strengths in pitched battle. The plan was also incomplete, as the men were ordered to take up defensive positions and to wait to see what materialised.

One of the reasons no one, including Robert, spoke up was because Whitelocke had become increasingly unhinged. He was seeing enemies everywhere and convinced Gower and a cabal of disgruntled officers were attempting to usurp his command. His paranoia was such that he was spending more time with non-commissioned officers and ingratiating himself to the men. They saw through this for what it was and despised him for it. The atmosphere at Whitelocke's command area was increasingly bizarre and highly unsettling. Reluctantly, though they had little respect for Gower, the senior officers believed he was more reasonable, though inexperienced and were forced to defer to him as Whitelocke's conduct deteriorated further.

His behaviour proved dangerous and ultimately fatal for the army when he ordered a delay to the attack in order to provide not one, but two separate offers of surrender to the people of Buenos Aires. This resulted in Robert Craufurd advising Whitelocke with as much restraint as he could summon, that a second offer only served to indicate possible weakness on the British side. Nevertheless, the parlays went ahead and the people of the Buenos Aires, who naturally refused to consider capitulation, were given two more days to strengthen the defensive constructions in the city. These two days would prove crucial.

The city was laid out in rectangular blocks each 130 yards square, the eastern side of the city facing the Rio de la Plata. Several high buildings dominated the view and were occupied with defenders armed with bricks, grenades and burning hot pitch. The Spanish plan was to draw the attackers into the narrow streets towards the Plaza Mayor, neutralising their effectiveness in superior training and discipline. Cobble stones were prised from the roads and used to build barricades. Fortifications were packed with sandbags and bales of wool. Cannon were placed in the Plaza Mayor and surrounding streets. All citizens were mobilised, armed with every type of weapon imaginable.

At dawn on the morning of July 5th 1807, the British attack finally began. The men, ordered to leave knapsacks and greatcoats behind, shivered while awaiting the orders to advance. Robert Craufurd, with his light brigade, received a relatively gentle beginning, only receiving sporadic musket fire as they worked their way through the streets of Calles Correro, Catedral and San Martin. Less than two hours after the order to attack, Robert and his brigade reached the Rio de la Plata. Unfortunately, his experience was one of the few exceptions that bloody morning.

The 88th regiment was sent into the city without flints in their muskets at the behest of Gower. Their colonel, Duff, unable to believe the preposterous order, soon had his hands full as his men were shot and attacked from the roofs of buildings. Without the ability to shoot back, they had to wait until Duff sent an officer to the rear to find as many flints as he could lay his hands on.

The 87th regiment, in advancing into the city, first heard little sound. As they entered the El Retiro district, the tightly packed column in the narrow street was devastated by a deadly discharge of cannon fire which tore through the ranks, killing dozens and wounding more.

In some quarters the British made progress towards their goal, but in others, were held back. Through a mix up in orders, a column of the 95th under Denis Pack blundered towards the no go area of the Plaza Mayor. There they faced opposition the experienced Pack later described as the most unequal struggle he'd ever fought in, as his men were cut down by an apparently unseen enemy and forced to retreat back.

On hearing the close by gunfire, Robert Craufurd turned his brigade from the beach at the river mouth and went back into the city. He ran into Pack, clearly in distress.

'Christ, Bobby! We've been cut to pieces. The entire city's a death trap.'

'Calm yourself, Denis!' Craufurd ordered. 'Tell me what occurred.'

Pack recounted hurriedly his experience and also what he had heard of the fate of other columns. He ended his highly agitated discourse with an appeal to Craufurd to himself retire from the city before suffering a similar fate.

'Never! Not a chance. I've not come here to do a runner. Get your wounded back to safety, Denis.' Unwilling to argue, Pack offered his good wishes, turned and made off with the remainder of his force. Robert called Major Trotter over and advised him of his intentions to make for the church of Santo Domingo. Soon after they spoke, a unit of the 45th regiment led by a Colonel Guard arrived on the scene. They joined forces, and after some heavy fighting, made their way to the church.

Robert stopped and turned round to look at the column. If it now could be described as such. He made his way slowly along it. So many now struggled on barefoot. How they did it was beyond his understanding. A few fell out while he walked past, no longer caring. He went over to one of them.

'Can you go no further, Rifleman?'

The man, a soldier of the 95th, was himself barefoot, his feet blue. He was using his Baker as a crutch. His face was gaunt, his eyes staring out of his head.

'Your honour, forgive me. But I am just resting. I will be up again presently.' The words in a Welsh accent seemed torn from him. He was an older veteran, about his own age. Robert recognised him but could not remember the name. He cursed his memory for letting him and the soldier down. He unscrewed the cap from his near empty canteen of rum and poured a drop into the cup.

The soldier wearily reached out to accept the drink, grimacing in pain as the harsh alcohol stabbed his parched and painful throat. He wiped his mouth and returned the cup.

'Bless you sir, for a true soldier.'

'Try to keep going, man. It isn't far now. You must keep moving. Soon we'll be at the harbour and the ships to take us home.'

Robert screwed the cap back on and assisted the man to his feet. He then returned to his horse at the head of the column. He needed to refill his canteen.

The church of Santa Domingo proved a death trap as Pack's prophetic words were realised. Having been forced to blast the wooden doors open with a 3 pounder gun brought with them, Craufurd and his men took up defensive positions inside. He was unable to stop the looting that began almost immediately. All the gold, silver and ceremonial plate disappeared and a monk was shot trying to defend the property of Mother Church. Eventually order was restored. The 95th regiment's renowned marksman, Private Thomas Plunkett, took up a position on the roof and a flag was raised. Unfortunately, this attracted unwanted attention and soon the church was under sustained musket and cannon fire.

The streets ran with blood as casualties on both sided mounted. Inside the church, no one was safe as marksmen had taken up positions on roofs where they were able to shoot through windows. Outside, a lone gunner valiantly worked on the 3 pounder to keep the Spaniards back. Plunkett continued to ply his deadly trade.

Around 1p.m., Craufurd noted a large column moving down the Calle San Martin towards the 3 pound gun with intent to capture it. Robert drew Trotter's attention and the major immediately volunteered to lead a force from the church to confront the enemy. Craufurd believed it suicidal but Colonel Guard of the 45th detachment also requested to take part. Robert could not refuse and it was a decision that would haunt him for the rest of his days.

Eighty men volunteered, and led by Trotter, they charged out of the church where they were hit by a volley from the Spanish who soon fell back. But just as he reached the Calle Rosario, Trotter was shot dead. Another good man wasted.

Unable to make any headway, only twenty men made it back to the church. Sickened by the losses, Craufurd prepared to sell himself and the remainder of the occupants dear.

By 3p.m. the sound of firing all around the city had fallen away. Craufurd could only draw one conclusion. Inside, the church was a charnel house. There were close to a hundred wounded men and water and ammunition were running low. Robert called for a meeting of senior officers and the decision was reluctantly made that surrender was the only option left to them. It was clear the attack on the city was a failure. It was time to prevent the useless loss of more lives.

Terms were agreed shortly after with the Spaniards. Robert Craufurd led his command from the church, the wounded were left inside. Outside, a mob gathered and Craufurd had a first look at his vanquishers. They bore little resemblance to any enemy he had ever fought previously, even in India. They were ordinary Spanish civilians, hurriedly raised, barely trained militia, women, even children, Indian levies, slaves, creoles and a few professional soldiers. A rabble. A rabble from the gutter that had humbled the world's finest infantry.

Walking alongside Robert was Colonel Guard, whose sword was shattered as he led the attack with the gallant Major Trotter. Guard mourned his loss and lamented the ruined weapon.

'Should I send the repair bill to General Whitelocke?'

Robert Craufurd, unable to control his passions, spat. 'Aye. Do that. As for my men, I'll let them know if anyone sees him, they have my permission to shoot the bastard dead.'

The weather was relentless, the terrain was relentless. The hunger, the misery and the pain were relentless. But the man who drove them on, almost alone, was equal to it all.

Robert had men flogged all the way to Orense. Two of them, after a plea by their colonel on their behalf for mercy, were made to draw straws. Craufurd relented. He only flogged one of them. Even in that he relented. He stopped the lash at seventy five rather than the one hundred strokes he normally proscribed.

He was not slackening. He had his reasons for every action he took. But he never explained. He never opened up. Robert saw no need for any of that. It was weakness. And weakness cost lives.

He rode down the column, stopping at men and staring intently at their faces. No words were spoken. He rode further and told another group of men to remain together at all times. No straggling. Maintain line discipline. Disobedience costs lives.

Whenever they came to a water obstacle, he demanded they march through at the point of arrival. They were not to stop and look for another crossing area. Men waded through, in some instances, up to their necks. But they got through without wasting time or using up precious reserves of strength. Soon this became second nature in the light brigade.

One overweight, elderly officer made the mistake of his life in ordering a soldier to carry him over a stream. Robert saw them, ran over and screamed at the officer to get off the man's back. No soldier in his division was to be used as a mule by any fat arsed bastard, however exalted his rank. He made the officer wade across the stream twice. Private soldiers observing, laughed and thanked God to be led by such a man.

Once they left Orense, they came to country so barren, so harsh and forbidding, the Irishmen among them made the sign of the cross and Protestants in the presence of evil, spoke the Lord's Prayer aloud. Their spirits sunk lower, their resolve lessened as they weaved their way around mountain tracks like an army of ants, so many tramping barefoot, the path ahead illuminated by fresh bloodstains. More often now they witnessed scenes so harrowing, they stopped registering in their addled minds. It became the only way to go on or they should all go mad.

A family, the woman and child unable to continue, sitting in the snow. The soldier husband remaining with them, awaiting approaching death in silence. Groups huddled together, unclothed or covered in rags, dead where they collectively stopped together to give up what remained of their spark in order to end their suffering. A beautiful young girl with long blond hair, sprawled dead, her baby miraculously still living, lying in the snow beside her. How many walked by her still body no one could say until an officer of the 43rd stopped and picked the child up and carried it with him to take home to England. The little one was fortunate. So many others were not so lucky.

All this Robert Craufurd witnessed, stony faced. To those observing him, he appeared without a shadow of pity. They were wrong. He was not pitiless. He stopped the floggings after Orense. He knew he could not ask any more of them. He was not Napoleon Bonaparte. He understood much better the limitations of human beings, what they could endure and how long they could endure it. Now he became softer. He passed his canteen to the men more often. He searched his tired mind for ways to aid the few women and children remaining. Robert requested officers climb off their horses to make way for the sick and needy. He continued to pass up and down the column, inspiring, encouraging, cajoling.

'Stay in your ranks, lads. Keep together. It's getting close now. I can smell the sea. First man to spot the mast of a ship shall be rewarded a guinea.'

It was on the 12th of January 1809 that Robert Craufurd washed away the stain of South America from his soul forever. Walking ahead alone, on reaching the brow of a hill, he found himself looking down on the harbour below and the ships sailing for Coruña. He had lost less than four hundred souls on the march. For the size of his force, this was a remarkable achievement. Robert proved his methods worked. They hadn't met any serious French opposition. But the route they took, with no supply depots anywhere along the way, through far rougher country than the main column, was an epic of human endeavour.

The path of Robert Craufurd had led him from the broiling cauldron of a city of the new world, to the snow and ice of a freezing winter in a peninsula of the old. It was to a place called Vigo, fate carried him to his redemption.

He touched his face, then licked his finger. There was salt there, he was certain of it. He'd spared himself a guinea. Black Bob Craufurd took a deep, satisfied breath and smiled happily.

Chapter Twenty – Five

The army was disintegrating. Sir John Moore had to do something.

They were no longer soldiers. They were mendicants. A barefoot parade of tramps shuffling through snow and ice adorned in rags and cast offs from dead men. Officers indistinguishable from rankers. Bearded, ragged haired, eyes red-rimmed or inflamed with snow blindness. Cavernous cheeks, the stark imprint of privation and hunger. Heads cast down under the pitiless load of fatigue. Spirits fading to despair. Souls welcoming of death's cold embrace.

The sixty mile march from Villafranca took the army across the Cantabrian Mountains and over formidable land masses such as the defile of Piedrafita and Monte Cebrero. They surmounted rivers and streams and traversed near bottomless gorges. Outside the village of Cerezal, Edward Paget was forced to order £25,000 worth of casks filled with silver dollars from the army's treasury, to be smashed and their contents dumped over the side of a ravine. He threatened to shoot anyone who attempted to help himself to any scattered coins.

This stretch would be remembered as the 'March of Death' and the point of the retreat where discipline broke down completely. Dead bodies of human beings and animals scarred the entire route. Men fought each other like beasts for scraps of food or over a pair of shoes. Line discipline was non-existent. Groups of men fell out of the column to wait at the roadside to surrender to the advancing enemy. The weak and needy were beaten and robbed. Officers went in fear of their lives if they attempted to intervene. Very few children were left alive. Three women who found shelter in a small hut were raped and murdered by French cavalry.

After a tense conversation with Thomas Graham on the perilous state of the army, Moore decided to fix a position outside the town of Lugo and make a stand. Soult was close and stabbing at the British reserve. Moore was ready and willing to show his claws. He had earlier received a report from his senior engineer recommending Coruña as the most suitable port to embark the army. It was well provisioned and its geography made it highly defensible. This would be vital during the embarkation period. Davy Baird argued privately with him that Vigo was the safer option, but Moore believed it lacked defensive capabilities. Baird got his way and his and the other divisions turned west. The report now vindicated Moore's preference. The navy was requested to sail for the northern port. Moore sent an urgent message to Baird who was presently at Nogales, ordering him to make for Lugo. The rest of the divisions were advised accordingly while mention was made of Moore's intention to make ready for a poke at the French.

When word got out about the forthcoming clash, an army of vagrants was transformed. Men who formerly ignored or abused their superiors, now jumped to attention instantly and obeyed every order given to the letter.

There was a large supply of ammunition and rations in Lugo, but yet again the commissariat was ill prepared and many men went without adequate replenishment. This was set side in the excitement after they were led above a sloping valley, broken up by hedges, lanes and stone walls. They were flanked by hills on one side and a deep river on the other. It could only be described as a highly favourable position to hold.

Marshal Soult arrived to take up the challenge set before him. He made determined thrusts towards the British line. At one point, he came close to a breakthrough but was beaten back in time. He then ordered the recall and forwarded a message ordering Marshall Ney to join him with his twenty thousand men and fifty guns.

For the rest of the day, the armies did nothing but glare at each other. By nightfall, Moore recognised Soult was attempting to pin him while awaiting reinforcements to arrive. As darkness fell completely, he ordered the army to withdraw and continue on the retreat. He gained a twelve hour start on the unsuspecting French. But the sullen, resentful mood of the army returned almost immediately. Moore had once again made the correct decision but the men he led would not forgive him.

Two nights later, Moore ordered a halt in Betanzos, less than twenty miles from Coruña. Messengers arrived from the port with mail and despatches from England. Moore's heart leapt when he was handed a letter from Lady Hester Stanhope.

If ever there was ever a moment when his flagging spirits needed reviving, it was now. Hester's letter provided the uplift as only she could. It was the usual chatty (and catty) missive along with perceptive commentary on the political scene. She advised him that though news was circulating in England of difficulties in Spain, he retained the full confidence of those that mattered within government. He remained much admired by the Whigs who would vigorously defend him against any Tory mischief making. She also asked him to send her warm regards to her two brothers, Charles, a major of the 50th regiment and young James. The letter ended with a tantalising allusion on the subject of marriage.

Hester's devotion infused him with a much needed boost to his waning morale. Her letter offset another piece of news less pleasant. The mother of Caroline Fox, the beautiful girl in Sicily he came close to marrying, had finally succumbed to a long and debilitating illness. Moore was greatly saddened as Marianne and Henry Fox were highly valued friends and confidants during his time on the island.

By tomorrow he would have brought the army to its destination. There was stocks of food and stores in the port and God willing, the ships to carry it home. The French were not far away, but he would build a defensive shield while embarking the army. If the enemy wanted a go at him, they were very welcome.

Arm in arm, Andrew Berry and Archibald Miller dragged themselves along together on the roads of death.

There were now barely five hundred men of the 42nd left in the column by the time it reached Betanzos. The remainder of the original nine hundred men of the battalion were either dead, prisoners, or among large groups of stragglers trailing in its wake. McQuater was promoted to sergeant. Iain Colquhoun was given temporary rank of corporal to Tomàs Killane's great relief. Apart from his wife, the prospect of obtaining rank was the only thing on earth the man from Longford truly feared. Andrew

Berry assumed the dominant personality once more with his remaining friend from the original three.

His shoes were now tied together with strings pulled from his kilt. Due to the condition of his feet, he daren't walk without them and was continually stopping to make adjustments. Archie, normally physically tougher, was marching barefoot. The new shoes had fallen apart after two days. They were originally sent from England for the Spanish army. The contractors skimping on costs and manufacturing ultra-cheap shoes filled with a clay base above the threadbare leather soul. Evidently, their Spanish allies' welfare was of little consequence when it came to the profit margin. If the little girls and women slaving in factories in Northampton and other sweat shops for barely a living wage could see where their unending toil ended up and why, they may not have been surprised. Archie was fortunate, some of the shoes gave way only hours after their owners took to the road.

Ordinarily, lack of good shoes could have proved a potentially fatal prospect. Archie grew up without footwear most of his life, consequently, tramping bare shod was less of a hindrance for him than for others. But he was now weakening. Fortunately for them both, Andrew had discovered a fresh resolve.

The news of the horrific manner in which his uncle lost his life transformed Andrew's outlook on surviving the ordeal. He was now consumed with a deep, obsessive hatred for the French. What kind of people could hack at a man stumbling around with his head bandaged? They were nothing less than savage, inhuman beasts. He desperately wanted to face them man to man to gain some measure of retribution for both his uncle and Joshua. Not the cold, the snow, rain or hunger would hinder his thirst for vengeance. His normally soft, kind heart, coarsened into something bitter and hardened. Ironically, such a transition would prove the key to survival for both Andrew and his remaining friend.

The men were given permission to throw away the hated knapsacks. All they carried now was ball cartridge ammunition and horns filled with powder stuffed into their belts, along with bayonet, musket and wooden canteens. They turned their blankets into ponchos. Andrew refused to part with his uncle's French knapsack or any of the precious belongings it contained.

At Lugo, Andrew stood with the regiment, elated his opportunity had arrived to meet Frenchmen in battle at last. It was not to be as no part of his line was engaged during the encounter. Instead, they stood shivering the entire day awaiting a decision from the commander. When it arrived and with the retreat order given, Andrew was as bitter and spite-filled as any other man. Archie was less sanguine and said little.

They returned to the march. There was no period of the retreat worse than the stretch from Lugo to Betanzos. More men dropped out in agony and exhaustion than at any point. It was only the hate that burned in Andrew's soul that kept him going. Archie was slowing by the hour. Andrew took the lead and led them both on. Any food they were fortunate to find, he gave most of the share to his friend. Needless to say, apart from the odd frozen turnip, they found little. Men were dying of dysentery all along the road. By God's grace neither Andrew nor Archie were afflicted. Andrew insisted that they never suck any of the snow but only drink from their canteens. His mind was entirely clear in what he had to do to survive. His strength of character received its brutal flowering on the road to Coruña.

He followed the instructions of Mr Innes, the assistant surgeon. But he noted that his toes were beginning to darken and a blister appeared on the little one on his right foot. It was beginning to hurt but he refused to bow to it.

An indication that something had changed in Andrew's character was a highly distressing incident involving himself and Archie. They walked through the village of Bamonde, stripped bare by those before them, but word was the next village contained supplies. The rain teemed down inexorably, the road, already badly churned, dreadful. Archie pleaded with Andrew to stop to rest up.

Looking around the tiny settlement, Andrew shook his head. 'We can't. We have to get to this next place. There's food there. If we hang about here, there might not be anything left by the time we arrive. I'm sorry, Archie. I promise we'll stop at the next village.' The Fifer nodded his head slowly in acceptance, but his movements remained unsteady and laboured.

They carried on and left the settlement behind. They walked at Archie's slow, shuffling pace which suited Andrew as his feet were hurting. They were constantly soaked and he had almost forgotten a time when he ever felt warm or dry. As he tramped along he tried to fix on absolutely nothing in his mind. Thinking about anything wasted energy. The only things that were real were the next step in the road and the pain from his feet. He never thought of Gabriela now. He tried not to think of Joshua. The image of his uncle and the death blow that killed him burned into his mind for a time, fuelling him, but even that was now fading.

As they walked along they noticed a woman and a child of about seven years old struggling alongside them. This was now an unusual sight, a living woman and child. They were usually dead. The child was beyond exhaustion and had to be dragged along by the hand by his mother. She had to stop to coax him to continue, lacking strength to carry him.

'Please soldier, take my child. Take him with you.' She begged without response to the shuffling scarecrows who passed by, ignoring her.

'Only for a while. Please carry him. To the next village. Please, good soldiers. My husband is dead. Please help me.'

As Andrew came to the spot where she stood, he tried to block out her pitiful entreaties. Go away. Please go away. I can't carry anyone. He tried to quicken his pace and move beyond her. He walked on a few steps before he noticed Archie was not with him.

Exhaustedly, he stopped which often hurt more than marching, turned and saw to his numbed mind's disbelief, Archie speaking with the woman. Angered now, he paced towards the three people standing to the side of the moving column.

'Archie! Why are you stopping?' The woman looked at Andrew and then back at his friend.

'I'm going to carry this wee lad a bit until the lady feels stronger.' Archie replied simply.

Mouth open in astonishment, Andrew walked up to Archie and stuck his face into the Fifer's. 'You're doing what? Have you lost your mind, you stupid bastard? You can hardly carry yourself! Do you want to die out here? Do you?'

Archie shoulders dropped and he turned away from the woman's desperate stare. He'd never seen his friend so enraged. His tired mind returned to the fight in the brothel in Salamanca. It was dangerous to cross Drew.

'Soldier,' the woman pleaded, her hand out to Andrew, 'it's only for a short while. Then I'll take him back. Please, I beg you, kind soldier!'

Shaking and furious, Andrew turned to the woman. 'I'm sorry. We can't. My friend is barefoot! Can you not see? We can't help you. Wait for the reserve. It's their job to assist you. They won't be long in coming.' The last was an exaggeration to say the least. Andrew grabbed Archie by the arm and pulled him back on to the road. They both did not look back at the two lost souls stranded behind them.

Andrew brooded on the incident obsessively for a time. He was bitter at the woman. Who did she think she was? Risking his life and that of his soft hearted friend? They were soldiers, not mules. If you couldn't march, you died. It was simple as that. His mind was temporarily in a state of derangement.

They continued until they arrived at a collection of non-distinct huts called Guitiriz where groups of soldiers were congregated around a wagon containing salted fish. There were casks of rum split open and canteens were being filled. Andrew noted the acrid stench of vomit.

'Best leave it mate, on empty guts it'll make you puke.' A soldier of the 51st explained, pointing to the wagon. There were men rolling around in the snow and mud spewing and holding their stomachs in agony.

'Is there anything else here to eat?' Andrew asked.

'Bastards ahead been through like a plague of locusts. You'll find little 'ere, mucker.'

'It's better than nothing.' Andrew walked over to the wagon to collect chunks of fish and placed them in his knapsack.

'Your funeral, Jock.' The man replied squarely. Meanwhile Archie was filling both their canteens with rum, Andrew decidedly no longer tee-total.

A lone, elderly officer stood observing the scene. He bellowed to the groups of soldiers. 'It's to Betanzos that you must head now, boys. Only twenty miles to the ships after that. No stopping till Betanzos!'

As they marched towards that town, the country began to change for the better. They had finally arrived at the temperate coastal land of Spain. The temperature rose, wild flowers, rye and small country lanes replaced snow, ice and desolation. The men sensed the pull of the sea and their spirits rose. On entering Betanzos, for the first time since leaving Astorga, Andrew began to believe he was going to make it home alive.

There were plentiful supplies. New shoes for both and a blanket each. The commander ordered 11th of January 1809 a day of rest for everyone entering the town. The halt would allow stragglers to arrive and re-join their regiments. The 42nd found a monastery as a billet and after eating their fills, the men took advantage of Sir John Moore's generosity to sleep.

The relationship between the two boys strained after the incident involving the woman and child. Archie would heed whatever Andrew advised but in a passive, almost sheep like manner that Andrew found disconcerting. Now in the monastery, Andrew felt himself unloaded of the awful stress of trying to keep both of them alive. The consequent psychological burden made of him fell away and something of himself began to return. The woman and child soon haunted his thoughts. He seriously considered going out on the road back to Guitiriz to look for them. This was madness of course, and he knew it. But the shame burned him and the ecstasy of arriving in Coruña and a ship home the next day, was tempered somewhat by his feelings of guilt. He knew he had to reconcile with Archie over the matter. He had lost two people very close to him and he would not countenance losing a third.

He asked how Archie was faring. They'd hardly spoken since arriving in the town.

'I'm alright. Good grub that was. Feel full up again.' Archie was referring to the generous meal they'd just consumed. Like most of the regiment, both were now bedded down in the billet. Andrew leaned up on his elbow.

'I want to say sorry to you for what happened. My mind was addled for a while out there.' Archie remained silent. 'We can't let it gnaw away at us. It happened and it's only now I realise what I did.'

'You looked like you wanted to kill me, Drew.'

Andrew was not expecting such a response. 'Did I? Christ, forgive me. What was going on in my brain? I was only thinking about staying alive. My mind was such that I would do anything, no matter how bad to achieve that.'

'I wouldn't. There are things you can't do. No matter what. They're against God's law. Only Satan prospers when good men commit evil.'

Andrew was now shocked. 'Was what I did evil?'

Archie didn't reply. But Andrew demanded a response. He felt Archie's sanctimony misplaced and faintly ridiculous. 'I asked you. Was it evil?'

'Ask yourself that.'

Andrew snapped. 'Damn your piety! You're alive aren't you? How many of God's laws have I broke? Where was God on the march? What mercy did He ever show us?'

'You shouldn't blaspheme like that, Drew.'

Andrew got out from under his blanket, put his new shoes on and stood up. He needed to urinate. 'You must have undergone a transformation on that march. From whoremonger and despoiler of lassies to Saint Archibald of Fife. You're in the right country. They'll worship you here. But not me. I bestow no adoration on hypocrites!'

Sir David Baird had some explaining to do.

He was with John Moore and Thomas Graham in the commanders quarters in Betanzos. He turned up to the summons rather sheepishly. Davy was not looking forward to the confrontation. He had to answer for a calamity involving the loss to the army of four hundred men, women and children.

When Sir John sent Major George Napier from his staff as messenger to advise Baird at Nogales that his division was to proceed for embarkation to Coruña and not Vigo, Davy was not best pleased.

'Christ!' He exclaimed while reading the despatch in bed. 'Will the bugger ever make up his mind? Like some damnable woman who doesnae ken whether to offer up her quim or no'!'

Fortunately, Napier had difficulty comprehending the heavy Scots invective, but was left in no doubt of the gist of the generals' feelings on the matter.

'I suppose you'll be wanting to carry the message to Hope and Fraser too, Napier?' Baird grunted resentfully.

The major wasn't ordered to do so by Sir John, but more than happy to oblige. If General Baird didn't have anyone in mind from his own staff, he would be perfectly willing to carry the message on personally.

For reasons known only to the general, Baird exploded. 'Oh dae ye now? Well let me tell you, George fucking Napier, I dinnae require any pretty boy chaser o' floozies and shagger o' scrubbers tae dae my work for me! I've got many a muckle lad perfectly capable! Now leave the despatch wi' me and bugger off!'

The major bravely stood his ground, insisting as he knew the roads and as the instructions detailed in the despatch were of the highest importance, he believed he should carry them.

Napier would later describe the general's face as turning purple. 'I told ye tae fuck off, didn't I? Now beat it, before I fling this piss pot at yer heid!'

Major Napier retired to safety and Baird despatched a dragoon with the message. Only, the dragoon got drunk along the way and failed to deliver the message on time. Fraser's division had set out for Vigo and were ten miles on the road before they received the belated order. They turned back and in the darkness, lost four hundred casualties to death from the bitter cold and to straggling.

Now Davy Baird had to account. But there was another black mark against him. Embarrassing gossip was spreading throughout the army. While commandeering a house for the night in Guitiriz, the general sent down his cook to prepare a pot of tea by the fire. A number of exhausted officers from various regiments were allowed to use the downstairs accommodation as shelter for the night. The cook had trouble squeezing in between the slumbering men and could not reach the fire to boil the general's kettle. Returning to his master, all those downstairs were awoken by Sir David's outrage.

'Then tuft everyone o' the bastards out! They can sleep in the fuckin' cauld! I want my tea now and I'll be damned if I care if a bunch of (expletive deleted) freeze their baws aff for it!'

The cook was sent down to present the general's feelings on the subject. He was sent packing and there was a tense stand-off between officers and commander. Sir David finally relented, had his tea, and honour was satisfied.

Amusing as this last anecdote was, it pointed to the wider issue of Baird's competence and the fragile state of his health. Moore and Graham now accepted between themselves he was struggling with illness. They knew him as profane and moody, but always highly effective. It was known that he never spoke to the men in such a fashion, no matter the reason. They loved him dearly, partly because he spoke as they did. He could be forgiven the odd outburst. But the incident with Napier at Nogales had to be addressed. It was too serious.

'Have ye calmed doon, yet, Davy?' Thomas Graham asked testily. He was given the pleasurable task of dressing down his old rival.

'Tam, Johnny. What can I say? I'm truly sorry. I am.' Baird pleaded. 'Those poor laddies! Their lassies and wee bairns. I keep seein' their faces in my nightmares! If only ye kent how upset I am?' Moore said nothing but glanced over to Graham to continue.

'Ye're nothin' but a bad tempered auld goat, Baird! Christ man, anyone wid think ye were steamin' hawf the time! The way ye dealt with yon boy Napier was a disgrace! He's one o' my laddies and I dinnae take kindly tae a foul moothed, auld mairbag threatenin' tae lob pish bowls at him! Where dae ye think ye are, man? At a regimental bash doon the Grassmerket?'

Davy stood and accepted his verbal thrashing admirably. He knew it was deserved and allowed Graham his moment.

'And what's this aboot a cook? Whae is the man? Some culinary genius oot o' Paris? Is feedin' yer gob wi' honest sojers fare no' guid enough for ye? Can ye no' make yersel a cup o' tea wi' oot disturbin' hawf the airmy? Fuck me, Davy. Yer gettin' soft, laddie. Next thing ye'll be wantin' a dozen virgins tae take turns wiping the shite fae yer erse wi' silk handkerchiefs!'

Moore and Baird could not help but snigger at the last. The air was now clear and they sat down to discuss future plans. Moore then advised of an urgent despatch he had only just received from Coruña.

'The ships have not arrived in port yet.' Graham gazed impassively ahead.

Baird responded. 'Well? When will they?'

'Maybe another four or five days. There are ships waiting but nowhere near enough for the entire army. My plan is this. To begin defensive preparations for the likelihood of attack while embarking the wounded and sick on the ships already there. Gentlemen, we have work to do.'

Chapter Twenty – Six

Andrew Berry limped agonisingly through the last few steps into Coruña. He was in too much pain to take in his surroundings. He did not care about women cheering and handing the soldiers food and drinks. He was barely cognisant of a particularly beautiful girl stopping and placing a flower in his bonnet, then kissing him. All he desired was to halt, remove his shoes and allow cool air at his blistering feet.

He did not march the last stage of the retreat with his friend. Archie snubbed him and refused his apology and handshake the night before after Andrew offered to make amends. The friendship appeared to be over. What Drew said could not be unsaid, Archie responded in a self-righteous tone. Andrew didn't bother to reply and rolled himself up in his blanket, turning his back.

Instead he marched with Killane, Dod Melvin and Hugh Scott. The latter two were still recovering from wounds suffered at Bembibre. Andrew felt a certain comfort to be close to men who had known his uncle so well.

Word spread there were only enough ships in the harbour to carry away the wounded and the cavalry. Everyone else would have to wait for the fleet to arrive. But Coruña was a veritable paradise compared to what they experienced on the march. There was food, drink, supplies, clothes and a new musket for every man. Discipline was being enforced once again, but most of the men would be allowed to rest before they boarded their ships. There was a rumour that the commander was about to sign a truce with the French to allow safe passage home. A type of Convention of Cintra in reverse. Needless to say, the rumour was scurrilous but there was talk that a number of corps commanders had approached Sir John to ask him to make just such a request. Conversely, there was a feeling among a few of the high command that the French would not attack and allow them go home unhindered.

In fact, Sir John Moore was seen riding outside the town on his cream coloured horse surveying the landscape. He was preparing his defence of the town regardless of any rumour or opinion while scouting suitable positions to draw up his plans.

Andrew cared little for any of it. His ears perked up at talk of the sick being embarked first. He was suffering from frostbite and was calculating whether that was enough to get him on a ship. There was talk of a battle on the horizon. He'd still have the chance to kill two Frenchman. That was the number he fixed on in his mind. One each for Joshua and his uncle.

On arriving in the town that afternoon of January 12th, they were found surprisingly pleasant billets in a former convent. Each man was given a clean set of uniforms, shoes, stockings and fresh linen. They were then invited to burn their worn out rags in a bonfire built outside the town.

On removing his worn shoes to examine his feet, he found the three toes of the right foot swollen. Each appeared to be nothing more than a large, red blister. Walking barefoot on the cold floor of the convent gave some relief.

The men were given facilities to make their ablutions. Andrew washed his entire body thoroughly, paying particular attention to his feet. He felt better afterwards and went to consult with Mr Innes. The assistant surgeon was pleased to see him and asked after Archie's welfare. Andrew mumbled he was doing fine before Mr Innes began his examination.

'That's good, Andrew. I see you've been following your instructions.' Mr Innes said with an air of satisfaction after completing his inspection. 'Fortunately there won't be any more marching for a good while. The toes, though blistered and swollen, have not reached the stage where they risk becoming gangrenous. That as you know is when we may have to remove them. On board ship and with fine sea air, I am confident the healing process will begin. As for tomorrows expected action, I cannot say I am entirely comfortable allowing you to take part.'

Andrew's elation at the good news about his feet quickly turned to anxiety. 'Sir, I could not in all good conscience abandon my friends at such an hour.'

'Such decisions are not for you to make, *Private Berry*!' Mr Innes' tone, to an older man, would have been heard for what it was, ironic and humorous. But Andrew believed him deadly serious.

'Sir! The shame…what would Iain or Tomàs think?'

'Or Colonel Stirling, or General Moore, or his Majesty King George himself for that matter?' Mr Innes laughed out loud. 'Very well, Andrew. I would not wish such a burden on *my* conscience. But wait here a moment. I have some small bandages for you to append to your feet. I would not want your urgent desire to meet the enemy spoiled by your tripping over your own shoes before facing them in battle.'

Relieved and grateful, Andrew watched as Mr Innes demonstrated how to use the bandages effectively and after giving thanks, left his quarters. Feeling euphoric that he no longer need fear amputation, he went out for a walk alone around the town.

Sir John Moore returned to the house in the Canton Grande where he made his quarters in Coruña. It was previously occupied by Davy Baird when first arriving in the town from England. Situated in the Pescaderia quarter, it had a windowed balcony (now missing a pane or two) looking over the port to the little island of San Antòn. He noted men still coming into the town, stragglers mainly, looking to join with their regiments. He'd need every one who could hold a musket.

After making his survey of the ground outside the walls of the town earlier, he accepted with only sixteen thousand troops able to bear arms, he did not have the men to spare to adequately cover both main features of Monte Mero and the Peñasquedo ridge. The land was undulating, strewn with gorse and boulders with furrows and small patches of field enclosed by walls making it tough country to traverse. It was not ground for cavalry. He stopped to gaze thoughtfully at a small settlement below Peñasquedo's heights. Less than three miles from Coruña's gates, Elvina was a village of scattered farms and houses with a church with an open belfry containing two bells. It was a maze of dry stone walls surrounding its lime-washed properties and gardens, and a veritable warren of narrow side streets and little pathways.

On his left was the estuary of the river *Mero*, creating a natural barrier. At his centre, the French would use the heights of Peñasquedo to look down the sloping valley onto the lower but raised British position on the ridge opposite. That's where they would come at him. Two of Moore's divisions would be placed there. The French advance would cut through

Elvina lying between the two opposing forces. Pickets and skirmishers took up positions in the village.

He then had to offer the carrot. His right flank was wide open to a turning movement which could cut him off from the town. The village of San Cristobal lay in the heart of this area and may prove enticing. It's certainly what he would do if he was Soult. To combat this obvious threat, he would place Fraser's division of six thousand men on the outskirts of Coruña. His remaining division under Edward Paget, he would use as a mobile reserve placing it in front and to the left of Fraser. If the threat increased on the right, Paget would spring to his aid. If Soult managed to gain headway along Moore's left, then Paget would make his way there to block his path.

Moore only had nine guns. The rest were aboard ship. He gave three to Paget and placed the rest along the ridge facing the heights above Elvina. They would add nuisance value, if little else.

Thomas Graham entered the room just as he was finishing his lunch. He sauntered over to Moore's table and poured himself a glass of wine. He swallowed it in one go and smacked his lips in satisfaction.

'You're looking cheery, Tam?' Moore noted.

'I am that. I'm pleased to humbly report to the honourable commander, that the fleet from Vigo is in sight and will be enterin' harbour before ye know it.'

Moore jumped eagerly from his chair and looked through the balcony window. 'By Christ, so it is! We can start loading tonight with luck. I wonder how Bobby Craufurd's faring. How I'd love to see his gurning face again!'

'Och, dinnae worry about Boab. He'll be fine.' Graham tutted. 'Worry about this. I've somethin' else to report. Johnny Colbourne's returned from patrol. He reckons Soult could be here by the morn. And he'll no' be stoppin' to attend Sunday service either! He'll be lined up and rarin' tae go. It's going to happen, Johnny. There'll be a scrap this time.'

Tam pulled a chair and stretched his long legs out. 'Have ye got it all in yer heid? What you'll do, like?'

Back at his desk, Moore filled a wine glass. 'I believe so. We don't have to win. We only need to contain him long enough to get the army aboard ship. I won't allow myself to be sucked into any attrition battles for position. I don't have to. As the old saying goes, what we have, we hold.'

Graham was quiet for a while. 'And after, Johnny? When we get back.

Are ye as well prepared for *them*?'

And there lies the rub if you're John Moore, that man thought. But hasn't it ever been the case? Corsica, Sicily, Sweden and now Spain. All of them explainable and indeed explained or else why would he be here now at the pinnacle of his career? Who were his rivals? Davy Baird was finished as his health was giving out both physical and mentally. Wellesley? Banished to Ireland with the stink of Cintra clinging to his tails. The up and coming men, Hill, Craufurd, Hope were years behind him in the lists.

He thought of Whitelocke at his trial. How pathetic a figure he cut. Moore could face a similar enquiry. But would he really? In her letter, Hester confirmed what he now believed himself that Castlereagh was fully in support of him. And he ran the government. Not Portland. Moore was *his* man.

Reports were still coming in but it looked highly likely that he'd lost above five thousand men of the army. Five thousand men and he hadn't fought a battle. But the king lost that many a year to disease in the West Indies. No enquiries were held over that.

He had come very close to Bonaparte, or rather, the Emperor had got close to him. Moore found that he held no fear of his reputation. He knew the fighting capabilities of his army were second to none. He was confidant of his own abilities. Though it would have been something to confront the man on the white horse.

Two days before, he wrote a last, bitter letter to Castlereagh. He poured out all his anger and frustrations. Explaining himself the victim of circumstances, of unforeseen events out with his control, writing it left him spent. Almost as if he could expel no more energy on the matter. His last testament of sorts.

And if they did want a head to roll, and if were to be his, what then? He'd find himself some sinecure. Shorncliffe. Then marriage. Yes, married to Hester. And children. He would be a contented man with all of that. He had money. He smiled. But never enough for Hester! She'd have to adapt. He smiled again. To watch Hester adapt would be something, too.

What had it all been worth? He'd been chased around the Peninsula from one place to the other, losing thousands of men and women along the way. What next for them? The street for the maimed and sick and the poorhouse for the women back in Britain. What were his troubles to theirs?

He still burned in shame over how he spoke to the colonel of the 42nd that day outside Bembibre. How he described ordinary men in such ill-considered words, born less fortunate than he. It was unforgivable. If he could take anything back that would rank high. The failure to send all the woman and the children of the army home before entering Spain was his biggest regret of all. The scenes he'd witnessed! He knew they would haunt his dreams forever. Poor souls. Those *poor* souls! God, please forgive me and bring them peace.

Now melancholy after the exuberance over the sight of the fleet, he turned to a response to Graham's question. 'I'll leave it to them to decide what they wish to do with me. I usually do well to come out the other side. I've always been fortunate that way, despite the scrapes I found myself in. I just hope they do me justice. That's all I ask for.'

The first thing that Andrew could not fail to notice on his stroll was the damage caused the town by the enormous explosion the day before. The commander ordered that all stocks of gunpowder, some 1500 barrels kept in a warehouse one mile outside the town, were to be destroyed. The engineers laid their charges but the subsequent explosion belied the amount of gunpowder held in store. There were in fact 5000 barrels.

Believed to have been the largest man made explosion in European history to that date, the blast sent shock waves to Coruña's harbour where some ships slipped their cables and rocked dangerously. Many windows in the town were blown out. Two huge columns of smoke hung around for hours before finally drifting out to sea.

Andrew hobbled carefully round the broken glass that still lay on the cobbles, slowly wandering through the centre of Coruña in no particular direction. It was a welcoming, vibrant place in comparison with the gloomy, unfriendly towns and villages passed through during the retreat. It reminded him of Salamanca.

He had money in his sporran. The men were paid for the first time since leaving the university city. Andrew went into a shop and bought writing materials. He found a small café, ordered coffee and began a letter to Gabriela.

He wrote in simple language, aware she would need to seek an interpreter. He told her he loved her, and would one day come back to Salamanca with the army to marry her. He asked her if she would wait for him and if she was willing, to write to the Toll House in Barbauchlaw.

The girl at the counter of the café was young and pretty like Gabriela. She had a little English and he was able to make her understand with the help of gestures, that he would wish to pay her if she were to have the letter mailed for him. She would only accept the money for the mailing of the letter but invited him to buy another cup of coffee in lieu of payment. They both laughed together, shyly.

He left the café feeling content and dreamily walked the streets. Soldiers were everywhere doing the same in groups or as individuals. Restaurants were filled with singing and good cheer. Officers smoking large cigars strolled about studying the architecture.

He went into a church, seeking some quiet for reflection. Andrew had little to celebrate other than being alive. He looked at the pews, mostly filled by women, praying for whatever they prayed for. He wanted closeness with his uncle and Joshua again. Now, here in Coruña, he was safe. They were all safe. What good did their deaths serve? If they had all arrived here to embark over the next days, why did God not allow Joshua and Sandy to do the same? What was their crime?

But hadn't Joshua and his uncle committed offences according to God's law? Adultery and fornication were mortal sins. Andrew looked at the crucifix above the garish altar. The Christ was horrifically real, as in all chapels in this strange country. Why did they base their faith on pain and torment? Andrew was without the base sins of his friend and uncle. Was that why he was spared? He wanted to do things with Gabriela, of course. Thought about them. Dreamt of her naked body.

He left the church, having found no peace. He turned and began to walk towards the harbour. Wagons and other equipment were being thrown over seawalls to be destroyed. He found a spot and remained for a time watching the fleet from Vigo arrive. Andrew found the movement of the sea brought him a measure of calm. The air was invigorating, too. He soon started to enjoy himself watching the ships tacking and coming about, marvelling at the skill and courage of the tiny figures working high up the masts and rigging.

He began to hear gun shots from below and wondered if ammunition was being fired off. He noticed the sound of clip-clopping behind him and turned to see a parade of horses being led to the beach from the harbour. He watched as the procession made its way down and decided to follow on behind. A stroll along the dunes would be pleasant.

When he arrived on the beach he found a vision of hell. The horses of the cavalry were being led to slaughter. Only a few could be brought on board ship and the remainder were to be destroyed to prevent them being taken by the French.

Naturally, the exercise was botched. They were killed by bullets or by having their throats cut with sabres because the men couldn't bear to shoot them and made a mess of their pistol shots, leaving the beasts in agony. The sounds of screaming, terrified animals rent the air. The smell of blood and steaming droppings was overwhelming. Many horses broke loose, galloping down the beach or attempting to go back up into the town. Hundreds of carcasses lay along the sands. Officers and men wandered about lost, distraught and in tears, cursing God, cursing themselves. Andrew closed his eyes to it. He stood swaying unsteadily. He wanted to weep tears for all the horses, oxen and mules, for all the women and little children, for all the poor soldiers. For Gabriela and his lost friendship with Archie. For Joshua, for Uncle Sandy. For his mother and father whom he pained so much. But there were not enough tears left for any of them. Not even for himself.

The following day, the 42nd began their preparations for the defence of Coruña. Sir David Baird and his brigade commanders were given a first look at their position in the field. It would be the forthcoming battle's fulcrum point. The ridge on the slopes of Monte Mero, looking across the village of Elvina to the heights of Peñasquedo.

The three commanders, Warde, Manningham and Sir William Bentinck were made aware the initial onslaught was expected to head directly for them. Manningham's brigade would take the left, Bentinck's, the right, with Warde's Guards behind Sir William in reserve. The 42nd would be fixed in the very eye of the coming French storm.

Andrew spent the day trying to erase the memory of the horrors on the beach. He slept little the night before, reliving over and over in his mind the dreadful sounds of the horses and the endless streams of blood soaked sand. Fortunately, he was kept busy by Sergeant McQuater, constructing huts and tents the entire day up on the ridge. Archie was employed delivering crates of ammunition and supplies from the few remaining wagons to the 42nd's field position.

The day passed in good fellowship. A battle followed by a ship home. Morale rocketed. There was plenty food and flirtation with the females offering wares from baskets to the hungry kilties. After returning to the billet that night, Andrew was healthily shattered after an honest day's work and fresh air. His feet were no worse for it and memories of the day before had receded.

That evening, Andrew and Archie were summoned to the colonel.

They met with Captain Crozier first, who assured them they had done no wrong but the colonel wished to meet them to discuss a matter of great importance. Andrew and Archie had not spoken and avoided each other since their fall out. They both now stood together with the captain outside the room in the convent allocated to the commanding officer.

The door opened and they were led in by Crozier. The colonel, a man in his forties with wavy brown hair and an attractively boyish face, welcomed them to stand at their ease. Crozier took up a position behind and to the right of his commanding officer.

He was evidently well briefed. 'Well now, Mr Berry and you, Mr Miller, it's a pleasure to make your acquaintance at last. It reflects shame on a mere colonel that he's taken so long to introduce himself to two such notable paladins as yourselves! Can you forgive me?'

The boys now relaxed, though still mystified somewhat, both mumbled that they most certainly could.

'Well, that's fine then. Oh, Captain Crozier! I'm somewhat relieved. I've been worrying about this all day! It's off my chest now, thank the good Lord.' He winked at the boys and both found they could not hide their grins.

'Now, lads. The reason I wish to see you is that I would like to admit you both into a secret. Are these young men good for holding their tongues, Captain Crozier?'

'In my humble opinion, they are, Colonel Stirling.' Crozier replied on cue.

'Why that's just fine! Well, then, here it is. And hush mind! No' telling anybody. Not even your sweethearts! That includes the wee darlin' o' yours in Salamanca, Master Andrew, eh?'

Now thoroughly enjoying the colonel's banter, Andrew gave his assurance heartily.

'Boys, the news is that when we return home, I shall be resigning as colonel of this regiment.' Andrew and Archie merely stared, emitting no response. 'Oh, I see it has shocked ye's both into silence.' The colonel turned and rolled his eyes comically at Crozier. 'Anyway! The *rest* of the regiment will be in tears at the news. Whether it's tears of joy or sadness remains to be seen! But anyway, my replacement as colonel is yet to be decided, though I've a fair guess who it may boil down to. But as far as you two are concerned, here's why my leaving matters.

'As departing colonel, I must prepare a report for the new man. In this report I shall make recommendations to the new colonel which, by all the traditions of regimental protocol, he is obliged to adhere to. These recommendations regard the performance of enlisted men as well as officers.

'Andrew, Archibald. I am pleased to advise you that both your names will appear in my report.'

'Thank you, sir!' Andrew cried, Archie also making the colonel aware of his gratitude.

'Thank *you*, lads. I've received many reports from your superiors about your attitudes to duty, to your friends and to your non-commissioned officers. In particular, I draw attention to reports from Sergeant McGillivray, a man of inestimable value to this regiment. A man of great worth whose opinions I valued above all others. I know his loss is a source of deep hurt and sadness to you both, as I know you regarded him highly and respected him deeply. I only wish he were here to see this moment. As I know he would wish the poor laddie who was your friend, young Joshua Whitfield, of whom the sergeant also greatly esteemed. Indeed, he described you to me as his 'terrible trio' with some affection. You were his pride. He deemed you boys as future men of consequence in this regiment.

'When we return home and the new colonel takes up his post, I have recommended that you both be transferred to the light company. While there, you are to fall under the guidance of the senior sergeant and corporals where you will be trained in the dark arts! You will advance along the path to leadership where I fully expect you both to be promoted corporal in good time. I have no doubt you will be successful. Now then, boys. How does that sound?'

Excited, they could only mumble embarrassed platitudes. The light company were skirmishers, screening the battalion's front and flanks. Light company men were the particular envy of the younger recruits. There was a mystique about them. They were elite troops, wearing the green *tourie*. Andrew and Archie had arrived in the regiment. They were now recognised.

'Humble. Eh, Captain Crozier? Nothing daunts these lads! I'll now come round and shake you both by the hand and offer my congratulations!'

After he did, the colonel turned and sat on the edge of a small table facing the boys. His mood changed.

'Tomorrow or the following day, there may well be a battle fought. Our regiment has been honoured with providing the defence of a vital section of the field. There is no doubt the enemy will target that ground in order to destroy us. You will both confront Bonaparte's columns. You will be tested to the limits of your courage and fortitude. I know you will not let me down. If God willing, we are successful and repel the French, then with His grace, we shall all meet again and head home. On behalf of myself and my officers, I pray for the safety of all in this regiment. Go with God, Andrew, and you, Archibald!

'Now return to your billets and clean your muskets one last time. Both of you try to get a good sleep. For tomorrow may be the longest day of your lives.'

Lying in the billet later, Andrew turned over the colonel's words in his mind. The meeting and news of their good fortune changed everything. It meant he now had a bright future. Some men tried for years to get into the light company and failed recommendation. Now he was in it though he'd been in the army less than six months. Once gain he blessed his uncle's memory for looking after him. He didn't really know what it was that he had done so well. He only ever did as he was told.

It meant he would now stay in the army. He'd reckoned on his frostbitten toes being cut off and then discharged as a cripple from service. He had wanted that on the march. It was a price worth paying to escape the hell he was suffering. But he accepted it was the cruelty of the roads that caused him to aspire to such an extremity. After Mr Innes' encouraging diagnosis, with good luck, he now need not fear such an outcome.

What about Archie? He had to try one more time to patch things up. It was like a running sore. They were a trio as the sergeant described.

Indispensable to each other. That's how they made it this far. Then they lost Joshua and lost part of themselves. They both had that inside them. They needed each other still.

He barely thought about the battle to come. Twice he'd been prepared to face the enemy and twice it proved a damp squib. It might happen again. Though it would just be his luck to be killed in his first battle after being told of his transfer.

Everything prepared for the morning, he wrapped himself in his bedroll, ensuring enough straw lay under him. He didn't want to wake up aching on the day of a battle. He had only just settled when he felt something prodding his back.

'Drew.' Archie stood above him carrying his kit and bedroll.

'Archie. What is it?'

'Can I bunk down here?'

'Aye, of course.' Andrew moved himself along to allow room. Archie silently made up his bed. Unconsciously as always, Andrew pushed some of his straw towards Archie's bed space. Archie glanced at it and returned to his kit.

'Tomàs says there won't be a battle tomorrow, but the day after. Iain, too.' Archie declared as he climbed inside his blankets.

'They could be right.'

'If we make it through that, we'll go home and join the light company.'

'Aye, that'll be fine'

'Do you get more money for that?'

'Not sure. I'll ask Iain tomorrow.'

There was a silence. Then Archie spoke. 'Pals again, Drew?'

'Of course. Always will be, Archie.'

Chapter Twenty – Seven

After breakfast the following morning, the 42nd were paraded and inspected outside their billet. They carried all their implements of war. Ball cartridges, powder, bayonet, and musket.

They then marched out of the town. The locals watched in silence as the kilted men made their way through the streets. Girls walked out and stuck flowers in their bonnets and coats. Older women stopped and kissed them as they would kiss goodbye to their own sons. Many shed tears, crossing themselves vociferously.

They passed the café where Andrew wrote his letter. The girl who served him stood outside watching. Andrew caught her eye. She smiled bravely, then put her hand to her mouth and hurried back inside. Andrew remembered Salamanca and the cross now around his neck.

There was something else precious hanging there. When looking through his uncle's knapsack, he found wrapped in a piece of plaid, a broach that opened up to reveal a lock of sandy brown hair. It was his mother's colour. Alexander kept it with him all these years. Andrew believed as long as he wore it, his mother and uncle would protect him. Gabriela's cross would do the same. Together with Gods mercy, he would make it through the trial of fire to come.

The morning was dull and damp, the ground they marched over difficult, but they made the two mile hike to their position in good time. Senior officers on horseback milled about discussing the events ahead. Andrew recalled Killane's prediction.

The French finally appeared later that day. Soult's twenty thousand men took up position on the heights of Peñasquedo and Palavea as British pickets involved in fire fights were forced back to Elvina. A heroic but futile charge by the 5th with fixed bayonets ended with the colonel of the regiment killed.

In the event, the Longford man proved prescient. There was no battle. It was said Marshal Soult was high up on his hill, enjoying himself watching the English fleet beat about. He was too much of a gentlemen to launch his army before the British made their preparations. Good manners mattered to the *Duke of Damnation*, as he was known to his enemies.

Andrew and Archie lay that night in bivouac on the ridge. Only officers were allowed tents. It would be later on in the war before the men were afforded the same luxury. Each slept fully clothed, using their knapsacks as pillows. Archie lay awake next to the snoring Andrew. He was overjoyed they'd reconciled. He'd had time to think, which he tried not do too often. He concluded that everything Drew said about him was right. Archie *had* been a stupid bastard.

He knew he came close to dying on the last stretch from Lugo. If it wasn't for Drew, he wouldn't have made it. He understood now that in undergoing such an experience, the mind mattered as much as the body. In the early part of the retreat when Joshua was with them, Archie was physically strong, but now accepted carrying Joshua as far as he did weakened him. He'd used up reserves of strength needed for the final haul. Archie now accepted Joshua's death had saved the other boys' lives. Tears ran from his eyes as he remembered his dying moments.

As for the incident before Betanzos, he now accepted it had served a purpose. He did not stop to speak to the woman with the child for altruistic reasons. He only noted interest in her the moment she mentioned her dead husband. Women in her predicament were fair game, available to anyone in the army. It happened all the time. Some newly made widows married another man the day after their husband was killed. It wasn't unusual. When he stopped to look at her, he saw a youngish women with long dark hair who matched his fantasy of having one to keep for himself, to do what he wanted with her anytime he liked. She'd also wash and clean for him and keep house.

He used the child to get to her. Carry the boy, be a hero and she would be his. The shame of his behaviour gnawed at him. Plus it was utter folly. He did not know how far he could have carried the boy before collapsing from the effort. Even if he didn't, how on earth could he keep a woman and child alive on that march? Drew was right. He could hardly carry his own diminishing weight.

What he would not tell Drew, was that soon after the incident, Christ spoke to Archibald Miller. He did not appear physically, but his voice came into his head and told him if he wanted to remain alive, he must change his ways towards females. They were God's creatures, not playthings to assuage his lustful urges. They were wives, mothers, sisters and daughters. The Lord's son spoke in Joshua's voice, warning him hellfire awaited fornicators and abusers of girls and women.

He thought about what Drew said about being a hypocrite. Those words affected him deeply. God was speaking through Drew, to warn him further. It took him time to comprehend all that happened. But it all fit into place after they met the colonel and received the good news about the light company. The Almighty was trusting him to change his ways. He was showing him the correct path to take and rewarding him in advance. Now it was up to himself not to let God down.

It was then he believed he underwent his rebirth. He could clearly see the path to his salvation ahead. The first thing he had to do was make amends with the beloved friend who'd saved his previously worthless life. Drew had shown the strength of his character and his inner goodness by accepting him back as if nothing happened. But something *had* happened.

Archie had no fear or concerns for the battle tomorrow. The Lord, in leading him on the journey to this place called Coruña, was saving him for something important. Maybe it was to perform a supreme act of heroism. Bonaparte was a Godless atheist. Everyone knew that. Their bestial slaughter of McGillivray, a man Archie idolised, confirmed it. His was the army of Darkness. Tomorrow, with the newly found faith and purpose God granted him, he would strike a fatal blow against His enemy while gaining revenge for Joshua and the sergeant.

At 10a.m. on the morning of 16th January 1809, the French came down from the slopes and formed into two large columns above Elvina.

They began their artillery barrage at 12p.m. Andrew and Archie were out of the line receiving their lunch when they heard the cannonade begin. They were with a group of men from the company about to enjoy their ration of delicious *labscuse*, a thick soup of minced beef and potatoes, seasoned with pepper. Andrew had his spoon to his mouth when a nearby hut he had worked on the day before was hit by roundshot. Splinters and sticks of wood flew into the air as the structure collapsed within itself. Fortunately, it was empty of occupants

'Stand to!' a voice roared loudly as bugles sounded the alarm. Andrew hurriedly lifted the bowl of soup to his mouth and drank down as much as he could, before gathering his kit together. Along with Archie, he made his way to stand in line with the regiment.

Andrew stood behind Killane, Melvin and Scott. Colquhoun was at the rear to ensure any gaps were closed up and to prevent anyone fleeing the field.

'What's happening?' Andrew asked Tomàs as he took his place.

'They're finding the range. Then there'll be hell to pay.'

Despite the soup he consumed, Andrew's mouth began to dry. His canteen was filled with rum but he didn't know if he would be permitted to take a drink. He looked ahead. Two columns of six hundred men each in dark blue stood against the green slopes behind the village before him. He shook involuntarily. He was looking at death heading his way.

Such a size of a force would swamp the little red line he formed part of. How on earth do you stop that? There were only two British cannons with his brigade and they were with the 4th regiment, far to the right of the line. Why did they get them and not us?

'Will our cannon return fire?' He asked nervously.

'I dare say they will, for all that they might as well blow peas. Two guns won't stop those columns.'

Andrew wondered what would stop them. The village maybe. If we get behind a wall, we can slow them down. No, we'd still be overrun. Andrew wracked his mind to think of a tactic that could be used to destroy such a formidable enemy. They had no cavalry to use either. Only seven hundred muskets.

They might have well stayed to finish their lunch. The French columns, now fully formed, remained at their positions as the ranging cannon shots ceased. The 42nd stood in line and considered the next move. Archie spoke to Andrew.

'Why are they just sitting there doing nothing?'

'Maybe they're eating their snails and frogs-legs.' Andrew replied.

The thought of such things made Archie queasy. Other than that he felt fine. Whenever he felt disturbed in any way now, he said the words from the Lord's Prayer to strengthen him. Those were the only words from the bible he knew. They comforted him as he looked at the hordes of Satan ranged before him.

They stood for over an hour and a half. Andrew asked permission to leave the line to defecate. He passed Corporal Colquhoun on the way back.

'All's well, Drew?'

'Aye, Iain. Wish you were standing with us.'

'I'll be about, don't worry.'

Andrew wondered if Iain and Tomàs were thinking of their families. How do you fight a battle with a clear mind if you know your death will bring possible destitution to your kin? Do you hang back and not go full tilt? But Andrew had kin too. He remembered Killane telling him that you must go in so hard, you think of nothing other than killing. Weaken for an instant and you'll be dead.

His thoughts were interrupted in devastating fashion when round shot ripped through the 42nd on the right. He caught a glimpse of two men being knocked backwards and a red mist appear above them. There were shouts of 'close up!' and two smashed bodies were carried to the rear. The French had opened the ball.

Andrew was grateful he only just emptied his bowels as the urge to go again hit him, though he knew it was only nerves. He returned to the line but now shot was homing in on the entire brigade. The 50th in the centre was taking its share but the 42nd were also receiving hits. Men moaned and dropped to their knees. Others shouted, when are we allowed to lie flat?

Andrew was now face to face with the ultimate test. He felt his chest tighten. The hand that held his musket was soon soaked in sweat. His left, at his side, rubbed the plaid of his kilt. I don't know how long I can stand this. Oh God, please let it end soon. He saw men drop their muskets and fall down to lay flat. Tomàs and the two others in front remained stock still, unmoving. They did not speak.

A shot went sailing over Andrew's head. He instinctively ducked and was glad he was able to do something. He reached with his shaking hand to the canteen at his side, but found he couldn't release his sweated grip on the musket with the other in order to unscrew the cap. He tried to follow Melvin and Scott's lead before him. Standing rigidly, facing the front. He emitted a soft moan as a man fell back to his left. He was completely unaware of Archie's presence at his side, so absorbed was he in his own terror. Make it quick if it happens. Don't let me suffer. Oh, Lord Jesus, my saviour, please allow me to get through this and never again will I take your name in vain. He lifted his trembling hand to the locket of hair and rubbed it. Please protect me, Mother and I'll come home to you. He touched the silver crucifix. I love you, Gabriela. Please let me live to see your beautiful face again. He was now shaking uncontrollably.

Killane turned his head. 'Stand firm, boys. It won't last.'

Sir David Baird watched as Moore and Graham rode towards him. The French cannonade had just begun. Davy thought it would be an expensive ball that landed on this spot in the next minute or so.

'Johnny, Tam! Fine morning for it.'

Moore steadied his cream coloured horse with the black face and mane. He looked for movement over at the French columns behind Elvina.

'Aye. It'll be a hot yin, the day!' he declared thoughtfully. 'How are the laddies bearing up?'

'As to be expected. But I'll no hold them too long to be mauled like lambs, Johnny. Give me the word and I'll take them forward!'

'You'll receive word in good time, Davy, I promise you that.' Moore confirmed and rode off with Graham towards the 42nd.

A shot crashed over Baird's head. Aye, you bastards, ye see me, do ye? He nudged his horse gently forward away from his position behind the 50th regiment. He wanted to observe how his fellow countrymen were faring. The 42nd were taking a pounding. It pained him greatly to see fine boys knocked over before having the chance of getting at the enemy as only they could. Davy rode forward and turned in to face the front, when he felt his left side hit by a hammer blow that nearly knocked him from his horse. His left arm lost all feeling and he leant forward in shock. He was then knocked back as another blow punched into his side. He felt sick and seemed to take a lifetime to ease himself off the horse. He leaned against its haunches and then felt himself lowered to the ground.

The stunned young face of his aide told him all he needed to know. 'Sir, Sir! Please don't move. We're sending for the surgeon.'

'Aw, bugger.' Davy sighed wearily. 'Tam's goin' to have all the fun!' He then passed out.

Unaware of Baird's wounding, Moore rode out in front of the 42nd. He watched them absorb the shock of the cannon fire and looked up at the ridge before him. He wondered when Soult would make his move. He had an inkling it was nearly time. But he would try something in an attempt to speed Soult's decision making processes.

A ball took the leg off a highlander in the front of the line. The man screamed dreadfully and a gap opened up as men moved away from him in horror.

'For the love of God, see to the fellow, someone!' Moore pleaded. The opening created could lead to worse. Men might begin to bolt. Three soldiers ran to the wounded man's aid, who continued crying loudly.

Moore reached down with his hand to the stricken soldier. 'My man, try to bear the pain a little better. You'll now be cared for. God go with you.'

Grabbing the reins, Moore rode to the rear of the 42nd line to look for Colonel Stirling. Meanwhile, Thomas Graham was receiving a message from an aide of David Baird's.

'Johnny, Baird's down. It's bad.'

'Oh, Christ! Poor Davy!' Moore put his hand to his forehead. 'Send a message to John Hope. He is to command the army should I fall. Do it now, Tam.'

'Aye. The lad's on his way.'

Moore's eyes found the 42nd's commanding officer. 'Colonel Stirling. I would be pleased if you would be so kind as to request the 42nd to lie themselves flat just below the ridge line.'

Shortly after the incident involving Moore and Stirling outside Bembibre, the colonel was summoned to the commander and an apology was offered for his unfortunate choice of words. Stirling was prepared to forgive, accepting the general's responsibilities were great and such men were allowed to blow out once in a while. It was impossible to bear a grudge or feel anything other than affection for Sir John Moore.

'It'll be my pleasure, sir!' Much pained at the punishment his men were taking, a relieved Stirling hurriedly called his officers over. The two lines were ordered to turn about and march ten paces. They then dropped to the ground just below the ridge line. They were now to all intents invisible to the French artillery.

Men reached for their canteens and drank deeply. There were a few nervous laughs and jokes but the feeling of relief was palpable. Iain Colquhoun appeared, anxiously searching for his friends.

'I knew they wouldn't get you!' He shook hands gratefully with Killane. 'And you four strapping lads! Not a scratch! You lead a charmed life, indeed.'

Melvin and Scott nodded over deep drafts of rum. Archie lay with his head down, praying. Andrew's face was buried in the gorse. He was hyperventilating and having difficulty trying to catch his breath.

Colquhoun knelt over him. 'Drew. Are you well?'

Andrew slowly turned around. His face was pale and there were strands of grass in his hair and bonnet. 'Yes…Yes, I'm better now.'

Iain rubbed his shoulder. 'You're a soldier and a man now, Andrew Berry.' He crawled over to Archie and spoke with him quietly. They were not out of danger as a cannon ball skipping across the gorse could still inflict grave damage. But they were now in a safer position under cover.

They lay only ten minutes recovering when the guns fell silent. There was a strange unnatural calm as the men looked about them. The two French columns then began to come down from the slopes of Peñasquedo. The 31 *leger* regiment of the French line commanded by General Mermet, led by *voltigeurs,* advanced directly towards Elvina. Andrew heard the sound of drums and music. This was the infamous '*Old Trousers*' the term British soldiers gave to the marching songs of the French army. He could hear the tramp, the jangle of twelve hundred belts and knapsacks. He would have seen the bayonets glisten in the early afternoon light. He heard but did not view the bitter struggle as French and British skirmishers fought it out in the village. Eventually, weight of numbers told as desperate red-coated figures emerged from Elvina, scuttling towards the British held ridge.

The French were now making their way through the deserted village. Its inhabitants had left days before for shelter in Coruña. The blue coated men climbed over walls and traversed the labyrinth of side streets. On reaching the outskirts, they stopped momentarily to reform, then began the advance up the slope to confront the red-coated brigade.

'Well. There they are, Johnny.' Thomas Graham observed. 'Are you goin' tae do the honours?'

Aware of what was required, Moore looked to his right where another column of French left the slopes in an attempt to cut off his flank. He ordered Harry Percy to ride to the colonel of the 4th regiment to request he throw back his right wing, effectively forming an 'L' shape, to protect against an encircling movement by the French.

More worryingly, Moore noted squadrons of cavalry riding forward on the tail of the column. He sent John Colbourne to Edward Paget asking to him to move his division forward in order to reinforce the right flank. Fraser had already began his march from Coruña.

Now to the issue at hand. He had to put a stop to the French advance from the village and hold them on the slopes below his position. Artillery was now out of the equation. The French had shown their hand with their cavalry. He hesitated to tempt fate, but everything appeared to be going to plan. So far.

He rode over to the prone men of the Royal Highland regiment. 'Brave lads of the 42nd! You have unfinished business with the enemy. Now is the opportunity to gain revenge for Sir Ralph and your comrades at Alexandria. Hold fast! The moment will arrive soon.'

Moore was reminding them of Egypt and the heavy losses the regiment incurred in their victory. It had an immediate effect as veterans minds turned back to their beloved commander, Abercromby.

'The bastards! Sir Ralph and Alexandria!' One man roared aloud.

'God bless the memory of that saintly old man.' Killane crossed himself in respect. Melvin raised his canteen. 'To the auld boy.' Scott remembered the bitter day and lost friends.

Sergeants and corporals crawling on their bellies, moved among the men, ordering them to fix bayonets and get ready to stand up. The three *click, click, clicks* of cold steel affixing to muskets sounded throughout the ridge. They were to fire one shot and then charge the advancing Frenchmen. It was traditional highland warfare of Tippermuir and Prestonpans. The stress of earlier moments turned to acute excitement as men prepared to kill. A few thought happily of the booty they would take from dead officers. Some looked forward to taking the canteens of wine from soldiers. All were prepared for an almighty scrap.

Andrew checked his musket was ready for firing. Ramrod where it should be, not left down the barrel. Pan filled with the correct amount of powder. Bayonet secure. This was it. He thought of Colquhoun's words on his new found manhood. His time had arrived. He was unafraid of the next phase of the battle because it would be man to man. He had stalwart friends at his side. They would cover each other. His entreaties to God, his mother and Gabriela held up. He didn't want to kill anyone. But he knew he couldn't afford to think like that any longer. He must do whatever is required to remain alive as he did on the latter stages of the death march. It was all or nothing.

'Are you ready, Archie?' He asked.

'Aye. Stay close, Drew.' He laid his hand on his friend's shoulder. 'God's watching over us. We're in his hands.'

'All set, *a grà?*' Killane grinned wickedly. 'We've suffered the pain. Now it's time for the pleasure.'

Andrew lay on his front with the musket before him. His breathing became heavy and his heart began to race. But where before it was abject fear, now it was almost ecstatic excitement. All his previous life now led to this supreme moment. Come on, Frenchmen. Hurry up!

He heard strange voices shouting in tandem, *En avant! En avant! Tuez! Tuez! Tuez!* They were upon them, Andrew thought expectantly. The time to avenge Joshua and Uncle Sandy had come. They were here!

'42nd CHARGE!'

Colonel Stirling's roar was followed instantly by the front row rising to its feet followed by the rear. Every man raised his musket and waited for the word. To the astonishment of the men of the 42nd as their muskets pointed down the slope, the blue jackets of the *31 leger* were only yards in front of them, marching on steadily.

'FIRE!'

The volley crashed out as the front row squeezed their triggers. Andrew steadied his musket, aimed and the rear rank followed suit. He felt himself lurch backwards as the shocking recoil hammered into his shoulder, his senses stunned and hearing momentarily shattered from the explosion. Billowing smoke blinded him as it poured from seven hundred muskets, the sulphurous stench of rotten eggs clogging his nostrils.

After the rear rank fired, the front row instantly screamed death cries and charged forward, bayonets bristling. Andrew followed close to Killane, Melvin and Scott, Archie at his side. They were soon among the enemy. There were shouted commands in French as those at the rear of the column closed up ranks. Andrew watched Killane roar with berserk rage as he crashed into two men, bowling them over and swinging his musket from side to side and across shoulder to shoulder. Melvin and Scott were grappling with four Frenchman when two of them bolted and fled. Andrew was alone in space. He stopped to look for a foe when he heard screams to his right.

'Drew! Drew!'

He turned his head to see Archie on the ground. Two Frenchmen were trying to stick him with their bayonets. Archie desperately kicked with his legs out at the soldiers, frantically moving his body from side to side with his musket held out, trying to avoid their cold steel.

Andrew now instinctively held his musket in his left hand. He fired his shot right handed but in the intimacy of a face to face struggle, he needed to use every resource he had. He held his musket across his upper chest, ran forward screaming 'ARCHIE!' and smashed into both Frenchmen, knocking one from his feet and the other off balance. He raised his musket up and stabbed at the man on the ground but the bayonet point missed as he squirmed away. The man off balance recovered and turned with his musket and tried to slash him across the waist but Andrew jumped back in time. Now back on his feet, Archie put his head down and charged the off balance soldier, knocking him to the ground. Andrew raised his musket and plunged the bayonet point deep into the man's side. It tore through his blue coat, ripping through his liver. Andrew pulled and wrenched the bayonet out of the man's body. Just as the bayonet exited, he raised the musket to swing around to deal with the other Frenchman, when he screamed agonisingly as an officers sword came down on his right hand, holding the rifle's barrel.

Instinctively he dropped his right shoulder and barged the officer's mid-drift. He then heard the officer scream as Iain Colquhoun rammed a bayonet deep into his back. Dod Melvin stepped in to take lethal care of the other Frenchman. Andrew staggered backwards. He took his right hand off the barrel and saw to his horror the last three fingers flap lifelessly over the palm of his hand. It was only skin and gristle keeping them attached.

Colquhoun shouted to Archie. 'Take Drew to the rear. He's out o' the fight!'

In a ferment of shock and pain, Andrew watched Colquhoun and Melvin race off towards Elvina. After a stiff fight, the French pulled back to the village, leaving their dead and wounded behind. Barely five minutes after rising from their bellies on the ridge, the 42nd had stopped the vaunted French columns that conquered Europe in their tracks.

Chapter Twenty – Eight

Archie took Andrew's good arm and led him back up the slope to the top of the ridge. Other wounded men were doing the same. Andrew wept bitterly in pain and desolation. He knew what the wound to his hand meant. He was finished as a soldier.

As they gained the top of the rise, officers and aides observed the action below. Andrew held his bleeding hand inside his coat in an attempt to staunch the blood flow. He was beginning to feel light headed and asked Archie to stop and let him sit down.

'Stay here and rest. I'll try and find Mr Innes.' Archie left and ran off towards the tents and huts of the officer's quarters.

Andrew sat on the damp grass, bent forward. He took his hand out from his blood soaked coat and held it across his waist. He did not know how long he sat before a man on a horse looked down and spoke to him.

'You'll dae yersel' nae guid sittin, there, laddie!' He was a striking looking man of sixty years, wearing civilian clothing. Andrew had a vague recollection he knew him from somewhere.

'For the love o' Goad, that's a sare hand ye've got there, eh?' The man dismounted and pulled from around his neck a delicate scarf of Chinese silk. He began tying it gently around Andrew's hand.

'That'll dae the now. Until the surgeon sees ye, right?'

'Thank you, sir.' Andrew whispered his gratitude.

'First fight?

'Aye. And looks like the last.' Andrew replied tearfully. The old man grinned. He stuck out his hand and gently nipped Andrew's cheek.

'Ye're alive, son! You can go home tae your mother and sweetheart now.' The man winked. 'And ye'll have tales tae tell, eh?'

'Home.' Andrew mumbled.

The man peered at him. 'What's your name, boy?' Andrew told him. 'And where are your parents, Andrew?'

'The Toll House at Barbauchlaw.'

The old gentleman laughed. 'Och, aye! I ken it weel! Stayed ower one night, years ago. Oh, long before you were born, kiddo. But I might have spoken wi' your faither.'

'Maybe.'

'Aye, maybe! Chin up, Andrew. Ye're a well-spoken laddie fae a guid home. Ye'll go back and begin life again. Ye've a long way to go yet! Took me ower forty years to start livin' properly. See me now!' The old man chuckled heartily.

Despite his pain, Andrew smiled. He was only trying to raise his spirits. 'Sir, I'm sorry about the mess I've made of your scarf.' He'd never known cloth of such softness and delicacy. 'It's very precious. Is it of silk?' Shock was beginning to have an effect and his mind was starting to wander.

'What? The scarf? Aye. It's silk.' The old man's eyes became distant. 'But no' as precious as the lassie that gave me it.' He then returned to Andrew. 'But dinnae worry yersel' ower that, son. You just get yersel' better. And then go home, Andrew Berry of Barbauchlaw. That's your duty now.'

Archie returned with Mr Innes and each took an arm of Andrew's and led him to the hospital tent. It was filling up with wounded. Andrew could clearly make out the grate of the surgeons saw and the inevitable screaming.

'Do not mind that, Andrew.' Mr Innes advised. The assistant surgeon sat him down and gently took hold of the wounded hand, carefully removing the blood soaked scarf.

'Turn your head, Andrew. Archibald, take his other hand.' Mr Innes took Andrew's wounded hand, then turned it palm down. He then placed it flat on the operating table.

'Who was that gentleman you were speaking with, Drew?' Archie asked after a surreptitious nod from Mr Innes.

Trying to remember where he saw him previous, Andrew shook his head. 'I've seen him before but I just can't recall where... *Ah, Mother*!' Andrew's high pitched scream reverberated around the tent. Mr Innes had cut away the ends of skin and tendon that were keeping Andrew's three fingers attached.

'Hold tight to him, Archibald!' He ordered loudly. But Andrew had fainted.

The 42nd were heavily engaged on the outskirts of Elvina. They made some encroachments, but were now running low on ammunition. Major Charles Napier of the 50th regiment, standing observing impotently from the ridge, raged inwardly as he observed the highlanders repel attack after attack. Christ's teeth, those fellows can't hold out forever. Something had to be done. And quickly. Can't stand by and watch our people being overrun!

His men were restless, angry and eager to offer assistance to their Scottish neighbours. Napier was reduced to making them carry out musket drills to pass the time. The air was blue from the language emitted.

He approached a veteran former ranker, promoted to Lieutenant, named Montgomery. A Scot, Montgomery was considerably older than the young major, but Charles valued his counsel which invariably proved sound.

'Damn fine work from your fellows, Monty.'

'Aye, they could dae wi' a bit o' assistance though, ye no' think, Major?' It was the words Napier longed to hear.

'Buggers in command are sitting on their arses doing nothing, damn it all, man! My chaps are getting itchy. Can't keep them in check much longer or they'll go off the boil.'

'Weel, ye ken the auld sayin', Charlie, son.' Montgomery said craftily. 'Ye cannae go wrong if ye follow the Forty –Twaw!'

'By God, I will!' Napier turned around. 'Sergeant. Order the men to prepare to charge!'

Andrew awoke as Mr Innes was applying sutures. The pain was indescribable. Archie hugged him tightly as Andrew's good hands fingers dug into his friend. When it was over, Mr Innes administered a dosage of laudanum to aid him to sleep. He was led to a cot where the assistant surgeon left Archie to bed his friend down. Andrew lay looking over to Archie with his bandaged hand lying over the blanket.

'You saved my life, Drew.' Archie said simply.

'You'd do the same.'

'But look what it cost you! Why did God allow that? You're the best friend anyone could ever have. Why did this have to happen to you?'

'I don't know why.'

'You'll have to go home.' Archie gulped, forcing tears back. 'We'll never see each other again.'

Andrew didn't respond immediately. The shock and the laudanum were now working in tandem. 'You…you still have Tomàs and Iain…And Dod and Hugh. You'll be in the light company.'

'But it's not the same! First Josh and now you. It wasn't to be part of God's plan for that to happen. It was for both of us. To go on doing His work. Fighting His enemies. Together.' Archie now began to cry.

'I've done God's work. I killed a man, Archie. If you want God to succeed, you need to have some of the Devil in you.'

'That's blasphemy, Drew.'

'Might be the laudanum as well.' Andrew was beginning to drift away.

Archie stood up. 'I better go back.'

'No you don't. Stay here. Mr Innes will see you right. Please don't go back to the fighting.'

Archie smiled sadly. 'You're always protecting people, Drew. Look at what it did for you.'

Andrew resigned himself to Archie's leaving and gave in to the drug. 'Please stay close to Tomàs and Iain.'

Archie bent down and rubbed his shoulder. 'Goodbye, Drew.'

Andrew was now asleep.

John Moore needed to fill the gap in the line left by the 42nd.

Everything was going well. Paget had neutralised the threat to the right flank. The French cavalry was only now discovering how unsuitable the land was. The enemy cannon were impotent. All he had to do was hold and the French would soon sicken and pull back.

Young Napier of the Dirty Half Hundred was granted permission to lead an attack in support of the 42nd. He respected the lad, having great confidence in him. The 50th were ready to move, when Moore ordered Warde's Guards to march forward and take up the gaps in the line.

On the outskirts of Elvina, Tomàs Killane, Iain Colquhoun, Sergeant McQuater, Melvin and Scott remained unharmed. Captain Crozier had taken a ball in the shoulder from a *voltigeur* but was now safely in the rear receiving attention.

The 42nd were under the cover of the walls of the village. As long as they had ammunition, they would prove difficult to dislodge. But the enemy were getting closer to their positions. And as their numbers increased, the 42nd casualties increased accordingly. The Battle of Coruña was in effect, over. Both sides held their ground. The British had no desire to push out and the French found that they could not push in. Strategically, it was a win for the red side.

To men like Killane and Colquhoun, it was a fine distinction. They were going nowhere. The French in taking Elvina, would consider it a moral victory. Even if the game was up.

The men of the 42nd when not firing their dwindling ammunition at the French, were continually looking over their shoulders for relief from behind. It was then that someone shouted, '*It's the Guards! The Guards are coming.*'

As ordered, General Warde was bringing his two regiments to fill the gap in the line left by the 42nd and the soon to become engaged 50th. But a few men of the 42nd mistakenly believed the Guards were coming to replace them. The highlanders began to withdraw from the village back up the slope.

Just as the men were making their way back, Major Napier sounded the charge and the 50th regiment hurled itself down the slope into Elvina, passing the highlanders. Moore and Graham, along with other officers at a crossroad near the top of the rise which offered a clear view of the action, looked on at their countrymen in disbelief.

Moore grabbed his reins and rode over to the slope. '42nd, what are you doing? The enemy is there!'

'We've no' ammunition, sir! Oor pockets are empty!' A man declared to the general.

'By God, you have your bayonets and you are Scotsmen! Look! The 50th are about to carry the village! Will they say Englishmen can do what a Scotsman cannot?'

'By Christ, they'll bloody no', General!' another man replied angrily and turned back to the fight. The rest of the highlanders on hearing Moore's words did the same.

'Thank Jesus, I'm a smooth talker!' Moore chuckled to himself, allowing his chest to swell just a little proudly at how a Scottish private soldier could tell a general what he thought and get away with it. Aye, there's few like us.

Back with Graham at the crossroad, he looked down and watched the 50th along with small groups of men from the 42nd work their way into the village.

'Fine lad, yon Major Napier!' Moore declared happily to Graham. He turned to Colonel Stirling who looked on with relief as his men were reinforced.

'Colonel, give the order to recall the 42nd. Send ammunition down to the walls outside the village and keep the laddies there with their heads down. They've earned their drams the night!' He was feeling ebullient. It wasn't over but now knew he couldn't lose.

High above on Peñasquedo, a French artillery officer had been observing the crossroad outside Elvina. He noted it becoming a meeting area of senior British officers. Two in particular were spending time there, then leaving and returning again either alone or together. A man in a cape, red coat and sash with a bicorn hat and an old man in civilian clothing.

He calibrated the range and had already let loose a few balls. He believed he now had the distance and awaited the moment of maximum effect.

Archie made his way back to the ridge just as the 50th were preparing to charge down to the village. He now lost much of his religious ardour. What God had inflicted on Drew was unforgivable. Maybe he was right to blaspheme. God was cruel. A heartless being who tested men beyond their endurance. He was angry and wanted revenge on those who scarred his friend for life. With nothing better to do, he joined the end of the line of the 50th.

'Come to lend us a hand, Jock?' one of the men said to him.

'My best friend has a terrible wound. He's with the surgeon. I'm going to kill the bastards who did it to him.'

The man nodded his head. 'No worries, chum. You're welcome here. I've many a score to settle with them murderin' sods an' all. Stay close, brother.'

The order was called. Englishman and Scotsman together charged the enemy in Elvina.

After relaying his order to Colonel Stirling, Sir John Moore was blown from his horse as he was struck by a cannon ball. He landed beneath

Thomas Graham's feet. Tam leaped off his horse immediately and went to Moore's aid.

'The surgeon! Get the fuckin' surgeon here now!'

Moore sat up. He felt no pain, but put his right arm to his left side and felt an effusion of liquid. Graham held him around the right shoulder. Moore's cape fell back and Tam was horrified to view the insides of Moore's chest at work.

'Oh, Christ, Johnny boy. What have ye done?' Tam took Moore's red general's sash off and used it in attempt to stem the flow of blood. An aide of Moore's crouched to offer assistance.

'It's no use, Hardinge, I'm a dead man, son.' Moore said feebly.

By now a surgeon, Mr McGill from the 1st Regiment of Foot arrived to examine the wound. Moore's left shoulder was shattered, his arm dangling from a piece of flesh. His ribs were broken and bare as the flesh was torn away. Two buttons from Moore's lapel were driven into the shoulder.

McGill looked up from his examination to Thomas Graham and shook his head. Tam, decisive as ever, stood up. 'Hardinge, I'm goin' tae ride to John Hope to tell him he's now in command. Then I'm returnin' here. You take Sir John back to Coruña with all haste. Get crackin,' laddie!'

'JOSHUA! DREW! MCGILLIVRAY!'

Revelling in the ecstasy and freedom of the charge, Archie plunged down into the village with the men of the 50th. He knew he passed Tomàs Killane and Iain Colquhoun at the wall. He saw the shocked white face of Dod Melvin screaming at him to stop and come back. Hugh Scott grabbed his arm but Archie pulled away and ran on.

He followed the young Major Napier, screaming his friend's names in defiance. They were at his side, inspiring and empowering him. The French were running back into the village towards the slopes of Peñasquedo. Archie caught one in the back with his bayonet. It felt wonderful as it slid into the enemy who had destroyed one friend's life and killed another. They eventually stopped and regrouped deep inside Elvina.

Archie caught his breath and loaded his musket. He took a long drink from his canteen. He thought about the Fife hills and the view over the water to Edinburgh. He didn't quite know why God put that image in his mind. It comforted him to think of home, though he was unhappy there. He did miss the hills. He missed the lambs and calves he retrieved. Drew taught him you must protect the weak not just because it was right, but because no one else would if you didn't. That would be his life's work from now on. Drew would no longer be with him, but he would carry on along his road. He understood now that Drew's was the true path to heaven. It wasn't in seeking death and revenge. He would fight to stay alive, yes. But there would be no joy in killing.

The man from the 50th was at his side by the wall. 'Ye're a scrapper, Jock! Proud to know you. What's yer name?'

'Archibald Miller, light company of the 42nd.'

The man grinned. 'Light company. Might have known!'

A sergeant crawled over to them. 'Right, lads. I reckon we get out behind this wall and we're through the place. Get ready on my order.'

Archie checked his musket and awaited the word. When it came, he leapt up and dashed around the wall, following the man from the 50th. Frenchman popped up and fired back at them. The 50th charged forward to clear the Frenchmen out who turned and fled. Archie and the others followed them. They came to another wall. Archie looked around. Something wasn't right.

The man from the 50th noticed Archie's hesitation. 'What is it, Jock? We're through, mate.'

'It's not the end of the village.' Archie said, almost to himself. He looked up at the ridge above him and closed his eyes. He thought of Drew, Joshua and Sergeant McGillivray.

The Frenchmen stood up from behind the wall and laid down a deadly volley of fire directly at the men of the 50th regiment.

And the boy from Fife.

Chapter Twenty – Nine

They carried him in a soldier's blanket, slung between two poles by six men from the 42nd and their sergeant. He asked them to make stops along the way and turn him around so he could see how matters were at the ridge. As they took him back to Coruña, he asked each of them their names and where they hailed from. He made light of his pain and dreadful wounds.

Two surgeons approached who had been with the wounded David Baird. He asked them how his friend was. It was likely he would lose an arm at the shoulder, but may live should he survive the amputation. He smiled and thought, you don't know Davy. He then dismissed the surgeons as there was no hope for him, ordering them to return to the field to care for the men.

A spring wagon containing a wounded senior officer passed them and stopped. The officer asked who the men were carrying. When they answered, the officer, though in great pain insisted on climbing out and offering his place to Sir John Moore. The men of the 42nd courteously declined the kind offer. They weren't going to allow their Johnny to bounce around poor ground in a rickety old cart. The blanket, along with the devotion of his countrymen, would ensure the poor man a more comfortable, less painful journey.

By the time they arrived in the town's Canton Grande, the six men and their sergeant, all veterans, were in tears. They would return to the action determined on seeking retribution.

As he was carried into the house, his young valet, Francois was coming down the stairwell holding an unlit candle. The boy, looking at his master being carried in a blood soaked blanket, paused on a step. His face paled in shock.

'Hello, Francois. This is nothing, lad. Nothing.'

Andrew awoke in the tent, his hand throbbing mercilessly. It was the middle of the evening and the sounds of battle had ceased. All around were the groans of suffering men, talk from the surgeons and orderlies and wounded being carried in and out. The action had ended. Both sides held parts of the village of Elvina. An unofficial truce was declared and the dead and injured from each side were allowed to be carried off.

The Duke of Damnation had called a halt. The English were stubborn and it appeared in defence, well-nigh unbeatable. Those men in skirts were the very devil. He'd love a regiment or two of them for himself. He wasn't going to lose any more men and have to explain himself to the Emperor. He could just make out in the mirk the evacuation at the harbour beginning to escalate. He'd miss observing those delightful ships. *Au revoir,* Englishmen. Till the next time.

Andrew painfully and groggily rose from the cot. He desperately wanted news about his friends. He stood up and noted he was still fully clothed. The blood on his coat was dried somewhat. The bandage on his hand had a little red seeping through where his fingers used to be.

He didn't want to think of that right now. It was for later. His immediate focus was on Archie, Killane and the others. He wanted to thank Iain for saving his life. To know that Dod and Hugh were safe.

He looked around the tent. Mr Innes was working on a man's leg. Andrew turned away. Maybe if he could find someone from the 42nd they may have information. He then saw Willie Angus assisting an injured man to a chair. He walked over unsteadily.

'Willie.'

'Good Christ, Drew Berry! I'm awfy glad to see ye well, pal. Ah heard ye took a sare yin.'

'Have you seen Archie?'

'Archie? No son, a cannae say ah huv. But Iain and Tomàs are fine. Hughie's well too, but Doddie Melvin's in the wagon ootside. Go and help him in if ye can. Ah'v goat ma hands fu' the nicht!'

Andrew limped to the entrance of the tent. Men were being assisted down from wagons. He looked for Dod and shouted his name.

'Wae's that?' Melvin's unmistakeable tones replied.

'Dod! It's Drew Berry.'

'Drew?' A man climbed unaided from a wagon behind where Andrew stood. He turned and saw Dod with his arm in a blood stained sling. On meeting they embraced and congratulated each other.

'Och, its no' so bad. The ball went in and through. I'll no' lose it but I'm going to make sure Mr Innes sees me and no that auld soak, Ogilvie!' Donald McQuater, Tomàs Killane and Hugh Scott were back in the town preparing to embark. Iain Colquhoun was in Elvina supervising the clear up of dead and wounded.

'Dod, where's Archie?'

Melvin shook his head. 'He went off on his ain wi' the 50th. Aff his heid, he was, Drew. Wouldnae listen tae reason. All I ken is the 50th lost a lot o' men when they charged deep into the town. Just have tae hope he's wi' them somewhere.'

Andrew thanked him as the big man left and entered the tent. Angus was now back on the wagon holding the reins.

'Willie, can you give me a lift?'

John Moore was placed on a mattress on the floor of his bedroom. The surgeons who examined him botched matters and left him in extremities of pain. Paul Anderson, his oldest friend, held his hand and comforted him. John Colbourne hovered, his eyes misty in disbelief. Harry Percy was out in the field. He would arrive back late, to his devastation. Moore asked continually about the battle. Reports came in to inform him matters were faring very well.

He slipped in and out of consciousness through the afternoon and early evening. He awoke to Anderson's gaze at one point, pleading for his country do him justice. Then at 8p.m. he asked for James Stanhope.

Thomas Graham finally arrived at the house. 'Where is he?' he demanded. He entered the room and his eyes immediately fell to the man lying on the mattress. He looked over to Colbourne.

'He's asked for Stanhope.'

Tam instantly knew why, walked over and knelt down by the stricken man. 'Oh, Johnny. Ye're a trouble to me, so ye are!'

'Tammy, is Stanhope here yet?' Moore whispered, barely audible.

'Aye. Just comin'.'

'The battle won?'

'Of course. It was your plan, wasn't it?

'I suppose it was. How…How's Davy?'

Tam sniffed and wiped his eyes. 'He's fine. I've seen him. Givin' the poor surgeons hell!'

The faintest of smiles crossed Moore's lips. He was now fading, the light dimming from his eyes. A shadow crossed his face. He was only moments from the end. His life's path was dogged by injury and ill fortune. But he was leaving behind an extraordinary legacy of military genius that would echo down the ages. Along with that he left something far greater. A genuine belief in showing care and compassion for the poor. Ordinary men could walk proudly because of him. The old gentleman, down on his knees, his grieving begun, rubbed the fingers of his friend's hand.

'Say hello to my bonnie girl, Johnny lad.' Thomas Graham of Balgowan wept.

'I will, Tammy.' His mind was now clear. The visions and delirium of earlier no longer disturbed him. He knew it was his dearest friend Paul Anderson standing over him next to the inconsolable John Colbourne. He knew Francois was close, bravely holding up. He'd spoken clearly to Graham. He had a message to deliver for dear old Tam.

He did wish Bobby was here. Bobby could frighten the Devil. Probably had. But he was content to know he was safe in Vigo. Davy would live after having his arm removed at the shoulder. He knew Davy. Nothing to worry about there. Janie and brother Graham, his mother and all the young ones were safe. He hoped they felt him telling them he was safe, too.

Now he knew everyone was well, there was one thing left to do. *She* was not here. He knew that. She was asleep at home, dreaming of him. Oh, aye. She *knew*.

James Stanhope, who had suffered the death of his brother, Charles, during the battle, entered the crowded bedroom. He glanced at Colbourne who nodded and the young man approached the dying general, kneeling down before him. John Moore with one final effort, faintly brushed his good hand against the boys arm.

'James. Please remember me to your sister.'

They passed the ridge where torches and small fires marked the way towards the village. During the early hours of the following morning, the former positions of the British would be quietly evacuated. A few men would stay behind to ensure fires remained lit to fool the French into thinking the redcoats were still camped on Monte Mero.

Men of Bentinck's brigade silently walked in the opposite direction to the wagon back to Coruña. Andrew searched every kilted figure for Archie but by now most of the 42nd were accounted for. Angus pulled the wagon to a halt at a wall on the outskirts of the village. A pile of bodies of highlanders and 50th men lay along its edge, a lone corporal stood over them.

'Iain!' Andrew jumped painfully from the wagon and stumbled over to Colquhoun. They embraced. Iain hailed Angus at the wagon. 'No need to come down, Willie. There's no one else living to take back. All those remaining are with the Lord.'

'But Iain, where's Archie? Have you seen him? Is he with the 50th wounded?' Andrew asked, still not wanting to believe his friend lost.

Colquhoun unshouldered his musket and planted it down in the grass. In the torchlight, Andrew could make out the fatigue and strain etched on his face. Only hours before, the man saved his life. 'Drew. Archie's lying behind the wall. Men of the 50th brought him out with their own dead.'

'Dead...' Andrew moved towards the pile of corpses. Iain put his hand out. 'Don't, lad. Leave him be. Archie's with God now.'

Andrew stopped with Colquhoun's hand on his arm. He only wanted closure. He truly didn't want to view his friend's cold body. Tears streamed down. His body shook, his hand seared in pain and he was unaware of Willie and Iain gently helping him up on to the wagon.

They rode back to the hospital tent where the surgeons were now overseeing the removal of those deemed fit to board ship. Andrew walked over to the cot he had laid in to retrieve his uncle's knapsack. It was gone.

He searched frantically under the cot and the beds close by. There was no sign of it. He wanted to cry out loud his frustration and hurt. It contained his uncle's letter and belongings. He now remembered that Joshua's locket lay with Archie's body. Unless it too was stolen. He was unable to cease the flow of bitter tears. He saw Mr Innes at the far end of the tent. Andrew slowly wandered over to him to say his farewell and thank him.

'Andrew! Did you find Archibald safe and well?' Andrew informed him of his friends' death. Mr Innes' faced dropped.

'Oh, that's a terrible pity. You've lost both of them. Aye, that's a shame, so it is.' Mr Innes stopped and looked away for a moment. 'Is your wagon still outside?' Andrew nodded.

'Then we'll ride together to the harbour.' He looked around the tent and felt the tiredness of eternity cloak him. 'There's nothing left for me here now. The orderlies are more than capable. I believe we are both to embark on the same ship. That's good. I'll be able to observe your injuries.' Andrew was relieved to hear they would sail together.

'Oh, here's your knapsack.' Mr Innes reached down behind him. 'You left it behind when you went out earlier.' Andrew closed his eyes in a silent prayer of thanks for the surgeon's thoughtfulness.

'There's something else.' Mr Innes handed him a sealed letter. 'I'm resigning from the army when I return home. There's a paper I need to prepare for Surgeon's Hall. I wish to resume my practice in Edinburgh.' He then smiled. 'I also begin to miss my wife and family too much.' Wondering what this meant for him, Andrew took the letter in his good hand.

Mr Innes then explained. 'It's from myself attesting to your good character. It will be useful if you ever need seek employment. My practice details are appended. I would take it most remiss should you not pay a visit to inform me of your progress.' Overwhelmed, Andrew gave his thanks and placed the letter in his knapsack.

'I have but one small valise and my medical bag to carry me home.' For once, Mr Innes now appeared uncharacteristically absent-minded. 'All else was lost on the march. Oh, dear God! I nearly forgot.' He went to his coat lying over his waiting baggage. From it he handed Andrew a small item.

'Archibald gave it to me for safe-keeping. He wanted you to have it, should he fall.' It was Joshua's miniature portrait. With the priceless memento in his hand, Andrew felt the stirring of a healing process begin. He closed his eyes and again thanked Mr Innes from the depths of his bruised soul.

They loaded up the last group of men for Coruña on the wagon. Andrew and Mr Innes rode in front alongside Willie Angus. Colquhoun and Melvin on board, sat behind them. It was nearing midnight. Andrew now felt a strange but not unwelcome serenity. He was now only responsible for himself. He would allow the tide of events to move him to where they wanted him to go. He felt as if the entire episode of his life, from Lisbon to this moment, was a dream and only now he had awoke from it.

He clasped the knapsack tightly and rubbed the soft leather which soothed him as the wagon jolted over the uneven road. He now had three valuable objects around his neck. Each represented a precious life worth remembrance. The path of his own young life had led to deep personal loss. He had fulfilled his dream but at a cost of great sadness, pain and injury. If he could replay that day in Edinburgh when he first met Sergeant McGillivray and walked away from him, could it have been better for everyone? All three would still have died. They may only have passed away a little earlier if it wasn't for his presence. What difference had he made? They were questions only God could answer.

Conversely, had he walked away, he would not have known his first true love. He would not have known his two best friends. He would not have known men like Tomàs and Iain, Dod and Hugh. He would not have seen Lisbon or Salamanca. He would never have tested himself on the ridge. He would never know the dedication, professional ability and concern of Mr Innes. He would never have known the regard held for him by Colonel Stirling. He would never have discovered his father's brother and understood his parents better.

Andrew thought of the letter he sent to Gabriela. Should he not have waited till the battle was over before writing? How would he resolve matters now? Send for her using his discharge pay? Make his way back to Salamanca on his own? She may not want to marry him. But he was certain she would. She was telling him she loved him and would wait for him when she gave him the crucifix. He remembered the old gentleman, his kindness and wisdom. Who was he? He still had the bloodied scarf in his knapsack. He corrected himself. He now had four valuable objects. Andrew wondered who his precious girl was. He regretted he would never be able to return it to him. But the old man was right.

Andrew had a loving home to return to with his whole life ahead. Living was a duty. He had Mr Innes' letter. He may find a way of marrying Gabriela. Start a family. They would have grandchildren. One day he would tell stories to them of his youth. Their little faces would light up in enchantment as he told them wondrous tales of Portugal and Spain.

THE END

Printed in Great Britain
by Amazon

23764581R00179